Burnt

Basudev Sunani is an award-winning poet, writer and cultural scholar who represents a strong, articulate and engaged Dalit presence in the world of Odia letters. His numerous volumes of poetry include *Cast Out: Poems of Anger and Angst* (2021); two of his recent novels are *Padapodi* (2014) and *Mashani Sahara Delhi* (2021). He has also published critical works, including *Dalit Sanskrutir Itihasa* (2014), *Ambedkarism: A Way of Life* (2012) and *Dalit, Capitalism and Globalisation*. His works have been translated into English, German, Aboriginal Australian and Indian languages, including Hindi, Gujarati, Tamil, Marathi and Malayalam. He is the recipient of the Sahitya Akademi Award, the M. Karunanidhi Porkizhi Award, among others.

Raj Kumar is Professor of English at Delhi University. His teaching and areas of research and interest include Dalit Studies, Indian Literature, Autobiographical Studies, Postcolonial Literature and Odia Literature. He is the author of several works, including *Dalit Personal Narratives: Reading Caste, Nation and Identity* (2010), *Dalit Literature and Criticism* (2019), and *Bama: Writer as Activist* (2025), co-edited with S. Armstrong. His translations from Odia include *Bheda* (2017) by Akhila Naik.

Burnt

Beyond Return

Basudev Sunani

Translated from the original Odia by

Raj Kumar

Orient BlackSwan

BURNT: BEYOND RETURN

ORIENT BLACKSWAN PRIVATE LIMITED

Registered Office
3-6-752 Himayatnagar, Hyderabad 500 029 (Telangana), India
e-mail: centraloffice@orientblackswan.com

Other Offices
Bengaluru, Chennai, Guwahati, Hyderabad, Kolkata,
Mumbai, New Delhi, Noida, Patna

Originally published in Odia as *Padapodi* (Bhubaneswar: Pakshighara Prakashani, 2014).

First published 2025

041377

ISBN 978-93-5442-762-6

Typeset in
Cambria 10.5/12.6
by Le Studio Graphique, Gurgaon 122 007

Printed in India at
Avantika Printers Private Limited, New Delhi 110 020

Published by
Orient Blackswan Private Limited
3-6-752, Himayatnagar, Hyderabad 500 029
e-mail: info@orientblackswan.com

To Bedamati and Ishita
and
To all victims of caste atrocities

Contents

Author's Preface

IT WAS 21 JANUARY 2012. THE entire country was gearing up to celebrate Republic Day. Parade rehearsals were going on in the capital cities and in primary and high schools across the country. At 10 a.m. on that fateful day, forty Dalit houses of Lathore village in Bolangir district of Odisha were burnt down by upper-caste mobs, in a conflict that flared up over the small issue of buying a vest.

I was posted at Bhubaneswar at the time. The news was conveyed to me through a phone call. The people who lost their homes were my relatives. I also heard that the police and the local administration were not helping the victims.

Before I moved to Bhubaneswar I had been posted at Bolangir, and I was acquainted with most of the victims. We had worked together for social, cultural and literary activities on many occasions. So they rang me up to ask for help in their distress.

Through my personal connections I immediately contacted some IPS and IAS officers, and I urgently requested that they at once call the District Collector and the Superintendent of Police, Bolangir, to help the victims. But they did nothing.

Three days after the incident, I went to Lathore. The victims had been herded together into the village school buildings close to the railway station. Upon my arrival, Gouranga kaka, Bayash dada, Kapil bhai and Jitendra, my nephew, took me to the Dalit basti and showed me each and every house. I saw that some of the houses were still burning. It was a ghastly and haunting sight. The victims narrated the sequence of events in detail from beginning to end. While narrating the events they were inconsolable.

I stayed with them for half a day and returned to Bhubaneswar. But I felt restless. So after a few days I went to see my relatives again. As I interacted with them, more and more of the truth came out. I realised how hideously unjust and inhuman it was to burn down an entire basti for such a trivial matter. The caste angle to the incident was obvious. But there were economic, religious and political reasons as well.

The incident persistently played on my mind. I wrote a poem on it. But I was profoundly dissatisfied with it. I felt a kind of void in the undercurrent of the poem, for everything that I was unable to articulate in it, for all that remained unsaid. I was in regular touch with my relatives, who continued to share many facts about the incident. Finally, I decided to write a novel. That is how *Padapodi* was born.

All the events narrated in the novel are true. A few events might have happened at different times and at different places. But they are central to the story and relevant for the development of the narrative, which is why I have included them in the novel. All the characters in the novel are real. Many of them are still living. The narrator-protagonist of the novel hails from one of the slums of Raipur; in the course of writing the novel I visited Raipur to gain firsthand experience of living in a city slum.

When the novel was first published in 2014, 300 copies were sold within three days during a conference held at Anugul on 'Buddhism and Dalit: Vision of Modern India'. This was a record-breaking sale for any Odia book as Banoj Tripathy, the publisher of Pakshighara, later revealed.

It is heartening to know that a PhD student of the Central University of Hyderabad has included *Padapodi* as a primary text for her thesis. Students of other universities have also chosen the novel as part of their research project. In the meantime, *Padapodi* has already been translated into Hindi.

It is a matter of great happiness and pride for me that Professor Raj Kumar of the Department of English, University of Delhi, who is like my younger brother, has translated the novel into English and made it available for a wider readership. For this, he must be lauded. Another point which brings me immense satisfaction is the fact that he has undertaken the massive task of drawing the global audience's attention towards the heinous and abominable caste practices that proudly parade in dingy corners of our country to this day. This, to say the least, makes his role supreme, and his contribution unsurpassable.

Basudev Sunani
14 September 2024

Translator's Note & Acknowledgements

WHEN BASUDEV SUNANI APPROACHED ME TO translate *Padapodi* into English, I instantly agreed. Having translated the first Odia Dalit novel, *Bheda* by Akhil Naik, I was eager to translate *Padapodi*, for it encompassed the same discourse but from a different narrative viewpoint. Sunani and I both come from the same region of Odisha. So we share the same socio-cultural milieu. Moreover, we bond together over the cause of Dalit emancipation. So I began work on the translation with a lot of passion, and it took considerable time to complete. However, I have put in my best efforts to translate and to transcreate *Padapodi* into a work of literature that not only captures the essence of the original, but one that, I hope, also gives the reader a new and immersive experience.

Sunani has employed a colloquial language that is mostly spoken in western Odisha, particularly Bolangir and Nuapada, to give authentic voices to his characters. He has also used folk songs and proverbs. As much as these enrich and flavour a narrative that seeks to highlight a niche culture, translating colloquial words, idioms and humour is not easy. So my job as a translator was to find equivalents in English which came closest to what was conveyed in Odia. My primary concern was to not let this become a dry translation. So I have let the semantics and technicalities of verbatim translation take a backseat, and taken a few creative liberties in order to infuse energy and emotion into my work, which helped to turn *Burnt* into the powerful and gripping narrative I had envisioned. Having said that, I have not tampered with the original plot. The Odia novel has no chapters. I have chapterised the narrative in consultation with the author for a more methodical reading. Sunani has used both past and present tense to narrate events that go back and forth in time throughout the narrative. I have mainly used the past tense, and taken care that the sequence of events in the novel remains clear, coherent and connected.

I hope that readers will enjoy reading the novel, and that they will come to love the characters that people this narrative, the life worlds it inhabits and the indomitable spirit of resilience and humanity that it embodies as much as I do.

I am indebted to many people for having helped me bring out this book and I am grateful to them all. First of all I wish to thank Basudev Sunani who reposed faith in me, hoping I would be able to do justice to his novel. He constantly monitored the progress of the translation and guided me from beginning to end. I hope he is not disappointed.

I thank Animesh Mohapatra, Lalit Kumar, Moumita Sarkar, Madhulika Nirmal and Shibangi Dash who gave their time to read my draft chapters and offer their feedback. I wish to appreciate the professional help and encouragement I received from Moyna Mazumdar of Orient BlackSwan. She worked with passion and brought quality to the project. A big thank you to her. I also wish to thank Nilanjana Majumdar of Orient BlackSwan.

Finally, I wish to acknowledge my debt of gratitude to my family members, Bedamati, my wife and Ishita, my daughter. When I began to translate the novel, they were as excited as I was, if not more. They were my first readers and also my first critics. Whenever I would finish a chapter, and ask for their opinion, they would not give their approval unless they were thoroughly satisfied. They saw to it that the English translation was polished to perfection and met global standards. Vigorous, critical and determined, they spent months refining the vocabulary, refurbishing my sentences and transcreating paragraphs to ensure that the text embodied the essence of the narrative. So the work that you will read is as much theirs as it is mine. In appreciation of their labour of love, I wish to dedicate *Burnt: Beyond Return* to Bedamati and Ishita, the two beautiful women who changed my life.

Raj Kumar
5 May 2024

Translator's Introduction

IT WAS THE WINTER OF 2012, and India was preparing to celebrate its 62nd Republic Day. On 21 January 2012, forty Dalit houses of Lathore village in Bolangir district of Odisha were burnt down by upper-caste mobs, leaving more than two hundred Dalit men, women and children homeless, helpless and refugees in their own village. The atrocities deprived Dalits of their livelihoods, their dignity, and laid waste everything that they had struggled hard to achieve. Caste atrocities are rampant in Odisha. But the tragedy that struck Lathore was unparalleled in its magnitude and intensity. Published two years later in 2014, Basudev Sunani's novel *Padapodi*—from *pada* or locality and *podi*, which means burnt—is a fictional account of this incident that shook Odia society to its core.

While narrating the nature and degree of Dalit oppression in Odisha, Sunani depicts facets of Dalit lives, particularly from western Odisha, which are rarely discussed or written about. He also highlights the cultural heritage of the many Dalit communities in Odisha that have historically been pushed to the margins, existentially mocked and narratively invisibilised. *Padapodi* is thus a commendable attempt to document Dalit lives in Odisha, focusing on their history, myths, economy, religious and cultural mooring. Here, we briefly discuss some aspects of the novel, and how they converge into a gripping narrative aimed at rewriting a real-life brutality for history and for humanity.

The Context

A young Dalit boy was falsely accused of stealing a vest by an upper-caste shopkeeper, and badly beaten up. When Dalits protested, the upper-caste villagers got mobilised and, to teach them a lesson, torched the entire Dalit basti at Lathore. Before dousing the houses with petrol and diesel and setting them on fire, the mobs looted and vandalised the colony. The Dalits, who saw their houses burning right before their eyes, had to flee for their lives, and were forced to take shelter in the village school for months together. Despite such large-scale violence perpetrated by the upper castes in plain sight, the local administration was slow to respond to the victims' urgent pleas of help. They took their time to reach the village, and made at best feeble attempts to rehabilitate them, and only after they had lost everything in the arson. After more than a decade, the victims are still waiting to be rehabilitated. Sunani's novel underscores the victimisation and marginalisation that Odia Dalits face to this day at the hands of the upper castes, who continue to exercise power.

The story begins with Makaru, the narrator and protagonist, an Odia Dalit migrant living in one of the sprawling slums of Raipur, the capital city of Chhattisgarh. He works as a peon, and lives with his father Manglu, who pulls a rickshaw, and his mother, Sabesh. They live a simple, hardworking life of self-respect, patience and perseverance. As the narrative unfolds, we learn that Makaru originally belongs to a village called Banjipali, which is close to Lathore where the caste atrocities took place. The victims of the violence are close relatives who share a common family bond. Deeply disturbed by the news, he catches a train and heads for Lathore, a journey that is unforgettable.

On the train, the narrative becomes dynamic and non-linear, moving back and forth across time and space, as Makaru begins to recollect his childhood in Banjipali. He recalls life in the feudal village, how his family worked like slaves for the *gauntia*, a cruel and exploitative Brahmin landlord. Makaru's father worked in the gauntia's fields, his mother did odd jobs for the gauntia's household, and Makaru tended their cattle. The wages they received for their hard labour were not sufficient to feed them even two meals a day. They were impoverished but alive, just barely scraping enough together to survive. This changed when, in a twisted turn of events, Makaru is accused of attempting murder, and the upper-caste villagers led by the gauntia are out baying for his blood. Makaru and his parents are forced to flee their ancestral home and village in the dead of night to escape their wrath.

Caste in Odisha

Makaru and his parents were lucky to have escaped the jaws of caste wrath. But not all Dalits in Odisha are as fortunate. Caste is a brute fact that impacts all aspects of life in Odisha, visible in myriad forms in both private and public spaces, individual and social life. While the upper castes are notorious for using their caste privileges to exercise power, the majority of lower castes, especially Dalits, are stigmatised by their low social status, oppressed by multiple forms of untouchability and other social atrocities, and live an insecure, uncertain life. Predominantly rural and illiterate, condemned to live in sub-human conditions, suffering economic exploitation, cultural subjugation and political disempowerment, they have become one of the most exploited and peripheral social groups. Angana P. Chatterji, who has done extensive fieldwork in Odisha, recounts the following experience:

> Among a list of incidents, I recall a Dalit community member being beaten for entering a Hindu temple in Bargarh district in April 2001, and fined 4,000 rupees. In Kendrapara district, also in Orissa, Dalits have been disallowed entry into the two hundred year-old Jagannath temple in Keradagada village. In 2005, four Dalit girls who attempted to enter the temple were physically assaulted and fined. In October 2006, faced with the denial of their right of entry into the temple, 1,200 Dalits instituted a "Dalit Manch" in the village, resolving to renounce Hinduism if the ban continued. In December 2006, led by the Orissa Mukti Morcha (Orissa Liberation Front, also battlefront), about 3,000 Dalits resolved to convert to Buddhism, in dissent to being refused entry to the temple by upper caste groups and Hindu priests. (Chatterji 2009: 69–70)

In such a hostile environment, Odia Dalits lead a life of constant hardship, struggle, fear, compromise, alienation and resignation. According to the last census, Odisha has 92 Dalit communities, constituting 18 per cent of the state's population. Following the Hindu caste structure, Dalit communities too have rigid internal hierarchies among themselves, and inter-caste dining and marriages are still not allowed between Dalit communities. Dalit politics in the state is fragmented as Dalits are divided into many groups and sub-groups, which prevents them from uniting to voice their grievances in common public fora. As a result, their demands go unheard and unaddressed by the bureaucrats and politicians.

It is unfortunate that even in the twenty-first century, Dalits in Odisha do not have equal opportunities for education or for employment. As per the 2011 Census, the literacy rate of Dalits in Odisha is just 56 per cent, as compared to the total literacy rate of the state, which is 72.9 per cent. This has led to serious structural problems. Apart from the inability to access secure jobs, due to their illiteracy Dalits in Odisha cannot avail many of the constitutional provisions that would guarantee them a life of dignity. For example, there is a general lack of awareness among rural illiterate Dalits about the various provisions of the Protection of Civil Rights Act of 1976, or the Scheduled Caste Atrocities Act of 1989. They fail to regard the practice of untouchability or caste atrocities as a serious violation of their fundamental human rights, and of the law of the land, and thus as a punishable offence. A 1994 study undertaken by the National Institute of Social Work and Social Sciences, Bhubaneswar, on the implementation of The Protection of Civil Rights Act, 1955, in Odisha revealed that untouchability practices are widespread and rampant in Odisha.

> As revealed in our study, some of the types of untouchability still practiced in Orissa are: denial of access to the Scheduled Castes to village pond, public well, bathing ghats, etc., denial of entry into the village temples and access to places of worship, burial ground, denial of entry into shops, hotels and tea-stalls, refusal of service by barbers and washer men etc. This list is suggestive but not exhaustive. What was even

> more painful for us to notice was that the ill treatment by the upper castes to the Scheduled Castes does not end with the imposition of these disabilities on them. It goes beyond that and the caste dynamics in the empirical situation is usually accompanied by and/or develops with physical violence and atrocities. (Dash and Kumar 1994: 91–92)

Rather than reporting such incidents to the police and other law-enforcing agencies, which is daunting for them given their disempowerment, most illiterate victims of caste violence take recourse to karma, blaming their fates, trying to live circumscribed within the inhuman and absurd social and cultural boundaries historically enforced upon them as 'low caste', and continue to suffer in silence.

Escape from Caste

In *Padapodi*, however, there are moments in the lives of Dalits who do try to break out of the oppressive caste structure and lifelong misery that it shackles them in, by migrating. Like Makaru, Manglu and Sabesh, there are many other migrant labourers from rural Odisha, such as Dambru and Neelia, who make the train journey to Raipur, and come to settle in the city's slums to earn a livelihood by hard work. The train in the novel is an important symbol of modernity and change, and a vital catalyst for Dalit emancipation. It is thanks to the train that Makaru and his parents escape imminent death. The train not only carries them to the city, but also gives them an opportunity to discover a new world. Though, as destitute newcomers from a small remote village, they find the huge city alien, cruel, forbidding and overwhelming, they eventually find a toehold and make Raipur their new home. They give themselves to the city, and it embraces them back: the unfamiliar gains a semblance of familiarity, even if partial.

Life in the city is very different from life in the village. In the city, not everyone asks what caste they belong to. No longer slaves to landlords and moneylenders, they find themselves emancipated to some degree—free to sell their labour and free to earn a livelihood, in real wages. Though they live in a slum where basic amenities are lacking, like thousands of other migrants in the city, they too somehow manage to get by. Makaru, who has some basic primary education, is hired as a peon-cum-security guard. It is not a well-paid job, but it is a departure from his illiterate father who pulls a rickshaw, and who slaved as a landless labourer back in the village. Later, Makaru educates his only son, Bishikeshan, who goes on to become an office clerk in Raipur, and joins the league of the Indian middle class.

Such positive social transformation reminds us of B. R. Ambedkar's clarion call to Dalits to leave their villages and move to the city—because villages in India were stinking hells.

> That they [village communities] have survived through all vicissitudes may be a fact. But mere survival has no value. The question is on what plane they have survived. Surely on a low...selfish level, I hold that these village republics have been the ruination of India...What is the village but a sink of localism, a den of ignorance, narrow-mindedness, and communalism? (Ambedkar 1994: 61–62)

Following Ambedkar's call, Dalits in Maharashtra indeed left their villages and moved to towns and cities, where they lived a life of relative caste anonymity. Baburao Bagul's famous short story 'When I Hid My Caste' (2018) and Narendra Jadav's memoir *Outcaste* (2003) are examples of how Dalits in rural Maharashtra escaped caste atrocities by moving to the cities. The call given by Ambedkar might not have reached Odisha then. But we hear echoes of it in *Burnt* when Makaru and his parents migrate to Raipur, and come to live a life that is more on their own terms, and that affords them a certain dignity.

Recollecting those days in Banjipali, Makaru imagines how his relatives in Lathore would have suffered due to caste revenge and, in doing so, he becomes conscious of his Dalit identity. It is no accident that this consciousness arrives on a train. As a product of modernity and mobility, the train is in significant ways caste-neutral, and hence a social leveller. As a Dalit, even if he jostles with or sits close to other passengers, occasionally coming into physical contact with them, nobody asks him his surname or his caste. Like the city, the train also stands for a certain egalitarian anonymity—at least for the same class of passengers.

When Makaru reaches the relief camp in Lathore, his caste consciousness is strengthened. He sees his relatives, despair and desolation on their faces. He meets Chitra—a poor Dalit of humble background who rose by virtue of his hard work, determination, intelligence, education and early self-awareness to become one of the richest, most respected and influential men in the village—who has now lost everything in the caste riots. During the few days he spends with Chitra at the relief camp, Makaru learns that the administration is treating the victims like criminals, while the actual criminals carry on as if nothing happened; that the government compensation offered to the victims is meagre in contrast to the huge losses incurred; that there is no Dalit unity in the fight for justice, and that a few educated Dalit youths among the victims who are managing the relief funds have now turned corrupt and cheated their brethren. This leads to a profound disillusionment, compounding the prevailing atmosphere of pessimism and helplessness, as Makaru realises that, despite all the constitutional laws available to them, as ordinary citizens, they cannot fight the state or the administration, for the whole system is entrenched in caste and tilted against them.

Dalit Culture and Life Worlds

In *Padapodi* Sunani celebrates Odia Dalit culture. In depicting their lives he also narrates their traditions, beliefs and the festivals they follow round the year. This is significant because Odia Dalits have a rich cultural heritage, which has however seldom found mention in public discussions, academia or in literature, until recently. Upper-caste and non-Dalit writers who have written about Dalits in Odisha—such as Gopinath Mohanty, Kanhu Charan Mohanty, Basant Kumar Satpathy and Parshuram Mund, to mention a few—have focused mainly on Dalit sufferings and exploitation, but not as much on their vibrant cultural and social lives as a community. Sunani, on the other hand, has meticulously documented Dalit lives and life worlds, in his poetry, prose and fiction, to highlight their unique cultural capital, encompassing their arts, crafts, music, oral traditions, and the distinctive aesthetic that they embody and live everyday. In doing so, he documents the legacy that Dalits in Odisha have inherited, owned and continued over the years.

Padapodi narrates the lives of three generations of a Dalit family who, in the face of caste prejudices and a world that is rapidly changing around them, struggle to preserve their ancient cultural beliefs and legacy amidst the daily battle for survival. Dalit characters in the novel who continue to celebrate traditional customs and who speak the local dialect are spokespersons of their community: Chitrasen who organises a grand *gadi* puja in the village to remember and venerate his Gana ancestors; Sabesh who steadfastly continues to worship her family deity Nialimali after her arrival in Raipur, and even after others switch to worshipping Hanuman; Manglu who wishes to be buried as per old Gana custom when he dies, and not cremated.

In the course of the novel, Sunani also subtly traces how, with changes in time, an oral community becomes a part of the written community. While narrating stories of the first generation, Sunani makes evocative use of oral forms like folk songs, folk tales and proverbs to emphasise the richness of Dalit folk culture in Odisha. Conversations between characters reveal glimpses of a language that is nuanced, playful, ironic, at times witty and wry. When he narrates stories of the second generation, he uses words, expressions and idioms to reflect a language typical of the first generation of Dalit literates. The use of songs, music and dance continues into the second generation as well, but certain idioms and expressions gradually become formal—a significant departure from the informal language and speech used by members of the first generation. So when we read Sunani's Odia novel, we realise that while his rural characters who live in villages speak the colloquial native Odia, their urban counterparts in Raipur, in trying to fit into their new environment, emulate the speech habits of the city and speak in a mix of Odia, Chhattisgarhi and Hindi. Unfortunately, these intricate linguistic transfers and nuances are lost in translation into English. Throughout the novel, Sunani traces how Odia Dalit culture has interacted and engaged with other cultures and evolved over time. It may be noted here that Sunani has published a volume on the history of Dalit culture in Odisha, titled *Dalit Sanskrutira Itihasa* (2014) an important contribution towards documenting a culture that is otherwise dying due to urbanisation, modernisation and globalisation.

Dalits in the novel celebrate several festivals such as Nuakhai, Puspuni, Dasahara and Bhai Jiuntia, among others. Sunani describes these festivals and their significance in Dalit lives. Whether religious or cultural, they are occasions for Dalits to break free from their harsh daily struggles briefly, to come together and rejoice. Each festival is governed by certain norms that are reinforced by the community elders, and followed by the young. Thus every festival is like a performativity that symbolically keeps the community alert, alive and together under the duress of the oppressive caste structure.

Significantly, in *Burnt*, Sunani also illustrates what happens when Dalits abandon their traditional religious beliefs and their inherited ancestral deities, whom they have worshipped generation after generation, and seek to embrace new ones, in the aspiration to emulate the upper castes or to move with the times, or both. In a historic break with tradition, when the Dalits of Lathore join the upper-caste villagers to worship Goddess Durga in a celebration which is organised on a grand scale, there are dire consequences that no one can foresee. Similarly, when Dalit residents of the slum in Raipur where Makaru lives enthusiastically pour their devotion, labour and resources into building their own temple for Lord Hanuman, they are eventually divested of the fruits of their devotion, though in a manner far less diabolic.

Whatever the occasion, Dalits believe in sharing their joys and sorrows by inviting the larger community of relatives, friends and neighbours. Communal feasts follow events such as births, naming ceremonies, marriages and deaths. In addition to worshipping numerous gods and goddesses, Dalits also worship their ancestral spirits and formally invite their ancestors and household deities for every occasion, and offer them food and drink before partaking of them.

Music, song and dance are an essential and inseparable part of every Dalit function and ritual. Dalit musicians are considered to be the custodians of Dalit culture. They showcase their extraordinary talents in playing traditional music instruments, singing repertoire songs from memory, performing dances and displaying acrobatic feats to entertain. In recognition of their multiple talents, Dalit musicians are respected by the community and given the honour of leading all processions. Sunani uses music as a vital aspect of Dalit creativity and self-expression in *Padapodi*, and details musical instruments used on different socio-cultural and religious events, especially the ubiquitous and popular *ganabaja*. All important events, whether celebrating life or mourning death, are marked by the use of traditional musical instruments, such as the *dhol*, *nissan*, *mahuri* and *tasha*, and Sunani describes each one of them and the distinctive sound they produce. Sunani, who has made an in-depth study of the subject, holds that the origins of Dalit music, musical traditions and creativity can be traced back to times when music and song was an essential part of any community event, and are as old as the history of the subcontinent itself.

Conclusion

Writing *Padapodi* could not have been easy for Sunani, who was a witness to the destruction caused by the riot. When he visited Lathore, some of the houses of his relatives were still burning. Seeing the gruesome scenes, he must have felt helpless like the victims. But as an activist committed to the cause of social justice, the writer-poet in him must have been moved and motivated to pay his personal tribute to the victims and to record the injustice. But more importantly, with the publication of *Padapodi*, Sunani was able to initiate a much-needed debate on the rights and liberties and the plight of Dalits in Odisha today.

Sunani narrates how a trivial incident snowballed into a monstrosity and a tragedy that would never have assumed such ugly proportions had it involved people of the same caste and social stratum. He shows us how deeply ingrained our presumptions of 'others' are and how deep-rooted our mistrust and hatred of them, built upon false social prejudices and misperceptions handed down and reinforced generation by generation. Taking a true event as the heart of his novel, Sunani weaves stories around Dalit subjectivities in Odisha. He narrates the lives of three generations of Dalits who witness many such events in their lifetime, and go on to participate in the making of the larger polity of Odisha, and India.

Reading the novel, one wonders how many more decades and how many more Lathores will it take before Dalits can lead a life as equal citizens in this country. In *Burnt*, victims of the violence do not get justice from the state. In reality, victims of the atrocities in Lathore have not got justice even today; for the upper castes believe that if the Dalits were to be rehabilitated, they will demand their dues, and hence become a threat to the upper castes. So the status quo continues. Caste remains an all-pervasive iron grid that deforms and mangles social existence and relationships in India. It is because of the stranglehold of this centuries-old entrenched system of hierarchy, power and inequity that Dalits are still treated as the 'other' in India. It is not surprising then that the victims in the novel are not hopeful of a future when they will not have to beg for their dignity and basic human rights. *Burnt* ends on a note that suggests time is the most powerful precursor of change. But one has to wait for that revolutionary, epochal moment to arrive. Or, one has to make it happen. Although much has changed in the near eight decades since Independence, caste continues to thrive in twenty-first-century India with new vigour and power, in forms new and old. It is, therefore, befitting perhaps that the subtitle of the novel is: *Beyond Return*.

Works Cited

Ambedkar, B. R. 1994. *Dr. Babasaheb Ambedkar: Writings and Speeches*, Vol. 13. Edited by Vasant Moon. Bombay: Education Department, Government of Maharashtra.

Bagul, Baburao. 2018. *When I Hid My Caste*. Translated by Jerry Pinto. New Delhi: Speaking Tiger.

Chatterji, Angana P. 2009. *Violent Gods: Hindu Nationalism in India's Present: Narratives from Orissa*. New Delhi: Three Essays Collective.

Dash, Anup Kumar and Raj Kumar. 1994. 'A Study on the Implementation of the PCR Act in Orissa'. Bhubaneswar: National Institute of Social Work and Social Sciences.

Jadhav, Narendra. 2003. *Outcaste: A Memoir*. Delhi: Viking.

Sunani, Basudev. 2014. *Padapodi*. Bhubaneswar: Pakshighara Prakashani.

Burnt

One

THE TRAIN WAS CHUGGING AWAY...CHHUK-chhuk-chhuk-chhuk... into the cold winter morning. The chilly wind rushing through the open windows made one shiver uncontrollably. A gentleman sat beside the window in trousers and shirt, a black muffler around his neck, gazing upon the scene outside and smoking a bidi. It was difficult to muster the courage to ask him to shut the window. He seemed completely oblivious to his co-passengers, as if he was the only one travelling on the train.

Why can't people be more sensitive to the sufferings of others, Makaru wondered. But the gentleman was lost in his own world. Even the tea seller's ear-splitting calls of "Chai! Chai!" could not divert his attention. The rhythmic movement of the train seemed to match the gentleman's incessant smoking perfectly. The thick smoke from his bidi was blowing right into Makaru's face, making him suffocate. But it was the icy cold wind that was in fact making him breathless. The train had meanwhile picked up speed. Makaru had already pulled out a towel from his cloth bag and wrapped it around his head. His ears were now well covered but his hands and feet were still exposed to the wind. The louder and longer the train blew its shrill horn, the more his heart shivered in cold fear. As if it wasn't just a horn blowing, but some awful unknown danger that was mercilessly crushing him into a thousand pieces. Everything went blank for moments—the earth, the water, the wind, the trees, the creepers, the thrum and throb of human activities around him. He could not even see his co-passengers who had packed themselves next to him on his berth. And the gentleman sitting beside the open window, oblivious to it all, was adding to his cold terror. Makaru had a sneaking suspicion that actually he was the one who was blowing the horn, and secretly enjoying watching everyone else suffer due to the cold, all the while contentedly pulling on his bidi and exhaling long puffs of smoke.

It was barely dawn. Yet the woman sitting opposite Makaru was already shelling peanuts and munching on them nonstop along with her three children. How could one possibly enjoy herself so much so early in the morning? *Arrey*! What have you got for common sense? Can't you at least throw the blessed shells out of the window? But no, she won't do that. Shell them, eat them and just drop the shells on the floor. What is more, her youngest daughter just felt like peeing right then and there. And so the peanut shells were in for a delightful swim. Now they were happily swimming towards Makaru's feet. On top of it the train's continuous jerks seemed hell-bent on pushing all that filth towards him, complete with peanut shells and the pee they were bobbing about in. Makaru lifted his feet up. But where would he keep his chappals? He was not going to hold them in his hands. Sitting with his chappaled feet up on the seat would be absurd. How about keeping his chappals on the seat? Well, that was out of the question. So what was he to do? With a flourish he cleverly pushed his chappals farther under the seat, safe from the treacherous liquid that had been floating dangerously close to them. Now the train started wobbling even more zealously. Thank God! The pee and the peanut shells now seemed determined to pay homage to the woman, and were headed straight for her now. Makaru was relieved. Meanwhile, the gentleman seemed to have had enough of his bidi and having finished smoking, he let the stub fall to the floor and crushed it with his shoe without another thought. The bidi went out and all that was left was the harmless stub and ashes. Aah, at last! If not from the cold, Makaru at least got rid of the suffocating smoke. Relieved, he took a deep breath.

It wasn't as if the smoke really bothered him that much. Makaru's father and grandfather were avid smokers of *pika*, an intoxicant made of strong tobacco. So he was quite used to being around tobacco smoke. In fact his family in the village even used to cultivate tobacco. Tobacco saplings were planted in neat rows made of mounds of soil moistened with a light sprinkle of water. In winters like these the greenish leaves would grow as big as winnowing baskets. Even the country chickens would hide themselves in the green realms of those giant leaves, so as not to end up on the dinner plates of the crows, eagles and ravens. The tobacco leaves were then cut with a sickle, soaked in water and expertly dried so that no two leaves were stuck together. This helped retain their powerful intoxicant quality. Makaru's father used to cultivate tobacco in their backyard. The potency of this tobacco when rolled in sal leaves was unparalleled. The smoke produced by a whole bundle of bidis was not a patch on what a single pika could produce. It almost reminded one of the smoke billowing out of a factory chimney. Being exposed to people smoking pikas, would the smoke of a mere bidi bother Makaru? But times had changed. After coming to Raipur, even the smoke of a bidi made him breathless.

He was thinking all this when someone abruptly moved his precious chappals out in front. As he put down his legs and bent to look under his seat, he saw a boy wearing a torn threadbare shirt sweeping the dirty floor with a tattered broom. Well, at least the urine, the peanut shells and the bidi stub would now get cleaned all at once. True, the shells had been swimming in urine unabashedly all this while. But the passion and vigour with which this dirty half-naked boy with a lanky frame was sweeping the compartment floor, literally sprawled over it, surpassed that too. People didn't clean their own faces with the enthusiasm that this boy cleaning the filthy, third-class passenger train floor demonstrated. Seeing this boy at work, Makaru's blood started rushing through his veins and tidal waves of something indescribable crashed over him, nearly engulfing him. It was true that he could not snatch the broom from the boy's shriveled hands and throw it away, nor fix the grimy buttons of his torn shirt, nor clean the boy's running nose with a soft kerchief—but the very realisation that he couldn't do any of these things burned his whole body in a scorching heat. His inner struggles made him forget the freezing cold. If the man had the brazenness to open the window in the biting cold of a chilly winter night, so be it.

After sometime, having tucked the broom under his arm, the boy came and stood in front of Makaru. He jingled the scanty change he had collected till now to draw the attention of the passengers. The trousered gentleman sitting beside Makaru lit another bidi. Exhaling a big puff of smoke, he swore angrily, directing his foul words at the poor boy, “Bastard! It is boys like him who grow up and thieve shamelessly, turn into ruthless dacoits and create disorder in society. Wandering prostitutes give birth to them callously in the filthiest nooks and crannies one can imagine and then just dump them in the gutters...just adding to the population...Chhi!”

But the boy wasn’t there to listen to this tongue-lashing and had already moved on to another berth to ask for money. It was Makaru who had to listen to all this. The gentleman had been travelling in this train for so long, yet nothing had come out of his mouth till now except for smoke. And when he spoke, who was it for? The nation that the foul-mouthed patriot pretended to care so much about! Makaru heard him heedlessly. God knew how much the boy was hurt by those offensive words, but Makaru’s heart had been wrenched open like a raw wound. He was so enraged he thought it would have been better had he thoroughly soaked his slippers in the urine and given the disgusting man a few hard slaps on his cheek. “Sala! Call yourself educated!” he hissed under his breath, “If you have so much knowledge and are so well-mannered, then why the hell are you smoking and throwing the ashes inside the compartment? Don’t you even have the sense to throw them out of the window? And when you crushed the bidi stub on the floor did you think that your father would come and pick it up for you? Sala! Civil fucker! Lecturing big instead of giving a few annas...If that boy is a bastard it is because some man like you sexually exploited his helpless mother and left her like a coward. Chhi-chhi-chhi...!”

Though his conscience was killing him, Makaru could not utter a word. Instead he played dumb and pretended not to have heard him at all. Tensed, his body started sweating profusely. By then the bright rays of the sun had spread their radiance everywhere; the pearly dewdrops had melted and mingled with nature; one could see goats and sheep heading towards the fields to graze. Makaru got up from his seat to use the latrine. He stood at the door of the bogey briefly, to gaze at the beauty of nature beckoning him and to savour that soulful moment. He saw a young goatherd waving at him and returned the gesture with a slight wave of his hand. After some time, the train reached Mahasamund station. The trousered gentleman deboarded. Makaru hastily lunged for the window seat. He felt relieved. Perhaps he had been waiting for this chance.

The train which had left Raipur at dawn was supposed to reach Lathore by 11 a.m. For most passengers, Lathore was a non-existent station. In railway parlance it was known as Harishankar Road. Only the locals called Lathore by that absurd name. Earlier, Makaru's ancestors used to live in Banjipali, a small village about three kilometres from Lathore. Because of a quarrel with the village *gauntia*, Makaru and his parents had left their village and migrated to Raipur long ago. Since then, they had not returned to their ancestral village. There was no trace left of their house in the village now. Two of his cousin brothers still lived in Banjipali. Makaru used to visit the village occasionally for marriages and social gatherings. But this time, it was neither for a marriage nor a gathering. The reason for his visit was grief. His heart was heavy with shock, sympathy and grief. All forty houses of the small Dalit basti in Lathore had been burnt to the ground by the upper castes. Makaru's relatives had become homeless overnight. He got this news only yesterday. Unable to bear it, he had taken the next train to Lathore, which had left early morning today. Leaving Mahasamund station, the train was now chugging on its way again, chhuk-chhuk-chhuk-chhuk...

Two

Makaru Suna's grandfather was one of three brothers. The eldest one lived in Banjipali, the second one in Lathore and the youngest in Larki.

Earlier, these three villages had been located in the middle of a dense forest. News of docile sheep and goats being abducted by predatory wolves was commonplace. Many had also been taken straight to the next world by hungry wild bears. Makaru had an uncle in Larki who had been doomed to live with just one eye thanks to an encounter with a bear. Sometimes cattle, and even humans, became prey to tigers. Even today a swear common to these villages is *baag dharaa*. When people got angry they would just say, "Tote baag dharu!" No, it wasn't some adage told to travellers before embarking on an adventurous journey into the unknown. It simply meant, "May the tiger get you!" or "May the tiger make a good meal of you!" Makaru could recall being told by his grandfather that tiny villages dotted the outskirts of the seemingly forbidden forest, for few could muster the courage to live right next to it when they didn't know whether the next morning's sun would kiss their eyes good morning, or bid their shrouded corpse good bye. Whilst the king reigned in the area, he had appointed one each of a *gauntia*, a *makaddam*, a *jhankar* and a chowkidar in every village. The king was cunning and possessed discretion, but a biased one. He chose carefully. Thus all the posts of gauntias and makaddams were handed over to the upper castes. The responsibility of jhankars was thrust into the hands of the Gonds, Sauras, Malis and Kondhs. That left the post of chowkidars with the Panas, Kandaras, Ganas and Doms—that is, those who happened to be, through no fault of their own, lower in the caste strata.

Unfortunately, no suitable candidates for the post of a chowkidar could be found for the village of Larki. Lathore, too, seemed to be cursed with the same fate. And so, Makaru's middle and youngest grandfathers were appointed as chowkidars in Lathore and Larki, respectively. And that is how they ended up leaving Banjipali. However, their new assignments and locations could not estrange the brothers from each other. They often held family get-togethers and bonded over family functions. And what better way of keeping in touch and sharing events of each other's busy lives than at social gatherings! Their cordial family relationships had continued right up to the third generation—now represented by Makaru.

A *gudi* puja had been organised three years ago. The Suna family had invited acquaintances from near and far, be they relatives, relatives' friends, in-laws, in-laws' friends, friends of the ancestors, or just family friends. Essentially, anyone who had ever known the Suna family or its ancestors was invited to the puja. The head count had reached a staggering three thousand. They had all assembled to pay homage to their *duma*, their ancestral deity, at the site where they believed their ancestor had come and first settled down. The gadi puja was held every five, seven or ten years to pay tribute to the ancestor of the family in question. But, you couldn't just show up with your beautiful face and expect to be treated to a lavish feast. Every attending family contributed rice, sacrificial goats, hens, new clothes, *pithas* and money for the puja, as per their budget and capacity. Pious parents whose vows had been fulfilled by their venerable gods would perform their children's *mundan* on this auspicious occasion. Goats, sheep and hens brought by the attendees would be sacrificed. The elders would patiently sit and animatedly narrate the stories of the origin and spread of their clan, so that the newer generations would learn at least a little, if not more, about their ancestry and their vibrant past. The ancestral spirits would be invoked by playing traditional musical instruments, and invited to bless the immense gathering.

The chief organiser of the last gadi puja had been Chitrasen Suna of Lathore village. As Chitrasen was much older than him, Makaru called him 'Chitra-da'. Chitrasen was widely respected in Lathore, despite having failed his matriculation. Mind you, at that time, even being a ninth class pass was no mean feat. Chitrasen was one of the few men of Lathore known for their humility, civility and dignity. His good public rapport had twice earned him the coveted post of the sarpanch of his village. His concerted efforts in working for the people's welfare were quite popular with the villagers, and these tales never left their lips well after he had satisfactorily finished serving his tenure. So it won't come as a surprise if one was told that people in and around Lathore would still often fondly address him as the sarpanch. Chitrasen advocated good farming practices on the chowkidari *jagir* that he had inherited from his father, and his thriving farming business was solid evidence of the same. He was known as an experienced and wise cultivator, with sound agricultural knowhow which helped him reap rich benefits from his land. A prosperous man, in times of need, people took monetary help from him, be it on the occasions of Nuakhai, Puspuni, a marriage or any other occasion. The same Chitrasen had organised the gadi puja so well, with such seamless perfection and generosity that the event had touched the attendees deeply at the core of their hearts, and its memories stayed with them for years to come. Even today, people of Lathore don't shy of singing praises for the grand and joyful festivity, and for its head organiser.

The more educated the youth had become and attained reasonable jobs in the bustling cities, the farther and farther away they had drifted from their community, their culture, their ancestry and traditions. To make them aware and remember, a *birtia* had been called. He had eloquently narrated family stories through his enrapturing songs accentuated by the beats of his trademark *damru*. Chitra-da had then himself beautifully explained the meanings of those soulful melodies. Makaru had attended the puja alone for he had been unable to bring his family along. Chitra-da had advised him, "My dear boy, the gadi puja does not take place every year. It is good to bring your family along to such jamborees. What better excuse to mingle with your acquaintances and friends? You can always hop into a train and just come and pay a visit that is long overdue." Makaru was touched by those loving words. Who can mouth them in the absence of genuine warmth and intimacy? Thereafter, Chitra-da had called his only daughter-in-law, who worked as a *shiksha karmi*, and introduced her to Makaru. Not only that, he had also asked her to bow to him respectfully. Makaru was overjoyed. He had really regretted not having brought his family along.

The upper castes have torched all the forty houses of the Ganapada, including that of Chitra-da. Now all of them have been rendered homeless.

Compared to his other brothers, Chitra-da of Lathore was the only one who was well-to-do. The family in Larki was the poorest. The ill-fated man who had lost an eye in a wild bear attack was known as Larkia kaka. He had a brother who left for the Assam tea gardens with others for work, and never returned. Whether he was alive or dead was still a mystery. Despite being blind in one eye, our Larkia kaka went to the bamboo forest next to his village every day for work. It was a small hillock full of bamboo trees. A bamboo company had set up its operations there. Larkia kaka was eventually appointed as a guard-cum-sweeper in the company. All he had to do as a sweeper was clean the houses of company employees. As a guard he often had to travel in trucks loaded with bamboo. Once, a loaded truck got upturned and crushed ill-omened Larkia kaka to death.

Larkia kaka had once brought his better half to Banjipali to see a *badipala*. He had gone to every household and showered them with his love. He had recounted numerous anecdotes about the dense bamboo forests and the bamboo company that he worked for. Makaru must have been five or six years old then. Even at such a tender age, Makaru used to tend and graze cattle belonging to the Arasthi family. It would be evening by the time he got back home from work. Back then there was neither electricity nor money to light a kerosene lamp at his place. So his house was bathed in eternal darkness. All people could do was light up an *antra* and sit around the somewhat feeble light of its flames. The memories Makaru had of Larkia kaka were all of the time when he used to sit in the evening, the soft light of the small fire creating a halo round his auburn face. Larkia kaka used to traverse the entire distance from his village to Banjipali on foot. By the time he reached his destination, it would be pitch dark. When Makaru would get up early next morning, eager to see kaka's jovial face, he would have already left for the fields. Their meeting was left unfinished forever. Little did Makaru know that he would never meet his dear old kaka again. However, he did meet kaka's daughter, who had come to attend the gadi puja. Yes, the very same one that his beloved Chitra-da had organised so efficiently and well.

Banjipali had a different story altogether.

Makaru's father had another brother. An elder one. He was the chowkidar of Banjipali. It would be quite a quotidian thing to say that Banjipali was hit by drought almost every year. Once there had been a severe drought—worse than anyone could recall or think of in their wildest imagination. People were forced to flee to the forests to collect what scanty grains of wild rice the bamboo thickets could offer and cook them to survive.

That was also the year that the *khenjed* had come wandering to Banjipali. No one knew where these vagabonds had come from. They were a seemingly random and motley group: big beefy men, headstrong women, jolly children, married couples, spinsters, bachelors, the aged, toothless toddlers. Since one could make neither head nor tail of their origins or their settlement, they were simply called khenjed: the poor, the homeless, the ragged, the dirty. The women would strap their toddlers to their bosoms, like fleshy backpacks. Their language was nothing more than cryptic babble to the villagers. With an aggressive demeanour and a fierce temper always perched on the tip of their noses, like some intimidating Maoists, they would go from house to house and demand the freshly cooked food right off the blazing hearths. Their unnerving belligerence came quite handy here, of course. And then, as if they had come casually strolling to their neighbourhood grocery store, they would cart away every speck of ration they could lay their hands on.

As for villagers who had money but would refuse to part with it, the khenjed would heartlessly crush their own children to the floor—cheap emotional blackmail, if you ask me. Their children, having survived more sentimental wounds than bodily ones, would dissolve into a flood of tears. Hearts wrenched by their copious cries, the damned hosts would be compelled to give away some of the fruits of their toil. Still discontent, the khenjed would turn their roving eyes towards the neat vegetable patch next. They would greedily pluck cucumbers, ridge gourds and pumpkins, even as the villagers looked on with broken hearts, seeing months of labour disappear in a matter of seconds. If they caught sight of any hen or goat the khenjed would instantly cull it and take it away. Such cold cruelty was something that the simple villagers dared not challenge. More often than not, they preferred to maintain their distance. A courageous protest could result in dire circumstances and even be fatal. Knowing this, the villagers bore the aggressive nomads as much as they could, like silent martyrs. People were forced to hide inside their own homes whenever news got around that the khenjed were nearby. Children, of course, were locked in.

It was in such an adversity-ridden year of drought that Makaru had made his way to earth. His father had aptly named him Makaru: 'the one born during drought'. With a drought occurring almost every year it was difficult to manage life and tend to a family with what he earned from a small plot of land. Makaru's paternal uncle, or Bada Bapa as he affectionately called him, had already sold off the chowkidari land. Only the homestead was left. Later, even that land got divided between two brothers. In one portion lived Makaru with his parents and in another, his Bada Bapa's family.

Makaru was just a young boy then. All he knew was adversities and hardships. His family was so poor that four days a week they had to make do with just one meal a day. Throughout the year, their bellies remained half-empty. Once, on a Nuakhai feast, having thoroughly filled his belly to his satisfaction, Makaru let out a happy burp and said, "Ma, my stomach is gleefully full today." With glistening eyes his mother had pulled him into her lap and let her fond caresses add to his joy.

It is not that Makaru's family alone had to face this. Other Ganapada households encountered similar deprivations as well.

Makaru's father worked as a *halia* in the *gauntia*'s house. All he got for the hard labour of an entire year was six *khani*s of paddy and sixty rupees. Needless to say, six khanis of paddy were hardly sufficient to feed a family of three who slaved like bullocks all day. If they managed really tightly, that is to say till the family was on the brink of starvation, they might, and I am saying might, have lasted a maximum of six months on it. And to top it all, like unpalatable green icing on a rancid yellow pineapple cake, there were other expenses to meet as well. So his mother was left with no option other than to take up odd jobs here and there.

But the gauntia family knew very well that a halia could not toil hard unless his stomach had been attended to. So the maid of the gauntia's house gave Makaru's father a meal of rice gruel in a big bowl every day. Every morning, when Makaru's father went to the gauntia's fields to work, he would brush his teeth with a twig broken from a neem tree on his way, and rinse it off with water from the fields. Sprinkling some salt on the heady mix of gruel and rice, he would drink it to his heart's content. With a full belly, he cared not a pice how hard he slogged. Whether he had to level the fields with a heavy plough, uproot the arrogant weeds under the scorching noon sun, sow the seeds by hand across the vast expanse of the fields alone, he did not give a damn. He toiled like a buffalo, uncomplainingly.

But, no matter how hard they toiled or how much sweat and blood they poured into their job, who ever appreciated the labour of the lower castes? Take Makaru's father, for instance. He had tilled the land in pouring rain. He had transplanted the paddy standing knee-deep in muddy water. He had cut cartloads of paddy and transported them on his tanned back to the *khala*. He had spent sleepless nights harvesting the crop. No matter what he did, would the insults and abuses ever leave his trail? Praise and appreciation were a far cry. Like the other halias, all he got at the end of it was a six-feet-long coarse dhoti on Nuakhai and stale leftover pithas on Puspuni—and that was all.

Once while chopping wood, the axe slipped and the blade hit his leg. Blood started flowing freely from the deep cut, and it took quite some time to staunch. What harm would have been done if the gauntia family had taken him to the doctor? After all, it was they who had hired him. But no, why would they ever do that? It was against their dignity and model code of conduct! Makaru's father had to tend to it himself. Every day he would burn some wild *bheluans* in the fire and press them to his wound to disinfect it. A cleverly contrived remedy of nature, but it took its time, which was allegedly too much for the gauntia household. The mistress of the house found a good excuse to scold and humiliate her employee every day and missed no opportunity to rain abuses on him. When she cunningly complained that there was no firewood in the house and that no food could be cooked without it, Makaru's father was forced to go and cut wood despite his serious injury and his weak, still healing leg.

Even today, Makaru cannot dismiss that other diabolic mishap of his childhood from memory. Recalling even a moment of the incident makes his head explode in pain, as if a million pincers were stinging him at once. His whole body shudders with cold, as if some terrifying unseen force was murderously squeezing the life out of his soul and tearing it apart with unimaginable coldness.

Like any other day Makaru had taken the gauntia's oxen to graze that morning. They were up to their throats with the lush green grass from the backyard and the fields. The paddy had already been harvested, so he didn't have to keep a sharp eye on the cattle in case they had a mind to munch on the ripe golden crop instead. Makaru gathered them into a herd and having left them at that, he headed towards the *tendu* tree. He saw fat bunches of mouthwatering, soft succulent tendus hanging from the tree, beckoning him and his growling tummy. It was already lunch time. Makaru couldn't control himself. Intent on quelling his gnawing hunger, he lifted his plough shaft and flung it at the ripened tendus with all his might. It went up with hurtling speed aiming straight at the tendus, but unfortunately got caught in the dense foliage. Not a single tendu fell. The ripe tendus had also caught the eyes of the gauntia's grandchild. He must have been about ten years old. Tempted to eat them, the boy tried to playfully mimic Makaru by picking up a small stone and throwing it. But to his bad luck, nothing fell. Makaru could not bear this insult. If the gauntia's grandchild wished to eat tendus, Makaru felt he must ensure that he had some, come what may.

Makaru started collecting stones to hurl. He then aimed carefully chosen stones at the tendus that he desired so much. The first stone brought down three ripe tendus. The gauntia's grandchild lunged at them greedily. Makaru felt relieved that he had been able to preserve his dignity. He hurled another stone at a bunch which hung high above the ground, but the stone did not reach its target. Not one tendu fell down. Then he gathered all his strength and hurled a stone for the third time at the biggest bunch that he could set his eyes on. Although the stone did not fall, loads of tendus fell to the ground. The gauntia's grandchild gleefully ran to gather them. The tendus were raining down. There were so many of them that the stone had in fact got stuck in them. So, when the tendus fell, the stone also came down along with them. Unfortunately, it hit the child on his head. The child started wailing as loud as he could, fit to burst his lungs, "O my god, I am going to die!" Seeing the bright red blood on the child's head, Makaru's heart started throbbing painfully inside his chest as if his very life were ebbing out of his numb body along with the blood trickling from the wound on the child's tender skin. Hearing his dear grandson's agonised scream, the gauntia and the people working in the fields nearby rushed to the spot. Makaru could not bear to look at the scene. A stark reality loomed before his black eyes. He had thrown the stone that hit the boy's head: so he was undoubtedly the culprit. With tears streaming down his eyes, he ran from there as fast as his legs could carry him. Soon he reached the dense jungle. With no other option, he hid there with a heavy heart and a guilty conscience. Afraid of jackals and bears, he climbed up a tree and stayed there till midnight.

Meanwhile, Makaru's mother cried her way to unconsciousness. All the villagers were convinced by the spreading rumours that Makaru had shrewdly lured the gauntia's grandchild with a promise of ripe tendus and then smashed his head with a stone.

The gauntia's son Nandakumar was a school teacher in the nearby village. He was the first from Banjipali village to have passed the matriculation examination, not to mention that he was the very first person to get a decent salaried job. The gauntia had him sent to a hostel in a far-off village so he could pursue his studies. While staying at the hostel, Nandakumar had a discreet affair with the daughter of one of his teachers. Unfortunately for him and his lover, the affair was not as discreet as he thought it to be. His teacher came to know about it and he promptly expelled Nandakumar from the school. And so that's where his studies came to an end. The gauntia's household had no problems at all, monetary or otherwise. They had plenty of everything—land, cattle, goats, sheep, houses, gold, silver and what not. And naturally, the heir would be given the best of the best. He was served rice with spoonfuls of ghee every day. That made him look big, beefy and dashing like a macho man. The gauntia had chosen carefully, and finally married his son to a girl who came from an even more well-to-do household than his own. The grand spectacle of Nandakumar as the bridegroom, sitting all bedecked atop his glossy black horse looking like a king, was a memory that would never be erased from the villagers' minds. Long after his marriage procession had gone, the onlookers were left still gaping at the dusty empty path like stunned goldfish.

When the gauntia's daughter-in-law was pregnant she suffered terrible pains in her bowels. Every conceivable effort was made; quack doctors and sorcerers were frantically called. But it was all in vain. Giving birth to a baby boy, she glided away to heaven. Thankfully, the child survived. The gauntia looked after the motherless child with all the love and affection that his heart could muster. He loved his grandson more than he had ever loved his son. The child is now in the fifth standard of the village school. The boy's pleas would invariably melt his heart; he could never say no to him. The gauntia saw to it that all his wishes were fulfilled. Tendu was just a fruit. Had his grandson said so, the gauntia would have planted the biggest tendu tree in the world laden with ripe succulent fruits right at his doorstep. But, quite contrary to his optimistic dreams, his darling grandson went out to eat tendus and got his head wounded in the process. The gauntia was smoking fire! "How dare that lowly halia's son hit my grandson on the head? What was the poor boy's fault?" he bellowed.

Nandakumar wasn't home yet. He was still busy teaching his students at school. The gauntia sent a manservant to inform his son about the tragic incident. The man ran to Nandakumar as fast as his legs could carry him, and repeated the grievous incident that had taken place in the village.

Nandakumar could not believe that his halia's son had the nerve even to touch the princely heir of the gauntia household, much less to crack his head open. Incredulous, leaving his schoolwork unattended, he immediately rushed to his trusted bicycle and its old worn out tyres sped away squeaking to his son's aid.

You could search far and wide in Banjipali and no less than at least five of its neighbouring villages, but you won't find a single bicycle—that is, except the one owned by the most dashing Nandakumar. Its once-pure-leather seat innocent of even a speck of dust, and its tyres...well, we all know what a pleasing sound they made. There it would stand, glinting humbly under the admiring sun, in the gauntia's garage, if you could call it that. When

Nandakumar used to cross the villages on his sleek black bicycle, children would run after him with their mouths agape in awe, screaming, "Bi-skull! Bi-skull!" Seeing Nandakumar pedalling away fast, raising a cloud of dust behind him, one would think that he might put a superfast bullet train to shame. Now, having heard the news of his son's cracked skull, he pedalled even faster, perhaps in the hopes of shaming a supersonic jet today. Perched on his bicycle with knitted brows and eyes that didn't so much as blink, he reached his village clocking record time.

His son was sitting on his father's lap and bawling uncontrollably. Seeing his son's wounded head and the trickling blood, Nandakumar felt his eyes moisten with helplessness and silent rage. Meanwhile, there was considerable unease in the village at the fact that a mere untouchable Gana boy could dare to try and batter the head of the great gauntia's grandson. For the villagers, this was fairly shocking news to gossip about, with stunned expressions of disbelief, yet also an interesting one they could cleverly lend their expert opinions and comment on. Unable to believe the news that was now spreading like wildfire, the villagers started thronging near the gauntia's house. Knowing there was nothing more they could do, they were making sympathetic clicks and noises of "Aha...Oho..." No one could imagine Makaru's intentions or picture him trying to smash the child's head. What was he thinking of, that servant boy? What was he but the son of a lowly halia? No one hesitated to fling the vilest obscenities they knew at the black-hearted culprit. So charged was the atmosphere that, blinded by their collective rage in sympathy for the gauntia's family, had the people found Makaru there, they would probably have torn him into pieces and scattered them for the vultures and jackals to feast on.

In contrast, who was there to witness the pitiful state of Makaru's by now almost deranged father, leave alone support him? Manglu knew that the gauntia's grandson was the apple of his eyes, more precious to him than life itself. It would become difficult for his family to live in the village now. Manglu had been the gauntia's halia for as long as he could recall. If his family could eat even one square meal a day, they were indebted to the gauntias for it. He knew the gauntia and his son Nandakumar very well. They were not the kind of people you would like to mingle with, if you had a choice. They could burn the earth down for the sake of a tiny whim. The insurmountable question hovering in his mind was: what hell on earth possessed Makaru to dive into such turbulent troubled waters?!

Manglu was acutely aware of his situation. He was low-caste. Their basti was located at one end of the village. It was called Ganapada, a Dalit basti. The upper-caste villagers would wrinkle up their noses in disgust even at the thought of passing by it. If they needed some work to be done, they would simply call them out by name from a distance. Manglu had been working at the gauntia's house for years now. But he still couldn't muster the courage to meet the gauntia's eyes, much less answer him back. Once, having split the firewood for fuel, Manglu was storing it in the backyard when he had inadvertently brushed past the gauntia's wife. She had almost fainted with anger and snapped back in cold fury, "Look where you walk! Just because you work in this house doesn't mean you become its member!" And she had rushed inside to bathe and change her clothes in some haste. After all, her purity had been stained! Then she had performed an elaborate ritual of sprinkling herself with holy water. Only then had she returned to a calmer state of mind. Manglu was severely reprimanded for not having followed the caste rules. Since that day, he had been walking on tiptoes and being extra cautious never to commit such a crime again. How terrible, how unfortunate this black day was! Makaru had stoned the beloved grandson of the very house that had been providing for their livelihood since heaven knows when. O god! Manglu did not dare imagine what the consequences would be.

Here, Makaru was untraceable. No one knew his whereabouts. Had he run away, that insolent coward? Or had he purged his sins and drowned himself in the village pond? Good that the brute is not around. Had he been spotted, he would have been beaten black and blue. The villagers would have chewed him alive for sure. Wherever that coward is hiding, let him be.

Manglu knew well that his son was not the belligerent, easily provoked type who would answer anyone back, let alone beat up a child. No, no, not at all. Makaru was a simple, silent boy whom you would in fact get tired of provoking but won't be able to get even a swear word out of. However much you incited him, roused him or dangled a carrot in front of him, Makaru was not the one to raise his hand or open his mouth. Till now, not a single complaint against him had come to Manglu's ears. How could then such a quiet, such a peace-loving, docile boy create such a big nuisance?

Makaru's mother, Sabesh, seemed half dead. The only signs of life were her pitiful groans and tearful whimpers. Her greatest fear was that she would never be able to see her only son ever again. If only she could meet him, caress him...she would hide him somewhere. She would not let this ill fate befall him. The gauntia household would stone him to death. No! No! Sabesh couldn't even bear to think of it. Even if her son had accidently thrown the stone, it had just grazed the child's head. And here are the foolish villagers making a mountain out of a molehill. The child didn't get killed, did he? Makaru was just a small boy and he was innocent. He'd made a mistake. Could he not be excused? These were the feverish musings of Makaru's mother as she sat on the verandah, cursing her poor son's evil fate. And a step or two above her sat Manglu with a heavy heart.

Just then, Nandakumar flew in fast as a javelin. He was flanked by a group of villagers. Boiling with rage, paying no heed to the rigid caste rules he otherwise so piously followed, he ran straight to Manglu and kicked him square on the chest. Manglu fell headfirst onto the ground, and yet folded his hands in submission, helplessness writ large on his face. Nandakumar thundered, "You devilish mother-fucker! Out with your bastard son! That sadistic wretch dared lay hands on my progeny! Now I will drink his blood! What was that bastard thinking?" And he started raining blows on Manglu again. Manglu was getting mercilessly battered in the dust, but kept his hands folded. When his wife came to his rescue, Nandakumar bellowed, "You prostitute, what kind of bastard have you given birth to? He dared touch *my* son! Out with him! Let's see who saves him from my wrath today!" Saying so, he again started kicking the prone Manglu. His fierce blows and furious, hate-filled words would have frightened anyone to death. The men and women of Ganapada stood as mute spectators; no one raised even an eyebrow at the sight of the bloodied Manglu being rolled about in the dust like a piece of meat. Instead they chastised him, saying, "Being an untouchable, even touching an upper-caste boy is an abhorrent crime for Makaru, not to mention the assault."

Nandakumar charged into Manglu's house. He searched every nook and cranny, even looked behind the door and underneath the cots. In his mad rage he broke all the pots and pans. His search, though extensive, turned out to be fruitless. In his exasperation, Nandakumar took off his slipper and started beating Manglu with it. With bruises on every inch of his skin, Manglu was pleading for mercy, "Forgive us, master. Just this time, master. We have always been subservient to you...you are our God. My son committed a terrible blunder. Forgive him. Mercy, prabhu, have mercy..."

Hearing Manglu's pleas for mercy, Nandakumar's anger reached a climax. His voice had turned hoarse due to continuous shouting. He was drenched in sweat. But this did little to douse his fire. He abruptly got up and turned to leave for home. One could hear him mumbling like some homeless lunatic, "I will drive that mother-fucker out of the village. *Sulu*! How dare he set his eyes on my beloved son! Cracked his head open! I won't leave him!"

Manglu was grief-stricken. His heart stung much more than the bruises that Nandakumar had inflicted upon him. It ached for his son. His absence was too much for him to bear. They had no other child to call their own. Their son had to be protected by all means. But where was he to find Makaru? Who knew where he was? Where did he go?

Evening set in Banjipali. Like docile hens, all the villagers returned to their homes. There was pin-drop silence. No one knew what the consequences were going to be. The sharp chill of the winter evening could now be felt. Hundreds of fireflies could be seen glowing on the moringa trees. The moment the house sparrows had ceased their noisy boisterous chatter in the backyard, the eerie yelps of the jackals could be heard from deep inside the forest. The first call of huti-huti was followed by many more.

Just then Kirtan Gana's loud voice pierced the silence. "Come over to the *beheran*—the village meeting is about to commence," he was repeatedly announcing. The beheran was almost always held in the evening; you couldn't very well expect people to be harvesting their precious crop on one hand and gathering to discuss mundane village matters on the other. This was the one part of the day when they could take a brief breather after a hard day's toil, lounging on the coarse carpets laid out for the meeting, and participate in the beheran.

Manglu's heart started pounding in his chest. He felt as if it was not Kirtan Gana but God Yama himself calling out loud. The hearth at home seemed cold and unused today. The house looked deserted, a chilly wind was billowing about and an eerie calm prevailed, as if someone had been called away to heaven.

After having shouted the announcement through the entire village until his lungs were fit to burst, Kirtan Gana came over to Manglu's. The one because of whom the meeting was being called had to be personally invited, so that at least he should be present even if no one else was. Village etiquette, as they say. Following the gauntia's orders, Kirtan Gana was here to do the same. Of the many powers the gauntia held in his robust palm, being the head of Banjipali was one. He presided over all the meetings and then passed what he thought to be the most apt judgement. Today the gauntia himself would decide what punishment was to be given to an untouchable Gana boy who had plucked the courage to stone his own grandson. After Kirtan Gana left, Manglu was in a dilemma. Should he go to the beheran, or should he go search for his dear son instead? But as they say, it is not good to live in the water and make an enemy of the crocodile. He knew well that the gauntia was a ferocious crocodile, a venomous cobra, an angry tiger or something far worse and more fearsome. A creature whose path a man with the slightest bit of sanity would never dream of crossing.

Despite these dark and pessimistic thoughts, Manglu went to the beheran. He was despondently accompanied by his helpless partner, Sabesh. Everyone had already arrived. The reigning lord and *debata* of them all, the gauntia arrived last, flanked by his son Nandakumar and his grandson. Manglu paid obeisance to everyone and sat down in a corner. Normally the residents of Ganapada were never invited to the village meeting. Even if they came, they simply shrank silently into a corner, like Manglu.

They could never voice their opinions. On the very rare occasion that they mustered the courage to speak, the villagers would just wave it away in hysterics. So all they could do was play dumb and listen to whatever cock and bull story was being enacted out there. As usual, Manglu crouched into a corner, while Sabesh hid herself against a wall near the margins, silently praying that she was invisible to all. Not a soul got to know whether she had come to the meeting or not.

The meeting commenced. The gauntia, the very personification of law and order that the villagers looked up to, cleared his throat to begin his speech.

Gauntia: "Have all the villagers come?"

Kirtan Gana: "Yes, huzoor."

Gauntia: "Hey Manglu, do you hear me?"

Manglu: "Yes, huzoor."

Gauntia: "Your son Makaru beat Nandakumar's child with a stone and bloodied him."

Manglu: "Yes, huzoor."

Gauntia: "You all are the Gana community, the untouchables. According to the holy caste system meted out by the Creator himself, you are at the lowest rungs of all. Even if the upper castes so much as touch you by mistake, they rush to take a bath and change clothes. And that son of yours, forget about touching, he straight went and broke an upper-caste child's head! This is a heinous crime. For having committed this sin, you must bear the punishment that is due."

Manglu: "Yes, huzoor."

Gauntia: "Because your son has broken my own grandson's head, I will not pronounce the punishment myself, for if I do so, it will be accused of partiality. So let the wise gentlemen of the village decide the quantum of punishment for this gruesome act. What do you say, gentlemen?"

Everyone: "Yes, huzoor."

Gauntia: "Then gentlemen, tell us, what should be the punishment?"

Shashank: "Huzoor, according to custom, when beaten by a Gana, the victim loses his caste. A community meeting is organised to undo the grave mishap befallen on the victim.

Communal brothers from no less than five villages are invited. The victim's head is tonsured and he is given a ritual bath. Wearing a new dhoti, he is given sacred waters of the Ganges to drink. Only then can the cursed soul regain his lost identity. What happens thereafter is no mystery to you, huzoor. The perpetrator gives the community six khanis of rice, a he-goat and 120 rupees as a fine for having committed the heinous crime. This also helps cover the expenses of organising the feast."

Hearing this, Madan Mohan shouted: "There is more to it! As the victim is a mere child, Manglu's son's head must be smashed to dust, right here, in front of everyone. This, when done in addition to what was earlier suggested, is the only way to secure justice for the gauntia household."

A man sitting beside Nandakumar like an obedient puppy angrily barked: "Let Manglu go and bring his son here at once! Or he must confess where he has hidden the coward. Only when he surrenders his son to this august gathering will justice be done."

Having heard the discussion, Sabesh felt the walls closing in around her. If the villagers start insisting upon finding her son, or worse, get lucky in their search, what would befall her poor lad? Today heaven had shown mercy and her husband, on the brink of death, was somehow spared alive. But if Nandakumar found her son, he would chew him raw like a ravenous horse. Oh God! Save us from this calamity, please!

Here, Manglu could not utter a word. Six khanis of rice, a male goat and 120 rupees in fines...These accounted for more than two years of his income. How would he ever manage to give so much? And the people seemed to be salivating at the thought of finding his son. What if his nightmare came alive? What if they found him? Would he be spared alive from their bloodlust? While he sank deeper into the bottomless pit of such dark thoughts, an invisible voice spoke up: "And if Manglu does not deposit the amount by tomorrow morning, he will have to slave at the gauntia household for two years for free."

It felt as if Indra had himself descended from the heavens and cut Manglu into two with his thunderbolt. Even if he somehow agreed to work for two years without wages, what were his son and wife to live upon? How would they survive? They would surely die of hunger. What was he to do in such a situation which was closing in on him like floodwaters from all sides?

Having heard the last suggestion, the gauntia shook his head categorically and said, "No, No. Hereafter I will never ever employ any Gana halias. I will not allow them to enter my fields. Today, they have beaten up my grandson. Tomorrow, who knows, they might even beat me up. All these years I had kept Manglu in good faith, but not hereafter."

Manglu, with all the humility a man in his position could muster, paid a small courtesy to everyone again, and said: "Debata, kindly forgive us this time. We would never dream of committing such a wrong again. I agree that my son is the culprit. I will pay all the expenses of the community meeting in installments."

At this Nandakumar barked: "Not in installments, you fool! By tomorrow! By any means! How long will my son remain casteless due to that vile dog you call your son?"

Those present let the committee know of their consent. The meeting ended with a collective shout of "Haribol!" Manglu's elder brother was also present at the beheran. He had toiled as hard as possible to make ends meet. But thanks to the villagers and their revered gauntia, he no longer held the chowkidari post. He had heard every accusation hurled against his younger brother, but not uttered a word in his defence. What could he have said? Manglu himself had been rendered speechless. Even if he had spoken up, he wouldn't have been heard, so what was the point? Manglu tried to console himself. He suddenly remembered his dear departed father, who had once said: "Remember son, the God of Death Yama himself is easier to handle than these foolish bloodthirsty hellhounds of the village." The wretched conspirators! The whole village is run by the gauntia, and so are its people. So why won't they back him? What the gauntia utters the village echoes.

It was dark as death in the village. Wading through the blackness, Manglu could be seen as a morose figure stumbling on his way to his hut. He felt as if his eyes had been gouged out. His hands felt numb as if they were nothing more than rubbery flesh. His legs seemed to have turned to lead. He felt sick. Sick of himself. Sick of the situation he had landed in. Sick of the world.

The strength with which he could crush massive stones now seemed to have left him; his blood seemed to be pounding in his head like an angry gushing river. His eyes seemed to be staring into the abyss; everything turned grey and then black. He couldn't remember where his home was; instead, the wilderness seemed to beckon and call out to him.

When Sabesh put her hand on his shoulder to console him, Manglu reeled back in shock. He wanted to console her, to wipe her tears, to reassure her, but his body seemed to be no longer his. The shouts of "Haribol!" were tearing his eardrums into shreds.

Hari belonged only to the upper castes and the rich, Manglu mused. He neither belonged to the poor nor to the untouchables. Makaru was just an eight-year-old boy. He had committed a crime—if it could be called that—unknowingly. Was there no forgiveness for him? Couldn't the heavens show him just a little mercy? Tending to the haughty gauntia's docile cattle for years, Makaru had become quite like a calf himself. Who knew, perhaps the stone had hit the wrong target, after all. Now where was Manglu to get six khanis of rice, a full-grown male goat and the princely sum of 120 rupees from? He couldn't even conjure up that much money if he sold off his entire homestead. How was he to arrange for it all by tomorrow morning?

What if the villagers meant to kick him out of the village? Manglu somehow found his way back to his hut. He dropped dead on his cot and curled up like a dog whose teeth had been wrenched out of his mouth, without the smallest whimper or moan of pain. What could Sabesh, who had heard about the fine, have done to help Manglu recover from his wretched state? The yelping of jackals could be heard from the distance. The crickets were chirping ceaselessly. The moonless sky seemed to emphasise their doomed luck. Only the stars were gazing at him helplessly.

There was no sign of Makaru. Where was he? Was he alive or not? If he had returned, Manglu would have got his breath back. His innocent boyish face would have provided him solace. He would have got to know the actual turn of events. Manglu's fear and apprehension seemed to have found a way out of his numb insensate body in the form of tears.

Suddenly, there was an urgent knock at the door. Manglu's fear gripped him even tighter. The mad thirst for blood which seemed to have possessed Nandakumar might well drive him to Manglu's hut in the middle of the night to exact the revenge he desperately sought. He might even rape his wife! Ashen-faced, Manglu mouthed to Sabesh to hide under the cot. She wordlessly obeyed.

The knocks grew frantic and started raining blows. Manglu had no choice. His voice edged with fear, he asked, "Who is it?" In a barely audible whisper came the reply, "Bapa...It's me, Makaru!...Open the door!" Manglu could not believe what he heard. The murderous shouts of "Haribol" were still playing in his ears. Rushing towards the only barrier separating him and his lost son, he stealthily opened the door and quickly pulled Makaru inside. He peered outside to ascertain that no one had witnessed this union. If Nandakumar got to know that his son was home, Makaru would be dead in a blink. There was a sea of blackness as far as the eyes could see. Not a human limb or movement in sight. He silently prayed to the heavens as he swiftly bolted the door, "Oh, Goddess Nialimali! Please, please don't let anyone have seen my son!"

Sabesh wept, not letting go of her son for a moment. Her hands wouldn't stop caressing his listless body, nor would her tears. Her poor child had been starving all day, but she had nothing to offer him. The hearth was as cold and empty as his stomach. But be that as it may, all is well that ends well. So what if her son was hungry? At least he was alive and well! At least she was no longer clamouring for him, going mad not knowing where he might be, how he might be, or worse, searching for him on this earth when he may be serenely looking down at her from the heavens. What could be better than the return of her only son! Goddess Nialimali had herself bestowed her blessing on her darling son. She had protected him!

It seemed as if the walls of the simple mud hut had been bathed in the soothing glow of an earthen lamp. The warmth of intense relief and life itself coursed through Sabesh's veins. The moment Manglu saw his son, he too got back his lost energy and felt ready to crush stones with his bare hands if need be. It seemed that his limbless inert body had sprouted arms and legs again. He was ready to confront every damned obstacle and challenge that the world could throw at him.

Makaru narrated to them the turn of events, not leaving out even the smallest of details. What his parents had suspected right from the beginning in the depths of their hearts was indeed true: Makaru was completely innocent.

But, clearly the villagers did not share their view. For them, Makaru was the most wretched scoundrel they had ever set eyes upon, and luckily for them he had been caught in the blasphemous act. Even if he told them the truth, he would still be branded an arrogant liar. People would believe themselves to be so clever as to point out that Manglu was making up this cock-and-bull story just to evade the fine he had to pay. And, for certain, if Nandakumar ever set eyes on Makaru, he would not think twice before rendering him lifeless, leave alone pausing a moment to consider showing mercy. This deep crimson fire of revenge swirling dangerously in the orb-like eyes of Nandakumar would reduce Manglu's small family to ashes. Would Manglu ever bear to step on the very earth on which the gauntia's progeny would crack Makaru's head open? And Sabesh? That her anguished heart would burn in eternal despair and hellish agony would be an understatement.

The decision taken at the village meeting was no bad dream: it was stark reality. Every single villager was a witness to and a participant in the grossly unfair punishment meted out. Their vengeful souls would not rest content till they saw blood on his son's head. Was there any alternative, any way at all to get out of this mire? There wasn't a man in the neighbouring villages who could think of dueling with the powers of the gauntia household. How could he, Manglu, a mere halia, who fed himself and his family on the leftovers they threw at him with pity, even dream of locking horns with them? That would be more like embarking on the insolent quest to drain the seven seas of the world with the battered, rusty metal bucket that he bathed with.

Manglu was engulfed in darkness. Banjipali was sleeping, with just the occasional satisfied burps and snores to mar the tranquil silence. Even the trees, the creepers, the water and the wind were fast asleep. Nothing moved or stirred. But then, could the train thundering through the night, shrilly blowing its piercing whistle, be left far behind? The sound reverberated off each sleeping leaf, piercing through the silent night and travelled right up to the glittering skies. At times its high-pitched whistle shook the eardrum and made it tremble in fright; at other times it felt as if the heaving, crashing bellows of the night train were inviting you, beckoning you, calling out to you. The call of this train has resonated powerfully in the hearts of hundreds of people in this region, who pack their bags and head to Raipur and other big cities in search of work.

What native land is that where not a soul resides who will shed tears for your sufferings, or console you with a caress of understanding? Such a mountain of miseries had crashed over Manglu's head, and not a whimper of pity crossed the villagers' lips. But, were they really to be blamed? It is the gauntia who had clasped the entire village in his sausage-like pudgy fingers. Without his consent it seems even the rains were forbidden to fall. As soon as the first rays of the sun kiss this ominous land good morning, Manglu will be left a jobless man, with a fine bigger than the assets he could imagine possessing in his wildest dreams hovering treacherously over his head, the guilty father of a wretched criminal. Every single resident of Ganapada was aware of the twisted turn of events. But they too depended heavily on the gauntia for sustenance. If someone spoke a syllable against the man or his son, he would have to pay dearly for it. He would perish, left with nothing but starvation to escort him to his grave. So why would anyone be mad enough to support the ill-fated Manglu, who seemed to have reached the end of the rope already? It was in fact rather like trying to caress the hood of an angry cobra. But who was Manglu to blame? Had the sides been reversed, even he would have backed off like a coward from offering the unfortunate victim any help. Whatever one may say, it was the naked truth. It was not an act of heroic courage; it was what any man with even an ounce of sanity left inside his skull would have done.

Manglu's elder brother and sister-in-law had stood huddled in a corner, watching the joyful yet pained union of the accused with his family. All the language they had ever mastered seemed to have deserted them. And courage? They had forgotten what it was. They stood there, cowering under the waning light of the earthen lamp, like Egyptian mummies who had been dug out of their tombs: fear, grief, regret and sympathy seemed to have enshrouded them in silence.

Manglu's wife was a picture of misery and helplessness at that moment. Try as she might, Sabesh could not shake off the proceedings of the beheran. Even if it was an event too unnerving and macabre to contemplate, time and again her fickle mind would morbidly probe and imagine the execution of her son, each time more diabolic than the preceding one.

Finally, Sabesh could take it no longer and screamed out in agony, and started planting desperate kisses on the prone figure of Makaru lying on her lap. All at once, she made up her mind. With steely resolve, every letter spitting out hatred, she said to Manglu, "We must leave this beastly village, forever."

Manglu looked up at his wife, his wrinkled face riddled with disbelief. But where were they to go? Questions of where soon gave way to questions of how. However much he reasoned with himself, Manglu knew that leaving this village with a sobbing woman and a young boy labelled 'criminal', under the very noses of the villagers who seethed with hatred even at the mention of his son, was nothing short of a fantasy. However, Sabesh was determined. Folding the handful of clothes she had with steady hands, she repeated, "Let's go."

Manglu finally pried his locked jaw open to say, "It is not as easy as you think. Besides, this is our native land. It has given birth to us, nurtured us..."

Sabesh half-shouted in her impatience, interrupting him, "No one is desperate for us to stay in this barren land! In an hour or so dawn will break and the cruel fate awaiting my son will feast upon our melancholy! Those wretched scoundrels will eat my son alive and scorch him in their burning hatred! What is left here for us to stay on? We will go somewhere. Anywhere! Do some work to earn our bread and butter. Do anything other than stay on here, holding our heads in our hands, waiting for the beheading of my innocent son! What monstrous obstacle is there in leaving this village, over which you prefer to watch the murder of your only child?"

Manglu tried his best to pacify her, "Listen, Sabesh. There isn't anything you can do if you blow your head off with impatience. Goddess Nialimali will surely show us the way. Let it be morning. We will think of something. All these years I have slaved like a bull in their fields. I have shed my blood, my sweat, my energy. Will they not heed my pleading? They were enraged and spitting fire today. Their hearts will surely melt tomorrow morning. I will go ask for their forgiveness once more. I know they will pardon us."

Sabesh said, "Go ahead, there's no one to stop you. Go crawl and grovel at their feet. Rub your nose on the ground. Do whatever you like. I am leaving. I don't care if anything happens to me. But no one shall dare put a scratch on my only child, else my soul will drift far from my body."

It was not that Manglu was being foolishly hopeful and naïve and trying to stop Sabesh without having a clue of the reality. They would surely kill the boy and harass his family. There was no doubt about that. But...he couldn't just pack his bags and herd his family away into the great Unknown in the middle of the night, could he?

As if on cue, the train blew its horn long and loud and clear, calling them as it went chugging, chhuk-chhuk-chhuk-chhuk...

If they hung back now, his son would be as good as gone. How could he push his own son into the pit? Why cling on to a life that offered them nothing? Sabesh was right. Wherever they went, they could sell their labour for a living. There was no free food here. By the sweat of their toil they would at least be able to put something on their plates. Leaving this village suddenly seemed like a far, far better option.

Mustering all his resolve, Manglu said, "Fine, let's leave the village." He gathered the handful of essentials they could call theirs and dumped them into a rusty tin box. Sabesh went straight to collect her marriage jewellery, her *katria* and *bandria*. Then she bundled up their few utensils in a tattered saree and thrust it into a rucksack. Manglu collected about two *manas* of rice and knotted them into a piece of cloth. He also found the *patta* of his homestead land, which he carefully tied to a bamboo pole and dropped into the tin box. After he had collected all his belongings, he took a handful of rice and went to the *pidar* to pay his last respects to his ancestors. He sprinkled a few grains of rice, saying, "O ancestors, I am leaving this house and going elsewhere. Give me your blessings. I would like to take you along: come with me."

He called Sabesh and Makaru to pay their respects to the ancestors. He then collected few grains of rice and put them in his pocket. He also put some rice on their foreheads as a good omen.

After worshipping his ancestors, Manglu felt lighter. He felt that his burden was now over. Perhaps his decision to leave the village was right. The ancestors wouldn't condemn him because he was leaving the village. After all, ancestors were ancestors. Lifting the battered tin box onto her shoulder, Sabesh stepped out of the house. Makaru followed with the bundle. Last to come out was Manglu. After closing the door he touched the bamboo wall and stood for a while leaning against the door. He bolted the door behind him. He caressed the old mud walls. He pressed his forehead to the door to let its coolness soothe and calm him. His eyes welled up with tears. This was the land on which he had woven his entire life. And now he was leaving it...forever. No, it was not the land which was to be blamed. It was the people. It was they who had forced him, like mindless brutes, to leave the homestead he had been born and raised in, and where he would have preferred to die.

Manglu was shaken out of his thoughts when Makaru came up and reported that Sabesh was way ahead of them by now and that they would need to catch up with her fast. Manglu impulsively hugged his son tight and replied, "Yes, son! You go on ahead. I am on my way. And don't forget to tell your mother to pay homage to Ma Nialimali on the way." Nialimali was the village deity of Banjipali. Everyone worshipped her. In a small hut on the outskirts of the village was housed a stone which symbolised her presence. Every time that Manglu left the village, he would pay his obeisance to her, once while going out, and once while returning. This gave him immense peace. He felt that the goddess was always nearby and would come to his aid when he needed.

The villagers worshipped Nialimali during Dusshera, on the full moon day of Phaguna and on the day of Nuakhai. During Dusshera, the goddess went from house to house, lovingly decorated and beautifully adorned, in a magnificent procession called *buel.* As per popular belief, the soul 'possessed' by the goddess sanctified anyone who approached her with wishes, offerings or simply to seek her blessings. Gana music played an important part in her worship. Never did the goddess materialise to possess a soul before some Gana music had been played. The steady thrum of the instruments propelled her to come and the rhythmic beats of the *dhol* and the *nissan* made her feet go tap-tap-tap. Manglu's father was the leader of the troupe of *mahurias*, the trumpet blowers. As part of the ritual he would blow his trumpet right at the earlobe of the person to be possessed. It was no mean feat discerning the subtle relationship between the goddess and the Gana musicians. Perhaps there was a divine language that both of them shared. When the lahili-lahili of the trumpet resonated in the air, the hairs at the back of the person to be possessed stood up eerily, announcing the eagerly awaited arrival of the divine spirit.

The goddess often used to run, with the Gana musicians close on her trail. And behind them came the awed and joyful villagers, following reverentially. On countless occasions, from his childhood till present day, Manglu hadn't missed a single opportunity to seek her blessings. True, after his father's sad demise, he hadn't inherited his father's passion of blowing the trumpet. But that didn't mean that he shied away from playing the nissan when he got his hands on one. He believed that the art of playing instruments at the deities' processions was one of the highest services one could render to them. And so, naturally, Manglu would jump at any opportunity of playing an instrument that was offered to him.

It was the selfsame goddess before whose altar Manglu now bent down and prostrated himself. He offered her the grains he had carefully pocketed, placing some on the jagged stone that embodied her divine presence. Then he repeated what he had done before. Sabesh and Makaru were already there. He put a *teeka* on his wife and son to ward off any evil that may be on its way to their disarrayed lives. They too paid obeisance to the goddess, and said, “Ma! We depend on you. All we seek is your protection and your blessings.”

Manglu had once heard from his grandfather that the goddess Nialimali, in the form of the large jagged stone signifying her presence, had been installed in Banjipali under the joint enterprise of two elders, one each from the Gond and Gana communities. No one knew when, but it must have been done well before the railway lines had been laid was what he had been told. Nialimali had been guarding the village ever since. Today, he had been compelled by circumstances to leave that abode of the motherly goddess, his own ancestors, and the land that had anchored his whole life—everything. But surely, Ma Nialimali would know all this.

The night was eerily still; not a ray of light pierced the dark. Human snores buzzing like angry wasps stirred the infernal silence now and then. The ever vigilant street dogs that usually started barking ferociously even at the sight of a harmless house lizard seemed to have sewn their muzzles shut. Instead, they were faithfully following Manglu at his heels in docile silence ever since he had stepped outside Nialimali’s altar. In accordance with the superstition that his father had once told him about, Manglu had exited her altar putting his left leg out first: it was for good luck. Besides, he had been doing this since his childhood. But today, he wasn’t stepping out of his mud hut hoping for a good day’s work at the gauntia’s house. Today, his steps were leading him out of his...village. Manglu’s determined footsteps seemed somehow at odds with the torrent of emotions inside him, waiting to burst. He led the way for Makaru, and in the end came Sabesh, as they headed to meet their uncertain fate with nothing but the memorabilia of the life they had seen unravel with their own eyes. Out there, against the endless vault of the dawn sky, Venus was shimmering brightly in all her glory. In a few moments, the morning sun would have risen to unveil another day.

The train to Raipur came at dawn. They would board it, on their way to the new life and the livelihood it would offer...

Manglu, Sabesh and Makaru reached Lathore railway station. It was dawn already, though the foreboding air was still swathed in patches of dark. Manglu shuddered at the thought of someone spotting them and informing the gauntia of their escape. Of course, he would eventually get to know, when Manglu would not turn up at his house for work in the morning. But all that he wanted for now was a clean escape from his claws.

Manglu's guilty secret was still a secret, buried within the walls of his painfully pounding heart. Not a soul knew of their escape. Not even his own brother. Manglu's heart felt leaden with melancholy, but he urged himself to keep going. He knew his brother would have never agreed to this act of cowardice and abandonment. But under those circumstances, anything dire would have been allowed to befall Makaru, and Manglu did not wish to know or see what it could have been. But then, his brother would certainly have blinded himself before he saw his own nephew's execution. He was pure as dew. He didn't speak much; his eyes did that for him. But he was hardly any different in that; most of his brethren did the same. They didn't speak, or else they would be branded loudmouths by the rich. Their eyes were forbidden to shed tears, for if they did, the rich would crinkle their noses in disgust at the very sight of them. So they cried into their hearts in silence. For who would want to be the laughing stock of the village? And so, Manglu's brother did the same.

The train arrived at Lathore station on time. Sabesh had never before heard a sound so monstrous. The loud harsh bellow of the horn almost dried up her marrow. What was the poor woman's fault? Only the distant horn of the train and its name had managed to penetrate the quiet life she had cocooned herself in. The ferocious beast was charging towards her like it was on its way back after having reduced a million rib cages to dust. Its ceaseless chugging sounded like, "chhachha paisa…chhachha paisa…chhachha paisa…chhachha paisa…"

The often quaint village beliefs went somewhat like this: if a woman's labour pains were stubborn enough to last longer than they should, the villagers brandished a train ticket at her, or simply stuffed it in her hair bun. And lo! The baby was out in a flash!

Sabesh had been writhing in pain when she was due. A renowned genius of a *gunia* had materialised with a ticket from the local train station, chanted some incoherent words, and then tucked it into her tangled bun. And soon Sabesh found her rubbery hands clutching Makaru, her eyes streaming tears, when she had felt her life ebbing out of her just moments ago. Oh no! It wasn't the train ticket which ladled out babies with expert efficiency. One thought of its monstrous never-ending metallic body, ear-splitting shrill horn and meteoric speed, and women found their blood teeming with fear. This made them panic, and out popped the baby. Sabesh could feel that old fear now coursing through every vein of hers. Couldn't they have gone to Raipur on foot? Anything other than this humungous hungry beast was preferable.

Manglu half shouted in urgency, "Go on! Board it, quick!" Taking good aim, he threw his belongings into a bogey. He turned to grab Sabesh by the waist and hoist her up, but she was busy performing an act of obeisance, or fear, or perhaps both. She faced the steps of the compartment—the steps leading them to their destination—joined her palms, bowed down and touched them reverentially. Then she climbed them up. Helping Makaru board, Manglu got on last. The train blew its whistle and pulled out of the station.

Shuffling into the corner of a seat, Sabesh sat huddled with her legs up on the seat. As she peered out of the window, she saw the greens rushing past her. She fixed her saree, covering her head, and her thoughts turned to her son. At least the poor lad was safe. Alive! He would now be far away from the evil eyes of the gauntia household. The gentle morning sun was kissing the earth joyfully. The cool breeze fanned her face. She stroked Makaru's head and took a deep breath.

Whenever Makaru travelled by train, his thoughts would spin back to what had compelled him to do so for the very first time. That painful farewell to his home, his village, that eerie, fearful walk to the station in the dead of night, that long, arduous journey they had undertaken...it would all come rushing back into his head regardless of how much he tried to stop them. The loud ghar-ghar of the train didn't do much to distract him. His memories were like those winged ants that anthills teem with at the first spell of rain. And of course, his thoughts would eventually come to rest on the gauntia, his son Nandakumar and his grandchild, the very same child whom he had so fondly offered to pluck tendus for. And that very fondness had forced his father to leave his roots, his ancestors, his village behind, something he had never dreamt of doing, ever.

Three

Whenever Makaru's past came to haunt his thoughts, restlessness would grip him like a vice. He felt haunted, vulnerable. His enthusiasm seemed to fade into the grey expanse of the sky, a fearful ghoulish feeling would take hold of him and all his interests, emotions and desires would disappear into a bottomless pit of despair.

The train clattered into Komakhan station. That it wasn't an important stop was evident from its size; a small and insignificant station. Of all the passengers travelling on that train, only four deboarded at Komakhan. The four who got down under the watchful eyes of Makaru appeared to be a close-knit nuclear family. There was a middle-aged woman with her man, huffing and puffing under the weight of their luggage, and two children, aged perhaps between nine and fifteen. It was the man who deboarded first. Then came the smaller child, who was lifted down carefully onto the platform by his father. Then out jumped the older boy, and finally his mother climbed down. She started putting their bags in order and counting them. Who knows, perhaps they too had come all the way from Raipur? And Makaru was again pulled into his past, to a day when he too had got down dishevelled and bewildered, with his parents shivering at his side. As Makaru slipped back from the present, an indescribable helplessness caught hold of his disturbed soul like raw, visceral fear.

That day, when the train had halted at Raipur station, and Makaru had stepped uncertainly onto the platform, flanked by his parents Manglu and Sabesh, the fates that awaited them back in their village suddenly seemed to be nothing in front of what they faced now. The city had an aura of its own. It breathed a wholly different air, teeming with thousands upon thousands of people, all strangers. Nothing, not one thing around them seemed familiar, recognisable. Terrifying thoughts smothered Manglu's heart. People were swarming on the roads like houseflies, but there wasn't one amongst them that they could pluck up the courage to approach. Where were they to go? Who were they to ask for help from? What fate awaited them in this sprawling beast of a city which held no corner that was familiar to them? Makaru could almost see his father's wizened face burdened by the overwhelming weight of these thoughts—never before had he wished more fervently for the situation they found themselves in to be better. To this day, he felt his soul being strangled by that heart-wrenching sight of his father, utterly at a loss.

It was true that the panic threatening to smother his soul had compelled Manglu to flee Banjipali with whatever little they could gather at the eleventh hour. Ensuring his son's safety had been topmost on his tormented mind at that dark hour that witnessed his arrival with his family here. But now that they had arrived in Raipur, what was he to do? How was he to earn a living? How was he to settle and feed his family here? With this swirling, overwhelming chaos of questions following him around like a dark cloud, they stumbled out of the railway station. As they came to halt near the rickshaw stand, the three plonked down their luggage, which seemed to grow heavier by the minute under the weight of the desolation and uncertainty strangling their hearts. Clueless, they sat down on the side of the road, wordlessly gazing at this alien new realm they had entered, feeling disoriented, dazed and stupid. The vehicles whizzing past furiously, threatening to run over one another yet not colliding, seemed extraterrestrial, as if propelled by some intangible divine mechanism; their loud harsh honks were an assault on the ears. The concrete highways stretching to eternity, the thousands of vehicles snaking their way through the endless grey expanse of the road, the huge hoardings, the people milling past them aloof without a glance, the unfamiliar language...everything seemed to push them to withdraw even further into their cocoons. Not one tiny minuscule element of their surroundings seemed familiar enough to touch and caress.

Manglu felt utterly helpless.

Makaru said, "Father, I am thirsty. I want water." Manglu looked around, but could not see any tube well or tap nearby.

Suddenly, Manglu was struck by a train of thoughts. This was the same Raipur from where the brothers Neulia and Balia used to travel all the way to Banjipali to visit their relative, and Manglu's fellow villager and Ganapada resident, Nakul Dom!

When in Banjipali, Neulia, or Neelia as he was called by the villagers, was almost always seen wearing full pants, and speaking an atrocious mix of broken Hindi and Odia. The children used to follow him about everywhere just to listen to his colourful anecdotes about the city. Neelia would narrate vivid tales of the larger-than-life heroes and heroines of Hindi movies, and the children would listen to him entranced. There was no cinema hall around. Then how could they have any idea of what a movie was? So when he narrated scintillating stories of adventurous heroes who expertly manoeuvred their speedy motor bikes fearlessly over falling bridges and jumped down from high mountains to bravely kill gold-toothed villains with their bare hands, in the hushed, enraptured silence of his young audience you could hear even a leaf fall.

The villagers, however, would eye Neelia with disdain and wrinkled noses, for he had the odd habit of wearing the same shirt and pair of trousers for days on end. So fond was he of his trademark clothes that he did not bother to change them even when he went to the fields to relieve himself, swinging a bottle of water. The villagers did not approve of such 'ultra-hygienic' city habits, and would shudder in disgust at the sight of him.

The gauntia's family owned an enormous pond that was demarcated into several *ghats*. Each ghat had been assigned a specific purpose: some served for the villagers to bathe; others were for bathing their cattle; yet others were meant for ablutions and cleaning up after defecating, and so on. Cleanliness was their highest ideal, next to godliness. Neelia, however, couldn't care less; he remained exasperatingly and willfully (or so the villagers thought) oblivious, refusing to take any lessons from the ardent devotees of such godliness. He simply did not bother to change his clothes. So he ended up being labelled and teased as a "Raipuria".

In fact, the villagers went a step ahead and started subtly berating other villagers of Neelia's league too by mockingly calling them Raipurias.

Now Manglu knew that this famous Raipuria, Neelia, worked as a rickshaw puller somewhere in this vast city. His sixth sense whispered that Neelia was perhaps his only hope, before the quicksand of hopelessness in this mad metropolis swallowed him alive. He fervently wished that he could meet him. But how?

Manglu was aware that once the railway lines had been laid in Odisha, thousands of workers headed for the neighbouring states to find jobs in the industries and new construction works that had intensified at the time. The districts of Bolangir, Kalahandi and Nuapada, for instance, were home to millions of half-starving desperately poor Doms and Ganas. The huge newly built Bhilai Steel Plant gave these vagrants the incentive to hop onto the next train and set off for Raipur, Bilaspur and other big cities to work as daily-wage labourers or try their luck at other odd jobs, as rickshaw pullers, road workers, sweepers, helpers and dishwashers at roadside eateries and teashops, railway workers, or factory workers. But finding any of them in this monstrous city was like looking for a needle in a haystack. There wasn't one face that was known to Manglu—except that of Neelia. But where was he to find him? He didn't even have his address. Perhaps he should have asked Nakul Dom for it. But where was the time to do so, what with his fear of the gauntia and his desperation to put as much distance between him and the village as fast as possible.

Right now, his son was dying of thirst. He simply had to get water from somewhere. There was a bunch of rickshaw pullers gossiping a little distance away. Manglu walked up to them and, in an incoherent jumble of Odia and his negligible Hindi, asked, "*Bhai*, where can I get some water?" The expressions of his listeners clearly said how odd they thought him to be. They put two and two together and quickly surmised that this man standing in front of them was an Odia, new to Raipur. With mild irritation, they enquired, "Why don't you speak in Odia?"

Having heard these unfamiliar people speak in a familiar tongue, Manglu was so relieved, he felt as if half his problems had already been solved. He almost shouted in joy, "Oh! So you all speak Odia, too? I...I thought that the people of Raipur knew nothing beyond Hindi. That is why I did not speak in Odia," he finished sheepishly.

One of them said, "Never mind. What happened?"

Manglu answered, "Bhai, my son's throat is parched from thirst. I need some water. Is there a tube well nearby?"

Another asked, "Where have you come from?"

"I am from Banjipali village in Bolangir district. I have come to Raipur for the first time. I arrived today," Manglu replied.

Just then a passenger arrived, and the rickshaw-wallah who had been asking about Manglu's hometown went away saying, "Got to go...got a passenger waiting."

Manglu's spirits were dampened again. But he wasn't going to let go of this golden opportunity that fate had bestowed upon him. He turned to another rickshaw puller and asked, "Bhai, is there any chance of getting a job here somewhere? I am new to this city and haven't got a clue as to how I should earn for my family."

The man replied, "How is it that you just packed your bags and hauled yourself together with your family into the great unknown? Fond of adventure, huh?"

"Oh no, bhai! Actually there were some problems back home. So I had to leave the village and come here. I will be forever grateful to you if you could arrange for some work for me."

"You know how to pull a rickshaw?"

"Well, I have never tried, but I am sure I will be able to learn how to within a day or two."

Pointing at a tube well far away, the man said, "See, there is a tube well. Go quench your son's thirst first. Will talk to you later."

That man, Manglu was to know later, was Dambru Tandi.

Manglu untied the bundle of utensils that they had brought along and, finding a bowl, headed in the direction that Dambru had pointed to. Mother-son duo was sitting with their chins cupped in their hands, listening to the conversation listlessly. Everything was new to Sabesh: boarding the train, the train journey, setting foot in a completely new city, gaping wide-eyed at thousands of motorcars...and people. Sitting beside a grey strip of road enshrouded in uncertainty and helplessness was a first in her life, too. But despite all this, Sabesh tried to console herself and held on tenaciously to a fragile hope, thinking: wouldn't Ma Nialimali be kind enough to bestow a tiny home upon them?

The mellow evening tickled the air. It was time for the goats and cattle to return home after grazing. Had she been in the village, she would have gone to someone to collect wages. Or she might have gone to the jungle to collect fuel wood and some fresh *muti, bahal* and other leafy vegetables and succulent greens to cook for their meal. Here, however, she felt the pincers of despair clawing at her flesh, threatening to tear her mortal shell apart and the vital pearl white soul residing within. The constant honking of vehicles only added to her vexation. Where the hell were all these people going, or returning from, anyway? Still cocooned within the tranquil confines of the rural village milieu that she had been brought up in, Sabesh could make neither head nor tail of anything in this huge noisy city. And there wasn't a soul around to help her go about it either.

Returning with the water, Manglu handed the brimming bowl to his son. Makaru thirstily downed half the bowl in one gulp, then he passed it on to his mother. She drank some and splashed the rest on her face. The cool refreshing caress of the water rejuvenated her.

Makaru must be hungry by now, Sabesh thought. They had brought some rice from home, but where was she to cook it? She had neither a hearth, nor fuel wood. Perhaps she could make a rough temporary hearth with a few stones; the wood could also be arranged. But what about the rebukes she would have to deal with? She saw a policeman fiercely blowing at his whistle some distance away. There was no way he was going to let her go if she went about lighting a fire in the middle of the road. But her poor child had had nothing to eat for over a day. All that had gone into his growling belly were a few grains of stale rice yesterday morning when he had taken the gauntia's cattle out to graze. His stomach had been empty all this while. His face, wilted and withered like *bhaji saag*, had now turned pale as the last remnants of energy were being drained out of his frail body.

Sabesh looked at Dambru hopefully—that stranger seemed helpful. What would she lose if she asked him for help? Bundling the last ounces of her shaky courage with hastily gathered conviction, she went up to Manglu and said, “Our son is hungry. We’ve got some rice. If only we could make some cooking arrangements here...” Dambru said, “If you start clanging your pots and pans here, the policeman is sure to rain lathis on you. Let me help...I will show you a place nearby. You can cook there in peace, undisturbed. You will even find some fuel wood there.”

And that brings us to the Raipur Medical College. It had gathered much acclaim in the past few years. People from far and near undertook arduous journeys to get diagnosed and treated in this safe haven of syringes and hospital scrubs. It drew a lot of poor people to its premises too. This destitute lot with more misery in their life than money in their pockets couldn’t dream of enjoying a wholesome meal in the cheap makeshift eatery nearby. All they could do was cook their own food in the hospital compound.

Like Manglu, Dambru too belonged to Bolangir district. Having offered to help, he was obliged to take them to the Medical College compound. Satisfied at having performed the role of a good samaritan, Dambru left them there to make preparations for food and went his way. Manglu, on the other hand, was awash with relief and gratitude for having received such unexpected kindness from a total stranger. With a swelling heart, his mind drew the natural and perhaps inevitable comparison between the rich gauntia, whom he had known and served for years and whose cruelty had forced him to flee his native land, and the poor rickshaw-wallah, whom he had never met before but who was making every effort to try and make this alien land seem a little less unfamiliar, if not the same as his native one.

By this time, all three of them could feel the stony grip of starvation wringing their stomachs painfully. Sabesh conjured up a crackling fire with the few sticks she could find, and quickly set about her business. They gobbled up each half-cooked morsel hungrily. True, it was nothing like what they ate at home, but what went into their bellies somehow assuaged the diabolic hunger churning inside for now at least.

This humble J-shaped organ grandly named the stomach is what every creature walking this earth goes berserk trying to win some food for. What's more, the claw marks of its perpetual insatiable hunger follow us to our very deathbeds. Even as you are burping in contentment having consumed a satisfying lunch, the hunger pangs of dinner make their presence felt. You eat dinner, and soon it demands breakfast. Breakfast over, you find the stomach already growling for lunch. And so on. Man keeps running endlessly in search of that elusive moment of fulfillment in this eternal cycle of bodily needs. He never seems able to lay his hands on that one solitary meal that would put this constant cloying, omnipresent and annoying presence of hunger to rest forever!

Dambru had long disappeared. Now that he was gone, Manglu wondered if it would in fact have been better to have enquired about Neelia from him. Just that it had completely slipped from his mind. But never mind, he had plenty of time. He would find Neelia sooner or later. What he really had to devote all his time and energy to now was looking for a job.

Suddenly, Manglu set his eyes upon a shoddy eatery nearby. There he struck up a conversation with the owner. The latter assured him a job, but not before having asked him for some residential proof. Manglu had none obviously. So he hung his head in silence. The owner said, "A lot of job-seekers come to us every day. How can I just give them a job without having a clue as to where they live? We have no way of knowing if they are genuinely unemployed or merely looking to earn some easy money. Some work here for a few days and then just vanish with the hotel money. Yet others come here to hide the skeletons in their closet. Such recruitments invite nothing more than scrutiny and tarnish the reputation of our hotel. Slowly and steadily, even the numbers of our trusted customers have been on the decline, to say nothing of the losses we have to bear. All this has to be kept in mind. I will employ you as soon as you give me some proof of where you live."

Manglu's head was a whirlwind of thoughts. On the face of it, this Dambru seemed like a decent and considerate person. He even belonged to Manglu's community. Giving Dambru's address as a reference, Manglu could have easily secured this job. He should have asked him for his address; it was really foolish of him not to. The shock of recent events must have eroded his presence of mind. Manglu felt a twinge of embarrassment. And so he left.

His next stop was a grocery store. There, too, he was refused work, for the same reason. He had no better luck with the rickshaw owner either, who said, "No rickshaw for unknown people. What if they go and sell it off to some rogue in a cheap bargain, or worse, land me in the middle of an accident case? So we need a trusted agent who is in contact with us and who can keep track of the workers that we employ." Manglu found himself stuck once again. No. There was no way out—he simply had to ask Dambru for help.

Manglu's mind was whirring busily. Here there were scores of jobs, but not a soul to count upon. The city was not gullible like the village, which simply distributed work by face value, or by muscle value for that matter. Here, even an ox of a man could be swept aside to make way for a handicapped one, if he had an acquaintance by his side who would guarantee his honesty and suitability for the job. Recommendations alone could get you any employment in this city.

The evening seemed to have stripped herself of all mirth as it mellowed and aged on its way to black night, embellished only by the brilliance of stars. Where was Manglu to spend the night? Back in the village, even in times when they were refused aid, there were familiar faces around them who reinforced their sense of security. If nothing more, at least they had a jagged roof to call their own under which they could sleep soundly without a care. The small but boisterous village now seemed a thousand times more vibrant and inviting than the vast city, which seemed cold and lifeless like a desert to Manglu's eyes.

Still not having come to terms with his new abode, Manglu couldn't help comparing where he used to be, and where he was right at this moment. He caught himself red-handed many times and berated his soul for pining for the very village whose barbarism had forced him to abandon the only home he had ever known. Why was he longing for that heartless clump of huts with such passion? Why couldn't his heart keep silent in gratitude that all three of them had escaped alive with their bodies and souls intact? Why did he have to constantly keep thinking of his village and his hut and longing for it? Why?

To his uncomplicated mind, the endless vault of stars that stretched above them was not half as sheltering as the crude thatch that they called their roof. Even so, at least here his son was not running for his life or turning to cold sweat in fear of those wolves hell-bent on his blood. This thought alone gave his heart the unaffordable luxury of relief. Manglu couldn't muster the courage to imagine what his son's life would have been like had he chosen to stay back in the village. No, there was nothing wrong in what he had done. Having dipped into this sea of thoughts for a moment, Manglu went about consoling himself. Still dissatisfied, he sent up a brief prayer to Ma Nialimali.

Manglu felt encouraged by the thought that thousands came to these streets every day, and that nothing stopped them from turning these never-ending strips of tar into makeshift kitchens or even a home for a night. All he had to do was spend a day or two at the feet of the gulmohar tree. Didn't this huge city play host to hundreds of large-hearted men like Dambru who could help him in his search for a job? Speaking of which, Dambru had mentioned that almost all the rickshaw pullers and the women working at the eatery here could trace their roots back to Odisha. More than half of them were even from the same community. If his luck obliged, Manglu could strike gold, or better still, perhaps even meet Neelia one of these days. Makaru had committed no crime, and the heinousness being attributed to his act was plain exaggeration. He was innocent. Manglu was innocent. And at the core of his heart, he knew that Ma Nialimali knew it all.

After arriving in Raipur, Sabesh had become more reserved. The blissful reminiscences of Banjipali constantly tugged at her heartstrings. All she could think of was her big burly rooster who practically shook the whole village when he crowed, threatening to reduce it to dust. He too had to be left behind. There would be no one to open the door of the barn to let him in when he returned at dusk. Poor fellow, his legs must have given away with the effort of standing and waiting for her to come. Those heartless goons of the gauntia must have made a meal out of him by now. Not in favour of arranging impromptu 'luxury' meals for guests who arrived unannounced at her doorstep, Sabesh always kept a tiny reserve of green gram bundled up in some corner; she couldn't bring that along either. Her neighbour had once lent her two *seer*s of rice, for which Sabesh was still indebted to her. Punia's daughter-in-law had sent her tasty fish curry in a bronze bowl. Wanting to return a full bowl rather than an empty one, Sabesh had delayed sending it back. In her procrastination, she neither cooked a delicious meal for her neighbour, nor returned the bowl to her. As if the fates were determined to make their lives miserable, that bronze bowl had perhaps sprouted legs and come running to be thrown into her bundle along with the other utensils that Sabesh had hastily packed up to bring along. Who knew whether she would ever get the opportunity to hand it back to its owner or not?

Such minuscule yet strangely significant thoughts were what occupied Sabesh's troubled mind. There were millions of such tasks that she was yet to do, yet to complete before she had set foot upon this strange land. The fact that she hadn't been able to was filling her heart with the dark poison of excruciating remorse; yet all she could do was look on as her soul turned blue-black. This hurricane of thoughts seemed to have sucked all her words into an endless void of silence, from where they glowed like the red embers of smouldering charcoal whose fire had been extinguished long ago.

Having spread out the threadbare *kantha* at the base of the gulmohar tree, as if seeking its blessings for the night, Sabesh tried to get some sleep to enter her prone body, just like moonlight slipping through the shutters of a window traces delicate patterns. Next to Sabesh slept Makaru, and at the far end of the miserable bed they had made for themselves lay Manglu. But try as they might, his heavy eyelids could not curtain sleep, that played truant and remained elusive. After a tortuous session of tossing and turning, he propped himself up on his elbows to take a peek at the mother-son duo, only to find that they were fast asleep. Unable to take it anymore, Manglu sat up on his haunches. Gazing up at the sky he inhaled deeply of the restless night air and plunged headlong into an abyss of colourless thoughts. He had somehow managed to spend his very first day in this city. But his survival instincts were making him uneasy. He couldn't just while away the second day in mundane chores like cooking and sleeping, could he? Tomorrow, he would have to do what he was really here for. He would have to find a job that would enable him to feed and settle his family here.

Sabesh's voice abruptly cut through the silence, startling him, "What is it? Can't sleep?" Manglu had naturally assumed that she was asleep, but clearly, that was not so. She had been merely feigning sleep, her eyes wide awake behind those tired eyelids. Manglu replied, "No. Not one bit. Can't stop thinking about what I am going to do tomorrow." Covering her sleeping son carefully with the sheet, Sabesh sat up. Suddenly, they heard the loud shrill siren of a police van nearby. The guard who had been snoring jerked awake from his dreams and started blowing his whistle so hard that a pack of street dogs, frightened by the sudden cacophony, started barking themselves hoarse in an attempt to cover up for their cowardice.

The dogs barking on top of the police siren is definitely not a good sign, thought Manglu. Who knows what mishap might befall us? The police may herd us out of this compound, and then we will have nowhere to go to. Entangled in this volley of thoughts, Manglu whispered urgently to Sabesh, "Quick, get back under the sheets. We don't want the police shooing us away at this time." And so they made desperate but futile attempts to fall back to sleep again as they lay huddled under the covers, which did practically nothing to cover them up.

The next morning, Manglu woke up to some noisy altercation. Still not acquainted with the hustle-bustle of the city, he couldn't bring himself to shrug it off. He turned to face the source of the commotion, and found a rickshaw puller bargaining with a gentleman. He heard snatches of their argument: "Sir, a journey from the station to this hospital adds up to a total of five rupees. You have given me just three. Kindly give two rupees more." This is what the customer had to say in his defence: "You thought that I was some foolish new arrival here, and left no potholed underpasses and bumpy *kachcha* roads that you could find. And then you have the insolence to charge a whole two rupees more! Three rupees is three rupees. Not one *paisa* more."

Thoroughly satisfied with his not-so-gentlemanly bargaining, the man dropped three rupees into the withered hands of the poor rickshaw-wallah and trotted away in a huff. As Manglu's eyes adjusted to the bright morning sunlight, he recognised that this fellow, who had clearly been wronged, was in fact none other than Dambru. Breaking into a run that Budhia Singh would have been proud of, Manglu came to a halt near his newfound friend and, out of curiosity, enquired, "What happened, my friend? What were you two haggling about?" With a broad smile that said much and hid more, Dambru replied, "This is the fate that awaits each one of us, my friend. How is it that these people never flinch from parting with their precious money when it comes to hiring luxury four-wheelers, or shopping in fancy malls big as cricket stadiums, or slopping cartons of imported liquor into their bellies till they are on the verge of a meltdown? How is it that only the rickshaw rides threaten to eat up all their hard-earned money! That is when all their bargaining skills are put to the test. Why, we even end up learning some cuss-words for good measure! That is how colourful our lives can get at best." The bitterness in his voice was smartly peppered with nonchalance.

All the rickshaw pullers of the city had formed a union of sorts. It was led by a man who, in most cases, did not have to pass his day ferrying rides, but managing the monetary aspects of this business. Each rickshaw puller had been assigned a designated stand for all the hotspots of the city; Dambru had his own next to the station. He too, like other members of the union, was expected to pay a sum of ten rupees every month to the union leader to be able to own his stand. Oh and by the way, a rickshaw puller could not, under any circumstances, have his own independent business. If you owned a rickshaw, the union owned you. You had to be a part of it. Otherwise, you would end up losing your stand, not to mention your rickshaw. The union decided a fixed rate for all the rides that crisscrossed the city, which was the minimal amount one had to charge to stay alive in this urban sprawl. But these low rates would often dip further below the minimum support fare. For instance, a nominal sum of five rupees had been fixed for a ride from the station to the hospital. But that crook of a customer haggled it down further to three, adding his bit to Dambru's already poverty-ridden misery.

By some effort of will, Dambru brushed it away with a deep sigh and, in an attempt to sound casual, asked Manglu, "So, how did you spend the night?"

Manglu answered, "Just find me some work, my friend, and I will be obliged to you for life."

"I was thinking of you last night. In fact I shared your tale with my wife yesterday. I live on the outskirts of the city, right next to the railway station. I have secured a place for you there. You need to move your things from here as soon as possible. There is no way you can live here in the hospital compound for more than a couple of days. Let's get over with this task at hand first, then we will think of a job for you."

Manglu was overjoyed, to put it mildly. He just couldn't bring himself to believe that such angels in disguise actually existed in the city. Back in the village, he had often heard the white-haired old venerables say that in times of need, it was the community that always came to one's aid. That large-heartedness and generosity of spirit for members of one's own community was what bound people together. For Manglu, this was what Dambru was living proof of.

Apparently oblivious to the absolute veneration with which his fellow Odia now viewed him, Dambru ferried the three newcomers on his rickshaw, that screeched to a halt near his tiny shanty. Handing the man of the house a spade, he showed Manglu to a stinking, rotting mound of garbage and, like a dutiful chaperone, said, "Just clear this up and make it all nice and homely. We will talk about a job for you later." Then, having introduced Sabesh to his wife, Dambru sped away on his rickshaw towards the station.

Overwhelmed by gratitude, Manglu spent a moment in a hurried prayer to goddess Nialimali, "Thank you, Ma! You anchored my hapless directionless boat and guided it to shore amidst the raging storm! I cannot imagine where I would have been had you not sent Dambru my way!"

Then, offering an elaborate and fervent appeal to all his ancestors and gods, Manglu proceeded to give the spot he had been shown a good once-over. The place looked and smelt about as habitable and pleasant as a hybrid between a septic tank and the U-bend of a commode. The unbearable stink said it all. Splattered with the refuse of digestion, it was evidently used as an open toilet by those who lived nearby. Naturally, they couldn't resist dumping their daily household garbage there, too. Shouldering the spade he had been lent, Manglu suddenly felt clueless as to where he should begin with the clean-up.

But, it is only in the muddiest of waters that the lotus unfurls its sublime petals to reveal its fuchsian glory. Each one of us is, shall we say, a storehouse of shit. What goes in as ambrosia comes out as shit. Whose mortal intestines are clean of it? Excrement is inevitable: it transcends all classes, castes and professions; it does not spare gauntias, high officers or even the honourable Prime Minister himself. So who was he, poor Manglu, to wrinkle his nose at it? Rather, he counted himself as blessed that his devotion to Ma Nialimali had earned him the acquaintance of someone like Dambru. Such a generous and considerate rickshaw puller could not possibly belong to a city; and yet, wonder of wonders, he did! For Manglu, this was nothing short of a miracle, a fortunate fantasy come true.

He would clean up this palace of human filth and make it his earthly abode; even heavenly, if need be. It would be his address, his identity, and perhaps even that precious proof of residence that he so desperately needed to get a job in this city, and an income. It would be the vital key to his vagabond identity that stood between him and a job like a solid door. Yes, it would get him a job. These thoughts seemed to reverberate through the morning air, the pearly dewdrops and the silken sky that glittered above him with a rainbow of spring colours. A job. Yes. He, Manglu, would get a job.

What was this in front of the enormous and arduous task that his ancestors had undertaken to clear the entire forest of trees that had once been where today stood his village, Banjipali? They had spent day and night clearing the dense forest, thrusting poles into the earth and hammering into place a divine shelter for goddess Nialimali to ward off evil spirits. When at long last their efforts had come to fruition, they had finally built homes for themselves and settled down in sequestered satisfaction. Today, history had come to repeat itself. A forest of trees or a mound of garbage—what was the difference?

Every ounce of regret, inhibition, doubt and despair that had accumulated in Manglu now spread its arms wide, grabbed hold of the spade in his hands and wedged it deep into the earth. Emboldened and energised at having rid his soul of all that was weighing it down, Manglu heaved and lifted filth and muck in a frenzy, and did not stop working for a staggering two hours straight. Bit by bit that odious ground filled with garbage, shit and rubble transformed as if magically into a neat, clean and livable patch of land. And how could it not? This was the very mortal shell that had spent every shred of its strength slaving on the gauntia's fields day after day, year after year. His muscles had hardened and his sinews had become steel breaking the biggest rocks, cutting the tallest trees and ploughing the roughest fields. To this day, every inch of the gauntia's meadows can be heard whispering how untiringly Manglu had poured his sweat and toil on them. This, really, was not a patch on the gauntia's fields. It was nothing. Oh no, no one was going to catch him complaining. This is something he was doing for his own family's wellbeing after all.

This train of thoughts greatly inspired Manglu, infusing him with fresh zeal. His starving stomach, taut with optimism, seemed as if to rapidly synthesise new energy. He was jolted out of his reverie by the bellowing horn of the passing train, which seemed to be hurtling past all obstacles with the sole intention of mustering every possible opportunity so the rushing wind could gently lift it and deliver it right at Manglu's (yet to be built) doorstep. Every bit of his effort seemed to add to this central event of his life. On hindsight, it was nothing more than clearing a few yards of land. But for the very first time in his life, Manglu was working for himself. Not for another. Not as a bonded labourer. Not as a voiceless, powerless slave. He was working as a man earning his keep—as a human being with dignity.

At noon, Dambru came home for lunch. To his disbelief, the mountain of sewage and garbage that he had left behind had vanished, to be replaced by a smooth, gleaming, clean spot that bore no resemblance whatsoever to what it had been just hours ago. Trying to mask his astonishment, he told Manglu, "Now all that is needed is to plant a couple of bamboo poles here, throw a tarpaulin sheet over it, and that will do for now. We'll improvise upon it later. At least the mother and her son would be able to sleep better under a makeshift shed, rather than spending all night gazing at the stars that adorn the naked sky."

Dambru's employer was a wealthy government clerk who owned no less than twenty-five rickshaws. He used to lend them out to the jobless who were willing to ferry rides in exchange for a deposit of thirty rupees every day. If you borrowed a rickshaw, you would have to attend to all the mundane repairs yourself. The major repairs were the responsibility of the owner, changing of tyres, tubes, wheels and the like. Dambru had been working there for the past eleven years and, over time, he had grown to be a loyal and trusted worker. The discerning clerk was shrewd enough not to loan out his rickshaws on leaps of faith. What he banked upon were recommendations. And that is where Dambru could come to Manglu's aid. In Dambru's opinion, there was a good chance that his employer might be willing to take Manglu under his wing. And this is why Manglu had an edge over other job seekers.

Soon the train clattered out of Komakhan station. Makaru, still lost in the memories of his father's first few days in that beast of a city that he had eventually come to embrace as his own, never realised when the train blew its horn, picked up speed and chugged off to its next destination, billowing fat grey clouds of smoke that were no more colourful than Makaru's thoughts.

Four

Midnight approached in stealth, laden with stars. At this eleventh hour the countless Raipuria footfalls seemed to have deserted the highway; youthful, lively and bustling with energy during the day, it now lay old, tired, bored, barren and grey. The bright neon lights seemed stitched onto this long jet-black road that slithered down from heaven to earth, bursting upon the horizon and then disappearing down it. Each street lamp stood at attention like a soldier, its neon eye fixed on that lone star in the night sky that rose high above everything, glittering like a diamond.

As the night deepened, the strays began to conglomerate on the streets. They were alert and experts at recognising passers-by. Attacking even one of them was like hurling a flaming spear into a hornets' nest. The pack would come together on the defensive instantly, ready to fight to death. And oh yes, getting away after running your car into one of them was no mean feat. They would take their time, plan their attack and come chasing after you like hell hounds the very next time you passed by. Yes, they had a superb memory. But if they had a good impression of you or were acquainted with you, they would still come after you, only this time their barks would be friendly and dripping with love.

Having got himself a bottle of country liquor, and having downed every last drop, Dambru set off along the deserted road, his jagged breaths in sync with his weaving, staggering gait. Trotting behind him faithfully were his silent companions, the infamous street dogs. Dambru was an old associate they had known for years. So as you might expect, not one bark or growl escaped their razor-sharp canines. Not even when he set out on some of his exploits at the tryst of dawn and dusk. On the contrary, if you saw him shush them, you would think he was a commander rounding up his jawans.

For now, this commander had handed over his rickshaw to his second-in-command, Manglu. The latter, having nothing else to do, was rolling the rickshaw along on the desolate road, feeling rather stupid. All one could hear was the rusty creaks of the old tyres as they tread the crunching gravel. These were the baby steps Manglu was taking to reach his goal: to be able to pull the rickshaw someday. But it was not that easy. The first hindrance presented itself in the form of Dambru's jawans, who couldn't resist snapping a bark or two every now and again at the new arrival on their street. But Dambru silenced them with an unsteady flick of the hand and an incoherent jumble of syllables that sounded like the whistle of a pressure cooker. A light playful breeze made the drunken Dambru burst into song, as if he was romancing the soothing gust of wind itself.

The gushing water hurtled
From one canal to the next
All I could think of was
He who had promised
To adorn my feet with *katrias*
And embellish my wrists with *bandrias*,
As my arms opened wide to embrace him
Yet, he lied
To me
To my love
Had I known
Would I ever have married him?
That liar ditched me forever...

Swaying in the heavenly abode of intoxication, Dambru brayed at the top of his lungs, fully empathising with the woman who in some folklore had suffered such tantalising heartbreak. To keep the momentum he added some random tune of his own, "*gadi gidi ginja gin...gadi gidi ginja gin...*" bursting his alveoli into a million drunken bits. To add to it, he even shook an unsteady leg to his own high-pitched rendition.

The inebriated Dambru apart, his second-in-command faithfully stuck to his duty of rolling the creaking rickshaw down the road in awkward silence, fumbling with the handles now and then. Finally, his teacher turned around to face him. At first the intoxicated man just stood there watching him with a blank expression. Then his face scrunched up in irritation and he howled, "You fool! I haven't brought you along to take my rickshaw for a walk down the road! Get onto it, man!"

Unnerved by this outburst, Manglu hurriedly hopped onto the rickshaw. Perched uncertainly on the frayed seat, he began with an earnest display of the biped, aerial version of the dog paddle. Naturally, the decades-old handlebars slipped out of control and the creaking tyres veered off the road, dragging with it a helpless Manglu shrieking in fear like an idiot.

Dambru was livid, to put it mildly. "You blistering fool!" he shouted shrilly. "What on earth possessed you to think that you could actually pull a rickshaw? *Sala*!"

Dambru could when drunk truly epitomise the heights of drunkenness. But only at night, of course. During the day, the saint in him would suddenly awaken from deep slumber and refuse to even look at a liquor bottle. His behaviour exemplified the bearing and etiquette of a perfect gentleman. And if you happened to have encountered him then, you would verily believe, "There goes a true gentleman. He's got those polished manners. No one else could possibly possess more courtesy." But it was night, and how gloriously drunk he was tonight! His happiness had climbed an unprecedented peak at the moment; hence the melodious braying and the giddy dancing.

His unsteady legs burst forth into a staggering sprint and took him to the upturned rickshaw. Suddenly a senile screw tightened into place, and Dambru was visited by a brainwave. Hopping onto the passenger's seat sprightly, he said, "I have known this cussed rickshaw for the past eleven years. It's a sucker for a *sawari*. Without a passenger, it just won't move the right way. So here we go. I am your sawari. Now ferry me to the station. Come on now, move it!" As Manglu proceeded to oblige, Dambru added, "But mind you, no matter how good you are at it, you won't get a paisa from your passenger."

Poor Manglu struggled, shifted his weight and made a feeble attempt at paddling. To his surprise, the unwieldy creature he was pulling actually inched forward a wee bit. Buoyed by this unexpected progress, he gathered all his strength and pushed as hard as he could at the paddles, his eyes never leaving the road, and he kept at it, until he got a genteel tap on his back. Manglu looked up and saw a ramshackle building looming before his eyes. His drunken sawari soberly patted him on the back and said, "You did it, mate. We have arrived. This is the station." Speechless with joy, a proud tear silently rolled down Manglu's cheek. There was a slight tremor in Dambru's voice as he said, "From tomorrow, this rickshaw is yours. You have earned it. Don't worry about me, I'll see to my needs."

Manglu simply could not believe that this was actually happening to him. And there was just one man in this world who had helped turn the utopia of his dreams into reality: Dambru. How would he ever thank him? What Dambru had done for him surpassed a thousand times what his own brother or father would have done for him. Manglu's clammy hands took hold of Dambru's dry ones. In an emotional voice, he said, "Bhai, to me you are a messenger of God. There is no way I could have settled here, or anywhere else in this city for that matter, without help—help which you have so selflessly extended. Call it coincidence or chance or some pre-ordained divine conspiracy, perhaps I was destined to ask you for directions to the tube well to quench my son's thirst. That eventually led me to find my identity, a home, and a job to anchor my ship without a mast in this sea of a city. Bhai, to me, you truly are God Himself in disguise."

With a sharp monosyllabic laugh, Dambru staggered out of the rickshaw and stood to face Manglu. "God...? You called me *God*? A healthy sense of irony you have, my man! I was a thief, do you hear me? A bloody thief! One hell of a thief I was!" He literally spat out each word in seething rage as he caught hold of Manglu by the shoulders and shook him hard, each word brimming with bitterness.

"Do you know people used to shudder in fear at the sight of me? My very presence was considered demonic, not just in my own village Semelpali but in those beyond as well. The moment I would set eyes upon something, that goddamn demon in me would not rest until I had laid my hands on it. My hands followed my hawk eyes everywhere. That is how good I was at it. Stealth. Thievery. Deceit. You name it—I excelled at them all. And you... you dare to call this piece of scum *God*? Hah! Even if this great almighty God of yours were to descend from heaven, I would not believe in him. This God that you believe in, He isn't there. Your faith is empty. If He had such immense powers, why didn't He ever help me? Or my family? Don't call me God! Your God does not exist. Not for me. Take that from me."

Dambru's chest heaved with the effort of this speech. Then he abruptly said, "Come with me. There's something I've got to show you." With that he hobbled away unsteadily from the rickshaw, pulling Manglu along with him.

Manglu felt that he was being followed. He turned around and saw that it was Fear. Black as a shadow. Black as death. As Dambru rambled on, Manglu felt seized by a sudden panic at the situation he found himself in. A new city he knew nothing about. Someone he had known for just two days. Someone who claimed he had been a thief, and who was now dragging him along to God knows where... With a sudden jerk he tried to free his sweaty wrist from Dambru's surprisingly strong grasp, but Dambru's long calloused fingers only tightened their grip. Manglu realised Fear was no longer following him—it now sat inside his heart.

They had come to a dusty cement bench. Dambru made Manglu sit down on it, and said, "Paint this bench into your memory. Never forget it, okay? When I came to this city, I slept here. I roamed about this station. I starved, surviving only on leftovers and rummaging for scraps through garbage bins. For three months, do you understand? For three whole months I lived like a dog. No work. No shelter. No food. And you here are calling this dog a god! I was a thief. And no one can wash off the stains of thievery. Not even your great God Himself."

Dambru's eyes welled up with sudden tears. They washed away his brazenness and bravado. His drunkenness. Made him seem vulnerable almost. Humane. Something rammed him in the back of his mind. A tightly knotted ball of thoughts and emotions buried deep. Dambru sat there on the bench, staring intently at his open palms as if studying them, unfurling with slow, infinite care the labyrinthine tapestry of memories that was his troubled past. That haunted him to this day.

Manglu felt awkward. Like a lumbering giant, a stranger in this small, private, intimate world of Dambru's, his anger, his bitterness, his frustration. Yet he also felt dwarfed by his emotions, by their sheer intensity and magnitude. Somehow, Manglu felt responsible, if not for Dambru's past then for his present, for his tears. He felt crushed by the thought that somehow, perhaps he was the culprit here. Manglu's thoughts relinquished their hold on his heart and flew out into the vast night. They went and sat on the crescent of the moon, stroking its magnificent silver curve.

Dambru's memories were like dark black clouds gathering on his mind's horizon, ready to burst into torrential rain. And so, jolting Manglu out of his reverie, Dambru broke his silence, cleared his throat and began his story.

"My grandfather was on the brink of becoming a pauper. Back then, the zamindars owned acres upon acres of land. They owned everything. Every hectare of fertile soil was under the name of the zamindar of Semelpali. His name was Lalbabu. Every now and then Lalbabu would pay our village a casual visit, to keep an eye on his precious fields. He would arrive with fanfare riding a bullock cart, his enormous fat belly heaving at every lurch, tormenting the poor beasts to death. His visit would not extend beyond two or three days. Lalbabu would never come alone. He was a man of status, ego and enormous pride, and there was no pride in surveying your fields with nothing and no one at your side but a pair of sweating bullocks. So he would always bring along three or four of his henchmen. Lalbabu would never arrive without making a grand entry. The echoes of his arrival would reverberate. Word would spread around at least five or six of the neighbouring villages. His stay would be welcomed at his magnificent *kothi*, or *khamar* as the villagers called it. Consequently, its caretaker had been christened the *khamari*. Each time that the zamindar set foot in the village, it would dutifully burst into festivity and celebration. You could actually smell that zeal, that gaiety dying to burst out of every villager. Not because it was real; no, not at all. If anything, it was joy that was killing every heart from within.

"Lalbabu had a passion for hunting. Donning high boots and armed with a rusty gun, he would head to the forest. He was good at it, too. At hunting, I mean. Be it deer, hares or wild boars, the moment they faced the wrong end of his barrel, they would find themselves face to face with Lord Yama himself. Back at the khamar, the souvenirs of his hunting exploits would be cooked with enthusiasm, served with submission and eagerly feasted upon with glee.

"The day that rolling mass of blubber would arrive on the village outskirts, the khamari would dutifully drag along a couple of musicians to welcome his majesty to the khamar with an atrocious smile plastered on his lips. Imagine a father-in-law welcoming his daughter's groom, and you will be able to picture the scene perfectly. The *ganabaja* would play nonstop for three days on end. The pomp and pageantry would continue well into the night and sometimes even into the wee hours. Liquor would be liberally poured and consumed and the music played at decibels that would deafen even a bat. And accompanying this loud blaring music would be the typical merry-making dance.

"Lalbabu loved music and dance and girls, especially the girls. A group of them would always be ready at the khamari's command to serve the zamindar's insatiable ravenous eyes.

"Sometimes the gluttonous Lalbabu would be unable to lay his hands upon the prize of his hunt. That is when the khamari would come to his rescue. He would arrange for the choicest meat delicacies that would put to shame the gourmet spread of any nawab. He would always have a supply of goats, sheep and hens at his disposal. No meal was entirely vegetarian. A platter of meat would always stealthily find its way in. No, make that a dozen platters actually. And one of them would also be emptied and licked to satisfaction at our humble hearth, thanks to my grandfather. He was the guard of the khamar, after all. Call it the perks of working for the filthy rich.

"My maternal grandfather, Dhubal Gana, had all the attributes of good health, strength and height. Even old age couldn't make him hunch or stoop. Once, he was on his way from Semelpali to Dangarguda. Back then it was filled with acres upon acres of trees. Our village was quite close to the *dangar* or the miniature forest, and hence the name Dangarguda. So...what was I saying? Oh yes, so once a large blackbuck was seen around the outskirts of our village. Keen to have it out of their fields and pastures, the villagers kicked up one hell of a ruckus and started chasing it with an assortment of stones and sticks. The creature itself did not scare them as much as its long dagger-like horns did. There was a staunch belief amongst the villagers that if those twisted horns happened to pierce someone's unlucky belly, they could disembowel him. The poor creature, clearly in the dark about the crime it had committed by growing horns at birth, was terrified and ran for all it was worth. As luck would have it, my grandfather was coming the same way.

"As if in slow-motion photography, the blackbuck was galloping full tilt towards my grandfather, who stood still in astonishment, his mouth open like a goldfish, wondering what he should do. Throwing the *potli* he'd been cradling, quick as a flash my grandfather grabbed the exquisitely beautiful creature by his most diabolic part: his horns. His adversary, equally quick on its part, threw my grandfather to the ground with one powerful flick of its neck. The man may have lost his balance, but he did not lose his grip. With maniacal audacity, his sinewy strong wrists grimly held on to those twisted horns. Somewhere at the back of his mind, my grandfather knew that a clock was ticking fast and that he had to get over all this soon. This battle begun out of the blue was draining his strength with every passing second. He could only hold on for a few minutes longer, and letting go was not an option. His rival still had its horns at its disposal, and grandfather was not too keen on losing his intestines just then. With a final heave of his tired lungs, he gulped in a deep breath of air and practically threw the blackbuck to the ground, never letting go of the daggers that were cutting into his palms and his patience. And there he lay hunched like a tired old man, kneeling before the blackbuck as if bowing to the beautiful beast, lathered in sweat and every muscle screaming like a newborn. Just when he thought his soul was deserting him and his sight gliding out of his closed eyelids, he heard a volley of shouts in the distance. He opened his eyes just a crack and could make out a crowd surging towards him, armed with whatever they could lay their hands on. Yes, go on, trample me, thought grandfather. But they came to a halt near him and the prostrate animal, and hauled it away from his now inert hands, taking those horns with them. As the huge blackbuck was being dragged away, its wide stunned eyes made it look more like a deer—a deer in the headlights. The path soon lay deserted, and my grandfather wanted nothing more than just to lie down on its bosom and go to sleep forever. But he couldn't. He had been the catalyst in this crime. He had given the predator his prey. In this battle that had ensued so unexpectedly and so needlessly, my grandfather had tried to save himself. So had the blackbuck. But in fact, it had saved my grandfather's life at the cost of its own. Somewhere deep down, my grandfather's heart bled and bled for the animal.

"Dangarguda was in for a feast. All thanks to the blackbuck.

"Dhubal Gana had fought a massive blackbuck, all alone! Talk of his exemplary courage, valour and strength naturally spread like wildfire. Lalbabu, who happened to be in the village on a visit, also heard of this brave and adventurous man who had fended off a blackbuck with nothing but his bare hands. He had him summoned to his grand khamar, generously let fall a few words of praise, and appointed grandfather the guard of his khamar. Ever since that day, my grandfather has been watching over the zamindar's khamar.

"My grandfather's small family comprised him, his better half and their daughter. I was to arrive on the scene bit later. Back then, I was living with my parents in Dangarguda. My mother died while giving birth to my sibling and took the baby in her womb with her to heaven. The people of my community are cruel madmen and worse. They let word spread that my mother had turned into an evil spirit and vampire overnight, that just before she breathed her last, her nails had elongated, her breasts had swollen and her eyes had reddened and burst in their sockets. The village *gunia*, that heartless monster, instantly declared her a *chirangul*. The villagers followed suit. As per village custom they proceeded to bury her. Mother's cot, which was bathed in her blood, her labour pains, her heartrending shrieks, was upturned and her lifeless body was tied to it. No, hammered is the word I was looking for. The human body that had sheltered and nurtured me for nine months and given birth to me was reduced to a carcass and its limbs were brutally hammered onto the cot with iron nails. Then they carried that bloody carcass to the riverbank and buried it as fast as they could. No, it wasn't out of good neighbourliness that they did it. For the villagers, it was good riddance. That is what happened to my mother.

"But don't think that I have been devoid of motherly affection all my life. No, bhai, not at all. Ma's mortal shell may have deserted me, but her ever loving soul remained. You wish to know where it sought shelter? In my aunt's flesh and blood. As luck would have it, my grandparents were bereaved of one daughter. But they still had another daughter to cling to. So they poured all their love on her. And it seems that she in turn channelled all of it to me. For compared with her love, even jaggery would taste like unripe bitter gourd. With whatever frugal resources she had at her disposal, my aunt showered her love and affection on me. We may not be rich, but I lived in extravagant luxury nonetheless. That's because of my aunt. She was rich from within, rich in her pure heart and rich in her sweet, generous soul. She was always brimming with love. Her motherly love for me never ran low.

"That was also because of my father actually. My father couldn't do without a woman in his life. And so he sat down for his nuptials again. That's right, bhai, father remarried. I was just a toddler of two then, still fresh from the loss of the angel and centre of my world. And, like the proverbial icing on the cake if you please, life bestowed upon me a completely strange woman, in whom I was supposed to find my own dearest mother. Fortunately for me, my maternal grandfather came to the rescue. Yes, he's the same Dhubal Gana whom I just talked about. He whisked me away to his own village, Semelpali. There, I would bathe twice a day. Once in the waters of the clear stream that I still distinctly remember, and then the entire day in my aunt's pure, selfless love.

"To this day, I truly believe it was the love that coloured her heart that infused her with the beauty she was so widely known for. Her beauty enriched her from within. Ever wondered what the earth might look like if it was bathed in the incandescent pearl-like light of the moon and the glorious golden rays of the sun at one and the same time? It would be a sight to behold, wouldn't it? But you don't need to rack your brains or strain your imagination. One look at my aunt Kalisundari's face, radiant with timeless beauty, and you would know.

"Let me tell you something about this goddess Kalisundari, the deity personifying the eternal beauty of darkness, a black beauty. We too worshipped her divine dark beauty. She was enshrined in a small *pidar* of our house. When the goddess would manifest, she would be lovingly decorated with accessories and jewellery, taken out in a procession and proudly shown at every house for people to pay their obeisance. That is how beautiful my aunt was! Or so thought the villagers. That is how she came to be called Kalisundari.

"Beauty is a boon. It carries your name from one hamlet to the other. But for my aunt, it proved to be a bane. And with her, it cast its shadow on my grandparents. And of course, with them it also affected me. That is how I came to be a thief.

"Lalbabu was the kind of man who believed in extracting every last particle of pleasure and enjoyment that he could wring out of life, if you know what I mean. He would stay in the village for three days, and he spent every moment in complete drunken revelry and hunting innocent creatures. At night the ganabaja would be especially played for him. If the spirit caught him, Lalbabu would even shake a wobbly leg himself. A troupe of young women dancers would be arranged for him to feast his eyes on. If a girl was lucky, that is if she was unlucky, she would be called to the khamar for Lalbabu to dispel his charged manhood. You know what I mean, right? Then she would be sent away with a wad of notes as *bakshish*. These poor girls would almost always be from the Gana, Gond and Gauda communities. Women of the upper castes would keep out of these matters. So chronic was this sick practice and perpetuated so unfailingly that it became almost routine, like a custom.

"Apart from such shameful and cringe-worthy tastes, Lalbabu was a man of immense power. He possessed acres upon acres of land, which were a steady source of income for the majority of households in that village. The people were landless after all. The much-needed wages for feeding their families and meeting their living expenses came from the hard labour with which they brought up the zamindar's bountiful harvest. Forget about working for that monster, if you had to collect any firewood, *char*, *mahul*, *kendu* or mango, you could not take it from anywhere else except Lalbabu's meadows. Forget firewood, even if you had to defecate or take a piss, the best and most obvious place to go to was of course Lalbabu's fields. In short, his lands were widely used and their master eternally feared, not just in our village but in the surrounding ones as well. This gave him power, untold, immense power: the power of exploitation. So it should come as no surprise that if a girl was offered a nocturnal visit to the khamar, and she turned it down, her life would become living hell, to say nothing of her family, which would face tyranny, a social boycott and worse. In other words, going against this *asur* was like picking a fight with Yama himself. Hence, the demon was not only feared, he was venerated and worshipped like a god, with every villager in the rat race to try and appease and please the beast the most.

"This nauseating custom was something that my aunt and her mother were blissfully oblivious of. Until it came to wreak havoc in their lives. Being an insider and part of the zamindar's system, as the guard of his khamar, my grandfather, however, was privy to considerably more than he would have wished to be. He would, in fact, even have to arrange for the girls himself at times on the orders of the khamari. Not that he willingly played the boatman ferrying the poor creatures to Yama himself. But he had to—he had no choice; his role as a servant demanded that he do it. It is not that every woman would tear at her flesh, curse her wretched fate and with feigned courage turn down the dreaded proposal. For a handful of them, desperately poor as they were, even the frugal bakshish would prove to be a powerful lure, for it would mean at least one full meal for a family, drawn by which they would obediently turn up at the khamar without a word of protest, but nevertheless with acute hesitation and fear.

"My aunt always steered clear of this vile business. And that was because of my grandfather. He knew the dire consequences of sending her to dance at the khamar. And why would he push his daughter to the doorstep of hell with his own hands?

"But that evil butcher, that venomous snake of a khamari must have heard of my aunt's impeccable beauty. I am sure it was that bastard who let it slip to Lalbabu. And so began the prelude that was to lead up to the ultimate disaster of our lives. One day, my grandfather was summoned to Lalbabu's chambers, and asked, 'Hey Dhubal, why is it that your daughter never comes here to dance?'

"My grandfather's imagination went haywire. He had known and feared this was coming. He had to think of something fast. '*Huzoor*, my wife is an old hag now. She cannot think of managing by herself and spending even a night all alone. My daughter gives her company.'

"Lalbabu said, 'So what's the big deal, eh? Bring her along as well. We've got a feast on here in full swing. There's nothing to be afraid of once you've got a plate of steaming hot food in your hands and fun and frolic all around! Now bugger off.'

"And that was it. There stood my grandfather, stone still, his brain having short-circuited from the cold realisation that there was nothing he could do about the situation he now faced. But surely, oh surely, there was something he could do? A hasty plan…a half-baked strategy? He knew very well what hellish fates awaited his wife and daughter, and especially his daughter, if he thrust them into the hands of the khamari. Suddenly, somewhere in his head, a bolt clicked into place. The khamari. Perhaps it was not the end of the world, after all. Grandfather's desperation was so great that he could bring himself to believe that the khamari could provide the magic solution to this ghastly predicament that had befallen his otherwise untroubled life. He had been living in his vicinity for the past many years, and his allegiance to him was untainted. Wouldn't he show at least a bit of heart to help him out? Patching up his frayed hopes and hastily gathering them into a wary bundle, he approached the khamari and let his woes spill out of his lips.

"The khamari heard him out, and replied, 'Brother, these are royal whims and fancies. They are implicit and irrefutable; there is no way we can question them. Lalbabu is not short of girls, as you know; he's got plenty of them at his disposal. But he has gone to the lengths of choosing yours. This is a sure sign that he is satisfied with the services you have rendered him. Why, this could even be a blessing in disguise! Who knows, this may change your fates forever! So go running as fast as your legs can carry you and fetch your daughter before our master changes his mind!'

"Grandfather's hopes shattered. Imagine you are holding on for dear life onto a branch which may snap any moment and, as if luck was your long lost enemy, the whole tree itself is uprooted and comes crashing. That was how my grandfather felt at that moment. He had come in a desperate state of panic and despair, hoping against hope to find a solution to his problems. But the exchange between him and the khamari had only made the situation far worse. The black void of hopelessness sucked him in and shredded his soul into a million bits; then, it churned him in a potent pure rage. What emerged was a man grimly determined, holding on to his last conviction. One thing was clear to him: the khamari would neither empathise with him nor be of any help. So, my grandfather surmised that it was about time he straightened things out and let the naked truth do the talking.

"He took a long deep breath, cleared his thoughts and chose his words with care as they marched out of his lips in a polite but firm line: 'My wife and my daughter will not be coming to this khamar, sir.'

"A monstrous wave of anger seized the khamari, who simply could not believe that Dhubal Gana had actually dared to rise above his position and voice his protest. His mind reeled in panic at how incapable and ineffectual he would be considered if he could not fulfill such a simple desire of Lalbabu's. He was the khamari, the master of the granary, no less. His entire career could come crashing if his services displeased or dissatisfied Lalbabu. With a strong sense of foreboding, his heart whispered that this was precisely what was about to happen. Channelling all the uncertainty weighing on him into his voice, and sounding much more nonchalant than he felt, the khamari lashed out coldly, 'Dhubal! Do you have any inkling who you are speaking to? Do you know the implications of what you are saying? If you have the foolish audacity not to bring your wife and daughter to this feast for Lalbabu's entertainment, you will be thrown out of your job before you can whimper an apology. And mind you, you wretched rogue, every thing you have ever possessed, from your income to your house itself, will be snatched away in a matter of minutes. One click of my fingers, and you will find that you can no longer call this village your home. Understand?!'

"My grandfather was engulfed in a torrent of rage. One look at his eyes would have revealed how desperate the volcano inside him was to erupt and destroy everything, everything around and everything within. As his vision cleared, and the khamari came into focus, my grandfather felt a furious itch in his fingers, an itch that travelled all the way to his spine shuddering with rage. At that moment he wanted nothing more than to just crush the beast in front of him to the ground, rip out its tongue and toss the piece of flesh at the feet of that man-hunter who called himself Lalbabu. Oh what a sight that would be! My grandfather savoured the sweet taste of revenge that was pricking the back of his parched throat. Then, like a lunatic who had just relived the accident leading to his insanity, he answered back, 'Do what you want to, but nothing in this world can make me push my own daughter into the hands of that hungry monster. If you are so concerned about satisfying his carnal hunger, then why don't you make him a present of your own daughter?'

"If you had been a fly on the wall, bhai, you would have had to shield your eyes from the glare of the white-hot wrath pouring out of the khamari. Gripping the lathi he always had by his side, he brandished it ferociously and ran head-on into my grandfather like a ram. As the man stood before him, vulnerable and uncertain, he rained blow upon blow of the weapon on grandfather. This, as was later revealed, was only a prelude to the violence that ensued at the khamar, and naturally, news of it marched straight to the ears of Lalbabu. Seething with fury, he ordered, 'Tie up that bastard and beat him so that he reeks of the hiding for years to come! And you damn well make sure that even his shadow does not enter the threshold of the khamar from tomorrow. And he must not be able to find any work in this village as long as his wretched soul lives! Get it, you milksops? Now bugger off and don't dare show your faces till you bring me what I want!'

"As if to amplify the significance of the moment, the ganabaja reached shrilly high decibels that day. Bathed in the intoxicating sounds that seemed to shake the ground like seismic waves of terror, Lalbabu and his cronies gyrated to a slow drunken rhythm. Somewhere deep in the shadows, a wailing body was being beaten black and blue. The powerful arms that had once overcome the lethal horns of a massive blackbuck were now bound by cruel ropes that were cutting into their bleeding flesh. With iron resolve, grandfather was biting his tongue, his mouth clamped tightly shut in a brave attempt to silence the screams that threatened to pour his helplessness into the merciless abyss beyond.

"The victim steeled his glance and gauged each of his assaulters one by one. None of them would have stood a chance against him in a one-to-one combat. No, he was being too generous. He could, single-handedly, have them all down on the ground at once. And yet, here he was sagging under his own weight, his body silently shrieking in pain. With surprising humanity, Dhubal Gana reasoned with himself: these men are duty-bound. They are flying blind, powered only by Lalbabu's orders. With that thought he shut his eyes and clenched his jaws with such force that they threatened to draw blood. Lalbabu. The khamari. If he was hung here like a lamb for slaughter, it was because of those two vile souls. If he was being flayed alive by a bunch of half-bred youngsters, it was on their command. He could sense vomit forming at the back of his throat as he imagined two triumphant grins displaying crooked teeth covered with odorous yellow plaque. Yes, he was being beaten. His assaulters stood in plain view. But he knew who really held their reins.

"How cheap were the girls of Ganapada, Gondpada and Gaudapada that they could be served a summons by anyone who wished to fuck them at his will? The only motive for Lalbabu's visits was to quench his monstrous appetite for meat, wine and women. And that beast of a khamari was nothing more than a pimp who would arrange for the girls for his master. Not one man had plucked up the courage to utter so much as a word of protest. Except perhaps grandfather. It wasn't only his own family's wellbeing and dignity at stake that made him stand in denial. There were previous occasions as well when, driven by his own complicity and guilt, he had attempted, by a smooth mix of subtlety, flattery and truth, to dissuade his master from this loathsome habit: 'Master, who in the universe would be foolish enough to leave such delectable platters of meat, such divine wine and such utterly delightful music? I am sure the mistress would have liked to be here too. Why don't you bring her along someday? Both of you could conjure up a night to remember, that too without your having to consort with these lowly maids! Prabhu, you are a man of such high position and prestige. By mingling with these power-hungry untouchables, you are putting a lot at stake. It is better to be safe than sorry. Prabhu, you won't even realise when they steal your power from right under your nose, and before you know it you'll find yourself doing their bidding.'

"He had tried to politely and quietly register his protest and his disapproval on numerous occasions in different ways. But he was just the guard, after all. No one paid the slightest heed to his remarks and shrugged off his suggestions with good-humoured guffaws. But today, the war of words had turned into a battle of blows. His gut instinct told him he had caused a considerable dent in Lalbabu's metallic ego. If it weren't so, why was his flesh being bloodied right now? Even so, however excruciating the lashes might be, oddly enough they soothed his soul from within and gave him a peculiar satisfaction. Through clenched teeth he challenged his tormentors, 'Yes! Yes! Go on raining your blows until your arms are wrenched out of their sockets! You can't kill me twice, can you? My death won't bring the world to a standstill. And why would it? What have I ever done for the world, or for Mother Earth who groans beneath the weight of my sublime existence? All I have ever done has been for the khamar and the khamari and for your most virtuous Lalbabu. And today, I have been bestowed the rare opportunity to learn what my sacrifices have wrought. What I have deserved all along is in the open for everyone to see.' One could actually taste the diabolic sarcasm that glinted in his pained eyes.

"As the first rays of the young sun looked earthwards from the east, grandfather was released from the khamar. His lips stayed sealed on why he was beaten. So his wife and daughter remained clueless about what had happened. And, as you might have guessed, he stopped going to the khamar. No one in the village was eager to give him work. If there was any household that he went to of his own accord, holding a small bundle of hope, he would be told to return right from the doorstep; no one wanted to incur Lalbabu's wrath.

"Grandfather was the sole breadwinner of his family, or he used to be in better days. His sixth sense flagged warnings at every step that his daughter was not safe anywhere except in the sanctuary of her home. Wherever she went, her eyes never seemed to lose sight of a pack of men, their vile gaze following her everywhere, sullying her modesty. Grandmother, who was afflicted with rheumatism, could not spend long hours working in the fields or loading and unloading heavy basketfuls of soil because it was painful for her to bend her back, not to mention her knees; one could say she was practically disabled. The only member of the household who was truly capable of earning an income to sustain the family was my grandfather.

"The golden harvest in Lalbabu's fields was swaying with the playful breeze. Flocks of birds like parakeets, doves, mynahs, munias, sparrows and pigeons had started conglomerating in the fields in large numbers. There was a time that they wouldn't have had the audacity to do so; because my grandfather, the loyal guard, would diligently stand watch with alert eyes, brandishing his lathi at the slightest flap of a wing. But it was not so now. So the intrepid feathered folks landed in the fields in droves and piled up grains in their tiny bellies, even as some others nonchalantly stood watch. Having eaten their fill, the birds would fly off to rest on their designated branches in the trees nearby just beyond the fields. And that is what gave grandfather the seed for his master plan.

"Armed with an axe and an almost infectious determination, my grandfather set off for the forest. Finding an old peepul tree, he cut off the bark and carefully collected the oozing latex, which looked to him like white tears. He brought the treasure home and boiled it with some castor oil. What now sat before him was a heady adhesive mixture which the villagers grandly called *chopkania*. Mind you, you don't want to go anywhere near this. It's damn sticky—strong enough to trap bird's legs. Grandfather went back to the forest to pour the freshly prepared mixture on several carefully chosen tree branches that stirred the tranquil woody air, with the brazen hope that a bird or two may get stuck to it. At least he would get some bird meat to silence the growls of hunger that had enshrouded his household of late.

"The gentle morning sun had undergone a gruelling moulting and was now shining down mercilessly on a blazing afternoon. But not one insolent feather had stuck to the glue, let alone a whole bird! A wave of panic seized my grandfather. What ill-fated times and what terrible luck had befallen him that even the birds knew of it? Unless...and then, a thought struck him out of the blue. Two faces materialised before his eyes and every blow of the lathi came back to haunt him. Was it those two wretched beings who had ruined what he had so meticulously planned? Had they forewarned the birds about the chopkania that sat waiting for their oblivious talons and shooed them away from the trees where he had so carefully planted his weapon, waiting for it to explode into action? A wave of fury crashed over him. So that was what had happened. Fine. If his fates were conspiring to make this a neck-to-neck fight, he would ensure that he made it one. In angry frustration, he resolved: You go on feasting on paddy, my folks. Just wait and watch, if I can't have you, I will have your paddy itself. Shaking in ferocious angst, he traced his steps back home.

"Just one hour from midnight. A cold wind waltzed around the fields. Shimmering beads of dew fell on the soft carpet of grass and leaves swaying gently in the wind. The eighth day of the fortnight heralded the hour that would witness the sinking of the moon; that moment was just round the corner, stealthily watching from the shadows. The deep nocturnal silence amplified the softest intake of breath. Every once in a while the intermittent howls of a jackal would rattle the air. The faithful halias of the khamari would have long inspected the immaculate stalks of the ochre crop that stood at attention, and gone back home to lie in a delicious cocoon of slumber.

"A perfect setting for a romantic adventure.

"My grandfather's adventures, however, turned out to be disastrously far from romantic. But first let me recount his elaborate preparations.

"With eyes that glittered with anticipation, his sinewy arms lifted a sickle from an unnoticed corner of his hut, its serrated blade gleaming with cunningness in the moonlight. He carefully turbaned his head to contain the errant strands of hair that had bristled themselves for the moonlit escapade. With silent dexterity he unlatched the door and stepped out into the night. His eyes swept over all that they beheld and finally, reassured, he surreptitiously set out for Lalbabu's fields, his feet treading softly over the ground. Those very fields where the ripe paddy stood meekly as the birds feasted on the grain with a hunger that never seemed to cease. Today, it was his turn. Dhubal Gana had set his eyes on the crop. Soon, it would be in his hands. That bloody

Lalbabu, who would feast on the harvest, hadn't given an ounce of his effort to raise the crop. Oh no, it was people like him, Dhubal Gana, who had poured their toil and sweat and blood like water upon the soil, but who had to survive on meagre wages instead. Today, he had come to get back what he had lent. His sweat. His blood. His labour. And most of all, his dignity.

"Stealthily, he set foot into the paddy fields. Out came his sickle and set about swiftly slicing the crops from their stalks, which seemed as if to melt on the touch of the iron blade. The water standing in the fields seemed to possess a soul of its own, created from the darkness of night, and sloshed about impatiently as if waiting to unleash its fury. The howls of the jackals were stirring the night air. Any moment, a wild boar might come crashing through the sea of golden crop, and the intruder would have to run for his life. And then there were the halias to consider. If they chanced to come prowling on an inspection, he was done for. But Dhubal Gana did not care. With firm steps and a determined heart fired by anger, he softly tread the ground that held his treasure: the treasure he had grown by his hands; the diamonds that would adorn his plaguing hunger. He cut an entire *bhara* of paddy, bundled it up in the cloth of his guilt-laden turban, loaded it on his head and trotted back home fast.

"In urgent whispers, he told his wife and daughter to get up. Both were astonished to see the bulging bundle. The sharp pincers of hunger had poisoned their sleep and not allowed them a moment's rest. I too joined the lot. Each of us briskly settled down to work. Stamping on the paddy as if our feet were crushing hunger itself, we went about separating the paddy from the stalks. Then we set up a crackling flame and the grains were in for a delightful roast. My aunt, cradling a pestle in her beautiful palms, pounded the roasted paddy, which turned into succulent sparkling white rice. Finally, it was cooked in an old pot, which hummed a joyful tune as the boiling water bubbled merrily juggling the grains of rice. My grandfather downed every grain of rice, gulped down all the gruel in his bowl, and letting out a contented burp, declared, 'You goddamned hunger! You can't sit around lounging in my belly for long!'

"Secrecy, the quintessence of thievery, could only be embraced in the blackness of night. By then I was fourteen, and could make some sense of what was taking place in the world around me: Lalbabu's ruthless exploitation, the khamari's covert spying, grandmother's failing health, and aunt's fading dreams for her youth, her life.

"As the days passed by and our circumstances remained unchanging, grandfather fell prey to the habit of thieving paddy. I would often go along with him. Under the scorching sun, we would look for ripened paddy during the day, and come back to claim possession of it by night. Just see how the fates tilted—it took almost no time for a conscientious and committed guard, a caretaker of paddy at that, to turn into a shrewd and dexterous paddy thief. Oh, and yes, he even went ahead to teach and train the heir who would inherit his noble profession: me.

"But luck is not like sunrise; it doesn't greet you every day. The victims of thievery turned detectives, wondering who could have possibly had the audacity to steal their beloved paddy from right under their noses. My grandfather's trail would be marked by stray tell-tale ears of paddy that would fall from the bundle restraining them. The people weren't blind either; they also noticed the growing heaps of straw that now occupied his backyard, like souvenirs of his helpless dishonesty. No better proof was necessary. A village meeting was called. Grandfather had no choice, and soon admitted his crime. A case was filed. Grandfather was sent to jail. A few months later, he was released. But the name and photograph of Dhubal Gana remained on the *thana*'s notice board like an ugly blotch on the rest of his life. His dishonesty was branded on his flesh, on his bones, on his soul. Even distant thieveries would draw the police's attention to him, and they would spend no time resigning themselves to the fact that he was the accused behind it. He would repeatedly be served summons and made to undergo grueling enquiries. Grandfather was made to compulsorily report to the thana once every week. Such infamy did not help him get a job. What is more, no one came forward with the proposal to marry my aunt either.

"So, my grandfather gradually shifted his attention to burgling houses. First he would devour any stale cooked rice that he could find. Next he would go for the ration like rice, *chiwda* and pulses, and bring them home in a clumsy bundle. But he never touched an ounce of gold, silver or money. What business did he have with them? He had to settle the score with hunger first. If that was accomplished, it was more than enough for him.

"Thieves of that time nestled in their daredevil hearts a staunch belief: if the soil from a cremation ground on a moonless midnight collected by the bare hands of a bare-bodied man was placed in the house that was to be burgled, every creature in that house would for certain be gently nudged into deep sleep while their belongings were lifted with ease. So it would come as no surprise if I told you that my grandfather too fell prey to this 'shortcut' that would help him do his job with expert ease, ruthlessly depriving another of the fruits of his sweat and toil in the process.

"Every act of thievery costs the victim something. This time, however, it was the thief who had to pay.

"One night, as always, my grandfather set off for another heist. Preparing a mix of a pinch of the precious cremation ground soil and a few priceless grains of rice, he murmured a prayer to his goddess and let the potent dust fall onto the imposing porch that stood before him, as the particles danced in the tranquil air carrying the soul of the night. With the stealth of a stalking predator, he dug a hole in one of the walls of the house. His sinewy wrists rose up leaving the sides of his thighs, hovered in the air in front of the gaping hole and like a hissing serpent they slithered into the little void of darkness that stretched before them. Then, slicing through the colourless silence came an immaculate swoosh. Cold metal against warm flesh. An excruciating blinding white pain shot through grandfather's wrist, coursing through his veins. And oh, his face! Contorted in agony, his mouth released a rush of bloodcurdling screams and a desolate 'Aaaaahhh!' filled the night, as his arms withdrew from the merciless void that stood there silent, smiling a bone-chilling smile. Through a film of hot tears, his eyes beheld a hair-raising sight: blood. Warm thick blood. Spurting out of...an ugly stump of flesh where till moments ago his...palm had been. Blood flowing freely from his veins, his heart, draining his very life soul, drenching him. As the horrors of that night stood towering over him like some monstrous beast that had finally revealed its hideous true self, grandfather yanked his bereft hand incredulously, as if willing his lost palm to be restored. Then he burst into a sprint, running as fast as his shaking legs could carry him, deeper and deeper into the night, without once looking back, all the while his one hand nursing the other.

"Running like a man chasing his sanity, he crashed through his door and fell to the mocking earth. The gentle earth in whose lap he had spent countless nights and days drifting on the subtle currents of dreams, that very earth was now taunting him fit to burst his heart into a million shards as he lay writhing in agony. For three long tormenting months, he sat huddled inside his hut in shame. Dhubal Gana, who had guarded the khamar come rain or shine, who had conquered the fatal horns of a full-grown blackbuck, who was the proud breadwinner of his family, who had been thieving without a care to feed his family and himself... was now disabled. Dependent. Helpless. A burden. The mortifying humiliation bored into his skin, gnawing deeper and deeper into his soul. As the heartless months passed by his window, the once towering frame of Dhubal Gana began to shrink into the skeleton of an ageing man, a man who had stayed beyond his welcome on earth.

"My eyes witnessed each of these moments, each of these misfortunes that snatched a big chunk of our life, our joy away, never to return it again. I lived them, sometimes drowning in them, sometimes just managing to swim back to land and touch the shores of a mundane happiness, a brief calm, before the raging whirlpool of despondency sucked me back in.

"Sometimes from the dying embers of helplessness and black despair, a deep red flame rises up from my soul doused in the spirit of revenge, red as the red fluid dripping from the lifeless stump of flesh that grandfather brought home that night. That malicious flame of revenge is eating me up from within, and some nights when the voice in my head echoes the eerie laughter of that ever burning flame, I am tempted to let it break loose, and to let the Satan inside me escape.

"Temptation is powerful.

"But my identity is marked by the constant presence of another far more powerful force, something that has not left me all these years, and as it appears, something that is unlikely to relinquish its hold on me even in the years to come.

"Helplessness. Every minute of my life, I see this force radiating power, forever engaged in a silent tussle with my naïve temptations, always winning, and never very far behind my own shadow.

"Power is good. But it whittles down those subservient to it.

"And as I regain my balance after every stumble and trudge along the path of life, a wordless servant to the power of helplessness, I feel it slowly but surely whittling out my life from me. I see melancholy, the grey mixing with the black; but what catches my attention is nothing but a passing cloud of smoke, which is all that is now left of my soul.

"Little did I know that I would be completely engulfed by these emotions which would propel me further onto an even more hazardous path. As I was pushed further and further into the gallows, I started struggling with my identity. Then one fine day, in a perfectly ordinary moment, I realised what I had become.

"A thief.

"But it earned me a lot of popularity and fame. Hell, yes! You don't believe me? I was in every corner of the village: the pond, the *ghats*, the colourful weekly *haats* selling a dazzling array of merchandise, everywhere. My eminent persona became central to small talk and gossip, and with it came a heavy dose of scorn, of course. It ranged from 'What else can you expect from a thief's grandson?' to 'What more could he have been other than a thieving wretch?' and even 'I always knew that the fates would deny him any decent profession.' To add to it, nobody was willing to make use of my labour. Their rusted brains had suddenly clanged into action and they surmised that employing me to work for them would be like digging a hole for themselves. Suddenly I was this brand ambassador of thievery who was a walking advertisement for the gold one could strike in my profession, and naturally, they didn't want to end up being robbed by their own employees. And hence, decent, honest work began to sound more and more like a distant dream.

"Just the sight of me would make folks behave bizarrely. To men walking on the same road as I, the sky would suddenly become impossibly beautiful or important to ignore and their eyes would all be glued skywards, not climbing down to the ground until I was gone. Children who would be engrossed in their games until not a moment ago would disappear in the blink of an eye. Women's veils would swiftly come to the rescue of their precious jewellery, which apparently I was brazen enough to steal in broad daylight in front of every soul in sight. And livestock? Hens, goats, sheep, cattle, ducks, you name it. Dambru is around and suddenly everyone is frantically shooing their animals back to the barn or pen or shed in a trice.

"They all hated me.

"Then, adorned by a gossamer moon and stars dipped in sparkling silver came the fateful night.

"That night, I was planning another one of my exploits, which later turned out to be nothing of that sort. As the pitch blackness swallowed the stars and the moon, and the dark grappled with the light and won, I sneaked out of my house on a quest to lay my hands on something. I finally managed to secure a bundle of paddy. To avoid suspicion, I made my way into the verandah of the village school and started dehusking the paddy with my bare feet.

"And then I heard it. A soft footstep. Suddenly the night was filled with the hushed sounds of feet running. Then a shadow loomed into view. Then another. Then another. As my breath caught in my parched throat, I saw a hand shoot out of nothingness and before I knew it I was roughly pushed to the ground. Black shadows encircled me swiftly and started landing vicious kicks and punches on every inch of my body. There were sticks too. Thick as my wrist. Blow after blow. My body turned from red to blue to black. The shadows were merciless. The black night made them invisible. Invincible. Terrifying. The voices would have been recognisable perhaps, but my eardrums were frozen deaf with fear. And there I lay prostrate on the ground, alone and weaponless, writhing under the ceaseless blows, waiting for them to stop. And they did stop. For the better? No, for the worse.

"The malignant cosmic conspiracy that one grandly calls luck made the villagers come to the decision of sending me to jail. That very night. I must rot to dust in jail. I was a problem for the entire village after all. I deserved this.

"Three pairs of well-oiled muscles grabbed hold of me, every bead of their sweat glistening with the determination to deposit me in jail. And then began the nocturnal march to the thana, a good eight kilometres away from my village, something we were supposed to cover on foot. My brain was already whirring, trying desperately to come up with some strategy to break free and escape. But it just wouldn't come. Luck could be one hell of a devil when it wanted to.

"A murmur of sleepy whispers was floating through the air. Then the silence was broken by the voice of someone elderly, 'You boys, look sharp and don't loosen your grip on that audacious piece of flesh that you are escorting. I have heard scores of tales about these thieves. He'll just nip your arm and get away before you can say ouch.' And so, for one blessed moment, luck forgot how diabolic it was supposed to be. Here was my cue. A nip in the arm was what the muscles leading me to the thana would get.

"As if orchestrating a dramatic prelude, I slackened my arms and legs into a docile mode and walked along meek and obedient as a puppy with such submissiveness as if I was being led to paradise.

"Five kilometres left to the thana.

"And then came the golden opportunity. A pissing urge.

"One of those macho men escorting me got the call of nature. Shouting a warning to his companions to 'Hold on to him!' he melted into the trees to empty his bladder.

"One bloke gone. Only two left.

"I could actually feel the adrenaline pulsating through my canines. For the first time in my life, I regretted that they were not as razor-sharp as I would have liked them to be. The devil dressed as my luck was back again. But this time, I was the saint. One who was about to bite the poor chap next to him, who had no clue what was coming.

"And then, it happened.

"Thinking of the sweet, golden, succulent mangoes I used to relish come summer, I sank my teeth hard into the mound of firm flesh that sat on the arm nearest to me, and felt my canines pierce it with surprising brute force. A scream sliced through the silence, and the iron grip on my wrist loosened considerably. My other wrist shook itself free, and suddenly I was free. Without so much as a glance behind, I ran as fast as my legs could carry me. The pounding in my ears grew louder and louder and I felt I would either dissolve in the fear weighing my heart down or that my lungs would burst. I ran deeper and deeper into the jungle, past monstrous trees and poisonous herbs. I had no inkling as to where I was headed.

"Suddenly, I knew where I had to go.

"Willing my exhausted, aching legs to keep going, I ran straight to the one place in mind: Lathore station. I ran and ran till I lost track of time. And then at last I heard it.

"The familiar rumble of the train.

"Without another thought, I climbed onto the train that had just pulled into the station. Where was it headed, you ask. I had no clue. I saw a train. I climbed onto it. I got down at the first station where the train stopped. Yes—it was Raipur. I got down with a million thoughts clawing at my mind. Knowing nothing better to do, I just slipped onto a cement bench. The same one that sits with all humility in front of your eyes right now.

"To the world, it is just a bench. To me, it is the beginning of my life and my identity in Raipur. An identity I sought. An identity I sculpted myself. Right here in this city. And it all began from this bench.

"I am not God. No brother, I am just a thief. A paddy thief.

"It's been eleven years, and the bench that my life was pivoted on is just the same. It is where it was. But my life has changed. My grandparents are dead. All I have left with me from my village is my aunt. The barbaric fates were kind enough to let me bring her here. She lives in my cottage, a souvenir of days long past...days of which I want nothing more except just to press them to my bosom and never let go of.

"Call me an egomaniac if you will. I even give you my consent to call me a narcissist, but here's the truth, bhai: you are truly lucky that I was around to help you find your way in this city. When I arrived here, hungry, helpless, hopeless, there was no Dambru around to offer me any moral or physical support. My desperately lonely eyes ached to see someone familiar, someone of family, even some long-forgotten acquaintance would've done. But all they could do was linger upon the greasy bogeys of trains. I would watch them come and I would watch them go. That distant chugging of the bogeys that clanged with each other, that high boom of the roaring engine, the clamour, jostling, push and pull the platform witnessed each time that a train clattered to a stop: all this gradually ceased to be jagged shards scraping against my bitter, desolate heart, and gradually settled into a kind of solace in which I found some peace. It became a part of my everyday, my life. A quintessence of my survival.

"But man is a social being. He finds the most solace and succour in the company of others like him. My eyes soon stopped noticing the train and shifted attention to what sat inside it: the people. The rusted metal tap that stood stolidly atop a water service sink became my close friend. It would generously let water gush out of itself to serve my parched throat. Thirst is one thing; starvation is quite another. My rusted old friend the tap often helped me overcome my thirst, but the perpetual growling of my empty stomach was something I was losing to, every day. And so, to earn myself something that could silence my insolent belly, I decided I would lend my shoulders to carry the heavy bags of passengers. Quite a good business I would have done, had it not been for the possessive coolies. They practically tore my eardrums, shouting, 'Listen, you wretched piece of scum. Being a coolie doesn't mean you just pick up a couple of totes and get away with the money weighing down your pockets like rocks. You have to be a part of the coolie association first. Bugger off and don't show your shitty face till you register yourself there!' So what's the big deal, I thought. I went to the association. But those blokes weren't exactly eager to get me registered, and shooed me off like I was a funny little hen clucking about. But this is Dambru's story that you're listening to, bhai, Dambru. Was I just going to lose hope and weep on that bench like a pimply gangly girl? Oh no, not at all! I went up to shops, eateries, hotels and restaurants to try my luck and even to bloody hospitals. But the devilish fates were at work again. From everywhere, I came back downcast and low with rejection and misery. As the moonlit night would throw its black veil over the brooding sky, I would settle down in some not-so-private spot on the road to pass the dark hours. But even that was too much of a luxury for me. The local cops would materialise on the spot in a flash, breathing down my neck like hungry hellhounds, their lathis maliciously brutal on my broken skin. From there I turned to the footpath, but there too I was fed kicks and abuses. So all that was left for me to sleep on was this bench. But mind you, even securing this bench was no mean feat. I faced a lot of interrogation from the suspicious railway police. It cruelly reminded me of what my grandfather had to face back in his thieving days. These big posh hotels that we stare at so admiringly with eyes widened in awe, they are all a façade. I turned up at their plush entrance asking for leftovers, just leftovers, and they banged the door shut on my face. Imagine doing that to a helpless, homeless, starving child. Would you have the heart to do that? No, neither of us does. Well, as long as we still have a bit of humanity left in us. For three famished days, I roamed about like a hopeless ghost, my sanity and strength ebbing out with every step. For three whole months I had no roof over my head. It seemed like a lifetime.

"We belong to this city. But this city belongs to no one.

"Finding even a ramshackle shelter for oneself is one hell of a job. People say you'll find trust hidden in every corner of the world. Sure. But it's a bloody coward, because it is always trailing behind its more malevolent counterpart: suspicion.

"Suspicion, that powerful repellent which will tug at your heartstrings and try and push you away; away from what you have come seeking, away from the people you have come to with so much hope. Everywhere I went, suspicion would be lurking around ready to pounce on me and maul someone's compassion and my good fortune, and I would be left staring as it would whisk away yet another job that I could have had, yet another filthy dilapidated corner I could have called my home. Suspicion engulfs sympathy and trust, so no matter where I ended up, I found none.

"And ready to build and empower suspicion are two other emotions embedded deep in people's souls: selfishness and oblivion. Everyone is happy as long as you let them mind their own business. And let them be. They don't want to care about others. They don't want to know that others exist. They just want to think about their own greedy selves and all the while pretend that they didn't even know you existed.

"City life is golden, say some. For me, it's plain absurd. If you are the winning horse, congratulations; people will back you like you are their own son, their bosom friend. But if the fates have left you as nothing but a mule, congratulations again; no one will know you or have your back. You will find you are all alone. Well, almost. There will always be rebukes and thrashings to give you company.

"Don't mind me repeating myself, but I am definitely not a god. My true identity is, and will continue to be, that of a thief. A mere glimpse at you took me back in time, into my own half-deranged past when, thirteen years ago, I had staggered to a stop at this very station, my heart hammering with fear, my lungs ready to burst. What is it that I have done for you? Does my father own the palace I have given you to call home? Have I arranged a meal for you? Have I bought your wife a saree? Have I helped you send your son to school? No. Far from it. You had to clear out filthy garbage and shit from the spot I had shown you; only then could you think of settling down there. And I? I just cycled off in my rickshaw without so much even as a glance back. No, there is nothing I have done for you my friend, absolutely nothing."

Dambru had turned sober by now. In his distant eyes, Manglu saw what looked like unshed tears.

And so, we come back to Makaru, who sat by his window looking out, his heart flooded with emotions ready to overflow any moment. A soothing tune kissed his ears, which he realised to be a beggar's doing.

> O God of gods, when an elephant cried for your help from millions of miles, O Chaturbhuja, you heard his call immediately...

A smile lingered on Makaru's lips. He simply could not understand how this great 'God of gods' went about his work. If he turned deaf to the distress calls he had been receiving from so near, how could he have responded to one that had come from millions of miles away? He could not shrug off the uncanny feeling that it was all one big perfectly nonsensical lie. Beggar or not, this man certainly had a knack for singing. He knew how to hold people's attention with his melodious voice. And how could this poor chap possibly know about God's mysterious ways of doing things?

Makaru was reminded of drunken Dambru's soulful melody.

Choosing to ignore the rumbling and rattling of the train and the boisterous clanging of the bogeys, Makaru began humming the song he had been reminded of.

Blissfully oblivious to his song, the train chugged along.

Five

Fear is grotesque. And fear is beautiful. If you choose to embrace it, that is. Sabesh had never been one of the brave lot, so she never quite came close to embracing her fear. But what she did do was brave enough. She got used to the fear, and to the source of the fear itself. She had come a long way, from having witnessed childbirths that were believed to have been catalysed by the disgorging fear and the resultant labour induced in pregnant mothers by the sight of a mere train ticket, to living right beside the railway track.

For Sabesh, the village that she had left behind and this city were not incomparable. Here, difficulty lurked at every corner of the dark, uncertain times that she stood confronting, ready to pounce on her when she least expected it. But Sabesh learnt to shield herself from fear using acceptance. She adapted. She changed. And she trained her heart to make room for that one immensely significant element of her existence in the city: adjustment.

The human filth that routinely flew out of the train, snaking right past her hut. The jet black particles of soot that covered the food she cooked in a fine layer. The cloying, smothering stink that malignantly trailed behind the blissfully oblivious breeze, making her nauseous as it hit her nostrils. Every sunrise would bring them along, and Sabesh's soul would die many small deaths every day.

Once, Sabesh hated them. Today, they are her neighbours, her daily companions, with whom she cohabits every day.

Imagine an odd assortment of bamboo poles sticking out of the earth at awkward angles. Throw in a sheet of black tarpaulin; add an open bare hearth lying under the mocking clouds. There! You have successfully conjured up the humblest of humble abodes. You may also spot a threadbare mat lying around somewhere. Sabesh and her family sit out on it when the tumbledown shack they call home gets too hot and stuffy to stay inside. Mornings would see them trudging along to find a deserted spot near the railway track to relieve themselves, holding a plastic pot or bottle in one hand, and hopelessness in the other.

Like a faithful companion a water supply pipe runs beside the railway track, going all the way into town. Just where it comes into the vicinity of Sabesh's hut, this pipe nurses a puncture. Who has done it, you ask. Call it her neighbours' handiwork, or divine intervention if you will, but, procuring a more-or-less adequate and regular supply of water to bathe is perhaps one task less arduous in Sabesh's life. Come morning, water spurts gaily out of the blessed puncture like a fountain, putting to shame the explosion of firecrackers seen at big fat Indian weddings. And with it on the dot, immaculately punctual, arrive thousands of *baraati*s armed with buckets and mugs. In a matter of seconds, the precious pipe is teeming with half-naked men and women in various degrees of undress who couldn't care less about who is looking or the presence of the opposite sex. If you are so concerned that your *gamchha* should cover you properly, the water will run out, and you will be left without a bath! Well, perhaps they weren't that shameless either, and took care to expose only as much of their bodies as their already casual city mores allowed.

Sabesh admired the way the poor of the city bathed together in one place without any apparent qualms or hesitation. In her village, where people strictly followed traditional caste rules and where different caste groups bathed separately, this was unthinkable. The upper castes, who considered themselves to be the favourite of the gods, chose their own exclusive bathing ghats and ponds, barring people from castes such as Chamar or Gana from using them. Violation of caste rules was considered scandalous and the violators were heavily punished. However, the upper castes had no problems if pigs, cattle, dogs and cats entered the pond. But they would not allow the lower castes to step into their bathing ghats. Why—did they not qualify as human beings? What a marvellous system is caste!

Even today Sabesh clearly recalls the ugly fight that ensued in her parental village before her marriage. The reason was a trivial issue concerning the village pond. A Dalit boy from a neighbouring village had unknowingly entered the Brahmin ghat. The upper castes considered it a deliberate affront and decided to punish all the Dalits of the village. An emergency village meeting was called to decide the quantum of the punishment. It was only after the Dalits begged their forgiveness that they finally relented. As punishment, the Dalits had to clean the entire village for free, without any remuneration.

Sabesh remembered another event. Once the bore well at Ganapada had stopped working. So Dalits had no source of water. They begged the people of Gaudpada to allow them to collect water from their bore well. But their request went unheeded. After repeated pleadings the people of Gaudpada yielded, but on condition that, being untouchables, the Ganas would not draw water from their well themselves. They would wait at a distance with their pots and pitchers, until someone from the upper caste came along and poured water for them. While collecting water a young girl from Ganapada accidentally touched the bore well. That led to a riot in the village. The people of Ganapada were beaten black and blue. The Ganas filed a police complaint. But instead of registering a case under the atrocity act, the police negotiated a compromise. Had the case been registered, the people of Gaudpada would have landed in jail.

As per Indian constitutional law, untouchability has long been abolished. But even today, it lurks discreetly, or brazenly, in every village that dots the countryside. Sabesh, for one, has experienced it firsthand. Suffered it. Endured it. True, it was present here in Raipur, too. But here, it had been stripped of its inhuman dehumanising extremes. Or else, why would all the slum dwellers gather at the same water pipe for a bath? The fact that men and women could wash their bodies in front of each other without shame or harassment was also something worth appreciating, Sabesh felt.

As everywhere else, the rickshaw pullers of Raipur could either work in day shifts or in night shifts. Night-shift workers had to endure extra hardship. Other than having to sacrifice their sleep, they also had to encounter a rather colourful crowd: drunkards, drug addicts, pimps, prostitutes and what not. Which rickshaw-wallah wouldn't charge more to ferry such characters at night? The extra money aside, Manglu still preferred the day shifts.

Here is what Sabesh's morning rituals were like: an early bath at the punctured pipe; tossing the same old vegetables into a battered pan on the hearth, and making a humble offering of the same at the pidar. It is noteworthy that in that tiny shack, she had carved out a space the size of a winnowing basket for the pidar. She had purified that space by smearing it with fresh cow dung. She had beautified it by making an intricate *chita* over it with fine rice powder paste. This was an ages-old tradition. The Ganas, Gands, Gaudas and Kandhas had a deep and staunch belief that homes adorned with such beautiful chitas had the enigmatic power to please their family deities and ancestral spirits and convince them to make it their abode and rain blessings upon the household. No wonder then that every Gana house had its own pidar and chita.

Through all the trials and tribulations that had come her way, Sabesh had steadfastly stuck to this tradition. Countless changes had glided past her life on gauzy wings: the honking and hollering on these naked city roads that rushed about relentlessly; the metallic whining of the train that whistled and hurtled past her hut every day; the magnificent and magical images conjured up by the cinema and television with their titillating dances and lewd music. Yet, through all of this, one thing had stood with her like an obedient pet that refused to leave her side: her dedication and devotion towards her ancestral spirits and deities, and her steely determination not to let anything come in the way of her worship. With whatever she could lay her hands on, Sabesh had built a small symbolic altar to continue the priceless legacy of faith she had inherited from the culture and traditions she nestled close to her heart.

All she asked for in return was the rich sense of contentment that would envelop her heart every time she offered a handful of the day's cooking at her pidar. The deep tranquil joy of having pleased Goddess Nialimali and her ancestors with whatever little she had at her disposal was incomparable. Each time she did so, she felt reassured that the generous goddess would watch over and protect Manglu wherever he may go riding his rickshaw.

There was another tradition that the Gana community had handed down to Sabesh: the women of the community never addressed their men by name. So, Sabesh would never use the familiar first name for her husband. Instead, she addressed him as "*baburbua*" or the father of her son. More amusingly, since the local word for Tuesday, that is Mangalbar, sounded somewhat similar to Manglu, she had cleverly renamed it "Devirbar" or the day of the Devi.

After serving her family their meals, Sabesh would see her baburbua off as he set out for the day's work. He would ferry passengers round the city: I.G. Road, M.G. Chowk, Katra Talab, Kali Badi, the Medical College and hospital, the Collectorate, Gol Bazaar, and Babulal Gali were destinations he had now familiarised himself with. After all these mini tours of the city, Manglu would wind up at the Raipur station chowk and park his rickshaw there in his designated spot. Dambru also used to park his rickshaw there.

Having seen the breadwinner off on his way, Sabesh would get done with all her heavy chores. Her son Makaru was a considerate child who seldom made selfish demands, and would often remain immersed in a parallel world of his own, oblivious to what was happening around him. Dambru's aunt was an affectionate woman who never minded sharing a little chit-chat with Sabesh. She would recount how she, too, had found it difficult to adjust to this new life at first. And how she had by degrees softened and gradually fit herself into the city's humdrum rhythm, like a piece of a jigsaw puzzle does by forgetting its individual existence to paint a larger picture. And so on a sunny afternoon laced with a cool breeze, she would weave a tapestry of her past struggles to Sabesh.

"There wasn't very much left for me to do after finishing with my household chores. Poor Dambru had to bear the brunt of supporting the entire family with his derelict rickshaw. He could barely manage to make ends meet. Given this, I felt there wouldn't be much to lose if I looked for work somewhere so that I too could contribute to the household economically, and the stings of idleness would stop pinching me come mid afternoon.

"After a patient look-out for odd jobs, I was finally employed as a household help in a gentleman's home. My mistress was pretty indeed. I did every single chore you can think of: washing the utensils till they shone like silver, cleaning the house so as not to leave even a speck of dust, washing all the clothes and bed linen. I would leave at six in the morning, and by the time I would be done it would be eleven or so. They would offer me a cup of tea every day. Occasionally they would even toss me some breakfast. After months of having attended to them, one day I finally failed them. And do you know what let them down? My caste. It set their tongues wagging and they never stopped. 'You double-faced witch! What made you think you could have hidden your caste from us for ever! And look how we fell into her trap. Her decent ways and mannerisms pulled the wool over our face, made us think that she must be from a proper caste. We welcomed you with open hearts and open doors. The kitchen, the puja *ghar*, the bedrooms, you name it: where were you denied entry? Oh god, and she polluted it all! Just a casual flick of the wrist here and there, and we used to give you a full cup of tea every day! To think that we were paying her a hundred and twenty a month and that she was going about befouling our holy household! Dirty, greedy gold digger!'

"And that was it. They vowed never to let me set foot there again. Not that I would have wanted to after this episode, anyway. I hold my dignity close to my heart and there is nothing that comes in its way. God is witness: I never hid my caste from them. It's just that they never bothered to ask me outright. And I wasn't about to go digging my own grave and announcing it on my own."

Sabesh's fragile bubble of misconceptions abruptly burst. All this while she had been blissfully oblivious of the discreet workings of caste-based discrimination in the city, letting her heart believe the utopian vision that she witnessed at the water pipe every day. She had let her naivety guide her and thought that the educated city-dwellers couldn't possibly have anything to do with the ugly monster of caste, that she felt was constrained only to the rural countryside. No wonder then that the heartfelt narration of Dambru's aunt brought with it an ugly awakening and a rude shock.

Sabesh let her words form slowly, "So...then did you not go looking for any other job thereafter?"

Pat came the answer, "Of course, I did. And this time, I told the hotel owner upfront that I belonged to a lowly caste. If that did not bother him, I would be happy to work at his hotel. If it did, he better tell me beforehand to avoid an ugly confrontation later.

"To my pleasant surprise, the Punjabi owner gave an admirable reply and said, 'I don't give a damn about anyone's caste. You have come here for work, then work. Or else, you'll be driven out before you can say your name out loud.'

"Somewhere deep down, I felt a warmth spread slowly through my heart. With an inner zeal, I set about doing my job, which meant washing cups and plates. To top it all, we could have all the leftover *badas*, *pyajis* and *samosas*. We were an assortment of various age groups employed there, but I was the only woman among the fifteen-odd employees whose hunger had driven them to work at the hotel. Six or seven boys were young enough to be the age of my grandson. The rest were of my son's age. Being the only woman there, I was always particular about my attire and doubly careful that nothing was exposed. But it was difficult to always keep my saree tightly in place while working, particularly when my hands were wet. The young boys would often stare at me and crack lewd jokes. I did not realise that the hotel owner had evil intentions. He would give me five or ten rupees extra daily. Initially, I could not fathom his purpose. I thought he was pleased with my hard work. Whenever I had a little leisure he would come and talk to me with sugar-coated words. Sometimes he would hold my hands and talk. Then one day he groped me from behind and touched my breasts and thighs. I was furious and I shouted. All the workers came running. Feeling insulted, and to show how very virtuous he was, the owner concocted a story and started abusing me and shouting, '*Sali*! How dare you touch me, you filthy prostitute! You have no morals. Today you tried exploiting me. Tomorrow you will prey on these boys. Before the reputation of this hotel gets sullied, get out you old hag! I do not want to see your face here again!'

"But, to tell you the truth, it was not the Punjabi who drove me out. I left his employment immediately after this incident. Even if he had offered me double the wages, I would not have worked for that disgusting and vile man.

"Never ever believe these wicked men. My life has taught me this the hard way. I have never shared this traumatic past of mine with anyone else except you. After that horrible day, I lost my motivation and enthusiasm to look for work. The city started giving me the creeps. Even the mere sight of a man would make my flesh crawl, threatening to unleash memories of all the horrific male crassness and vulgarity that I had been subjected to. Our household had nothing to lose; my son's income from pulling the rickshaw just about covered the expenses. The municipality elections were held that year. And with it came the political leaders wooing voters with the intention of securing their vote banks. So here's the thing. The government officers, clerks and big businessmen are all busy *babu*s who don't have even a second to spare so they can get their finger inked and cast their ballot. So it is the slum dwellers that these candidates turn to. The votes cast from the *jhuggi-jhopdi*s determine who will hold political office. And our tiny hut and home was part of the slum. The voters' list was updated as always. This time, our names were included. And before we knew it, we became duly registered voters of Raipur! With that, we could finally access the government facilities that we had been denied so far: jobs, ration cards, and so on. There are several thousand Odias in Raipur who were granted this blessing in exchange for their votes. They work in the municipality, municipal hospital, electricity board, and other government offices. I, too, made use of this opportunity and got work as a sweeper for the municipality. I go to sweep the roads twice: once in the morning and once in the afternoon. I get rupees 1500 as my monthly salary."

This lit up a bright ray of hope in Sabesh's soul. She couldn't keep the enthusiasm out of her voice as she excitedly said, "If that is so, Mausi, how I wish I too could become a verified resident and procure a job like you! Then, I too can get to work with you, right? Right now all I do is sit at home and count the trains every day. At this rate, I might well turn into a walking train timetable! I could certainly do with a change in my routine. Even Makaru is a grown up lad now. I never had to worry much about him even when he was a child. He could manage quite well by himself. And he is educated, too. Studied up to class three."

True, Makaru's parents had indeed been responsible enough to send him to school. But their reasons for doing so weren't concerned as much with providing him the education he had the right to as they were with ensuring that he had food to eat. His school offered midday meals to its students, as per the government plans. Who would want to miss out on that? Sabesh, in her motherly concern, would even slip a plate and bowl into his school bag so that Makaru could eat to his heart's content at school. What education her son might be receiving there was beyond her concern, so when she checked his bag, it wasn't to inspect his books but just to make sure he had got back the utensils she had given him. Even when he started tending the gauntia's cattle after having passed his third standard, she would try and find days on which she could send him to school.

Sadly, this wasn't the case in Raipur.

Here in Raipur, boys of Makaru's age had already become wizards at surviving the game of life. They had found ways to sustain their grey lives and earn enough to live hand-to-mouth. Some were dishwashers, others were waiters in hotels. From helping in ration shops and going about hoarsely yelling for train passengers to buy their chickpeas and peanuts, to cleaning old rusty cars in garages and pulling rickshaws throughout the day, they had sacrificed their childhood and offered their hard labour at the altar of livelihood to keep body and soul together. Some others, however, had resorted to means that could be called more resourceful. They stole mounds of coal from goods trains and sold cinema tickets in black. Some had perfected the art of pick-pocketing, using their trusted knives expertly to slit open the pockets of strangers in a wink even as they walked away, blissfully oblivious. So what if there was no way of earning money? They would create one. They were clever enough for that. And our innocent Makaru, who no longer attended school but hung out with these boys instead, had also gained a newfound cunningness which manifested in his will to survive against all odds in this throbbing hustle bustle of a city.

However, despite the influence of his newfound peers, Makaru stuck to his morals and didn't opt for dishonesty. He found employment in a hotel where he was assigned the humble task of serving water to customers. This did not deter him from fulfilling his duties with earnest enthusiasm. His promptness and courtesy soon earned him a good name among the customers. It wasn't long before the hotel owner also came to recognise his immaculate work ethic and decided to appoint him the cashier. Makaru did this job just as diligently as the one before and never let a single coin go astray, and always put the cash records in order before he left for the day. So industrious was he that soon, the owner of the hotel started relying on him completely.

Now, Makaru too had joined the bandwagon of breadwinner along with his father. Sabesh found it easy to run the household smoothly. They no longer felt like someone else's slaves. No, in fact, perhaps for the very first time in their life, they felt refreshingly alive...human. Manglu felt liberated. Day by day he relentlessly pushed the pedals of his rickshaw and pushed through the obstacles that life put in his path, never once turning back. In the money that his passengers grudgingly or matter-of-factly paid him, he saw his blood, sweat and tears. Soon, the family started saving up for additional expenses. They would even treat themselves to a movie at the cinema once every month or so. Sabesh would occasionally visit the bazaar and return home treasuring a new pack of alta, sindur, face powder, hair oil, or some such trifle.

Now all that was left was to find Makaru a decent girl.

Their lives weren't entirely devoid of celebration. But whenever a touch of joy came to caress their lives like the carefree spring, they would also experience in their hearts a shade of melancholy, for no celebrations are complete without family. And happy as they all were in this city that they were quickly adapting to and settling into, they couldn't help but long for their home, their village, their own people.

And here was Makaru, on his way to his childhood village to meet his relatives, whose lives had been charred to ashes and scattered to the winds along with their anguish, their unfulfilled desires, their dreams, and their hopeless hopes.

Meanwhile, the Raipur passenger train had crossed Mahasamund, Komakhana and other stations. In sometime it would reach Lathore station, officially known as Harishankar Road.

Makaru's heart clenched with anxiety as the train sped ahead.

Six

Gadighini ghinja-ghin...! Gadighini ghinja-ghin...!

Lahili lahili...!

The melodious rhythmic sounds of the ganabaja reverberated loud and clear as its joyful notes danced upon the festive air. Music exuberantly, gloriously loud, loud enough to drown even the earsplitting horn blown by the train before its arrival. The irresistibly infectious beats of dhols, nissans, mahuris and *tasha*s flirted with the breeze, compelling the people of the basti to leave their chores aside and get onto their feet and move and sway in step together and dance their breaths away.

Gadighini ghinja-ghin...! Gadighini ghinja-ghin...!

As the railway basti of Raipur breathed in the music and danced away its woes, Makaru awaited perhaps the most significant moment of his life: his betrothal. He was getting married to Lakshmi, the beloved daughter of Nakul Tandi.

Like Manglu, Nakul Tandi, too, was an immigrant; he had come from Lachhipur village near Khariar. He worked as a sweeper at the Government Medical College and Hospital of Raipur. This marriage seemed to have almost been destined, for the Tandis lived barely eight or ten houses away from Manglu and Sabesh.

The proposal had been approved by both sides. From what she knew about the girl, Lakshmi, Sabesh was reassured that she was an obedient and docile girl who minded her own business. She had also completed five years of education in a Hindi medium school, and in Raipur, no less. Makaru liked her, too.

The holy bond was solemnised following all the customary Gana rites and rituals. First the elders brought sacred soil to lay the foundation of the *bedi*, a temporary rectangular marriage pandal, which was erected right in front of Makaru's house. The roof of the bedi was covered with branches of the jamun tree. A potter supplied the traditional *rukha batti*s or earthen pots and lamps, which were placed at the four corners of the platform. The *amera* or water pot was hung from the roof of the pandal. A branch of the mahua tree—said to be a sacred witness to the bond being forged for life—was worshipped by the groom's parents and then placed at the centre of the bedi.

This was followed by several other rituals. The first ceremony was called *unjli*, perhaps because the groom cupped his hands and held rice grains in both his palms as five to seven women took him along and made seven rounds of the bedi. This was followed by the *durla* dance. The groom was made to sit on a winnow, which was lifted up and down by some young women as the ganabaja played in the background.

Finally, the *baratis* took out the marriage procession. Once the groom and his family and friends had reached the bride's house, they were warmly welcomed and proffered a variety of sweets and delicacies. The nuptial ceremonies were performed during the night. The next morning, Makaru brought Lakshmi home. Sabesh welcomed them with a face-warming ceremony amidst cheerful ululations and the ever-present ganabaja.

Dambru, Manglu's neighbour and now close friend, enthusiastically participated in Makaru's marriage. The ganabaja playing in full swing amidst the celebrations brought back many fond memories. Dambru remembered the night that he had brought his aunt along to Raipur. Even in the chaotic rush of that moment and the crippling anxiety, he had managed to bring his dhol along. He was immensely grateful for the camaraderie and bliss that this faithful instrument had provided him in this alien, desolate city. After a tiring day of ferrying passengers to and fro, he would spend the evenings playing his dhol, humming along and sometimes singing his favourite song.

His neighbours, too, would be treated to his lively music as his vocal chords spilled forth his emotions and exhaustion of the day.

> Oh my beautiful damsel, where have you gone?
> Here a moment ago, and the next you vanish into air
> It was here that I saw you locking the door
> So tell me, tell me for the sake of this lore
> Was it the water of the well that you left to get?
> Or a beautiful youth who made your heart melt?
> Oh our beloved damsel, with beauty god-sent
> Was stolen by a young lad, much to our lament.

Dambru wasn't the only one who loved this song. A neighbour of his named Sebati liked it too. In fact, more than the song, she liked to hear him sing it. A native of Komakhan village in Chhattisgarh, this particular song and a few others that Dambru used to hum were relatively new to her as they were mostly sung by members of the Gana community. Yet, she loved hearing them. Dambru crooning those wistful lines was honey to her ears.

Sebati was fascinated by Dambru, to say the least. Drawn to him by his crisp baritone, his luscious black mustache, his gorgeous mane of hair, his supple yet strong physique, and his music, she found him enigmatic. Her attraction for him propelled her to learn more about the culture of the Gana people. She would try and learn their language and customs whenever she could. To her pleasant surprise, she found that there wasn't so much difference between her culture and his.

A maiden of eighteen, Sebati was fully aware of her desire for Dambru. Under pretense of going to fetching water, she would often surreptitiously follow him to the leaking pipe as he went there to take his bath. Covertly watching him bathe, his toned muscles rippling beneath his wet skin, her eyes would find it impossible to tear themselves away from him. Drops of water would splash onto her as Dambru bathed, giving her gooseflesh, and she would flinch. Struggling to mask the intense emotions swirling in her love-struck heart, Sebati would try and pull a false angry look. Feigning offence, she would say, "Can't you be more careful while bathing? Thanks to you, I am practically half-wet now!"

But our Dambru wasn't about to back down to the woman he had feelings for, and would get back at her with a cheeky reply, "Don't you fret about getting half wet, my sweetheart. If you wish, we can bathe together and get fully wet to your satisfaction. I'll make sure I scrub you to my heart's content so that your unblemished beauty glows even brighter under the sun and the stars."

Shy beyond measure, Sebati would splash him with some water and run away with her cheeks burning crimson. She couldn't believe just how giddy he made her feel! As her elated mind would take her back again and again to the encounter with him, she would catch herself wondering, "Am I really as beautiful as he claims? If I scrub my body enough, would my beauty really glow forth as he says?"

The warm splendour of these thoughts would make her heart swell, and as if in a stupor, she would start humming the song she had often heard him croon.

> Oh my beautiful damsel, where have you gone?
> Here a moment ago, and the next you vanish into air
> It was here that I saw you locking the door
> So tell me, tell me for the sake of this lore
> Was it the water of the well that you left to get?
> Or a beautiful youth who made your heart melt?
> Oh our beloved damsel, with beauty god-sent
> Was stolen by a young lad, much to our lament.

Whether the sky was adorned with the blazing sun, or the tranquil moon with its millions of twinkling stars, Dambru constantly occupied the back of Sebati's mind. Whenever he would leave for work on his rickshaw, an anxious Sebati would always be hovering around nearby to see him off. As the shadows would grow longer at sunset, she would be patiently awaiting his return.

One day, finding her alone, Dambru sneakily pulled her into his arms and placed a loving peck on her cheek. Taken by surprise,

Sebati's body lit up as if on fire as a shudder of pleasure coursed through her. She shyly whispered, "Why don't you...um, talk to my father about... about us? If he agrees to the...proposal, we can... we can live together forever." She stumbled over her words and her cheeks flushed furiously, and Dambru watched her with an amused smile and pure adoration.

He did take her words into account, though. One fine day, he went up to Sebati's father and respectfully asked for his daughter's hand in marriage. The elderly man heartily agreed at once. A few days later, Sebati and Dambru solemnised their relation and became man and wife.

Once, the top skin of his dhol got torn off. Without wasting a moment, Dambru ran to the butcher to get a raw goat hide. He nailed the hide onto the soft clayey ground, pulling it taut, and left it to dry under the scorching sun. Then he carefully cut away and removed the extra layer of flesh, blood, fatty tissue and membrane covering the skin. To keep off the flies waiting to gorge on the soft skin, he smeared a coat of ash on it. After the goat hide had dried, Dambru soaked it in saturated salt water and left it for two days, in impatient anticipation of his new dhol. After the salt had done its work and eliminated any water left in the fleshy membrane while also softening it, Dambru generously sprinkled salt over the flesh side and sundried it for the second time. Once it was completely dried, he set about cutting it into a circular shape so it was tailor-made to fit his percussion instrument. Finally, he fitted it onto his dhol, and tested it to see if it could spill forth the magical sounds it used to produce before. Dambru was overjoyed when he found that it did. His hard work had been worthwhile after all.

Not that he wouldn't gladly go through the tedious process once again if he had to. After all, it was thanks to this instrument that Sebati had fallen for him.

His efforts did not go unnoticed by her either. She could feel herself hurtling down a rabbit hole, falling deeper and deeper for his charms, unbeknownst to those around her. Not only could he sing and play the dhol, he could man up and repair it too if need be. His love for music was precious, and Sebati hoped for that kind of devotion from him for her as well.

That was a long time ago. Now that Dambru had come to embrace his senescence, he was spending lesser and lesser time with his trusted old dhol. He only played it in his leisure time.

Cut to the present: at Makaru's wedding, Dambru had his dhol swung across his lithe torso, and was dancing away to songs that he was belting out at the top of his lungs as he played his dhol. Ecstasy filled his soul as he swung around his luscious locks, moving to the mesmeric beats, rocking his body to and fro, high on rhythm. As the heady sensual music danced through his veins, he made Makaru wear a *khagla* handcrafted especially for the groom.

There is an interesting Gana folklore behind young lads wearing khaglas. As the handsome young Gana groom sets out to solemnise his marriage, his head adorned with a resplendent crown, he looks like a prince. So magnificent and pure is his youthful aura that even Indra, the king of the gods, burns with envy at the sight of him, and in his jealous rage he viciously strikes the unsuspecting groom to death with his thunderbolt, the *vajra*. What is the symbolic significance of this myth? What is the reason behind this ungodly bloodlust and hatred? No one really knew. Perhaps it was the fact that the Gana community, who were known to be non-conformist, had never shied away from defying the code of conduct established by the Aryans. In order to preserve the dignity of the Aryans and to ensure that the Ganas forever remained subservient to the Aryan norm, Indra targets newlywed Gana grooms setting out to build their life anew. The Ganas, of course, did not take this lying down. To protect themselves from the maleficent wrath of the deity, they adorn their community's young husbands to be in khaglas and arm them with bows and arrows.

That is the story. And so here was our Makaru, with a symbolically opulent crown on his head, a shiny new protective khagla around his neck, and a *kakan* of sacred mango leaves tied around his wrist to protect and to purify and grant prosperity, all equipped and armed to repel the evil envious eyes of Indra. It is a different matter that he couldn't find a bow and arrow and so had to settle for a modest cane instead, but that's not important.

With jubilant shouts and cheers, the *durla* dance began as the ganabaja belted out a lively rhythm for the dancers, "Tititi...tititi... tititi...! Ghingidin ghingidin ghinjan!". Dancing to the exuberant notes of the music, the laughing women swayed back and forth as they took Makaru around the bedi. The groom, perched on a winnowing bamboo basket, held onto the strong shoulders of the women who were carrying him, lest he should fall! Every time he was lifted up into the air, Makaru would playfully try and pluck off some jamun leaves from the roof of the bedi, which was covered with branches of the jamun tree. Every successful attempt would elicit another ripple of laughter from the audience.

Makaru's marriage was celebrated with much fanfare. All the people of his basti, young and old, men, women and children wholeheartedly and energetically took part in it. The ganabaja played all night, nonstop. The youngsters untiringly sang and danced to all the well-loved melodies. Uncles and grandpas traipsed around intoxicated, animatedly discussing affairs they knew a thing or two about. Manglu had slaughtered two enormous pigs for the big feast, so that everyone gorged on abundant meat and rice.

As Manglu took a satisfied look around with a smile on his lips, he felt fortunate to have been able to organise this huge celebration outside his ancestral lands. Back in the village, with the presence of that demon of a gauntia and his barbaric control, Manglu would never have been able to hold even a small feast for his son's wedding. No matter how much money his people would have generously lent him. His annual income added up to six *khandi*s of paddy and a meager hundred and twenty rupees. Even if he saved it all up for the wedding, he would still fall short by far. In other words, he would have had to sell himself and his labour to the heartless gauntia until death itself relieved him of his shackles. His son, too, would have had to follow the same path.

It was at times like these that Manglu felt relieved to have left his place of birth far, far behind. Yes, there were unfortunate conditions that had driven him to come and settle in an alien city all alone, but it had been worth it. Nobody here enquired about his caste. His only identity here was his occupation, not his lineage. Yes, his job as a rickshaw-wallah came with some drawbacks too. Some miserly customers just wouldn't settle on a reasonable price and would bargain for hours instead. Others would look down upon him and his fellow rickshaw pullers, their tone and mannerisms clearly depicting their contempt. But at the end of the day, at least he would have something put away in his pocket. At least he didn't have to wait for the whole long year to end, with his head bent low in servility and his hands extended like a beggar's, just to get his hard-earned pay. He toiled through the day, and he got his reward at the end of it. He could buy groceries and rations, and more if he saved wisely enough. He knew he could trust Sabesh for that. Another perk of working in the city was that he wasn't compelled to work under any duress. He could even be picky if he wanted and choose when he wanted to transport passengers and when he didn't, and where he wanted to go and where he didn't.

Perhaps the only thing that had bothered him for a while were those sleek vehicles that sped over the roads of this second heaven. Giant roaring beasts, they would often jolt Manglu out of his thoughts and he found their noise unbearable. But as the city embraced him more and more, her arms opening for him to melt into, he found himself embracing her back. It wasn't long before he found himself comfortable with everything. His past life, as he liked to phrase it, had taught him to value every facility that life gifted him, even if they came at the expense of a little compromise.

He was still the old Manglu, but stronger, more resilient. More mature.

His mature mind caressed his troubled soul and soothed it into a state of inner tranquility, and he found all his frustrations, his humiliation and his anger gradually melting into a pool of nothingness. It told him to forgive, and to forget.

And that is exactly what he did. Manglu forgot his arch nemesis the gauntia, and his son Nandakumar. He forgot what they had put him and his wife through. He forgot what they had put young Makaru through.

In a serenely tranquil moment of astonishing clarity, Manglu admitted to himself that yes, he was indeed immensely relieved that he had left his village far, far behind.

Seven

One day, Manglu ran into Neelia.

They had both come to the Government Hospital to drop off a passenger. Hence, the chance encounter.

At the sight of his past acquaintance, memories came hurtling towards Manglu.

Neelia's mannerisms had always set him apart in the village of Banjipali. His bearing, his attire, his habit of carrying along a bottle of water when he went to relieve himself. No wonder, everyone used to tease him as a "Raipuria". But these days, Manglu could himself feel the tug of these Raipuria mannerisms. Initially, he too had been averse to the idea of wearing trousers while pulling the rickshaw. But nowadays, he himself wore them. What to do—that annoying *dhoti* would slip off every time he slung a leg over the driver's seat or keep getting caught in the pedals or in the chain! So he had bought himself a couple of slacks and tees from the footpath. They were light on his pocket, and durable enough to last a year or half.

Manglu had blended well into the city of Raipur over the past few years. But now, seeing Neelia from afar, he was hit by a wave of nostalgia. The two men went and sat at a tea stall, and conversed for a long time, catching up on each other's lives. It felt just like the old days again, when Manglu used to meet Neelia on his visits to Banjipali. Manglu told him how the fates had pushed them to leave their ancestral land. As he was narrating the details of how Makaru came to be framed as a murderer, Neelia interrupted him to utter four words that rendered Manglu stone still.

"Nandakumar is no more."

Manglu sat there, speechless. He didn't know what he had expected to feel, but he definitely did not feel happy. Instead, he felt astonished. He simply couldn't wrap his head around the fact that a strong hefty man like Nandakumar could lose his life at such a young age. Manglu had firsthand experience of just how strong the man was. He still carried on his body the haunting souvenirs of Nandakumar's beatings. The infernal helplessness on the night of the beheran, the terrifying experience of being compelled to leave his village and his home by stealth in the middle of the night under constant fear of being seen and caught, the soul-crushing anguish of being pushed to board a train to an unknown destination at dawn against their wishes, the instinct and sheer will to survive that had driven them to such extremes, and his desperate determination to somehow save the life of his only child, his young naïve son…all these still rumbled in the darkest core of his heart like bubbling lava, as if waiting to stir awake and burst forth.

Yet, there were these faint murmurs of humanity that eerily whispered to Manglu's soul, reminding him that, after all, Nandakumar was human, too, just like him. And now, he was… gone. Just like that. He was dead. Departed from this earth for good, never to return. This stirred something deep in Manglu. He asked Neelia, "How did this come to be?"

Neelia shrugged in response, and set about telling his tale.

"I know the gauntia of your village. I have seen him many times before. He is six-feet tall, has a smooth tanned skin, a grave face and mien, and wears a clean new dhoti every day. When he walks, he surveys the road with squinted eyes and a nose wrinkled in suspicion as if there were thorns at every step.

"Once when I was very young, I was in your village, and ran into him on my way somewhere. He was returning home from the ghat after taking his bath. I made way for him so as to maintain a safe distance between us as he moved past. Instead, he halted and said, 'Hey, now look at this! Aren't you Suban Gana's grandchild, the one who lives in Raipur?' I was flustered at this sudden undesirable attention, so I just kept mum and nodded. He went on to jeer at me, 'So, living in a big city, aren't you, boy? Must have seen lots of motorcars and fancy things, haven't you, boy? So, do you think you could tell me how many wheels there are in a train?'

"I was flabbergasted. I mean, I knew that a train had a lot of wheels, but how in the world would I have known their exact number? I…I was ashamed. Sheepish, I kept my mouth shut. That seemed to further fuel that sadistic asshole's arrogance, for he continued to explain in a sickeningly sweet, mocking tone, 'Incredible, just look at this lad! *Arrey*, just the way there are two wheels in a bicycle, four wheels in a car, how many are there in a train? Shouldn't you know this much, huh? You live in a big city. Sheesh, to think that he comes from the city, in a train, and doesn't even know the number of wheels it runs on. Hah!'

"How I cringe now at my past self, thinking of that encounter. Silly me had understood the question, but couldn't figure out a smart answer to it. I knew that arrogant bastard of a gauntia was having a field day at my expense, for he said, 'Come on, answer up, boy. Oh wait—you folks pull rickshaws, don't you? Then how in the world would *you* know about trains?! Damn, I can be a bit dense sometimes. Of course, you wouldn't know how many wheels a train runs on. But the next time, make sure that you count them all and report to me, all right?' And then with a condescending smile, which I so wanted to scratch off his smug face, he left.

"Thereafter, I visited your village several times. Whenever I encountered him on the street or somewhere public, I would cross over to the other side or switch paths at the speed of light. I hated that man down to my bones. The very sight of him would deepen the profound disgust and loathing I harboured for that vile piece of crap. If I happened to spot him even from afar, my suppressed anger would venomously murmur, '*Sala!* So damn interested in a train...making me count wheels and all. Ever even sat in a train yourself?! Bloody bastard!' By then, I knew him only too well, of course.

"Then one day, while I was waiting for passengers, I caught sight of the gauntia getting off the train at Raipur station along with his son, and a servant bearing their luggage. Nandakumar looked extremely ill and emaciated. Gone was that burly physique, he almost resembled a skeleton. He also looked like he was in excruciating pain, and kept moaning and whimpering like a child. Those three were the last people I wanted to cross paths with that day. My history with the man wasn't something I wanted to be reminded of again. Yet, angry as I was, the old man's helplessness stirred something in my heart. My legs seemed to move as if on their own whim and before long I found myself standing in front of them. I bowed to them and offered my greetings, sans the intimacy.

"The gauntia, however, reacted quite differently to our chance encounter. Looking enormously relieved, he said in that sickly sweet tone of his, 'Oh my dear son! Take us to the hospital, will you? My son is dying of pain.' God, this man could be so unpredictable! 'But my dear sir, won't you get polluted if you step into this filthy vehicle of mine?' I so wanted to snap back at him, but I was rendered speechless. Before I could even respond to the man's 'request', he had already got into my rickshaw, huffing and puffing as he half carried, half dragged his sick son in his arms. Perhaps he had already lost his dignity and caste while speaking to me, so touching what I had touched wasn't such a grave sin anymore. I calmed myself down, sat on the driver's seat and set about ferrying these passengers that I had never dreamed I would meet in such circumstances, to the hospital.

"We reached our destination. I was about to leave them there, but the gauntia said, 'Son, we set out from the village this morning and haven't had anything to eat since then. Could we get something to fill our bellies with from around here perhaps...?' I nodded and said, 'Yes, there is a hotel across the road. Come, I'll take you there.' I expected him to come along, but wrinkles of dilemma were etched on his face. He looked at his moaning son, then at the luggage, and scratched his head. Then he looked at me with pleading eyes and said, 'Is it possible to bring us some food?' His helplessness was laughable yet soul-stirring. I responded, 'Yes, why not. Let's go buy some food.' But he wasn't about to leave his son behind and the servant was, of course, taking care of the luggage. He seemed to be weighing his options and finally having decided on something, he put forth a surprising proposal, 'How about you go and get it for us, my son?'

"This was new. How did he change from the infuriatingly haughty devil who would turn up his nose in contempt if he came within 10 metres of a Gana, to this soft-spoken man with pleading eyes requesting me, an untouchable, to bring him his food? Unable to hold back any longer, I said, 'But sir, as you know, I am an untouchable. Won't you become polluted if you eat the food that *I* have touched? Will you still eat it then?' But he seemed to have sorted it all out and calmly replied, 'My dear son, I am well aware of the laws that prohibit us from touching people of your kind.

But these are trying times, so what can we do but bend according to the circumstances?' I wasn't convinced, but I understood his reasons obviously, and as I half nodded in response, he added, 'Just...don't tell anyone in the village, all right?' With that, he put on his sugary sweet smile, and handed me a couple of notes.

"I can tell you, it took me all the self-restraint I possessed not to give him a truck-sized snort!

"Anyhow, I did buy them some *bara*s and *pakora*s from the hotel that I had mentioned. While the gauntia and his servant gobbled them up like starving cows, Nandakumar lay on the rickshaw, wheezing and whimpering helplessly. I left them at the entrance of the hospital. As I was going back to my rickshaw, I heard the gauntia call out feebly, 'My son, if you happen to come this side tomorrow, do drop by, will you?'

"It took much more effort to hold back the snort this time. I was certainly not keen to meet him a second time.

"But fate had other plans. I got a passenger who wanted to be dropped off at the hospital the very next day. Just as they were climbing off my rickshaw, I heard someone frantically hollering, 'Neelia! O, Neelia...! Here!' I turned around to see the gauntia's servant. So I went up to him and said, 'Calm down. Why are you howling like a madman? Where's your master?' Panting and out of breath, he explained, 'Bhai, his son passed away last night. He is weeping his heart out in the ward.'

"Guilt crept over me. I felt enveloped by remorse as I recalled how bitter I had been yesterday towards someone who was no longer here today. 'What happened to him?' I asked. The servant boy answered, 'The doctor said he had blood cancer.'

"My heart stood still, shell-shocked. I asked, 'So...then what are you doing here?' With panicked and pleading eyes, he said, 'The master has asked me to arrange for a vehicle. And I have no idea how to do that! I don't even know how to speak Hindi properly. Where the hell will I find a vehicle?'

"I understood that the old man was looking for a mortuary van to carry his son's corpse.

"I knew deep down in my veins that the gauntia was a cold-blooded bastard. I knew the deep disgust he held for my people, for no fault of our own. But here, he was utterly helpless. His pride had been shattered to dust and lay lifeless on the ground. His only son was dead. Perhaps fate had this in store for him as punishment for all the ills of his pride. It would have been morally wrong not to help him in this time of crisis. I mean, I too have a conscience, right? So I turned to the servant boy and said, 'Come, sit in my rickshaw.'

"We went to the mortuary and picked a van. After a lot of bargaining, I negotiated a deal. Then I brought the van to the hospital, to the gauntia. When he set eyes on it, a change came over him. His eyes, red and swollen with grief, had dried sometime ago, but as he turned to me, tears flowed afresh from his eyes in gratitude. His lips trembled and he dissolved into a quivering mess of emotions.

"The colossal hurt flashing in his eyes expressed what a thousand words could not have: 'Why O God, why did you do this to me? This isn't only my son that you took away! This is my pride, my dignity, my bloodline, my everything! All I have ever loved in my life seems useless now. And would it not—you took the one thing I loved most in this world! You took my child. That child whose hand I held when he was a toddler is now lying dead before my very eyes as I hold his hand for the last time! And I could not do anything to save him! Until now I had held on to some hope, dear God, and now I am holding his corpse! Why... why O God, did you do this to me?!'

"The old man never uttered a word. Yet, my soul heard everything his broken heart said, through his eyes.

"Nandakumar's body was loaded into the mortuary van. The gauntia and his servant helped lift him in. Then the vehicle, loaded with grief, despair and desperation, set off for Banjipali."

Neelia narrated everything in detail. Manglu listened to him in rapt silence. Then he said, "Ever since I have come to this city, I have not got a chance to visit my village. Let us see when an opportunity presents itself."

Nandakumar may be no more, but he had left permanent scars on Manglu's being. The pain, the anguish he had left him would haunt him throughout life. Manglu knew he would take those memories with him to the grave.

On returning home that evening, Manglu wasted no time in breaking the news to Sabesh.

He was astounded at her reaction. He had never seen her so happy.

In a moment of mad ecstasy, she released all her pent up fury as she half spit, half cursed, "Good, good that the bastard died! Son of a bitch! The village will at last breathe in peace. What a black sinner he must have been to have been zapped into the heavens before his father! That bastard wanted to kill my son! We abandoned our home, our land, our ancestors, our *everything* and came to this faraway city because of that piece of filth! What did he get by driving us away? He himself died outside his home village! And that godforsaken gauntia—he must be living in peace now that his pride has been ground to dust! Hahahaha! Serves him right!"

Manglu saw Sabesh go from being smug to hysterically happy to near deranged. She looked as if she would have torn Nandakumar's corpse to pieces had she set her hands on it.

Sabesh was no longer the docile, subservient woman who used to clean the gauntia's stables. She had grown strong-willed, independent and self-assured. She knew the markets. She knew the city. She knew its people. She knew her way around. Her exposure to the women of the slum and their chit-chat had taught her a lot. Now she knew her rights and also how to exercise them. She had learnt how to fight oppression, discrimination and inequality. No one could push her around so easily anymore.

Had the village meeting been held today, no helpless woman weeping desperately and begging for her son's life would have been seen there. Sabesh would have charged forth with conviction, and confronted the gauntia and the villagers like her very life was on the line—which, let's be frank, it indeed was.

Like a cyclone that dissolves into itself, Sabesh's emotions too quietened and withdrew into the darker corners of her heart. With eyes shining like stars and an eerie smile on her chapped lips, she whispered, "It is the gauntia's turn next."

Eight

The Jonk river serves as the geographical boundary between Odisha and Chhattisgarh. As the train hurtled over the bridge on the river and entered Odisha, leaving the Chhattisgarh border behind, a feeling of warm familiarity spread through Makaru's heart. It felt like home.

Having crossed the Jonk river bridge, the train entered the Khariar Road area. A slum ran alongside the railway tracks. As Makaru caught sight of a mosque, he realised that this was perhaps a Muslim basti. The slum reminded him of Raipur, and thoughts of home engulfed Makaru.

The slum beside the Raipur railway station has grown in size. Back when Makaru's family had first come to settle there, it was smaller. Now it has expanded considerably, with the row of dwellings steadily approaching the railway tracks. Between the tracks and the slum lay an open drain. The slum residents dump all their waste into it: human excreta, cow dung, polythene bags, household garbage, leftovers, scraps from the butcher's shop, you name it. Putrid thick black stinking water drifts sluggishly along the sewer the year round. Though, that hardly bothers the residents. Someone had placed two stone slabs at a spot over the drain so that people could step across it easily every day. In fact, people had grown so accustomed to the potent foul stench that they washed their utensils, cooked their rice and even ate sitting right next to the drain, not that they had much choice. These were usually the relatively newer residents of the slum.

The slum seemed to have been divided into tiers. Right next to the stinking drain were the dwellings described above, forming the first tier. If you moved a bit further in, another one made itself evident. The houses in this second 'strata' were small, really tiny; even those having two rooms were rare. Skeletal structures of bamboo with old hoardings thrown over them for support and a roof; occasionally, you might spot flex boards or cardboard cartons in these contraptions. The doors were tin sheets crudely cut and hammered into place. Every house had spots dedicated to cleaning utensils and cooking. The houses were built so close to one other that a newcomer could easily get lost in the winding labyrinths that snaked between them, which were so narrow that if two people happened to enter one of these lanes from opposite sides, one would have to make way for the other to pass. A bird's eye view of this part of the slum might have resembled a colony of large black bats hanging in absolute silence, for every dwelling had a roof of uniform black tarpaulin.

Now we come to the third and last tier. Here, the houses faced the city and away from the train tracks. These houses had cement floors and, often, even a small veranda overlooking the threshold, where women could be seen in the late afternoons or evenings combing their hair and chit-chatting about the day gone by. The *chulhas* were outside the house. Some residents had even constructed additional bathing places and designated spots for washing utensils. Almost all the houses here boasted televisions and music decks. Photos and pictorial calendars of deities adorned the walls of homes where people offered prayers and worshipped daily.

One could discern someone's class from their house, and their attire revealed which strata of the slum they belonged to. People of many castes, customs and backgrounds merged here in this assortment of poor human dwellings roughly cobbled together. One thing, however, was common: the lives of those who dwelled here were forever suspended in a stagnant time warp. No matter what they did or how hard they tried, it would take nothing less than superhuman effort to change their lives for the better.

The government had made numerous laws and introduced a variety of schemes for the people. But really, these were nothing but thin excuses for politicians to boast about when asked how they had brought change and progress to the poor. The basti was expanding at such a phenomenal rate that it was hard to say if the nation's explosive population growth was being witnessed predominantly in the villages, or in the towns and cities. If the ruling party had introduced such grand and benevolent schemes in the villages to radically better their lives, as they claimed they had, why did people still migrate to the cities in the thousands? And here, too, they were reduced to slaving as daily wage labourers surrounded by the stench and filth of an open sewage drain, with a train track thundering day and night metres away from their threshold, if they had one to begin with that is. Here, too, the politicians would come visiting them once every five years, wooing and begging ridiculously for their votes, promising rich dividends in return. "We will do this. We will do that. Your lives will change!" they would assure with hilarious sincerity. But, were their sugary words and tall promises ever realised, ever translated into action? No. The big city slums and the villages may be far apart; yet they were terrifyingly similar in that the people's lives in both were destined to be forever stagnant, as empty of positive change as these politicians' false promises.

One of the millions flocking to these urban slums as they migrated out of their villages was Farooq kaka. He was one of the older residents of the basti who had settled near the railway line much earlier, in the third strata of houses that faced Raipur city. His house, a lot like Dambru's, had a cement floor, better constructed walls and ceilings, and a proper threshold. Farooq and Dambru had built their houses in this slum at around the same time. And when Manglu came to settle here later with his family, he also made his acquaintance with Farooq and, over time, they forged a strong brotherly bond. Farooq addressed Sabesh as "bhabhi" while Makaru used to fondly call him "Farooq kaka". Sabesh, too, was close to Farooq, and would often share jokes and anecdotes with him.

So animated were their conversations and so free their laughter that no one would have thought that they lived in such pitiful and miserable conditions, in cramped dwellings so near and yet so far from the hustle and bustle of the city, barely an arm's length from the railway track and the train that would come shrieking and rattling along to jolt them out of exhausted sleep at night. No, their brilliant smiles and boisterous laughter painted their struggling, grey, nondescript lives with an iridescent light of hope and joy. As if the humble broken rice they cooked beside a stinking drain was heavenly ambrosia that even the gods would kill for. As if the threadbare thin mats they used to rest their tired backs on were a luxuriant bed of the finest teakwood, covered with the softest silken mattress that could lull anyone to sleep the moment they lay on it. Their exchanges were honest, open and frank, underlined by an unspoken mutual concern and regard that was hard to come by in this harsh world. And it wasn't just because they were inching towards more mature years. Farooq and Sabesh had maintained such good equations even when they were younger.

That day, the four o'clock sky looked magnificent in hues of lavender, pink and purple as white clouds brilliantly lit up by the sun swam lazily across it. Sitting outside her house, Sabesh was busy feeding her grandson a mash of potatoes and rice in a bowl. To her fond dismay, the toddler was obstinate and refused to eat. Every time she lovingly extended a morsel towards him, he would scrunch up his tiny nose and turn his face away. Just then, the familiar chhuk-chhuk could be heard in the distance. A female voice boomed on the speakers, announcing, "May I have your attention please! The passenger train heading from Waltair to Delhi is waiting at platform number one." Sabesh smiled winsomely and cooed at the child, "Look there, my love! That train is about to leave for Delhi! My darling little prince will grow up and go there too one day, won't he? Come now open your mouth wide, let's gobble this morsel up very quickly now!"

In the midst of all this cajoling and coaxing, Farooq kaka entered the scene, beads of sweat dripping from his chiselled face, pushing his trolley loaded with an impressive collection of discarded metal objects: tin boxes, brass buckets, aluminium vessels, copper wires, iron and steel articles, bicycle rims, and whatnot. He sat himself down near the busy grandmother, mopped his brow and mischievously asked, "And pray, where are you headed with this precious little ball of fluff? Leaving your husband for a youngster just because your old man turned senile, huh? And where is the man we speak of?"

Sabesh light-heartedly made a face and replied, "This one here is an obstinate one, Farooq. Doesn't eat a thing! I am trying so hard to feed him, if only this brat complied."

Farooq sighed as he nodded and said, "Yes, bhabhi. He who wants to feed himself has nothing to be fed with, and he who is being fed doesn't want to be, isn't it so? Think of this boy's childhood, and then think of the time when his father was his age. Things have changed so much, haven't they?"

"I couldn't agree more with you, Farooq. Who understands poverty better than we do? Who understands hunger better than us? Back in those days, I used to struggle so hard even to give Makaru just one proper meal a day. Those hardships, those struggles will be etched into my flesh and blood forever. I will never forget those days, even in my grave."

Farooq smiled, and was silent for a while, thinking about what she had said. Then he said, "Anyhow. I came here with something in my mind, bhabhi. A government officer has just been transferred. He sold his old cycle to me cheap. It needs just a little repair, but is in good condition otherwise. A replacement of tires and tubes, a bit of oiling, and it will be up and running. Ever since Makaru got a job as security guard in the factory, he has been walking to work and back. That boy works very hard, bhabhi. Give this bicycle to him. We will see about the payment later. At least Makaru will be able to reach his workplace in time without hassle every day."

Makaru used to work as a cashier in a cheap hotel earlier. It was only recently that he had landed a job as a peon-cum-security-guard in an iron factory. He was lucky to have found work in a private company. His salary was decent and there was no fear of retrenchment. But his workplace was eight kilometres from home. So he either took a bus into town or walked all the way to the factory.

Sabesh was acutely aware of Makaru's predicament. She couldn't deny that his new job paid him well, but reaching work on time without a vehicle of his own was a daily struggle. Being late meant the guard on duty before him would have to work beyond his shift hours. Sabesh recounted all the times that Makaru had to leave home with his breakfast untouched for fear of being late for duty. So, Farooq's proposal seemed truly god sent—and it had arrived at just the right time, too.

Sabesh was overjoyed and brimming with gratitude, said, "You know my lad and his needs better than I do, Farooq. Need I even say anything more in return? Leave the cycle here. Makaru will pay you the requisite amount."

Farooq simply smiled in response, a warm and winsome smile of camaraderie that lit up his handsome face. He left the bicycle there and pushed his trolley towards his godown.

As the sun melted into the horizon painting the clouds crimson, amber and gold, the day came to an end. Darkness fell softly over the city, though in Raipur, the difference between day and night was hardly felt. At dusk, hundreds of neon bulbs lining the roads lit up in unison to cast a warm glow on the streets and corners of the city. Everywhere, that is, except for the slum. Here, there were no street lights. Just a few naked bulbs guided the slum dwellers through its dark narrow lanes, so they had to walk carefully. But what the slum lacked for in light, it made up for in sound. It was like a cauldron of sound, constantly bubbling and murmuring with myriad voices that could always be heard from nearby or far. Privacy and solitude was a luxury here. But the slum dwellers hardly seemed to mind. They worked hard through the day as rickshaw pullers, coolies, construction workers, domestic helps, labourers, peons and security guards, and settled down with a bottle of cheap liquor under the stars so they could briefly wash away their worries and exhaustion of the day. The rich accused the poor of being lazy drunkards, but they couldn't care less. No one appreciated the tireless backbreaking labour they rendered to keep the rest of society in clean comfort. All people could do was point accusatory fingers at them and label them lazy, uncouth, uncivil and quarrelsome. Who had the time or patience to contest the absurd and ridiculous opinions of such hypocrites?

It wasn't long before Makaru earned himself the name of "peon Makaru" in the slum. Some even shortened it down to "the peon". Makaru's chest would swell in pride on hearing this nickname; he felt that it carried a sense of responsibility. Over time, even the workers of the factory came to see him as a responsible lad. They knew for a fact that every single job that Makaru was assigned, he completed with the utmost dedication and sincerity.

Makaru's father Manglu always told him, "Son, if it is worth doing, it is worth doing well. No matter what work you have taken up, whether it is pulling a rickshaw or lifting luggage at the railway station, give it your all and a little more. Work is work, something the gods have bestowed upon you; so hold it in the highest of respect." And that is exactly what Makaru did. His dedication and integrity paved the way for the rock-solid reliability that he was known for among his acquaintances.

If the people of his office admired and respected Makaru, his slum neighbours adored him. And who wouldn't? He was well-behaved, courteous and mixed well with almost everybody. Whether it was about showing respect to elders or becoming childlike and playful with the children of the basti, Makaru always found a way to make his interactions with his fellow slum-dwellers pleasant.

That day, our dear dependable peon was sauntering back home, humming the merry tunes of a Bollywood song. His wife Lakshmi sat under the porch, nestling their tiny bundle of joy securely in her arms as she breastfed him. The street lamp at a distance cast its modest light into their otherwise almost dark house. Except for the mother and child, the house was empty at the moment. Sabesh wasn't home. Manglu was also yet to return from work. Registering his parents' absence, Makaru quietly went up to his baby and very tenderly gave him a small peck on his petal-soft cheeks. To his dismay, his wife chided him, "You have just returned from the factory! God knows how many people you have come in contact with! Go wash your face and hands first! I won't have anyone fondling my baby with dirty hands. Go on, wash up first."

Makaru retorted mischievously, "Oh, what a shame! I had no idea that I was supposed to wash myself even to be allowed to kiss my baby." Still smiling, he suddenly drew Lakshmi into his arms as she gasped in surprise. Their breaths mingling, Makaru looked into her eyes with all the adoration in the world. Then, without warning, he placed a quick kiss on her lips.

Lakshmi blushed a deep red. But she composed herself quickly and, pretending to push him away, urgently whispered, "Oh lord, mother is here! Go, go wash yourself!" Makaru had only to hear the words to make him stumble away from his wife and go running into the house at full speed. Collapsing into a fit of giggles at her small victory, Lakshmi turned to her blissfully oblivious son and said, "See, your father is such a scaredy cat! Just the word 'mother' turned him into a timid mouse! How can a man this brave be expected to guard a whole factory?" she laughed.

Lights from the city glittered like specks of gold in the night. But darkness pervaded most parts of the slum. Darkness, the true and constant companion of all slum-dwellers. Truth be told, they were compelled to live in the dark.

Inside the house, Makaru searched for the kerosene lamp. Then he remembered that Lakshmi usually stored it near the hearth. Groping about in the dark, he finally found it. He carefully lit the lamp. It instantly bathed the surroundings in a warm glow. Makaru found his eyes fixed on his beautiful wife whose rosy cheeks looked radiant in the soft light. The child in her arms waved his arms about and started jumping up and down, as if he too had been waiting for the light.

Makaru's mind travelled back to the old days in the village. Back then, they didn't even have a lamp or kerosene. Lamps and lanterns were a privilege and a luxury that the fates had reserved only for the gauntia and his family. Makaru's people resorted to a cheaper alternative instead: firewood. Need some light? Just gather a few twigs and make a small fire! Is it too dark to see? Just light up a piece of firewood to dispel the darkness! Getting firewood wasn't a problem either. Even so, compared to life in the village, life in the slum was still better by far.

By the time Makaru had finished lighting the lamp and washed his hands and feet, Sabesh had returned home. She told Makaru about the cycle Farooq kaka had given him. His eyes glistened in sheer joy and gratitude. He knew how costly a new cycle was in the market. He didn't have 2,500 rupees just lying around for him to spend on a bicycle. He did consider buying one second-hand, but that plan never materialised. So often he had to plead with his colleagues and ask them for lifts. But now, all that was in the past. Now, he could commute to his office and back home as he pleased. Gone were the days when he had to wait for the bus or walk miles when he didn't have the money for a ticket. Immensely grateful, he had quickly left the house to go and thank Farooq kaka for his thoughtful, generous and timely help.

The soulful call to prayers of the namaz from the mosque reverberating off the walls of Khariar Road Station, "Allah hu

Akbar, Allah..." filled his ears, breaking his reverie, and brought Makaru back into the present.

Nine

A huge and majestic peepal tree stood towering right in the middle of the basti. Its vast dense network of branches, thick gnarled trunk and long aerial roots showed that the sacred fig had been there for a long time, much before the slum came up. In the early days, rag pickers from the slum would gather under the tree to sift through and segregate all the scrap and junk that they collected from various nooks and corners of the city. They would leave it there, and a private agency truck would come by to pick it up. As time passed, waste started piling up there in heaps. At present, the spot looked no different from an open scrap godown filled to the brim with rubbish.

Over time, the basti grew into what it is today. Not an inch of space was left unoccupied. The ancient peepal was a witness to the daily life and throb of the ever-growing slum community. Come evening, rickshaw pullers, daily wage labourers, rag pickers and other residents of the slum would gather around the tree to discuss news and events of the day, animatedly sharing anecdotes as they enjoyed a leisurely smoke of bidi, pika or ganja to pass the time. Sometimes their conversations carried on well past midnight, under the incandescent light of a silver moon.

If there was any crisis in the basti, the people would gather under the peepal tree for meetings to discuss the matter. Occasionally, someone would bring along their mridanga, dhol, cymbals or other musical instruments and strike up a beat, someone would weave in a tapestry of melody, and others would join in to make music and create a magical atmosphere so immersive that even the shrill blaring horn of the train would go unheard. After the gruelling exhaustion of the day, this joyful collective music and song, under the cool air of the dense green foliage, was like a balm that soothed their spirits, seeping into their bones and rejuvenating them from within.

Women of the slum regarded the peepal as sacred and worshipped it as they would a deity, bowing to it every time that they passed by it. Later, some started tying wish threads on it as well. Others, too, began to place pictures of their household deities under the tree. Gradually, the spot metamorphosed into a place of worship.

On the borders of Odisha and Chhattisgarh lay a small village called Kolabira. Goria Chamar, who had come to Raipur with his father many years ago, was a resident of this Kolabira village. Now of an age where he should have been resting at home, Goria spent his weary days pulling the rickshaw instead. Years had gone by since his father's demise. His two sons had grown into young men. But they were both wayward wastrels and unemployed, and all they did was while away their time, sharing worthless jokes and banter. When their father would return home exhausted in the evening, they would snatch his earnings of the day to buy alcohol. One of Goria's sons, a big burly fellow named Bunty, sold tickets in black. He was friendly with "special" people associated with the local MLA. Whenever the MLA needed someone to get into a brawl or a nasty fight, he would call on Bunty. His physique used to scare people away. If Bunty was ever unlucky enough to be dragged to jail, the MLA would bail him out. Talk about democracy.

Goria's other son, Chintu, was a pickpocket. Once he was caught red-handed in a train, and thrown into jail for six months straight. When he got out, Chintu pledged he would never indulge in such crimes again. To propitiate the gods and atone for his sins, he decided to visit the Ram temple adjacent to his basti. Now, people of the temple may not have known that Chintu was a pickpocket, but they certainly knew that he was a Chamar. While nobody took notice of him when he entered the temple, and offered his prayers to the deity, when he was leaving, they accosted him and started beating him up. They beat him up so badly in fact that Chintu peed in the temple premises. This only aggravated the situation further, for he got thrashed not only for having dared to set foot in the temple despite being low-caste, but also for having sullied the holy house of god. Doubly humiliated and wronged, Chintu was filled with righteous rage and spite for

Lord Ram. He thought, "This deity is indeed unjust. If he truly resided in this temple, he would have given these pea-brains some wit to begin with. But instead, he has sided with them. That too because they are the ones who have built this temple for him." In a fit of rage and aggrieved hurt, Chintu decided that he too, along with the people of his basti, would build a beautiful temple for god—one who would favour *them*.

Such unfortunate circumstances were not faced by Chintu alone; many others in this basti encountered them. Most were migrant lower castes like him, forever shunned and deprived, like wandering ships without anchor, condemned to eternally sail back and forth across the endless sea of life. Chintu now came forward with the proposal of building their own temple right in their basti, with their own initiative, their own efforts, and their devotion, so that the deity that chose to reside in that temple would also be theirs, and *theirs* alone.

And so, united by their shared distress, sense of injustice, emotions and beliefs, the slum dwellers set forth building their own exclusive temple. Ideas and proposals were discussed, pros and cons debated, responsibilities and tasks allocated. The humble basti suddenly turned into a thrumming hive of activity united by and working towards a single cause: building a temple. It was an idea so mundane, and yet as vast as the cosmos, for it bound people across communities and castes together. They pooled together their hard-earned money, going so far as to cut down their monthly expenses in order to realise their dream. Receipt books were printed and distributed, armed with which they split into groups and headed out into the city with a gigantic dream in their eyes and hope in their hearts. Shunning their inferiority, their anxiety and their hesitation, they went to every single shop, eatery and office they could, requesting strangers for kind donations. Every rickshaw puller in the slum was handed a receipt book to keep tabs on any contributions received from generous customers that fate perchance brought their way.

Come evening, they would meet under the peepal tree to count and tally every rupee, as the exhausted sun sank contentedly into the arms of the waiting horizon, painting the sky gold. Such was the tremendous excitement that they even sportingly competed with each other's "teams", laughingly showing off how much each group had managed to collect at the end of the day. Their zeal was infectious, like a ripple of energy that spread through the basti, transcending all human lines and divisions, touching everyone. A beautiful and wholesome manifestation of this common spirit of humanity was our dear old Farooq kaka, who generously contributed to the funds despite being tied to a different religious brotherhood. And it wasn't all for nothing. At the end of it, the basti people had successfully collected a modest sum that set their hearts ablaze with joy.

One evening as the amber skies were melting into a tapestry of stars, Makaru was returning home, after meeting Farooq kaka and expressing his heartfelt gratitude to him for the bicycle, when his eyes fell on the small groups of people huddled under the old peepal, busily counting and exchanging notes and coins. He walked up to them to see what they were doing. They welcomed him into their circle with lusty cheers and smiles, for Makaru was popular in the basti. The customary greetings exchanged, however, they fondly chided him for being too preoccupied with office work to even spare a glance at what was going on in his residential area. They complained that while all his time and energies were dedicated in service to his boss, he couldn't stop by even to ask to take part in such a majestic project coming up right outside his home. Makaru smiled gently at their amiable nagging, aware of the affection and regard his fellow slum dwellers had for him, though an outsider may not have been able to see this. Giving in good-naturedly, he promised, "All right, all right...I will try to take some time out in the evenings and participate as much as possible. And I will also try and contribute monetarily as much as I can. Happy now?"

And so the coming days saw Makaru adding his humble contribution and efforts, as did so many others. However, that was still not enough to build the temple of their dreams. They were still falling short by a large sum. So finally, they decided to approach the local MLA for help. They were considerably motivated and encouraged by the fact that he belonged to a party that was itself in the process of building a grand Ram temple in Ayodhya. Volunteers and workers of the party were in fact busy collecting funds for it, mirroring on a much larger and grander scale the small yet fiercely dedicated actions of the basti residents. So, they thought, it was only reasonable to nurture the hope that this MLA might support their humble initiative, too.

Approach the MLA respectfully, pay him your obeisance, talk about how great his party's initiative was, then slip in the proposal for their own little temple and humbly ask for financial help. Funds secured, mission successful! However, there was one small problem.

Remember Bunty, the big burly rogue who served the MLA and who had willingly or not-so-willingly made the jail premises his second home? He now stepped forward, finally putting his pea-brain to some use, and said that this was not going to work. It was all too straightforward. This was politics they were dabbling in, for God's sake, and when did politics ever associate itself with anything straightforward?! And so, he proposed a slightly different and a slightly more elaborate plan. Here's how it went: They would go meet the MLA, heap grateful tributes on him for having done so much for them, glibly toeing the line between genuine praise and blatant flattery, and invite him to visit their basti. Once he arrived, to a proper welcome with fanfare, they would share their worries, distress and stories with him under pretence of "opening up their hearts" to him. They would then mention the magnificent Ayodhya project, all the while liberally sprinkling him with sugary adulations, and then casually bring up the proposal of their own little shrine and humbly seek his help. Their saccharine compliments, coupled with the fact that their basti was potentially his biggest vote bank, would leave him no option but to accept their proposal and to rain funds on them! Well, maybe that was an overstatement, but they would definitely be able to overcome their economic constraints if they could get the MLA on their side.

Aside from the fact that Bunty was considered to be the most knowledgeable of them in matters like appeasing the MLA, the basti people actually loved the idea. Having enthusiastically approved of his plan, they all took a day off from their respective work to hold a meeting, and sent a select few as representatives to meet the MLA and invite him over as planned.

Suffice it to say that the MLA satisfactorily approved of the proposal. Firstly, his party was passionate about advocating the propagation of the Hindu religion, so any proposal involving building of a temple was something he should definitely support. Secondly, whether he liked to admit it or not, the bunch of haggard, scrawny people standing deferentially before him and crowding his office were the ones who had helped him win the post he held today. Thirdly, he hadn't paid this slum a visit since his election campaign three years ago, when he had loudly proclaimed his party's manifesto and modestly asked for their votes; so this might be a good excuse to change that. And lastly, of course, it wasn't as if he had to part with a single paisa from his pocket for their temple. Vast funds were rotting away in government treasuries anyway; so what harm would it do to divert a minuscule sum to these poor slum dwellers? Thus having shrewdly weighed every conceivable gain and loss that he could incur from this project, the MLA mentally gave it a nod, and with a plastic smile on his lips, gave them a date and time when he would visit their basti.

Bunty was roundly congratulated and applauded for his astuteness. A colourful tent was pitched under the peepal tree, and festive decorations and hoardings put up to welcome the MLA. A group of seven or eight women, including Lakshmi, was put in charge of welcoming him. Another group was given the job of garlanding the MLA. A *kirtan* band was also organised. The slum was swept and cleaned up. Bunty had further instructed everyone to stay at home that day and to attend the meeting without fail, for politicians loved crowds.

The MLA arrived amidst much excitement, clapping and cheers. He seemed pleased to see the beautiful decorations and preparations made in his honour, and the large crowd of hardworking basti people gathered to welcome him with garlands further broadened his smile. As planned, Bunty stepped forward and respectfully led him to the podium. Delighted by the hospitality, the politician praised Bunty. Basking in his appreciation, Bunty went on to show him all the photos of deities hung on the ancient peepal, and said, "Honourable sir, please see what pitiable conditions the people here are living in. They don't even have a proper designated spot to worship their gods, and are literally forced to worship them in the open. Please do something about this, sir."

The MLA looked around at the innumerable photos of Shiva, Hanuman, Saibaba and Anukula Chandra hanging from the aerial roots of the tree and placed all around its wide trunk, nodded sagely and declared, "It is the top agenda of my party to build temples. I will release some funds from the MLA grant for this holy proposition."

The audience broke into a thunderous applause.

The MLA added, "Our Raipur city has temples of every deity: Lord Shiva, Lord Ram, Goddess Durga, you name them. The only deity we are yet to devote a shrine to is Lord Hanuman. Therefore, I propose that we build a Hanuman temple here at this basti."

This time, the tumultuous round of clapping took even longer to die down.

The MLA continued, "You all live in this humble abode of a slum, serving the city diligently every day. The men ply rickshaws, work as daily-wage labourers and the women clean houses as domestic helps. Remember how during the *Treta Yuga*, Lord Hanuman served Lord Ram with utmost devotion and carried him in his heart? Each one of you is a Lord Hanuman in human form. So, it is only reasonable and just that we build a shrine for him here."

The people cheered and clapped ecstatically.

He went on, "You have all come from faraway places and settled down here. Not only are you burdened by the lack of financial resources, you are also cruelly deprived of education. Naturally, that also brings with it the inability to read the *shastras* and *puranas*, and hence the lack of proper knowledge of temple rites. But do not worry, for I will appoint a learned and experienced priest in your temple who will read the scriptures according to the norms and rules, and who will bless you all for your wellbeing, peace and prosperity."

And so, with a deafening round of applause, lusty cheering, hails to the MLA and hails to the gods, the meeting came to an end. Bunty proposed a vote of thanks, and the MLA departed from the basti with a send-off amidst cheerful ululation. Everyone returned home full of hope, optimism and excitement.

But not Sabesh. A frown on her face, she was deep in thought, pondering over what the MLA had said. For some reason, Sabesh could neither bring herself to embrace his logic the way her fellow slum dwellers seemed to have, nor share their elation. Something at the back of her mind kept nagging her and telling her that whatever this logic was rooted in was wrong. Completely, horrendously wrong. But she couldn't bring herself to express this to anyone.

Sabesh's household hummed with activity. Part of her mind registered Lakshmi moving around the house, doing the chores. Ever since Lakshmi had joined their family, Sabesh had more or less stopped doing household work. It is only when Lakshmi was confined during the dreaded days of menstruation that Sabesh would take over. As dictated by tradition, Lakshmi did not set foot in the kitchen for five days in a month, and at the end of it, she was expected to undergo a thorough ritual cleaning and purification by scrubbing herself clean (of God knows what), washing her hair and cleansing every piece of cloth that she had worn during those "heinous" five days.

Lakshmi was a very efficient housekeeper. But when it came to following the religious traditions, she failed to please Sabesh as the perfect daughter-in-law. For instance, it had always been an unfailing daily practice of Sabesh to offer their ancestors whatever she had cooked by dropping a small portion of it in the *chulha*. But this was not the case with Lakshmi, who did away with the practice altogether. It was not that Sabesh was deliberately trying to be orthodox or hard to please. Lakshmi was a girl from Chhattisgarh, not from their home state Odisha, and she did not belong to their clan. So it was natural and understandable that Lakshmi may not associate herself with the ancestral spirits that the Gana community had always worshipped. But what about Makaru? For Sabesh, no excuse could justify her son, too, mirroring his wife's actions when it came to his religious and ancestral duties. Forget the ancestors, Sabesh found herself sadly wondering if Makaru even found the time to worship Ma Nialimali.

No matter how much Sabesh may have embraced Raipur city as her own, it would never hold the place in her heart that her ancestral village did. Back in Banjipali, everyone knew everyone else and people were tied to each other by a common thread of devotion to Nialimali. Here, however, though people lived huddled together in cramped spaces, with barely inches separating their tiny houses, there was a huge gap in terms of that close community bond, that sense of affinity, kinship and solidarity that Sabesh so craved. Nialimali was her ancestral deity, worshipped by generations of her family, and Sabesh's love and devotion for this mother figure was deep and unquestioned. Ma Nialimali was the pillar of strength and wisdom who kept the villagers together, who infused in each one of them the sense of belonging, of being part of a shared world.

Staunch devotee of Nialimali that she was, Sabesh held little regard for Hanuman. The monkey god may well have served Lord Ram in the *Treta Yuga*, she thought, but what did that have to do with them, the Ganas, or other people of the basti? What had he done for them? And who the hell did the MLA think he was to tell them whom to worship and advise them who should be their ancestral deities? She knew very well who her deities were, and she had worshipped them sincerely every day of her life. And here was her son Makaru. Casting into oblivion all their great venerable age-old clan deities—Ma Nialimali, Chhotibuddhi, Budhharaja, Kanabhaera, Baburai and Mahalachama—he wanted to help build a shrine for Hanuman! Makaru was no longer a child. Then why on earth couldn't he judge for himself whom he should worship?

But then again, thought Sabesh, who was she to tell anyone? Even if it was her own son. She was nothing but a simpleton who would still have been tending to the fields or feeding the cows, had it not been for that extraordinary and catastrophic sequence of events that had landed her in Raipur. The MLA here and the older slum dwellers of the basti had more exposure to life, were more experienced, and they knew much more than she did. She certainly couldn't hold a candle to any of them when it came to formulating wise opinions, so how could she possibly be so stupid as to openly express her thoughts?

In the end, the volatile thoughts and counter-thoughts circling furiously in Sabesh's head subsided into a silent string of words that she felt were best left unspoken.

On the other hand, preparations for the temple were on in full swing. The MLA sanctioned the money as promised, and the construction work began in earnest. To facilitate and speed up things, residents of the basti enthusiastically poured in their support, even contributing their labour. The temple was completed. It was splendid and beautiful. The people's joy knew no bounds. A Brahmin priest was appointed as planned. He inaugurated the temple by performing a ritual *homa*, as the excited slum dwellers looked on eagerly from the sidelines. This was followed by a big feast collectively organised by the basti, which everyone enjoyed.

Soon, the temple in the basti became part of the people's daily routines. Before setting out for work, people would bathe, visit the shrine, offer prayers and express their gratitude to the deity, and leave with a vermillion *teeka* on their forehead, chanting Jai Shri Ram! Jai Hanuman! Some would devoutly slip a few coins into the donation box.

Life went on as usual. Everyone was happy. Everyone was content. But what is life without a fly in the soup? There was one little mole in this otherwise peaceful community, one individual who did not share the joy and contentment of the community—the temple Brahmin. He was not happy at having to serve at a place of worship visited by hundreds of untouchables and lower castes every day. Why, his priest community had even threatened him with excommunication for accepting a measly job in a slum full of untouchables. While the temple was still underway, the priest had tried his best to assure his angry fellow Brahmins that, of course, he would on no account allow any untouchable to enter the holy house of god; that was the best he could do to try and cool them down. However, once the temple was completed, his plan proved impossible to implement. For, how in the world was the priest supposed to tell worshippers to keep off a temple that they had themselves built? So, the miserable priest lived in perpetual anxiety and fear, trying to work out a safe path to delay and to possibly avoid his symbolic extermination.

One day, when the priest was about to begin his puja as usual, he spotted two rickshaw pullers entering the temple compound, carrying flowers they had freshly plucked to offer the deity. The priest stopped them right at the entrance. It was time now to bring out the brahmastra. With gestures and words that he thought were suitably impressive, he solemnly began, "Brothers, I have always wished only the best for each one of you and I always pray that may Lord Hanuman bless you and your families. But sadly, that is not what is happening at present. And, believe me, I did have a premonition of sorts, but last night it turned into conviction. We are sinning, brothers, we are all sinning!" Judging from the surprised and shocked faces of the simple basti residents who stood before him, the priest saw that his plan was working. In response to their questioning eyes, he began to spin an absurd and ridiculous yarn that he had himself concocted.

"Brothers, last night, Lord Hanuman visited me in my dreams. That's right, brothers, the great Lord himself! I felt truly happy and blessed. But the Lord looked anything but happy. No. He shouted at me angrily, 'How careless you have become, you worthless scum of a Brahmin! You have been worshipping me for years. Yet, you have the audacity to flout the basic principles of worship laid out by me! My worshippers here are all innocent untouchables. They wish only to seek my blessings. And in their devotion and ardour, they forget their caste and they do not know the rules. But you? *You* are fully aware of the rules, Brahmin, and yet you continue with this utter sacrilege! I command you to convey to my dear untouchable devotees the proper rules of worshipping me without further delay. I do not wish to deny them my blessings and I will never do so. All they have to do is to seek my blessings from outside the temple entrance, and I will freely bestow upon them all the happiness, health and wealth in the world that they desire.' Thus Lord Hanuman himself appeared in my dream and commanded me." The priest concluded what he believed to have been an Oscar-worthy performance, and he wasn't far wrong.

The poor rickshaw pullers were flabbergasted. Of course, they blindly trusted the priest. He was someone much closer to the gods, wasn't he? If the great Hanuman had himself taken the trouble to appear in his dreams, the matter was certainly grave.

Fine, they would not pollute the temple premises any longer. God was omnipresent and omniscient after all. He would certainly listen to their prayers even from outside the shrine. All that mattered was whether their prayers were sincere and offered from the heart. It was indeed disheartening and a terrible pity that they could not enter and worship in a temple they had built themselves with all their devotion, faith, love and toil. But... what could they do? They must heed the Lord's word. How could they not. And so, from that day onwards, the basti people started worshipping Hanuman from outside the temple. Soon, the entrance of untouchables and lower castes was completely barred from their own temple.

And Chintu Chamar? When he heard the news, he was surprised, but not very. He had once been nearly beaten to death for having entered another temple. Now, his brothers and sisters of the community were facing the same predicament, albeit with considerably less vehemence and violence. Moreover, the idea of stepping into a shrine for worship did not seem that appealing to him anymore. If he wasn't allowed to enter the basti temple, so be it. He no longer cared.

Meanwhile, and to Sabesh's great dismay, Makaru and Lakshmi had kept up with their weekly routine of visiting the Hanuman temple every Tuesday. The old woman chose to rebel, and stuck to worshipping her dearest Ma Nialimali. Still, every now and again, she would be pained thinking how her own son had gone astray. But Makaru, oblivious to it all, actually had no real, deep or definite purpose of visiting the temple with his wife. He did it simply because almost everyone in the slum did it too, and he wanted to fit in. And besides, for him, there wasn't much difference between worshipping Lord Hanuman and Ma Nialimali.

Cut to the present, where this same Makaru sat dangerously silent on his train seat, lost in thoughts of faith, religion and memories of his colourful past. He broke out of his reverie when a strange looking beggar entered his compartment. Clothed in saffron, with a dash of vermillion on his forehead and a string of beads around his neck, he carried a striking photo of Ma Samaleswari, which he held aloft as he begged for alms. Makaru immediately thought that had his wife Lakshmi been here, she would definitely have fished out a few coins and given it to the mendicant. But Makaru? He was different. His reason took over his sympathy as he told himself that hundreds of vagrants frequented these train bogies every day, and it was impossible to help them all. So he felt he was better off being passive than partial. He got up quietly and changed his seat unnoticed. He resumed looking out of the window, countless thoughts floating in the endless expanse of his mind, as the train chugged along on its way unhindered.

Ten

"O my beloved, o my king, where have you gone, leaving me bereft?" Sabesh wept inconsolably, her body wracked by sobs as she beat her chest. Manglu's corpse lay in their courtyard, wrapped in a dhoti as white as death.

Manglu had been bedridden for the past half year or so. The fever refused to let go of him, compelling him to remain confined to his bed. His once strong, muscular frame had grown emaciated and skeletal, his bones protruding visibly under the skin. He was coughing constantly and what little conversation he could manage was broken by intermittent coughs, wheezing and gasping for breath.

Ultimately, he was taken to a doctor for a check-up. He confirmed the worst: Manglu had contracted T.B. Nevertheless, he was prescribed some medication for relief. But it did not help much. His health deteriorated further and soon, Manglu started coughing blood. Sometime later, he passed away, leaving behind a family devastated by grief.

Manglu had led a hardworking life, a life marked by struggles, upheavals, hardships. But through it all, he had always believed in and embodied the principle of 'Work is Worship'. In the village, he had lent his precious youth in service to the gauntia, toiling relentlessly day and night. Yet, all he earned in exchange for his blood, sweat and tears was an expulsion from his motherland. He was at his wit's end; yet he chose to fight it out. In a completely foreign city, among foreign people who spoke a foreign language, with nothing in hand and no benefactor to back him, Manglu learnt how to survive. He chose to survive. Here again, life demanded a different kind of service from him. Here, his indomitable strength and unquestioning slavery were not of as much use, as something else that he learnt eventually to master: skill. The skill of pulling a rickshaw. The skill of keeping his cool when ungrateful, miserly customers bit his head off trying to bargain the fare down to half the reasonable price. The skill of embracing strangers as his own when they made his basti theirs. The skill of simply continuing to do what he had done all his life: working. Manglu was to his work what his shadow was to him: it stayed by his side from dawn to dusk.

The fates had never bestowed upon him brains, or beauty for that matter. But they had given Manglu a gift, an asset that he had sculpted to precision: brute manpower. It was something he made use of all his life, till his blood ran thin, oozing out of his mouth, and his limbs turned to lead and stuck to his deathbed. And he would be remembered for it, even beyond death.

Every man is a creature of the age he lives in. And though Manglu's age had come to an end, the legacy he had built for himself continued undiminished into the next.

Manglu, as you know, belonged to the Gana community from Odisha. So his death rites were performed in accordance with his clan's customs. Many of his rickshaw puller friends also came over to help with the rituals.

Originally, it was thought that Manglu would be cremated at the electric crematorium. However, Makaru conveyed to the community his father's last wishes. He recounted how, in happier days, his father used to say, "Lest paradise sends a summon for me, just dig a small patch in the ground and bury me there, son. But I don't want a funeral."

Ever since his feud with the gauntia's son Nandakumar, Manglu had changed his outlook. The upper castes burned the dead bodies of their loved ones by custom. So Manglu chose to rebel and wished to be laid to rest in the lap of earth instead. He had always been a follower of Nialimali and of Gana customs. Perhaps this was also why he chose not to contribute when the

Hanuman temple was being built, though he did not oppose it either.

Manglu would always say, "We are all children of Mother Earth. We farm on soil, cook on soil and we eat on it. Our goddess Ma Nialimali, too, is a goddess of the same soil. What better way to repay our holy Mother than by going back to embrace her in death and beyond?" Manglu's love for the soil was deep and immeasurable. In fact, even as he lay dying on his sickbed, he was insistent that he be buried so that his body could mingle and become one with the earth again. Even when swearing, he would invariably say, "*Maati kaati khaeba*: Lest I be lying, may the earth eat me alive." Makaru had heard all this innumerable times, and he knew what weight his father's desire for a burial carried for him. He wasted no time in sharing his father's wishes with everyone.

Dambru, too, agreed that Manglu should be buried according to Gana custom. He was an old man now. Nevertheless, he decided to accompany the funeral procession. He walked slowly and with difficulty, rendered breathless at every step. Every inch of his body told him to stop. But how could he? Manglu was a dear friend. No, Manglu was his dearest friend, if he must say it. As he stood to catch his breath, Dambru's thoughts went back to the old days, when they were both young and strong.

Manglu had just arrived in Raipur. He had nowhere and no one to go to. But Dambru had stepped forward like a guardian spirit, and taught him the basics of living and surviving in this city. He had helped him set up house, given him a rickshaw, got him a job, and thereafter, Dambru had always stayed by his side. Always.

Literally, till his last breath.

And now, Manglu was no more. Dambru felt hit by a tsunami of emotions and memories, knocking his heart askew, breaking it into countless pieces. As if in a trance, he somehow walked back home on unsteady legs, went in and brought out his old nissan.

Gathering his last reserves of energy, Dambru started beating the nissan with all his might.

Traditionally, villagers of the Gana community announced a person's death using this percussion instrument. Since the rural atmosphere is usually so tranquil and silent, the notes of the nissan can be clearly heard across villages, and relatives and acquaintances come running to the spot, guided by its beats. Sometimes, the drummer even climbs up on a rooftop for better effect.

But here in Raipur, with motorcars rushing past honking loudly, the train hooting and rattling down the tracks, and the city submerged in a constantly bubbling cauldron of sounds and noises, no one would have been able to hear the frantic beats of Dambru's nissan. Also, this was a foreign land, where no close kin or relatives of Manglu from his village, other than his wife and son, were present. Perhaps, Dambru beat the drum only out of his belief and respect for an age-old, solemn legacy that had been passed down over generations. Perhaps, he was soulfully pouring out all the grief of his bereaved soul onto the dry skin of the drum. Or perhaps both. No one really knows. But, in the middle of it all, the dam of mourning suddenly broke and tears ran down his face in rivers as Dambru cried out aloud for the heavens to hear, "Manglu, my brother, where have you gone? Take me along, too, o' Manglu...I don't want to live in this world anymore. I don't want to live anymore..." And holding his nissan tight to his chest, as if it somehow contained the precious soul of his dearest friend, Dambru dissolved into a sobbing mass of emotions as his heart painted a tapestry of beautiful memories that the two had shared.

Manglu's *telghar* and *dashaghar* were performed on the third and tenth day after his death, respectively. Gana musicians were invited to play during the ceremony. Many of Manglu's acquaintances and friends in the basti came. On the day of dashaghar, Makaru tonsured his head and wore a brand new white dhoti; a ritual feast was organised for all those who attended. At night, Makaru led a procession to the end of the basti, carrying an earthen lamp placed in an earthen pot hung from a rope. The Gana musicians outdid themselves and played exuberantly, not stopping even when the sound of the oncoming train blended into their music.

Ah, the train...It was a train like this one that Manglu had boarded with his family that fateful night that had brought him here, to Raipur. Raipur, where he had made friends, where he had built a house, built a new life from scratch. To think that one so resilient, so energetic and strong, so compassionate and alive was now a duma, a spirit being brought back from his burial site to be reunited with his ancestors.

A puja was performed at one end of the basti to rehabilitate his spirit. A moist dough of wheat flour and cow dung was prepared as an offering to the departed. Towards the end of the puja, they looked around to see if there were any insects to be found. The priest caught a fly, and thus it was announced that Manglu's duma had returned to earth in the form of a fly. Makaru captured the fly in an earthen pot, and proceeded to walk back home with it to their pidar.

A long thread had been tied from one end of the basti to the pidar in Manglu's home. Manglu's ancestors were weavers, so in the olden times they used cloth; but now since they could no longer afford new cloth, a thread was used for the purpose instead. Makaru walked back home along the path that had been demarcated by the thread. Manglu's duma was ritually installed on the pidar and it was announced that he had at last joined his ancestors' spirits, to be worshipped hereafter by his descendants.

All of a sudden, Lakshmi jolted into life. As if guided by an inner melody only she could hear, her body started swaying slowly and rhythmically, her eyes unseeing. Her eerie demeanour and movements reached a crescendo as she shuffled towards her husband Makaru, addressing him as her son, and blessed him. She went up to Sabesh and caressed her, calling her fondly by name and asking her how she was. She then asked for her "grandson" and, when he was brought to her, she gave him a loving kiss on his forehead. People watched with bated breath, but no one was surprised. It was an old Gana belief, after all, that the duma often came to possess someone who was pure at heart. Hence, Lakshmi's mystifying actions.

After sometime, Lakshmi returned from her supernatural high. She felt utterly exhausted and drained mentally and physically, she said, and that she had no memory of the preceding moments, her mind was blank. Those present satisfactorily deduced that Manglu's spirit had manifested through her, and had dispersed content.

After Manglu's departure, the house started looking empty and seemed enshrouded in a pall of gloom. But perhaps the one most affected was Sabesh. It seemed as if the demise of her life partner had drained her of all human emotions, leaving her as an empty shell of her past self. She lost all interest in life. Even when she seemed to be doing some household chore, any onlooker could see that she was just whiling away her time on earth.

Makaru observed all this in silence. He felt desolate and helpless, and haunted by this constant sense of foreboding that his mother may be inching towards her last days, too. That he could be rendered an orphan any time. Had he been in the village, the gauntia or some other diabolic being would have definitely exploited his helplessness. A tide of emotions surged over him, and for the first time in his life, Makaru felt vulnerable, like an orphan, as if left all alone to battle the harsh, cold reality of life without the constant reassuring presence of both his parents.

Makaru's eyes went to his little son. Now that he was a father himself, he could just begin to fathom to what impossible lengths his father had gone to ensure for him a secure childhood and a comfortable adulthood. He had some idea as to how many sleepless nights Manglu had spent for him, and to provide for his family. Makaru remembered how his father used to get him his favourite savouries like puffed rice and roasted chickpeas from the market whenever he could, tied safely into a knot at the end of his *gamchha*.

Sabesh had once shared with Makaru how he had learnt to speak later than other children of his age. They would be spouting words, rhymes and gibberish at the top of their lungs, while all Makaru would manage to utter were hesitant "hmms", relying purely on gesticulation for the rest. This troubled Manglu deeply, for which father would want his precious and only child to grow up dumb or stammering? He went to great lengths, travelling to villages far and near, seeking help. Then, he met a gunia, who suggested picking up stray grains of puffed rice from streets and marketplaces and feeding it to his son. Manglu obeyed. And lo! Makaru started speaking! Everyone was immensely relieved. Overjoyed, Manglu gifted the gunia an entire kilo of rice.

Manglu may have gone to such extents in following his fatherly duty, but for Makaru it didn't matter what thought lay behind his actions. All he cared about was how very fortunate he had been to have someone like Manglu for his father, who loved him more than life and always saw to his wellbeing. Had it not been for him, Makaru would never have reached where he was today. Whatever endeavour he embarked on, his father had always been by his side. Even when Makaru got a job as a peon-cum-security-guard, Manglu, being a rickshaw puller, couldn't offer him much guidance on the job, but he always lent him his wholehearted moral support.

His father's death compelled Makaru to introspect. He found himself thinking about what it truly meant to be a parent. Amongst all creatures, human babies were the weakest. They took the longest time to emerge from the protective cocoon that their parents wove for them lifelong, to venture forth into the world, and to live their own independent lives. They needed the utmost care and protection, something other animals provided their young for days or weeks or a few years at most. Manglu, too, must have felt bound by his duty as a human father to provide for him, Makaru thought. He must have spent all his resources, energies and time trying to provide what was best for his son despite the many odds that constrained him. This again was something Makaru was deeply grateful for. It would probably take Makaru a hundred lifetimes to repay his father, given all the sacrifices he had made for him.

That same father who had shaped and coloured all aspects of his life had disappeared behind smoke and mirrors and gone to heaven, leaving in his wake an immeasurable grey void and despondency. His beloved guardian was no more. Makaru felt as if he had been pushed into a black abyss.

Feeling his eyes turn misty, he pulled his son into his lap and caressed him, his heart brimming with emotions. Blissfully innocent, the child continued to play whatever little game he had invented to amuse himself. Makaru cast a glance at Sabesh, and pulled his son closer to his chest. Hot tears rolled down his eyes, like the anguish coursing through his veins.

Suddenly, Makaru was jolted back to the present by the shrieking of a train rushing past the one he was sitting in, and he felt as if he was being pulled fiercely towards it, as if it was dragging his dearest father further and further away from him.

Makaru shook himself awake. His father was in the distant past now. Yet, he haunted his senses, like the fragrance of a perfume that lingers long after the source is gone, just as if he were right there beside him, close enough to touch.

A monstrous wave of gloom washed over him, crushing him under its weight, throwing him into an abyss of loneliness and melancholy. And yet, it was terrifyingly beautiful.

And Makaru was ready to be terrified beyond his senses a million times over if it meant that he could meet his father again, albeit only in his memories.

He missed his bapa.

Eleven

Time flies.

Like the wings of a bird being chased by a hungry predator, it rushes past, dwarfing all human movement with its incredible speed.

The universe has been here forever, and it will perhaps remain more or less the same in the eons to come. But time, that infinite giant that exists and moves regardless of the human universe, has changed.

And so has Makaru.

He has now grown older. The advantages of that, as many claimed, was the maturity that came with it. But was it really so? Do we really grow wiser with age? Are we born to live, or are we born to die?

To Makaru, each day passing by in its hurried nonchalance seemed to be pushing him farther and farther into the jaws of death, whereupon his life, his whole existence would be swallowed into nothingness.

Makaru had already lost his father some time ago. Now, he was bereft of his mother too. Which tragic circumstance meant that he had to now take over as family head. Makaru's son

Bishikeshan had grown up into a young man. He had got a job as a clerk in a steel industry in Raipur, and had married a girl from Chhattisgarh.

The city belonged to no one. People came and went shrouded in anonymity, as if invisible to others. No one bothered about anyone else, about other people's lives, or deaths. They thought everything could be bought with money. They cared more about inert stacks of paper notes than for living flesh and blood souls. The city was crowded with human habitation, like a teeming anthill. It was jam-packed with people, and yet it felt empty as a void. Loneliness and desolation shrouded the city like listless grey winter fog. Sometimes, Makaru would glance longingly at the trains rushing past his slum, and his heart would scream at him to just board one of those and run away. Away to his village. The city was huge, and its hum and throb larger than life. But nothing could compare with the warmth and the familiar intimacy with which his village caressed his spirit.

Makaru longed for his village. Often in his free time, he would lie there daydreaming, his head filled with nostalgic memories. He would recall his old house on his ancestral land. Was it still there? Or was it now dilapidated beyond recognition? How would the village have changed over these past many years? Makaru would think of his ancestors, yearning to visit their duma. But each time that he would plan to visit his village, his job and family responsibilities would come in the way. And all he would be left with was an intricate loom of memories, and a yearning that ached, as he desperately held on to a fast thinning hope of ever being able to visit his motherland again.

Makaru would fondly recollect how in his childhood, while out grazing the gauntia's buffaloes, he used to go to the gauntia's pond along with his friends to bathe and cool off. In summers when the temperatures would soar to blazing heights, it would become impossible to walk barefoot on the ground without scalding their feet. So Makaru and his friends would collect tendu leaves and tie those on their feet. The leaves would protect and comfort them for a while, but soon get ripped off as they walked. As a last resort, the children would be compelled to ride the gauntia's buffaloes back home. The gauntia was never too pleased with that.

Another memory was that of fishing in the village pond. Makaru was an expert at that. He would wade into the pond, feeling his way carefully through the tranquil dark green waters, until his hand would brush against a fish. Then, with an expert grab, he would scoop the fish out in a flash. *Gadisha* were Makaru's favourite and, for him, their taste easily rivalled that of even the king among fish, the *ilishi*.

Once when he was chest-deep in the water, on the lookout for fish, his hands caught hold of a head. Delighted, he pulled it out of the water, only to find a *dhanda* snake thrashing about in his grip, its tail lashing the air furiously. Appalled, he quickly threw the angry reptile away, but not before it had bitten his middle finger as it disappeared into the dark waters. Makaru watched with horror as blood started oozing out of the snakebite.

Little Makaru knew that whoever got bitten by a snake died. Terrified, he ran home as fast as his legs could carry him, so he could have one last exchange with his beloved parents before he died. Whoever he met on the way was told, between gasping breaths, that he had been "bitten by a huge deadly snake!" When he reached home, as soon as his mother saw the blood on his wound, she burst into tears. When she learnt that her son had been bitten by a snake, she ran to a nearby anthill like a bullet train, returned with a lump of earth from it in her palm, and fed it to Makaru. The boy swallowed it without hesitation. To Sabesh's relief, he told her that it tasted pretty much like soil. The villagers believed that if someone was bitten by a snake, and if the venom had spread all over their body, anthill soil tasted bitter to them. And if it did not, they were safe.

Without further ado, she took him to the village *gardi*. The moment the man heard the news, he slapped her so hard on her cheek that Sabesh was stunned and almost fell from the impact. Seeing this, little Makaru was bewildered and seethed, muttering under his breath, "*Saala*! Why the hell doesn't he bring out his paraphernalia and do his wretched work instead of slapping my mother!" But he dared not say it out loud.

What surprised him even more, however, was his mother's response. She remained perfectly calm and unsurprised, almost as if she was expecting the slap. Unlike Sabesh, what young Makaru did not know is that it was a common practice among gardis to slap the messenger who relayed the news of the snakebite. It was believed that the sudden shock of witnessing the person being slapped somehow compelled the lethal venom to leave the victim's body.

The gardi then whipped out a magic concoction out of thin air and handed it over to a confused Makaru and Sabesh, who was still reeling from the impact of the slap. Then, furrowing his brows to build up suspense and anticipation, he said in as deep a voice as he could muster, "The boy was bitten by a non-poisonous snake. Fear not, he will heal soon." Enormously relieved, the mother and son returned home.

There lived about ten to fifteen Gana families in Banjipali village. All of them were poor and had no land to call their own. Perhaps the only one 'privileged' in this sense was Makaru's uncle, his father's older brother. But even his land wasn't enough to provide for his family the whole year round. So all members of the Gana community ended up working as daily wage labourers. Needless to say, none of them had the land or the money to dig a well for their farming or domestic water needs. So they made do with the water from the gauntia's pond.

The pond was huge and always filled to the brim with water. Except in summers, when the water level would go down and parts of the pond would dry up, and people from near and far would come, armed with nets and other equipment to catch the fish, crabs and other water creatures left behind in the shallow water and slush. Their collective activity made the pond muddy and smelly. It would take two or three days for the sediments to settle down, by which time the fungi and algae would spread their colonies on the surface of the water, causing an unpleasant smell. At this time of the year, needless to say, the water became undrinkable. The Gana people would have to painstakingly collect what scarce water was available in earthen pots and containers, filter the muddy water through cloth, and wait for the sediments to settle down a little so they could drink it after it had been filtered by this crude method.

What made the situation even sadder was the fact that the village actually had three wells, which had ample water the year round. The Ganas could certainly have accessed these wells, but their caste stood in the way. So, come summer, they would have to beg and plead for water from the upper castes as they fetched water from the wells for their own households. The Ganas had to patiently wait for a kind-hearted person to come along and pour some water into the vessels that they held out in such desperate hope. But life was cruel. They usually had to return empty-handed, or rather, with empty vessels. In such circumstances, what alternative did they have other than drink the muddy, smelly water from the stinking pond?

And yet, the plague of a harsh summer wasn't half as terrible as the crisis the Ganas had to face in a monsoon when the rains failed. Drought would strike, and the gauntia would mercilessly ask for the pond waters to be emptied into his fields for irrigation. This deprived the lower castes of water to a degree even worse than what they faced in summers.

As Makaru recalled a childhood incident, a low dry chuckle escaped his lips.

Once, Makaru and a few other boys of the village where grazing cattle in the fields. They were right next to the gauntia's farm, where he had grown maize and cucumbers. Tempted by the ripe golden pods of maize and green cucumbers, the boys chalked out a plan to steal them. One boy was assigned the duty of guarding the cattle; two others were to look sharp and watch out for anyone coming by and warn the others well in time. Of the remaining four, two were assigned the job of stealing the maize. That left Makaru, the youngest of the group, and another boy to steal the cucumbers.

Now, the maize plants were growing near the fences; so, as soon as they reached the territory, the two boys started breaking them off in some haste. This made loud snapping and cracking sounds, which alerted the gauntia, who came out running with a lathi, swearing, "You motherfuckers! Out to steal my crops again! Wait till I catch you, you bastards, I won't spare your life!"

The five intruders ran off as soon as they heard the bellowing man. But our poor naive Makaru was left stranded among the cucumber creepers. Cowering in fear, he quickly lay down flat on the earth, praying that the gauntia wouldn't see him, even as he kept thinking of the horrible consequences that would befall him if he was caught. How would his father react? Would they call a beheran? He shuddered in fright.

Fortunately, the gauntia couldn't spot anyone. So he went away angrily muttering, "Rascals! If the crops tempt you so much, why don't you grow some yourselves, huh? The lazy bastards!"

Makaru heaved a huge sigh of relief, checked if the coast was clear, and then ran for his dear life. After this near death experience, as he liked to put it, he vowed never to steal again.

To Makaru, his childhood memories were interesting, to say the least. They elicited excitement, joy and sometimes frustration and even sadness. But they were engrossing nonetheless. He chuckled at how innocent he used to be as a child, and wished that he could be a child again.

Suddenly, a cucumber vendor entered the train compartment, deftly peeling cucumbers and shouting, "Cucumbers, juicy fresh cucumbers!" A faint smile appeared on Makaru's lips as a vivid image of the gauntia's furious red face and his long lathi surfaced in his mind's eye. Struggling to suppress a giggle, Makaru turned his attention to the scene outside the window.

Acres and acres of lush green spread themselves before his eyes, stretching far into the horizon. The paddy crops had ripened and flirted with the wind, swaying back and forth gracefully in a slow dance. White storks could be seen perched patiently amid the stalks, scanning the standing waters in the fields keenly for fish. The waters of the irrigation canal sparkled in the afternoon sun. Makaru was quick to figure out that these fields followed a double cropping system.

Back in Banjipali village, the farmers used to grow just one crop. All of the irrigation was accounted for by the rains alone. Naturally, therefore, when the government decided to build a dam over the Sunder River, adjacent to their village, the people of Banjipali rejoiced greatly. This was also around the same time that children from their village suddenly started disappearing mysteriously. Many suspected this to be the doing of the *fushas*, the child-lifters. There was a blind belief that a powerful goddess resided in the area where the dam was to be built. To appease her and to seek her protection for the soon-to-be constructed dam, a child had to be sacrificed to the goddess at the site. Hence, the vanishing children.

Once this horrendous news broke out, the village was shrouded in a stifling atmosphere of pure terror. Children were shut inside their houses come dusk and not allowed to go out even to answer calls of nature. Fearful parents stayed vigilant and kept constant watch even at the cost of their sleep.

It was rumoured that the evil fushas would tie up children's hands and legs and gag their mouth with a cloth, lest they shouted for help. Then the poor helpless lambs were bundled into sacks and handed over to the bloodthirsty dam contractor, who would cruelly sacrifice them in the stealth of night.

Makaru too was just a child back then, tending to the gauntia's cattle. Being fearful for their lives, he and his friends would take all necessary precautions to ensure that they didn't let the cattle graze at the roadside, and kept well to the forests.

And they were particularly scared to death of ambassador cars. For some reason, the villagers suspected that the evil fushas rode in these large cars, carrying away with them the poor innocents that they had kidnapped and hidden. So every time the boys would spot one, they would scurry off the road like startled crabs and immediately hide behind some bushes or foliage. The ambassador car had even earned itself the name of *kechho*, for it resembled a tortoise.

Even now, whenever Makaru spotted an ambassador, he would be reminded of his childhood.

One good thing that did follow as a result of the dam being built was the compensation that the government provided. They gave money in return for all the land and homesteads that had been taken over by the government for building the dam. Even those who had the most barren lands, and were farming crops like *mandia*, were given cash in exchange for their lands.

For the desperately poor illiterate villagers, this unexpected bounty was surreal.

Those who didn't even know how to count up to hundred now suddenly had wads of notes in their hand. Needless to say, not knowing what to do with so much money, the villagers succumbed to a wave of splurging and excess. And with that came a brief season of indulging in food and drink.

A number of touts promptly arrived on the scene as well, worldly wise and shrewd, to dupe and exploit the gullible villagers. They lured them with things like new motorbikes, when the villagers couldn't even ride them, and convinced them to buy shiny speedy two-wheelers. Some poor folks even ended up breaking their bones. So they handed over their precious vehicles back to the touts, settling for riding pillion instead. And, perched on the two-wheelers, they would tour every eatery and bar they could set eyes on.

But, of course, the money did not keep flowing endlessly. Caught in a vicious cycle, the villagers were soon left stranded in their selfsame stagnant lives, only now they were both unwealthy as well as unhealthy. Left with no option, they were forced to sell off their expensive, newly acquired luxury goods cheap, to the same touts who had convinced them to buy in the first place what they did not need, and made them end up in this pitiable condition.

The dam was built. But the villagers remained naive and credulous. Other clever people came over from distant lands and big cities, and offered to buy up land there, which the villagers happily sold them in exchange for a little money. The new landowners knew how best to make use of and to harness the power and waters unleashed by the dam. The lands, that had barely been able to grow *mandia* before, were now thriving with two-crop seasons and producing truckloads of grains.

Most of the villagers lost their lands and their livelihood in the bargain. Eventually, they had to resort to selling fish that they caught in the canals of the dam, earning a measly twenty, twenty-five rupees a day. So, they continued living hand-to-mouth as before, and worse than before in fact.

And what happened to the touts? Well, each one of them became a gauntia in his own right, and a buyer of the fish that the villagers caught to sell.

Life is cruel. One has to be cunning in order to survive in this world. Makaru had long ago realised that his ancestral village hadn't taught him much of that survival skill. No, it was exposure to city life that had made him street-smart, smart enough to figure out how to make the best of a desperate situation, and to keep going. Perhaps, it really was for the best that he and his parents had been displaced overnight from their village.

And now, life had come full circle. He was on his way back to the very same homeland, to meet his own people.

The train slowed down and came to a halt. Makaru looked out of the window. It was neither a station nor a town, just a small nondescript hillock. So why had the train halted here?

The sun was blazing in its full glory. Some people were climbing off. Makaru too wished to stand under the bright sunshine for a few moments, to let its warmth seep into his tired bones and rejuvenate them. But just when he was about to get down, the train blew its whistle, and Makaru went back to his seat and sat down, resigned.

The woman co-passenger who had been sitting across from him all this while had also gotten down with her three children at the last station. In their place, new passengers had arrived to claim the seat. This was how a train journey was supposed to be, of course. Yet, Makaru couldn't help but feel slightly awkward in the presence of the new faces. Granted that the mother of three wasn't his acquaintance, but the train journey had rendered her one, albeit only for a while and in a superficial way. Perhaps, he would soon feel at ease with his new co-passengers as well.

The chilly wind blasting through the windows made him shiver. But, perhaps unknown to him, his shivers were more in anticipation of what he was about to experience, rather than what he was experiencing at the moment. He felt anxious, fearful and helpless. The train was hurtling him relentlessly closer towards his destination, whether he wanted it or not.

It is said that the greatest fear is fear of the unknown.

This is what was binding him in a vice-like grip that refused to let go.

Battling these tumultuous thoughts, Makaru found his train pulling up at Harishankar Road, or Lathore station—Makaru's destination. He got down. The train halted for a minute at the station, and then chugged speedily on its way.

The few passengers who had disembarked with him also headed off for their respective homes. After having travelled in a train filled with so many people all this while, it felt peculiar to be suddenly standing in the middle of a small station with no one around. Makaru felt lost and strange. He also had no idea where he was supposed to head for. There wasn't a familiar face in sight whom he could ask. He felt utterly desolate, stranded amidst the strange and the unfamiliar, taunted by fleeting glimpses of the familiar.

Makaru wanted to ask someone for help. But...what would he have said? He could not very well say he was someone who hailed from Banjipali. Their house in the village must have been reduced to ruins long ago. He could perhaps have asked for Chitrasen dada's whereabouts, but his house had also been burnt to ashes.

Makaru then spotted a solitary cement bench. His thoughts instantly went back to that fateful night, the night he had last been at this station. Was this that same bench where he and his parents had sat huddled together, waiting anxiously for a train that would help them escape their nightmare? His mental state at that time wasn't very different from how he felt right now. Anxious because of what had taken place, terrified of what the future held, and utterly helpless in the present. The bench seemed to be calling out to him like an old friend, beckoning him to just lie down there and let all his doubts and fears dissolve into nothing. As Makaru stood glued to the spot, his eyes fixed on the old cement bench, he strongly felt the urge and the need to sit there just for a few moments.

But he did not give in to the urge.

Just as how he had not given in to his fears fifty years ago, when he had been reduced to a miserable, hopeless wreck, sobbing as he sat here between his mother and father.

Makaru moved on.

Lathore railway station has a small footbridge to help people cross the railway lines and go on to the other side, which was Lathore village. But Makaru did not climb the footbridge. He simply started walking along the empty tracks towards his destination. He could faintly recall that Ganapada, the Dalit basti of Lathore, was only about a kilometre away. But to his exhausted mind, it seemed like a hundred never-ending kilometres.

Little did the world know that he was waging a fierce war against his own soul. As much as his heart wanted him to go running to his homeland and sink into the embrace of a familiar pair of arms, his mind held him back, refusing to let him proceed an inch further.

His mind was anxious, fearful, hiding from itself, hiding from what it knew, and from what it did not wish to know.

His heart was bleeding helplessly. And his soul, his soul was being sucked into a dangerous vortex, tumbling into the black void of hell itself.

Nonetheless, Makaru kept walking.

Twelve

Lathore High School was teeming with people.

The small school compound resembled a crowded market place, with more than two hundred people living there. Each one of them had been stripped of their home, their possessions and their dignity. They weren't crying or wailing out loud for the world to hear, yet the silence of their melancholy and despair was deafening. Their eyes were silent grey pools of screaming anguish.

When there's a raging forest fire and all hell breaks loose, destroying everything in its path, those observing it passively from the outside may feel for the animals, birds and insects of the forest running amok in fear as their homes are reduced to ashes in front of their eyes. But they don't really feel what the stricken animals experience. They cannot. Except, perhaps, in this situation. We now know what happens to the intricate fragile ecosystem that nature conjured with her own hands once those tongues of fire arrive, licking every bark, every blade of grass, every inch of soil clean.

A relief camp had been set up in Lathore High School, to house the people whose homes had been burnt down by other people.

Three police vans were parked near the gate, ostensibly to guard the survivors. To think that the law enforcement officers were sitting and idling their time here, when the damage had already been done, instead of bringing to justice those heartless men who had torched down their homes! Besides, the police's presence only served to intimidate the hapless victims, whose fear did not allow them even to express themselves freely, to unload the trauma and burden on their hearts. Without any outlet or succour for their grief, they were reduced to silent, angry, disconsolate wrecks.

The Anganwadi workers of the school in Lathore had been appointed by the district administration to cook and distribute food amongst the victims. Like the raging fires of the forest, the minds and bodies of the victims too were seething with unquenched rage. So much that they did not seem to need warm clothing despite the chilly January air.

The school building had a total of four rooms. In those four matchbox-sized compartments of cement and brick sat huddled as many as forty families. What they shared in common was loss, displacement and a bewildered incredulous innocence. "Why us?" was the only question that constantly plagued them. But deep in their hearts, they all knew the root cause of this inhuman act.

Crammed together in rooms among people linked to each other by a myriad interpersonal relationships, already struggling with the burden weighing their hearts down, they were also at their wit's end how to manage their intricate social customs and interactions. Odia traditions compelled women to maintain a distance even from their husband's elder brother. How were they supposed to fulfil such customs in these conditions?

True, their tumbledown huts were not palatial compared to these schoolrooms, but still, they were homes. There were always little rundown corners and spaces in each household that were designated for everyday chores. More than a shelter, it was a feeling: the feeling of having your own quiet little corner tucked away amidst the overwhelming chaos of the world, your sanctuary.

In torching down their houses, the black-hearted bigots and perpetrators of the crime had in fact burnt down something far more precious: their traditions, their customs, their culture, their identity.

Shaken to the core, their beliefs had crumbled.

Four large polythene sheets had been laid on the floor of the schoolrooms for the victims to use. When they would lie down on them to sleep, they eerily resembled dead bodies lined up for cremation, their souls sucked dry. In this strange hostile environment taut with unvoiced grief and anger, even the children struggled to sleep. Back home in the village, mothers could always lull them to sleep by diverting their attention to the stars, the moon, the birds, by telling them stories and singing lullabies. But here, in this unfamiliar, unpleasant, chaotic, claustrophobic environment, they all found themselves bewildered and at a loss, constantly grappling with their emotions. The children could hardly be blamed for refusing to sleep. Neither the children nor their mothers could catch a wink.

The men seemed to wander about like headless corpses, their sense of devastation so immense that they could neither bring themselves to eat nor sleep. The monstrous anguish weighing them down made them feel as if they were not supposed to have survived this ordeal of life. They no longer seemed to care about their surroundings or even notice their families housed in the same room. In their black eyes, there were no rays of hope—only glowing embers reminiscent of the leaping angry flames that had swallowed their homes.

Privacy is an unheard of luxury in a relief camp. The women had enough troubles as it is. The camp offered them a bare minimum of human dignity, compelling them to conduct their daily private activities, including bathing, in the open. They had been forced to flee with nothing on them except what they wore, and at most one extra set of clothes, and that was wearing thin due to continuous use.

A bunch of government officers visited the relief camp. They assured the victims that they were there for them, ready to provide them any kind of assistance they needed. They requested the victims to fully cooperate with the administration so that they could avail of any help that the government may offer them. They added that if they failed to do so, it could become very difficult for the officers to grant them any kind of aid.

Who the hell were these officers anyway? Did their jobs also pay them to mouth utter bullshit in order to pacify wretched victims of caste violence? And what was this great 'assistance' that they went on about? At best, they would dole out some half-cooked food or allot them some pokey Indira Awas houses. Could they restore the beautiful homes that they had built for themselves, whose floors they had plastered with cow dung with their own hands? Could their little sanctuaries of comfort, warmth and hospitality be restored to them? No. Then why on earth were these idiots blabbering on about their godforsaken 'assistance'? Somewhere, a nagging doubt crept up in their minds. Were these officers here to delay the investigation instead of facilitating it? Or were they here perhaps to quell the seething anger harboured by the victims, and to forestall any impulsive actions, lest they burnt down the upper-caste houses in righteous rage?

The devilish bastards, minions of the government.

Anyhow. Regardless of whether they wanted it or not, the government did offer them some relief by way of compensation. Help from civil societies across Odisha also poured in: from Bolangir, Khaprakhol, Maniguda, Kalahandi, Titlagarh, Haldi, Kesinga, Utkela, Khariar, to name some. Surprisingly, some relief packages also arrived from Jawaharlal Nehru University in Delhi. What was amusing was the different names by which the beneficiary recipient community had been mentioned. Some called them Gana Samaj, some Dom Samaj, some Lakhe Ghar Samaj. Despite the variety of names, the community was one and the same.

In the past, the Ganas were traditionally known as weavers. They wove distinctive and exquisite cloths, famous as *Gana kapda* or cloth made by Ganas, which they sold for a livelihood. The men were experts at weaving *Gana karia*, *Gana kapda*, *chandan kura*, *khadu* and *angchhi*, while the women crafted beautiful *antadors* and *jiuntias* to supplement their family incomes. Just like every story has a protagonist, every machine too has an essential, vital component. For the Gana weaver's loom, it was the *feni*, which had minute holes through which the thread went in and out, and one hole only had enough space for one thread. Weaving is an intricate process involving innumerable threads, and it was believed that the *feni* had as many as a lakh holes in it, if not more. And so, the Gana community came to be known as the 'Lakhe Ghar Samaj'.

More relief supplies were starting to pour in. Rice, puffed rice, soaps, oils, dhotis, sarees, and even cash, thanks to civil societies. The number of people arriving to visit the victims at the relief camp was also increasing day by day. After seeing their desperate and shocking plight, and talking to them, many of the visitors would become emotional and some would even break down.

It is not as if there are no homeless people in this world. There are hundreds of thousands. But these homeless people of Lathore found it difficult to live like refugees because, until very recently, they had homes to call their own. How does one go from living in a secure shelter that one calls home to sharing an empty schoolroom with ten other families overnight? If not for the open space adjacent to the school premises, where they could at least while away the daylight hours under the shade of the trees, the refugees would have had to spend all their time crammed together in the same room breathing the same stale air for days on end like in a jail.

So unhygienic were the conditions in the makeshift camp that many of the women and children had already fallen sick. They could not go to a hospital for help, and even the nearest health centre was thirty kilometres away, in Khaprakhol. Health workers were regularly sent to the camp for periodic check-ups. And they did their jobs as best they could, honestly and with determination, with the limited resources and manpower given to them. But in the face of such adversity, how much could they do? The medicines handed out to the refugees could at best temporarily cure what illness might have afflicted them; they could not change the filthy, cramped conditions of the camp itself, which were the cause of the health problems.

No matter who visited the camp, or whether they had come to console, offer help, or visit a relative, they always left with a heavy heart. Conversations were carried on in subdued tones. Those who came left with a sense of despair and anguish.

And then there were the schoolchildren.

Nestled right in the heart of the institution that bestowed them with knowledge, learning and understanding, and yet miles away from it. They were in school, but there was no knowing when they would resume studies. Their slates, bags, books, pens, pencils had all been lost or burnt down.

No, someone had in fact deliberately burnt them down.

Along with the stationery, their aspirations, hopes and young dreams were also burnt to ashes, leaving the children staring at a bleak future. What made it worse was that they were completely clueless as to why all this was happening. What had they done to deserve this?

It was January. A chilly wind rustled through the empty streets, sending shivers down one's spine and limbs and making the teeth chatter. The survivors bore the cold with what little they had on them, when tragedy struck their lives and they were forced to flee. Usually, in a winter like this, people would go about in layers of woollens, and use a thick sheet and blanket at night, looking like fat little rolls. But, here in the camp, they had nothing.

After three long freezing days and nights, the government finally woke up to their plight, and sent them some blankets. However, to their dismay, it was just one blanket per family. So even if you had an ailing mother, an exhausted wife, and three toothless balls of energy clinging to you for warmth, you still had to make do with one measly blanket, and a single one at that.

They might still have managed somehow, had the officials not forbidden them from lighting up even small *antras*, which would at least have lent a little warmth. That too was a privilege that was snatched away from them.

As were so many other things they held dear.

But then, a breath of warm air arrived: help from good Samaritans.

Non-governmental organisations, voluntary associations and civil societies sent in funds and materials to help them tide over the harsh winter. Some educated youngsters of the community diligently started keeping account of the relief being sent and used; the elders were neither in a state of mind to do so, nor, given their illiteracy, were they equipped to.

Like a viscous fluid, news of the atrocity spread. It was printed in the newspapers, broadcast on television, talked about on radio. Prominent public figures, civil activists, sensitive, conscientious citizens from around the country visited the survivors, to show their solidarity and lend moral support. Politicians and VIPs came, too. The school premises began to crawl with security personnel. Armed police manned the gates, recording every visit and visitor, date, day, time of entry and departure, and the visitor's relation with the victim if any.

To the sufferers, however, all the media attention, their near prison-like conditions, the high security, all this seemed to be part of some elaborate façade: one that screamed aloud that it is *they* who were the culprits, it is *they* who were the perpetrators of the heinous crime. It was the hunted being called the hunter. The oppressed, the oppressor.

Makaru reached the relief camp without difficulty. He registered himself as an acquaintance of Chitrasen Suna, at least, that is what he thought he had written in the visitor's register, and entered the school premises.

The tumultuous scenes that unfolded before his eyes upon arrival at the camp, however, were not what he was expecting. The place looked like a cattle fair.

Makaru set about looking for Chitra dada. What he witnessed broke his heart, for he found not one, but many Chitra dadas. Here he was, having somehow smothered his emotions into silence, having come all the way to console the only person he knew somewhat in this chaos of humans. But how could he have possibly known that the actual trauma of the victims was a thousand-fold greater than what he could even begin to imagine?

The atmosphere in the camp laden with shock, outrage and grief hanging in the air like hundreds of needle-sharp stalactites rendered him speechless. His words dried up from the tip of his tongue. His limbs felt heavy, leaden and numb. Not knowing what to do, Makaru went and sat down in a corner of the school veranda.

He noticed a small group of people huddled there, talking softly among themselves. Possibly visitors who had come to lend their sympathies, they were animatedly discussing in hushed whispers how grievously the Ganas had been wronged, the inhumanity of the perpetrators of the arson, the pitiable condition of the victims, and the grave injustice of it all. While Makaru agreed with them wholeheartedly, he did not join them or take part in the discussion. He sat apart in stunned silence.

What could he have said anyway? Such atrocities unmasked in all its ugly banal nakedness the animal hatred rooted deep in so-called modern civil society. So crude, so loathsome, so bone-chillingly evil that it gnawed away at one's soul. The same cold-blooded caste hatred that had riddled the perpetrators' souls and fouled them from within had also stripped its victims bare—not only of their shelter, their sustenance and dignity, but of their faith in humanity. With his clouded mind, grieving soul and bleeding heart, what could Makaru have possibly said that could have solaced these poor people?

Nothing.

At times like these, when the hatred of one people for another people scorched the very soul, it is empathy and compassion that holds humankind together. And true compassion cannot be heard. It can only be felt.

Makaru's eyes silently scanned his surroundings, searching for Chitra-da. He finally found him sitting alone in a corner.

All of six feet when he stood upright in his wiry, muscular frame, Chitra Suna was a handsome man, wheatish in complexion, with a thick mane of curls parted neatly on the left, and lips that always had a smile lingering on them. He was sixty-five, but could legitimately pass for someone twenty years younger. With a deep baritone and a dignified bearing, he was a frank and forthright orator who always put forth his words with conviction.

But now, he was almost unrecognisable.

A listless skeletal shell of his former self with empty, unseeing eyes, his chapped lips sewn shut, as if he was stranded on an island of brutal silence amidst a raging sea of emotions. His towering frame bent, as if under a terrible burden, as if he wanted to dissolve into nothing and disappear forever. His movements minimal and slow, as if laden with agony. His eyes glazed, brimming with all that he yearned to say and yet couldn't.

Like a long-forgotten, fragile, dusty masterpiece of an artist discovered years later, or someone seen in the delirium of fever, Makaru felt wary of approaching Chitra-da, lest he broke and crumbled on touch, or vanished altogether.

As he walked hesitantly towards the old man, their eyes met, and Makaru wordlessly bowed down to touch his feet in greeting. Chitra-da said nothing in return. He simply stared at Makaru, as if in a trance. He laid a heavy hand on Makaru's shoulder and looked up at the heavens wistfully.

Chitra-da's hand slipped down Makaru's shoulder, to his trembling hand, and gripping it firmly he got up and headed towards the gulmohar tree, with Makaru in tow. He sat down on the ground, and Makaru did the same. For tense long moments, there was only a stifling silence.

And then, the dam broke.

Chitra-da's chest heaved as his gaunt body was wracked by harrowing sobs. He let out loud heart-wrenching wails as tears streamed down his distraught eyes, vainly trying to douse the fires raging in his heart. His soul seemed to drown in grief, sinking to a bottomless void beyond the point of return.

Gasping between sobs, he said, "They have destroyed us, Makaru. They...they have ruined us. Reduced everything to ashes. Everything...our homes, our belongings, our possessions... everything. We lost everything. They ruined us, Makaru, they ruined us." His wrinkled cheeks were awash with tears as his face contorted in grief.

Try as he might, Makaru couldn't bring himself to speak. Every word that came to his tongue melted away, dwarfed by the magnitude of grief confronting him.

Having held on all this while, finally Makaru gave in and he let his soul embrace the pain. The pain witnessed, felt and experienced through the eyes of another, distant, and yet so close. He, too, started weeping.

He let his tears flow freely, unashamed. Flow like the tears of the man who sat beside him, drowning in his anguish, mourning his loss. Makaru let his mangled psyche consume his soul and let his pain become one with that of the victims, the survivors.

He had come here to console, but here he was, weeping like every other heartbroken soul, in need of consolation himself. But there was nothing more he could do. His tears wouldn't stop now. And he did not want to stop them. He too was human after all, and seeing others like him suffering and grieving made his heart long to join theirs in grief and become one with them. He cried and cried and cried, begging for the fierce ache in his heart and soul to ease just a little, but it did not.

And so he let his tears flow and mingle with those of Chitrada as they sat together under the gulmohar tree, in shared grief.

Thirteen

Remember Makaru's grandfather?

They were three brothers.

The middle one was Chitrasen Suna's grandfather.

He had migrated to Lathore from Banjipali a long time ago, when barely twenty or twenty-five-odd families had settled there. He started working as the village chowkidar, and was responsible for performing a range of tasks, such as announcing the beheran, relaying news to the government offices, disposing of the carcasses of cattle, birds, street dogs and the like. As the income from these jobs would often fall short in providing sustenance for his family, he would also work as a labourer.

Chitrasen's grandfather had three sons. When they grew up, the eldest took up the job of chowkidar from his father. The other two sons also found decent means of earning to support their respective families.

Now, the Gana community had a custom. When the children attained maturity and got married, they would move out of their parents' home to start life anew. What was significant was that this custom applied to both sons and daughters. So when Chitrasen's father got married and had to move out, he had to struggle to find an independent source of livelihood. After some thought, he and his wife settled on grazing goats and sheep.

Their 'job' entailed some basic tasks fixed into a simple daily routine. Come dawn, Chitrasen's parents would go to the homes of their employers and bring out their goats and sheep from their shelters. Then they would set off for the woods, where the animals would be left to munch contentedly on foliage glistening with dew sparkling in the rays of the morning sun. Having ensured that the animals had their stomachs full, the couple would lead them all back to their respective sheds. Then, they would begin their rounds around late noon, going to every house with a large bowl in hand, asking for their daily wages, which in local parlance was called *gani*.

Now you may ask, what was this gani? A local currency? A slang for a few coins or notes? No. It was the leftovers served to the goatherds in their begging bowls on the whims of their employers. They would dump whatever surplus food was left from the day's afternoon meal or the night before, or any edibles they wished to dispose of, in their outstretched vessels.

As the sun sank contentedly into the arms of the waiting clouds, painting the sky in rich hues of amber and bronze, the pair would repeat the process again: taking the animals out to graze, bringing them back safely to their respective spots, and going around asking for gani as alms. No matter how much their feet hurt, no matter how far they walked into the woods to ensure that the animals ate their fill, all they got as 'income' at the end of the day was food, a mere instrument of sustenance. It was a painful and pitiable existence, yet something they had to make do with.

There was nothing pleasant or alluring about grazing goats and sheep; on the contrary the disadvantages and hardships were too many to count. One of the unspoken rules of this occupation was that one had to be regular, since the animals had to be fed everyday. This meant that one had to disregard any other matter or eventuality that might pose an obstacle to being punctual, even if it meant ignoring a piercing headache or a bout of high fever. Also, there were always hungry predators that stalked the woods, and that could at any moment make an unsuspecting goat their unfortunate prey. The very prospect of an encounter with a wild carnivore would frighten anyone. But Chitrasen's parents were immune to it; for they had not only experienced such encounters, they had even engaged in nail-biting skirmishes with hungry beasts in order to protect the domestic animals entrusted to their care, at the cost of their own lives. What frightened them far more was the prospect of losing even one of these goats and sheep, treasured by their owners, for that could not only deprive them of their meal of the day, but also their job. And there had been times that this dreaded situation had manifested in reality, earning them harsh punishments from their employers and resulting in meetings of the beheran.

When Chitrasen was five years old, something happened in Lathore that changed the face of the village forever.

A number of Marwaris had been steadily arriving on the serene village landscape over the years. These foreign business and trading communities came armed with money and brass and bronze utensils to trade with. At first they would traverse the village on foot, going from household to household, exchanging vessels for money. Then, as they got a little better-off, they would go around on bicycles laden with vessels. Eventually, they would employ errand boys for the purpose.

However, straightforward business in metal goods and utensils wasn't the Marwaris' only route to a better life. As a side business, which, mind you, they invested more in, they started entering into agreements with the villagers to pawn their gold, silver and lands in exchange for some money in times of need. They would typically carry out their pawning and money-lending business in the village *haat* or at other places of personal convenience.

This itself could not have been such a bad thing, wouldn't you say?

Well, it was.

The Marwaris could not have disguised their entrepreneurial cunning for long. Much cannot be said about the community as a whole, but those who had come to the village with the hopes of finding prosperity were definitely shrewd to the bone. Exploiting the illiteracy of the naive rural folk, in the absence of any school in Lathore, they started pinning ridiculous amounts of interest onto the borrowers, making it practically impossible for the money borrowed to be paid back. The arbitrarily fixed cumulative rates of interest would come to such absurdly monstrous figures as compared to the measly dwarf-like principle sums that the poor duped villagers would end up losing all their jewellery or lands that they had pawned in exchange for financial aid. In sharp contrast, the money-lenders started building bungalows and *kothis* that reeked of the wealth they had unfairly amassed.

As the lives and lifestyles of the Marwaris grew more affluent, the villagers were pushed deeper and deeper into the pit of poverty and the trap of mounting debts. The opulence of one at the expense of another's want and deprivation was built on the façade of an honest business that hid in its treacherous depths deception and falsehood guised as entrepreneurial acumen and helping a fellow villager in times of need.

But then again, was this anything new?

The Marwaris, who had acquired the name of 'Seths', expanded their businesses further over time. They would exchange everyday items like salt, cereals and clothes for forest products like latex, resin, *mahua* and *char*, and pulses like *moong* and *biri* or black gram. They would then send them off in truckloads to distant lands, selling them at higher rates than they had bought them. Needless to say, this brought in vast amounts of wealth.

Over time, this practice became commonplace in the village. People here still depended mainly on exchanging forest produce for most of their daily needs and the barter system prevailed over the exchange of cash, which most villagers had little or no access to anyway.

It was therefore no surprise that Chitrasen's household embraced this system as well. Like the others, they too collected forest produce to exchange in return for groceries from the Marwaris. One fine day, Chitra's mother set off as usual for Ratan Seth's house with a basket of dried mahua flowers to barter for some salt. What she could not have anticipated, however, was the alluring offer that was coming her way.

Ratan Seth was an observant and astute man. He could size up every villager who came to him for exchange from their bearing and conduct, spoken and unspoken, their little tell-tale gestures, and gauge them with his shrewd entrepreneurial eye.

He was always on the lookout for a chance to profit from any opportunity that might present itself to him in any form. Ratan Seth had been observing Chitra's mother for past some time now, and he could vouch for the fact that she could hold her own in the sphere of business. He found her to be clever and firm, traits that were desirable in the industry he came from. So, it was not surprising when he gave her an offer to join him in the barter business. "Take some salt from me and go barter it in the village. In exchange, you can get me latex, tree gum, and other forest goods that the villagers offer. I guarantee that it will be profitable, and we can divide the surplus money amongst ourselves."

The offer wasn't bad. Salt was, after all, a necessity in every hearth. And the whole village was actively engaged in exchanging forest produce anyway. The only problem was the livestock grazing that she was engaged in. So Chitra's mother decided to trust her better half with the job alone, and to take up the Seth's offer. After all, he promised actual cash, while all she had ever got from grazing goats was stale leftovers.

So, with a bamboo basket laden with salt on her head, she would set off for the village, looking for customers. To her surprise, she never had to really persuade anyone to buy salt. She would be finished with her basket for the day without having to actively look for a customer. In fact, some days she got so lucky that she would have to make a beeline for Ratan Seth's house without even visiting all the villages that had been chalked out for her, for she would run out of salt early in the day. She would then sell the forest goods she had collected to the Marwari in return for some cash. This became a daily practice that benefited both Chitra's mother and her new employer.

This barter business was easily more profitable than the cattle grazing that she had slogged at for years. On top of that, the one basket of salt that she set off with was not enough to meet the needs of the adjacent villages. So, she decided to bring along her husband too. He readily left the job of grazing animals, and joined her on her daily journeys. While his wife would carry one basket on her head, he would carry two on a *bhar*. Granted that they would have to cover a couple of extra kilometres, but years of walking long distances in rain or sun with a group of animals in tow had rendered them immune to the fatigue of arduous journeys on foot. Despite selling thrice as much as they did before, they still ran out of salt, riding high on profits. Saving up judiciously, they put their hard-earned money to good use and bought a bullock cart to ease their travels.

They started frequenting the weekly haat, expanding their dominion further. It was literally raining profits on them, but there was one setback. Being illiterates, they were unable to calculate or know exactly how much money they had. This made Chitra's parents realise the importance of literacy, and hence they took the wise decision to send their children to school.

Their oldest son had already been appointed a halia, so they sent their middle son to school. Investing the most they could afford, which tested their financial limits, they sent him off to Kantabanji, miles away from Lathore.

This middle son happened to be Chitrasen.

And that is how our Chitrasen ended up staying in Kantabanji and studying in a hostel there. Far from home, he would naturally look for boys of his own kind, but he found none. That was because most people of his community were extremely poor, and could not afford to send their children to study, not even to the local school. As a result, Chitra found himself alone among the upper castes there.

He took with him a small tin box, two aluminium plates, one aluminium *lota*, two *kanthaa*s, and two pairs of pants and shirts. He eagerly looked forward to a new experience. But all he got was isolation and ridicule. He was given a grubby corner to sleep in, which nobody would pass by. He was told to start eating only when the others had finished with their food in the mess, and after he had eaten he would also have to clean his own utensils, which proved a difficult task for the small boy initially. And then, there was the perennial well situation. He was not allowed to draw water from it himself, and could only get some if a kind soul passing by poured some water for him purely on their whim. He couldn't even drink water when he was thirsty. At times, his classmates would perversely test his patience by deliberately refusing to give him water, which infuriated Chitra no end.

The rice served in the hostel mess was coarse and tasteless, and the *dal* runnier than Chitra's nose when he caught a cold. Sometimes, just to break the monotony, the children residing in the hostel would chop and toss some raw tomatoes, onions and green chillies in mustard oil to prepare a simple but tasty side-dish to go with the tasteless meal. Chitra, however, was not so fortunate. Being an untouchable, he was forbidden from entering the school kitchen, leave alone touching the kitchen *chulha*, so he would have to make do with whatever food the school gave him.

Chitra was supposed to follow certain rules in school that applied only to him, reason being his caste. Number one, he must never cast his shadow near the school's kitchen. Number two, he must never sit just anywhere in the line when they were being served food in the mess, but should go and sit at the very end. Number three, there was no way he could pick a fight with anyone for that would involve brawls, and touching anyone was a big no-no. Number four, he had to sit right at the back of the classroom, where no teacher even cast a glance and minimum interactions occurred. Number five, he could never even dream of drawing water from the well himself, because...well, he just could not.

But, despite all the difficulties that he faced, Chitra still managed to continue with his studies till high school. He was acutely conscious of the fact that he was from a lower caste and would always keep a low profile. He would meekly submit to every command, every taunt, every insult thrown his way without reacting, no matter how hurtful they might be. He taught himself to turn a deaf ear to all derogatory comments aimed at him, despite the fact that it made rage crawl up his bones. He went out of his way to avoid getting into any kind of arguments and altercations, no matter what the provocation, and would accept whatever opinion the opposite party would thrust on him.

But as Chitra grew older, he gained maturity. He was able to think and judge better for himself, and he began to analyse all the absurd irrational biases against him, only because of his caste. With that, an inner voice grew. A voice that told him to struggle, to rebel. To silence these biases. He no longer wanted to be a pushover or remain silent. He wanted to fight.

It was a public holiday during summer. The teachers had asked the hostellers to clean up the school premises. Accordingly, the students set about weeding the greens, trimming the grass and clearing the gutters. Chitra, naturally, was a part of all this activity it too. After the work was done, covered with dirt, hot and hungry, the boys were eager to take a bath and have food. They washed their utensils at the well and they bathed there, too. Poor Chitra alone had to go to the village pond, some distance away, for his bath. He patiently waited for someone to come and pour some water for him so he could wash his dishes, and then go have his bath. Much to his dismay, however, everyone was too busy to even spare him a glance.

Chitra was fuming now. He was already late for mess for he had to walk the extra mile to the pond. He could have put up with that, but what kind of brutish behaviour was this? He was human too, and he had as much right to use the well as the others, lower caste or not. Despite that, he had patiently waited for these useless fellows to pour him some water. And what had he got in return? Nothing! Boiling with rage, Chitra stomped to the well, drew water in the bucket, and washed his utensils vigorously, scrubbing them clean. While he was at it, he decided to bathe there, too—and why not? Having tasted a victory of sorts for the first time, he set off triumphantly for the school mess for his lunch.

This news spread like wildfire through the school. There was a hue and cry. The other students were angry. Many didn't think twice before hurling vicious abuses at Chitra. The hostel superintendent arrived on the scene and called for an urgent meeting.

And then there was Chitrasen.

Having carried out such a heroic act on impulse, Chitrasen was now beginning to regret it. So far-reaching were the repercussions of his actions that a meeting had been called in his name. What were the authorities discussing? Would they suspend him? Or worse, banish him from the school forever? No, no. This could not be happening! If his education was stopped midway due to rash behaviour on his part, his father would not be pleased. No, he would probably beat him to death.

Oh lord, now what should he do?

The hostel superintendent set about interrogating some boys to get the full details of the matter. Unsurprisingly, many boys expressed their strong discontent with this incident, even suggesting that brutal measures be taken against Chitra. However, some students also came out in his support, admitting honestly that they were, in fact, as much to be blamed, for they were the ones who had not poured out the water for him to wash his utensils, when he had been waiting for them to do so with the utmost patience.

The superintendent took all of this into account. He thought about the matter very carefully. If he announced Chitra as guilty, that would deem the well water to have been polluted, which would then require a thorough cleaning and purification by a pandit. That was too much work and involved expense besides. And then, the residents here were all children after all, and surely the caste rules did not apply to them so strictly. So, what harm would it do to just dismiss the whole matter?

Having acknowledged this train of thoughts, the hostel superintendent finally declared Chitra innocent. He admonished Chitra's classmates for not having helped him with such a mundane task, and said that they were equally to be blamed for what happened. He then recounted how Chitra had consistently been a model student, and that even now he had broken the code of conduct only because he was in dire need. The superintendent concluded the meeting by asking Chitra to ask for forgiveness. Chitra complied with evident relief and assured them that he would never repeat his actions again.

From that day on, Chitra gained a newfound confidence.

There is another incident he recalled from that time that brought with it countless unvoiced emotions.

During his hostel days, Chitra had a classmate named Nataraj Bedbak. Coming from a well-to-do family, Nataraj was one arrogant brat, forever boasting about his family wealth and whatnot. It didn't help that he was an upper-caste Brahmin as well. His affluence and class were prominently displayed in his clothes, and he was the only one in their batch who wore sandals.

Now, Nataraj had one exasperating habit: every time that he would pass Chitra, anywhere, he would always pull Chitra's hair. He derived sadistic pleasure from seeing Chitra hiss in startled pain and would grin like an idiot at the scowl of displeasure on Chitra's face. Chitra had time and time again told Nataraj not to do this. But he also had reason to believe that just the sight of his long hair worked like some sort of catalyst for Nataraj, who could not resist this annoying repetitive childish prank every time he saw him.

Chitra's long hair was not his fault. The local barber refused to touch his hair, much less give him a haircut. So he depended entirely on his father to trim his unruly mane. But since he seldom visited his village, that wasn't much of an option either. In short, his hair was bound to grow long whether he liked it or not.

One day, Chitra was going about his usual routine when he unfortunately happened to cross paths with Nataraj. Nataraj, of course, immediately turned to make a grab at Chitra's hair. But Chitra had had enough—he swiftly caught hold of the perpetrator's hand to stop him from yanking at his mane. Nataraj was stunned. Never in his wildest dreams had he imagined that a Dalit boy would dare to even think of touching him, a Brahmin. Despite this, Nataraj actually had the nerve to extend his hand again, with renewed determination, to pull his habitual prank. To his greater surprise, not only did his victim-to-be dodge him, this time Chitra also pushed him so hard that he fell.

Nataraj Bedbak was flabbergasted.

Ungracefully sprawled on the ground, he risked a quick glance at the pack of onlookers who had gathered, and realised they were all laughing at him. A shot of red-hot anger burst through him. Nataraj got up somewhat clumsily, and came and punched Chitra hard, right on his chin. Chitra's head reeled for moments, but he quickly regained composure and came back at his opponent, raining blows on him one after another, blows that only got angrier. Poor Nataraj was getting the beating of his life! But no one came forward to help him, for they knew of his mean and vicious ways.

Finally, having beaten him to his satisfaction, Chitra pulled himself away from Nataraj. On his part, Nataraj, too, realised how angry his repeated prank would have made Chitra over time, and having realised his mistake, he decided for once to extend a friendly hand. Once again, he was surprised when Chitra took his hand, if somewhat hesitantly at first, then held it firmly in his, and a slow smile spread on his lips as he agreed to be his *meeta*.

To say that the onlookers, fellow students from the school, were astonished would be an understatement. They were incredulous. They simply couldn't wrap their heads around the fact that a Dalit would even think of beating up a Brahmin, much less act upon it. They genuinely appreciated Chitra's courage to stand up for himself. After the well water incident, Chitra had already gained some popularity. Now, after this episode, his social stature grew considerably. The other boys started seeing him differently and somewhat more respectfully, as a human being like themselves, and they stopped throwing hurtful and derogatory comments at him. Observing this, even the teachers refrained from taunting him because of his caste. From then on, Chitra was allowed to participate in all school events like everyone else.

Chitra was actually quite good at sports. In fact, he was phenomenal at football. So much so that in the seventh grade he found himself enrolled in the school football team as the most sought-after player. So praiseworthy were his skills and dexterity on the field that his absence would cast a foreshadow of gloom on the team during matches. Forget the students, even the school headmaster enjoyed watching Chitra play.

The dreadful year of 1965 inched around the corner. The year of erratic monsoons and chaotic rains. Then the drought arrived in its full monstrosity, the parched earth cracked, the crops wilted, and along with them the people and livestock. The farmers and agricultural labourers were hit the worst. Stranded amidst a crisis with no resources to fall back upon, they were forced to migrate to the cities to look for means of sustenance. They were forced to sell off what little silver jewellery and brass and bronze utensils they possessed to the Seths for meagre sums. They also had to mortgage not only their cattle and livestock but even their homestead and land for money. But as the gloom continued to bleed into the long year, they failed to pay their interests and had to part with their land altogether. The Seths basked in the glory of their newly-acquired lands and turned haughty landowners. The poor were reduced to begging and scavenging. Poverty and hunger compelled them to collect bamboo rice from the forests and eat it to survive. As more and more people started resorting to working as cheap labour for income, the competition increased and daily wages fell further.

The salt trade of Chitra's parents stalled. They couldn't send Chitra's school fees anymore. And so Chitra had to leave his education halfway through ninth grade, and with a heavy heart, he returned home.

But then, a glimmer of hope shone through.

Back then, the police were recruiting tall and strong boys for the posts of constables and home guards. The DSP of Kantabanji police station had once seen Chitrasen playing football. So he gave Chitra's father an open offer to have him join the police force. But Chitra refused. Having grown up seeing the Marwari Seths amass huge amounts of wealth, he was drawn towards the business industry, and in continuing the trade that his parents had started.

Chitra already had a keen interest in business and trade. Now that he was forced to drop out of school, he took the plunge and joined his mother in the salt business. He would undertake long, arduous journeys, travelling from haat to haat. Proud of how quick her son was with accounting and calculations, his mother was happy with the investments and sacrifices they had made for his education, getting its worth back at a time of crisis.

If school had taught Chitra to be book-smart, this business taught him to be street-smart. Soon, Chitra knew all the neighbouring areas in and around his village like the back of his hand and had memorised the topography by heart. He became better acquainted with the villagers they used to deal with, and more aware of his surroundings. Regular interactions with the Seths also presented him with opportunities to observe their social mannerisms and entrepreneurial etiquette, something he tried to bring into his own dealings with customers.

A certain Seth used to frequent the marketplace. He would come along with his servants and two of his men—one in charge of weighing the goods and the other, of making the payments—to buy produce like wheat, char, mahua, groundnut, and so on from the villagers. Now, despite the fact that all the villagers would duly line up with their produce before this Seth, he would not hesitate to dupe them. So the villagers would invariably get much less than what their goods were actually worth. But in their fear of the powerful and intimidating Seth, and the rush of other customers scrambling to make a deal, they would accept whatever sum was offered without complaint or bargaining. Most of the villagers left disheartened, with no one to speak up for them.

Seeing all this troubled Chitra. Having witnessed first-hand the unjust treatment of the naïve villagers, he decided that it was time things must change. Determined to transform the lopsided and exploitative system of commerce, he resolved to join the market himself as a mediator on behalf of his people, quote the right amounts for their produce to the Seth, and make sure that they got their worth.

It was a well-thought out decision. After all, Chitra knew the villages and its villagers, and they in turn felt far more comfortable with him than with the Marwaris, and they trusted him. One catch was that Chitra himself also had to depend a little on the Seths, but that was alright. At the crack of dawn, he would set off for the villages he had mapped out and collect all the forest goods, grains and cereals that the villagers would hand over to him. He would segregate them and pack them carefully into different sacks himself. Then he would leave them at the home of a trustworthy villager. By then, it would already be nightfall.

The next day, he would collect all the entrusted sacks and take them to the Seths to be priced. This way, he could bargain and earn a reasonable sum for the goods. Whatever marginal profits there would be, he would keep for himself. The villagers were content, for they no longer had to physically visit the Seths to sell their produce, and what they earned was much more as well. The Seths were satisfied, for they got their goods in bulk, and no longer had to pay to have them segregated and packed.

Gradually, Chitra's hard work paid off and he prospered in this business, so much so that his parents left their little salt trade and came over to join him. People started believing that Lakshmi, the goddess of wealth herself, was presiding over his business.

Chitra started saving up, and, in due course of time, he saved enough to enable him to build a decent, spacious house for his family, in place of the tumbledown hut they lived in. Chitra's was a success story that even the Seths acknowledged and respected him for.

When Chitra got married, he organised two feasts, one for his own Dalit people, and another for the upper-caste villagers. The first one was held at his own home, where they were served mutton and country liquor, while the latter was organised in the schoolroom, which he paid for. People enjoyed the festivities and remembered his marriage for a long time to come.

Chitrasen's family did not own any cultivable land. After his business prospered, he decided to buy some land, because land would earn them respect and could reap rich returns. Thinking along these lines, he confided his desire to his parents. Of course, they were more than happy with his decision. And that is how our Chitra bought ten acres of land.

Now, he started managing his time so as to devote some of it to agriculture. According to the seasons, apart from paddy, he started growing a variety of vegetables like tomato, *kankada*, eggplant and chillies. Selling these in the markets earned him a good supplementary income.

The dusty roads of the village turned into pucca thoroughfares. Instead of a cart, Chitra invested in a jeep, to which he attached a trolley. This ensured both ease of commuting and carting his farm produce from one village to another without difficulty. This investment was well-made, and brought in additional profits. He also appointed one representative each in the villages that he did business in.

And so, the name of Chitrasen Suna started ascending higher and higher on the mountains of success. He began to be treated as one of the more respected members of the village.

Chitra's nephews were a bunch of good-for-nothings. Out of the kindness of his heart, he decided to help them by employing them in his business. But his nephews did not follow his principle of work is worship as diligently as he did. They only wanted to do work that was 'dignified' according to them, not hard physical labour. Naturally, they did not do as well as they wished to, or even as Chitra wished them to, for that matter.

When Chitrasen's first son was born, he celebrated the occasion with much pomp, surpassing what any member of his community had ever done, as they usually do not have the resources to hold a feast so grand. He also performed the *ekoisa* of his son, following Aryan customs. He called in a *kirtan* troupe to perform during the day, while the priest did the *homa*. At night, a Satyanarayan puja was held and a tent was set up in front of his house where a *pala* was performed.

Chitra also went the extra mile and employed an upper-caste cook so that everyone could heartily enjoy the puja meal. Needless to say, everyone enjoyed the food and praised Chitra for the arrangements. Usually when a child is born in the Dalit community, a ritual ceremony called the *aaenkh phuka* is performed to celebrate the birth where a few women of the community are called and served some *khiri* and *puri*, and, if possible, the head of the baby is tonsured.

It seemed that Chitra's first born was his lucky charm, and after the infant's arrival, his father's business expanded even more.

Once the government had built a network of roads, and the surrounding villages were well-connected by concrete thoroughfares, Chitra, upon his fellow villagers' suggestion, decided to invest in a new business venture. He bought a second-hand bus to ferry passengers around, employed a bus driver, and appointed his nephew as the conductor. This endeavour took off, and so well that Chitra decided to bring in two more buses, this time brand new, to meet the increasing demand of the passengers.

Humans are known to be haughty and fickle beings. Just one small improvement in their lives, one tiny step up the ladder, and they let it go to their heads. But there are some exceptional individuals who, regardless of how high they may rise in life, always stay humble and true to their roots. Chitrasen Suna was one of them. No matter how much wealth and social stature he acquired, he remained modest, approachable and affable. He remained just the same. If there was any change in him at all, it was his age. His hair was now peppered with grey.

Chitra had no bad habits and no substance abuse. All he was accustomed to was a cup of black tea in the morning. That too he had at the village tea stall, where he would meet up with friends and exchange the day's news, discuss politics and corruption and other current issues of interest.

During one such session, the incumbent panchayat sarpanch, who was a Marwari, brought up how enormously challenging it was to be a leader. He told his audience that they could invest in hundreds of business ventures and reap rich returns every time, but they could never experience the heady power of being at the top in politics. They could never be political leaders, he claimed. Chitrasen was somewhat piqued when he heard this. A spark of determination ignited itself within him, and he said that, if he really chose to, he could become sarpanch, too. Despite the jeers from the Marwari, he decided to enter the political fray.

Then, Chitra set about in earnest preparing to contest elections. He was already accustomed to visiting his neighbouring villages for buying and selling supplies. All his clientele knew him well and trusted him. So it was not difficult for him to approach them and to convey his desire to become the future sarpanch. Sharing some of the principles that underlined his work and outlining the projects that he planned to undertake in the village, he encouraged people to vote for him.

And, when the election results were out, Chitra won. He was crowned the sarpanch, not just once, but thrice in a row. He worked hard to justify the responsibility and power of his post, and he pleased the people with his just ruling. The villagers still remembered his tenure as the golden period.

Lathore may have been a small village, but it was near the railway tracks and it was connected to big cities like Raipur and Waltair. This meant that businesses had considerable scope of growing. Lathore, as a whole, prospered. True, the Marwaris were still the richest people around, but other communities like that of the Bhulias who were weavers also flourished.

As the number of rich people in the locality grew, they decided to invest in building a school. The Marwaris and Bhulias contributed generously to the project. Many boys and girls enrolled themselves and, over time, the school built a reputation for itself in the area. Encouraged by this, the villagers decided to build a college as well. Chitra-da was invited for all important occasions, gatherings and decisions, for he was a widely respected figure. No village meeting could take place without Chitra-da's presence.

It takes years to build a good reputation, but just a second to ruin it. For people are more easily convinced about the vices of others, but withhold themselves from trusting in another's goodness. But this trust was something that Chitra had earned. With his relentless hard work, his sincerity, his integrity and his generosity, he had earned a name for himself among the people as someone whom they could always turn to for help.

This same Chitra-da was the one who had lost everything, whose dignity had been toyed with, whose home and assets were now in ruins. The man who had always spoken his mind with clarity and conviction was now so disoriented that he could barely utter intelligible words. The one whom everyone turned to for help now sat listlessly on the ground, helpless.

Makaru so badly wanted to jolt Chitra out of this state and to somehow end the despair he was engulfed in. But he could not. He wanted to say, "Da, shall we go and see your house?" But the words stubbornly sat at the tip of his tongue, refusing to tumble out. So Makaru remained silent.

Makaru's blood boiled to see Chitra-da in this state.

Chitrasen Suna had indeed been undone.

Fourteen

Slow, reluctant steps masked the pounding heartbeats that threatened to propel their hearts out of their chests as Chitra and Makaru walked away from the camp, the blood in their ears roaring louder than their anxiety hollering at them to turn back.

They stopped at the *gudi*, the mud hut of the Pardeshen goddess. The villagers believed the goddess to be a powerful deity and worshipped her in good times and bad.

The goddess was known by many names: Pardeshen, Bastren, Pendragadian, Luhagadian. According to legend, Patna (then called Pataliputra) defeated the kingdom of Bastar (the Kakatiyas) in 1600 AD. Following this, the king of Patna adopted the goddess of Bastar, Ma Danteshwari, as his own deity. His subjects emulated him and they started worshipping her as well.

As Ma Danteshwari was brought from foreign lands, they started calling her Pardeshen. She was called Bastren after the land of her origin, Bastar. And she came to be named Luhagadian as it was believed she could protect anyone whom she possessed even from the injury of an iron weapon; if the mortal she chose to possess and reside in was stabbed with an iron sword, he remained unscathed even after it was removed from his body.

Chitra paid a full obeisance to the goddess even as he wailed out in anguish, "What did you do, Ma? What did you do? What sin did we commit that you punished us so? They attacked us and rendered us homeless. Why didn't you save us, Ma?" There was a sense of grim determination in his emotional and personal prayer to the deity that seemed almost audacious, as if he would refuse to get up until justice was served, or until Ma Danteshwari herself appeared before him to answer his questions.

As Chitra's prayers became more fervent, something stirred within Makaru. He wished to physically witness this destruction, this calamity that had befallen his people. But he didn't have the heart to ask Chitra to accompany him. What if revisiting the site affected Chitra-da adversely, did something terrible to him? What if his heart burst at the sight of his burnt house? No, Makaru would not risk it. So he set off alone, to see what had once been the Dalit basti he used to live in.

And so, leaving Chitra sobbing at the Pardeshen gudi, Makaru set off for Ganapada. All along, he felt an uncanny sensation tingling his spine, as if he was walking on a pile of dry bones and his feet were refusing to move forward. An eerie tension hung in the air; the silence was deafening. But as he saw the upper-caste people going about all their activities as usual, he couldn't help but feel disgusted and angry at how normal it all felt, how content and calm they all seemed. One was scratching his eardrum, another was cleaning his teeth with *gudaku*, a third was contentedly sipping his tea. Makaru felt wronged, betrayed. How could one world look so tranquil and put together when another had been ripped to shreds?

As closely as Makaru was taking in his surroundings, he himself wanted to be invisible to all eyes. As he walked around, people glanced curiously at the newcomer. Of course, there was no one there who recognised him, or knew where he came from. They were simply acknowledging his presence as he walked past them. But, to Makaru, it felt as if their eyes were piercing his soul, reading him like an open book. Even if one were to bring before him the gauntia's grandson, whose head Makaru had been accused of cracking open, even he would have failed to recognise this man as his former "attacker". For, Makaru had grown old and looked nothing like the scrawny boy who had left this village years ago. But this reasoning was beyond Makaru. He couldn't help but feel uneasy thinking that sooner or later someone would recognise him, and he would be subjected to the same treatment he had been given decades ago, that had compelled him and his parents to leave the village.

But, as Makaru fell into the rhythm of putting one leg after the other, he felt his emotions bubbling angrily like a potion brewing in a cauldron. Why must he feel so self-conscious? Why must he cower before these heartless excuses for human beings when he was the one who should be sizing them up? Who knows, perhaps it was one of them who had lit the flames that burnt down his basti. He could picture them viciously plotting the destruction of his brothers and sisters, and cackling like chimpanzees at the end of it. He had done nothing wrong, committed no crime. Steeling himself, he broadened his chest and continued walking, his eyes looking ahead, his head held high.

He felt as if he was standing at the edge of a cliff, being drawn uncontrollably, inexorably towards the abyss. All his emotions, his anxious anticipation were coming to a climactic end, like a huge tide about to swallow him whole and drown him. All that he had thought, envisioned, imagined and feared would soon be right in front of his eyes, whether he wished to see it or not. Would the situation be better than what he had imagined? Or worse?

Makaru wished that he had never found out.

But he did. And what he saw tore him into pieces.

As he reached the basti, he didn't know where to look. For there was nothing to look at. Everything was reduced to grey ash and black soot that one would thoughtlessly walk over. He choked on his emotions, a scream ripping through his soul, threatening to break through his lips as he looked around at the devastation.

Nothing had been spared.

How could human beings inflict so much brutality on one another? And what kind of brutality was this? It was beyond inhuman. His eyes were numb with disbelief at what lay before them.

Makaru's unsettled mind turned back again to an innocent time when, on winter mornings when bitingly chilly winds would blow, the children would light up tiny bonfires to keep themselves warm and huddle around it. They would put out the fire before leaving by stomping on the embers, leaving an insignificant pile of soot in place of the crackling flames.

But, those fires were not like this one.

These flames were not part of some innocent children's bonfire. These fires were rooted in feelings of irrational disgust, resentment, fear and loathing that one community harboured for another. These rose higher than the sky, surpassing the clouds of humanity and the horizon of compassion. These diabolic flames had burned down entire houses and every possession that their inhabitants held dear, and their embers were still smouldering arrogantly, as if mocking onlookers on behalf of the tyrants who had lit them.

Barring a couple of houses in the basti, the rest all used earthen tiles. These now lay battered into dust. Makaru knew for one that these tiles, baked in a kiln, could not just crumble to dust in a fire. Careful examination would have revealed that they were probably smashed using heavy rods and clubs before setting the houses on fire. The explicit destruction was there for everyone to see, but Makaru could also see how the perpetrators had struck a deep blow to the dignity and pride of his people.

The Dalits of Odisha and adjoining Chhattisgarh were experts at crafting earthen tiles. The hard work and skill that went into making these tiles was exceptional and the process was arduous. First, they would choose a special kind of soil and prepare it by stomping on it to get the right consistency for the mixture. Next they would pour the mixture onto wooden frames to get the desired uniform shape and size. Then the fresh tiles would be put out in the sun to dry. These were baked in the kiln at a precise heat and temperature to get the immaculate texture and shade. The colour of a batch of tiles indicated how well they were made. If dark and closer to blackish, it meant the tiles weren't very durable and could crumble or break more easily, while a reddish hue suggested strength and durability, which is what these tiles were known for. Makaru's heart broke to see how those barbarians hadn't spared even their tiles—symbols of their traditional knowledge and skill, their labour, their pride and their identity—now reduced to soot and dust.

As Makaru moved from one house to the other, with every step his heart sank a little deeper into a despair that felt all too familiar. He had come with the intention of gauging the extent of destruction that the upper-caste goons had inflicted on his people. But now that it was before him, he felt overwhelmed by its magnitude, for the damage done was far greater than what met the eye; the wounds inflicted on the soul and spirit were far deeper than the material destruction caused. Each step he took through the pile of rubble only marked his helplessness and mounting anger. He felt numb and stripped of his senses as he stumbled mindlessly through broken walls, half burnt logs of wood, half melted tin boxes, utensils twisted out of shape, half identifiable objects that once belonged. The Lakhe Ghar Samaj had been torn apart and ripped to shreds with such ferocity that it would take years to recover and rebuild itself.

Urging his feet to move on, he came upon an uncanny sight. A few feet away from him was a pile of old dilapidated bicycles thrown recklessly under a now skeletal roof. The shed had probably belonged to a bicycle repair man. Of the cycles once lent for repair, the tyres of several had melted into charred black rubber, leaving the spokes jutting out unceremoniously, like the ribs of a starving beggar pleading for alms. The handles and pedals were twisted. A layer of grubby soot had settled on everything, a noxious mix of rusted metal, burnt leather and rubber, and poisonous carbon particles. The sight eerily reminded him of human corpses, victims of an accident, with limbs twisted, burnt and blackened beyond recognition. Makaru felt the bile rise at the back of his throat, mingled with fury.

As his feet carried him forward, he saw a broken tailoring machine lying outside a partially standing veranda. He considered the painful irony: the instrument that stitched and mended clothes now lay broken, with no one to mend it. If the machine wasn't entirely burnt, the clothes certainly were. Pieces of apparel once fondly treasured by their owners were now blackened rags, clumps of thread and scraps of cloth that crumbled to the touch. Only a few pieces had been spared by some sheer luck, and those were covered in ash and soot.

Moving on, he walked into what was once the front yard of a house. The ground was dotted with dying embers blinking at him in the harsh sunlight. There lay a broken hearth, remnant of a home, a family that had once lived here. A family compelled to abandon their home, with cruel fate breathing down their necks—just like he and his parents had done, all those years ago. Makaru felt his heart clench. His eyes trailed back to the hearth lying in blackened pieces, like his heart. The hearth that once sustained life now lay lifeless because of an irrational hatred churned by some bigots into senseless violence. As Makaru's eyes took in the still smouldering logs that lay above the hearth, another bitter irony brushed past his perturbed mind: the very fire that had given this blessed hearth its origin and its identity had now stolen it back.

The utensils too had been reduced to the same indistinguishable hopeless greyish black mess that now coloured the entire basti. It didn't matter whether it was a bowl, a pan, a ladle or a spoon: all had been rendered misshapen, ugly, useless and vile, just like the vile hatred in the misbegotten perpetrators' hearts. Everything that his eyes registered: cots, tin boxes, pots and whatnot, all lay in a useless pile. He was reminded of a stray dog crushed by a speeding truck, its head smashed, its intestines spilled out of its gut and splattered onto the asphalt. Makaru reeled in sudden nausea.

He felt conflicted. His sickened heart urged him strongly to turn back, but his mind strangely prodded him to go on further. Why did he wish to go further when doing so only made him feel more hopeless and helpless? Unable to think, he mindlessly stumbled ahead.

His eyes fell on the remains of a document lying near an empty tin box, a layer of soft black soot partly covering what was once spotless white paper, its fragments so brittle they would fall apart on touch. One could just make out some letters at the top. Curious, Makaru leaned closer to inspect, and his heart clenched again at what he saw.

It was a land deed.

A piece of paper that had once linked arable lands to a name. A piece of paper that contained a legacy and a history, one that bloodlines waged wars for. A piece of paper that...was now nothing but.

Makaru moved on and spotted the corner of a tattered book peeking out of the rubble. It hadn't really been burnt, but it was not in usable condition either, the pages barely holding on to the frail spine, stomped on by many passing feet. He squinted at the title and barely made out the childish handwritten scrawl that read "*Mo chhabi bahi*": My first picture book. He stooped to pick it up very carefully, gently blew away the dirt and gingerly turned a few pages. Some were missing, others torn. As Makaru held the tattered scrapbook in his hand, he wondered how its owner would have felt had they been standing here in place of him. They would have felt bewildered and surprised. Confused. Hurt.

Angry.

Makaru felt the same. How detested did his people have to be that even their children had to suffer such cruelty? Those monsters didn't even spare a child's primer. Makaru felt his blood boil and everything momentarily stilled. He clenched and unclenched his fists to stop himself from hurling something to the ground or doing something he would regret. Heaving a deep sigh, he let his feet guide him further.

He saw an open fridge, its door barely hanging onto its hinges, and all that was stored in it shrivelled into blackened lumps. Makaru was vaguely reminded of how once a person was burnt after death, one could no longer identify who they had been, unless one had known them. The state of this fridge was such that only its owner would have recognised it.

Suddenly, he caught the smell of burning paddy. He followed it to a storage shed. The place was still full of smoke. As he moved through it, careful not to stumble over debris, his watering, stinging eyes fought with the smoke to register the sight before them. There lay numerous sacks of paddy, some stacked on top of each other, others lying on the ground. Many had been ripped open, with the paddy spilling onto the floor, mingling with the debris. Pale grains of paddy amidst dust, ashes and black soot. A juxtaposition of light and dark.

Good and evil. Life and death.

It looked like someone had stabbed a person brutally, with multiple wounds, wrenching their guts open, leaving them to bleed to death. This meant that the people of the basti were devoid of their sustenance not only for this year but the coming one too. The grains they would have used to sow next year's crop had also been burnt and destroyed.

Makaru felt a lump in his throat as his chest tightened. Those bastards knew what they were doing when they set fire to their harvest.

Then he saw something that made him pause. It was a small hut with its roof destroyed by the fire, but its walls were left intact. This meant that it had not been torched down and destroyed individually, perhaps. This made Makaru feel marginally better and somewhat calmer. As he stepped inside the hut, the air thick with smoke and soot hit his eyes and lungs. Lit by the dying flames, there lay a huge stone in the middle of the hut, with a vermillion trident etched into it. A few earthen lamps and a solitary iron chain lay nearby. Makaru didn't have trouble deciphering what place this was. It was the Gadia Gadapati's gudi.

Gadia Gadapati was the ancestral deity of the Suna clan, which Makaru belonged to. They had been worshipping him since the Suna family had first come and settled down in the village. To think that the sacred place of worship of their ancient deity had been defiled due to a needless clash between two groups.

Two generations ago, Chitra Suna's grandfather had come to settle in Lathore. He had learnt over time to blend in with the place, the people, the social environment, and moulded his person and his life accordingly. This was something he had taught his children, too. Granted that the upper castes went out of their way to avoid touching the Dalits. But, at the end of the day, they were two communities bound by the many inextricable bonds of cohabitation. Over time, they had come to share some of their customs, rituals, emotions, and consequently, their lives. But all it took was one tiny spark to start a fire. Just one small misunderstanding, and those fragile bonds of co-existence had been broken. If given a chance to go back to living together as they used to before, would they? No. For the perpetrators would have guilt eating into their conscience, and the victims would refuse to live with the same people who had wronged them so satanically.

Were the attackers even human? Would they call themselves human? What did humanity even mean? Was it so empty and vile a word that its meaning could be twisted and toyed with any which way, Makaru pondered as he fought the tears brimming in his eyes.

He was jolted out of his thoughts when he abruptly tripped over a low wooden cot that was lying upside down. This wasn't a good omen. In the village, when people died, their corpses were carried away on upturned cots. So a cot kept in this fashion usually signified death. Makaru chuckled humourlessly: perhaps the superstitions were true after all, for his basti had indeed turned into one large cremation ground.

Walking on, he saw an impressive two-storeyed house, standing tall despite the damage done to it. From the outside it seemed to contain several spacious rooms. Makaru guessed that it probably belonged to Chitra-da. It did.

Chitra Suna had accomplished much in his lifetime. One did not catapult to such success in one day. From his humble backgrounds as a goatherd's son, Chitra had come a long way to become the sarpanch. He had put in a lot of toil, effort and resources into building his beautiful *dhabaa ghar*, that now lay in ruins. With its ornate doors, elegant door frames, teak furniture, and a roof covered with the earthen tiles that Chitra took particular pride in, his house was an extension of his personality. Built using traditional skills and knowledge, and filled with natural air and light, his house was truly one of his dreams, and he was immensely proud of it to say the least.

The baseline architecture was so strong that it would last three generations at least, Chitra had thought. Take the roof, for instance. He had been told by the villagers many times to go for a concrete roof, which was sturdier and required less maintenance. But Chitra had politely refused, saying how he wished his house to reflect him as a person, and chose a roof of traditional earthen tiles instead. His house became an important hub for the villagers, who would come there to consult him on various affairs and make it a point to stop by. Chitra's humility and amiability made visitors praise him generously, although there were a few who were, naturally, jealous of him as well. Chitra Suna's dhabaa ghar marked a central reference point for the entire basti.

But now that house was no more. All it had taken was one moment to destroy all that Chitra had taken decades to build. All the bags of paddy he had stored were burnt to ashes. The steps to his house were littered with broken earthen tiles that once adorned its roof.

Makaru saw some people moving around the premises, clicking pictures. Anyone would have thought that these reporters were diligently and sincerely trying to tell the public the truth about the atrocity and arson. Knowing this was far from the case, he snorted in disgust. They would just write whatever they wanted to, or were told to; no one reported the truth unless it benefitted them or their bosses.

A police van was parked near the basti. A few home guards and constables were standing around listlessly, holding their lathis and looking utterly bored. They looked like they were guarding an unidentified corpse, not knowing when its particulars would be confirmed. But Makaru could not blame them. They were only doing their job. The ones he wanted to hold accountable were their higher-ups, those who held the power to do something about this situation. Those who were probably gorging themselves on food and drink, rolling in the ill-gotten wealth they had accumulated from the countless bribes they had taken.

Till now, Makaru had only heard about Chitra-da's phenomenal success from others. But now that he himself witnessed it—or rather, could only gauge from what little was left of it—even Makaru could not help but feel genuinely proud of his da. For he knew of no other Dalit who had achieved so much in their own lifetime; no one else of his community had built himself a home with so many spacious rooms and airy windows. All his adult life, Makaru had lived in a slum, ridden with poverty, and been subservient to the wealthy in Raipur. He could not believe that a Dalit, too, could scale such heights of prosperity and affluence, if he so determined. Chitrasen Suna had toiled very hard indeed to fulfil his dreams. He deserved his hard-won laurels.

Despite the fact that it was all now ransacked, destroyed and burnt beyond recognition. The almirahs and trunks had been toppled over, broken open, their contents emptied, ripped or scattered; the velvet boxes of jewellery had, of course, been looted without mercy. Makaru felt sorry for Chitra-da, and slowly began to understand his present plight.

As he moved on, his eyes fell on a puja room. Peering inside, he saw pictures of every conceivable deity adorning the walls. Makaru found himself wondering: why did Chitra-da worship so many gods? Was it genuine piety, or just a show of devotion on display for others? An atheist might have sarcastically asked Chitra, "How many more frames do you need up there before your devotion starts showing some effect and saves you?" Makaru knew nothing about that, but he humbly folded his hands and prayed, "Oh God, despite your benevolent presence, why did you let such a tragedy befall my people?"

Despite having been an active and energetic man, Chitra-da's age had now started telling on him. He no longer engaged in his daily activities of supervision and management. He had also gradually begun to reduce his businesses one by one. His buses had grown old, and new vehicles and taxis had come into the picture. So his bus transport business found fewer customers now. He wanted his son to study well, and couldn't find anyone to run his bus business. So, an expert farmer, he started depending mainly on agriculture. He invested in paddy, cotton, pulses, and vegetables like brinjal and *kankada*. He would transport the vegetables to Raipur, sell the paddy and cotton to Marwaris, and so on.

Chitra would always store his paddy for a year, and only sell it thereafter. Which is why there were those numerous sacks of paddy that Makaru had seen before—alas, all destroyed by the fire. Makaru was finally beginning to realise the reasons behind Chitra-da's silence, why he had been impassive like a stone when he met him, refusing to utter a single word.

Old age is usually accompanied with tell-tale signs: the balding and greying of hair, decaying of teeth, physical fragility, among others. Despite being in his sixties, Chitrasen Suna, however, hardly showed any of these signs. He still had his thick mane of hair, and his teeth, though starting to turn off-white, were all in good shape and intact. He still stood erect.

That is, until now.

It seemed as if his senescence had suddenly dropped on him from above, hitting him like a truck. Now, he looked too old for his age. With a bent spine and half-lidded eyes whose corners were encrusted with dried tears, he looked older than seventy. His salt and pepper mane showed more of salt now, and the extreme stress and insomnia since the tragedy struck had thinned his hair. His once boundless energy and indomitable strength had as if evaporated, for he had the lost the will to use it. His tall frame looked frail, gaunt, shrunken, almost skin and bones, and he seemed to have lost half his weight in the past seven days.

As Makaru's mind staggered through everything Chitra-da had endured over the last few days, and tried to make some sense of it, he went blank. Was it really surprising that Chitra-da was in this state given what he had gone through? At least he was still alive. Anyone less resilient than him would have probably died of shock.

Years of his hard work going up in flames overnight, smouldering helplessly as the satanic fires ate up everything he had ever struggled to build, everything that he was attached to.

Had he wished to, Chitrasen Suna could have taken revenge.

Futile, banal, toxic revenge. But revenge nonetheless.

Had he chosen to use his powers thus, the sarpanch could have easily called for an angry mob that wished to avenge itself with equally ferocious and brutal fervour. He could have stooped down to their level, meticulously planning to burn down the homes of the perpetrators in righteous rage and retaliation, channelling their volatile anger so it turned into white hot lava and swallowed their attackers whole, giving them a taste of their own bitter medicine.

But he did not do so.

No. He let his anger swallow *him* instead. He let it simmer so it cooled down to nothing but the darkest despair, melancholy and grief. Till his sanity slowly asphyxiated him, threatening to make him go insane, till his thrashing soul ate itself out of existence. He was teetering on the edge, and the only thing holding him back from the abyss was that one virtue he took pride in: patience. He had been patient enough to let his anger wither away, even if the remnant grief tore him apart. Patient enough to drown in his despair, even if his inner voice was screaming at him to rebel and to avenge himself.

Who would have thought such calamity would befall such a tall and patient man.

Why did it befall him? And all the people of the basti?

Makaru's exhausted troubled mind refused to bestow upon him any answers.

What were the inhuman workings of the diabolic human mind that caused this devastation? What manifested this bloodshed, this unfathomable hatred for his people that rendered them homeless? What singular explosion created waves so huge that they washed away his people's lives, stripping them of their dignity?

Like a time-bomb ticking with menacing regularity, the answers sat hidden in plain sight, waiting to be unveiled.

Fifteen

The month of Ashwin was just round the corner.

It marked a month of joyous festivities and celebrations when people worshipped their deities with enthusiasm. Several of their gods, and especially their goddesses, were taken around the streets in elaborate processions for people to get a glimpse of. The villagers would hold meetings on how to collect the funds required for these celebrations. There would be intense discussions where every detail would be intricately planned and immaculately executed. Whether it was goddess Nialimali, Pardeshen, or god Dharuabudha, people would teem in the streets and street corners or reach out from their porches, eager to receive the deity's blessings for their wellbeing. One indispensable element of all these processions was the ganabaja, the traditional musical instrument which made its appearance every year without fail in the month of Ashwin, gracing all the festivals with its ancient legacy and melodies.

People also remembered and worshipped their family dumas and performed their *shraadha*. One village was divided into several *padas* or localities, each of which honoured their respective ancestral spirits and deities. They would offer sacrifices of livestock such as hens, goats or sheep to please their gods and goddesses, and invite their relatives from neighbouring villages to participate in the feast afterwards.

Another important festival for the people of western Odisha was Dalkhai, which brought a lot of excitement for the young girls of the villages, who would be quivering with joyful energy like the dew drops that adorn the grass early morning. Throughout the day of the festival, they would fast for their brothers' wellbeing. In the morning, they would go to a designated spot to celebrate, have fun, dance and sing songs. At night, they would come together again to perform a special puja and worship goddess Dalkhai for their brothers. The next morning, they would go to the village pond for a ritual bath and follow it with another puja, making sure to return before dawn. Then they would come back home and tie sacred threads, called *jiuntia*, on their brothers' wrists, symbolising the holy bond that acted as a protective shield for the boys; this ritual was called *bhai jiuntia*. Only after this would the girls break their fast. Again, the ganabaja would make its much-awaited appearance. Apart from spinsters, married women would also be invited to their parental homes to enjoy the festival.

The ganabaja was the quintessence of Dalkhai celebrations. But usually, girls didn't have to go out of their way to book an instrument player. They had a different tradition instead. They would go to the homes of someone who had recently had occasion to celebrate in life, like someone who had got a job, welcomed a newborn in the house, or got married or received a marriage proposal, and so on, and politely request them to call a ganabaja player instead. This was supposed to symbolically serve as an auspicious beginning for the girls, from which they could reap rich rewards and fulfil their wishes in the future. All the young girls of the village would approach the family they had unanimously chosen, with a coconut and other paraphernalia, to formally request and appoint them for the task. The household selected would then happily call upon the ganabaja players, whose daughters would also come along so they could join in the festivities. They usually asked for a meagre pay, perhaps only a meal or two, in exchange for weaving magic in the jubilant air with the joyous beats of their ganabaja.

But the times had changed. People had gradually shifted from celebrating one day of Dalkhai to celebrating ten days of Durga puja. They would collect huge amounts of money by way of donations and invest them on erecting puja pandals and festive processions. People would throng at the pandals and enjoy themselves, melting into a sea of celebrations. While goddess Durga was worshipped during the day, many programmes and performances for fun and frolic were hosted during the night, including plays, orchestras, *pala* and *daskathia*. So immersed would the people be in the roistering that they would only return home at the crack of dawn. The last three days, that is *Ashtami*, *Navami* and *Dashami* were especially crazy. News of these grand celebrations soon spread far and wide through the village haats and bazaars, with people praising the few villages that would brave the ambitious task of organising such an extravagance.

Consequently, more and more villages started shifting from celebrating Dalkhai to celebrating Durga puja. Before too long, nearly all the surrounding villages of Lathore had discontinued the pious one-day ritual of bhai jiuntia. But Lathore remained humbly tied to its roots, for it couldn't even think of putting together such an expensive investment in the first place.

Pundit Binay Panigrahi was a well-known resident of Lathore, respected not only within his village but also beyond. People sang his praises because of his modest personality despite his vast knowledge of the scriptures. He was well versed with the Gita, the Ramayana, the Mahabharata as also the Puranas. People passing by would greet him with respect; women would make way for him and shift aside if they happened to meet him on a narrow road. Whenever his path would cross with someone, he would enthusiastically greet them with a Sanskrit *shloka* or two.

One day, as Binay Panigrahi was passing by the village chowk, he saw some people huddled together. Curious, he stopped by and asked them what they were discussing. They replied that they were talking about upcoming plans to celebrate their gods and goddesses for Dusshera. Binay Panigrahi smiled in anticipation. Suddenly interested, he proceeded to sit down among the people, apparently wanting to hear more of the discussion.

People gladly gave up their seats for him, and he gratefully sat down on one.

He said, "Folks, I have no objection at all to what you are planning. But listen, the times have changed. And so have the tastes of the people. They are constantly evolving to adapt to new practices. But though the culture is undergoing a paradigm shift, people have not been able to keep up with it at the same pace. So let's embrace the new culture, folks! For if we don't, how will we become culturally rich? How long are we going to stick to our old beliefs?"

The crowd respected Pundit Panigrahi enough to feel that what he was saying must surely be correct, but alas they failed to comprehend his words. One man got up a bit hesitantly and politely said, "Sir, we couldn't quite understand what you said. Would you please care to elaborate?" Panigrahi paused for a moment, then went on to explain.

"What I wish to convey isn't so difficult to understand. In the Gita, Sri Krishna told Arjun, '*Mamekam sharanam braja*' which means 'Take shelter in me, and you will attain salvation'. How long will it take for us to fathom the wisdom of these words? The Aryans settled down here thousands and thousands of years ago. Yet, here we are, forever stagnant in our beliefs and refusing to come out of the ignorant shell that we have cocooned ourselves in. How long will it take us to become refined, to become cultured? Granted, the Lathore of the present is not the Lathore of the past. Everything has changed, most of it for the better. The economy has grown several fold, and we now have schools and colleges to secure the future of the upcoming generations. In some respects, the lives of people here have definitely seen improvement and development. So why do our people have to go all the way to other villages to see their Durga pujas? We have hoisted ourselves to the position we are in today. So, why not do a tiny bit more and organise our own Durga puja too?"

Everyone appreciated Panigrahi's suggestion and praised him. One villager piped up and asked, "Sir, so do we worship goddess Durga along with the deities we already worship, or...?"

Panigrahi replied, "Boy, how long should we remain bound by the customs and traditions of the past? When the Gramdevi goes in procession, innumerable hens and goats are sacrificed for her. This is an ancient Dravidian tradition, totally un-Aryan. But now, we are modern and educated, and whoever is educated is Aryan. Therefore, our rituals too should be according to the Aryan tradition. If we learn to perform *homa* and *yajna* and chant *Harinam*, then we will be considered a cultured people. There lies our salvation."

After making his eloquent speech, Panigrahi left the chowk, leaving in his wake a confused bunch of villagers, their reactions varying from mild disbelief to shock.

So then, all their lives, they had been living as Dravidians?

All it took was a few words to tumble out of Panigrahi's mouth to render all their beliefs and rituals meaningless. Their hearts were now collectively thumping for a different cause altogether—to somehow try and become genuinely Aryan. Now their entangled thoughts had been ironed out into a single one:

they were ready to perform the monstrously significant homa and yajna, to kickstart their holy transformation into complete, pure-blooded Aryans, at the words of their most revered and scholarly Panigrahi *ji*.

Huh, as if.

Ensnared by the craze to transform themselves, they enthusiastically decided to call for a gram sabha to talk at length about the requirements and methodology of preparing for the now anticipated grand Durga puja in their village.

The meeting formally solidified the villagers' requirements in organising the puja. People excitedly started suggesting musicians and orchestra bands they could approach, citing instances when they had been impressed by the performance of those artists in other celebrations. Recommendations poured in, and with enough on the roster to refer from, the discussion shifted to the process of collecting funds, and exactly how much was needed for what.

It won't be very difficult to secure funds, they thought.

After all, Lathore had grown into a more financially secure village, owing to the advent of the Marwaris. Not only had they established their entrepreneurial roots there and given birth to new businesses that were flourishing to this day, the Marwaris had also brought economic development that had guided the village out of poverty as a whole. No matter what intentions they had originally arrived with, they had brought a better future for the place. Their business prospered as Lathore was well-connected through well-built roads and railway tracks to well-off towns. Which is why the villagers reiterated '*baanijye basati lakshmi*', or 'Lakshmi resides in the heart of business', and soon took up business ventures of their own. Today, almost all the households, barring one or two, were engaged in business. Hence, the gram sabha's certainty that collecting funds wasn't the biggest hurdle in planning this puja. They were sure of collecting at least 500–1000 rupees from each family.

The puja committee members were excited about planning their very first Durga puja. They left no stone unturned in collecting funds to ensure that funds do not fall short for anything.

They went to every household, every haat and marketplace they could, and collected money diligently.

Now at one end of the village stood the solitary country liquor shop of wine proprietor Bihari Seth. The puja committee demanded ten thousand rupees from him, and he happily gave it, for his business was profitable, and this was an occasion of joy in the making. The villagers also requested him to sell wine for free during the four days of puja, i.e. Saptami, Ashtami, Navami and Dashami. He happily complied, because the youth of the puja committee could be of help and handy when his drunken customers got into ugly brawls.

Groups of people used to frequent the markets to play *jua* or cards and *khudkhudi*, dice. Such gambling was illegal, however, so they would bribe the policemen to keep mum about it. Now what our puja committee did was to ask the police not to collect bribes for the week leading up to the grand puja. In return for this favour, they asked the *juawallah*s and *khudkhudiwallahs* to give them a ten per cent share of their profits. This ingenious plan ended up getting them lakhs of rupees from both groups combined.

Panigrahi was impressed, to say the least. With a beaming smile, he said, "See, all your hard work and dedication has paid off so well. As they all say, when there is a will, there is a way. You would be pleased to know that the money you have all collected could easily organise three well-prepared Durga pujas."

He was actually right. In a way, he had fuelled the piety in people and channelled their motivation the right way to have them celebrate Durga puja in their own right. The villagers were aware of it too. So it was no wonder that he was appointed the head priest for the extravagant celebrations. The villagers worked hard to build a permanent pandal for Ma Durga, for this year, and the ones to come. A glittering statue of the goddess was also installed there.

From then on, the quaint village of Lathore became crazed with joyous celebrations. Because Lathore had undertaken this project for the first time, many people from other villages were curious as to what exactly they had prepared. This meant a staggering footfall, and people generously offered *dana* and *dakshina* too, so Binay Panigrahi's house was practically overflowing with riches.

Everything was going really well.

So well that it seemed too good to be true.

Like the calm before a storm.

And then, like malignant tidal waves crashing at an unsuspecting seashore, tragedy struck.

Tragedy unfolds like a butterfly effect, sparking from the smallest of events, bleeding down the crevices of society's fallacies and cancerously growing into so monstrous a size that its fury supersedes all. Its effects may be so unreal they would blind, but its causes are mundane to the point of invisibility.

Tragedy was something no one saw coming, not even Binay Panigrahi, who sat smugly at the feet of goddess Durga on the *mandap* erected by the villagers, complete with his puja paraphernalia. Oblivious devotees thronged at the site, bringing along generous offerings. Some stood back and offered their prayers from afar, while some others who had come equipped with offerings climbed up the pandal to pay their obeisance, bringing tangible pieces of their piety along.

One of those was Shankar Suna.

He had gone to the village pond early in the morning and made it a point to swim through the frigid waters, in the cold month of Ashwin, mind you, to collect as many as twenty-one pristine water lilies. Laden with those beautiful flowers bejewelled with iridescent drops of water, puja items like *muan*, a coconut, some rice, and his devotional fervour, he enthusiastically set off for the mandap.

Oh, we forgot to mention something.

Shankar Suna was a Dalit.

Ideally speaking, this should not have been a problem. However, it was. Just as he was stepping into the pandal, he was stopped by the volunteers standing guard. They argued that he would 'pollute' the puja pandal. A distressed Shankar said that all he wanted to offer were his prayers and these offerings to Ma Durga, and that the goddess did not differentiate between devotees. But the volunteers argued back, saying that even if they allowed him to place his offerings there, as a Brahmin there was no way Panigrahi would touch them, so his efforts were futile. Shankar went from being dismayed to incredulous and finally to outraged on hearing the volunteers. When he saw how he had been humiliated in front of thousands of people, his vexation climbed a few notches higher. Livid, he returned with his basket in his tired arms.

Many came forward ostensibly to offer suggestions of getting 'justice'. They advised him to call for a village meeting, file a complaint with the police, or even hold a protest in rebellion. But Chitrasen Suna spoke up calmly with a wisdom and a restraint that set him apart from the others. "Shankar, you can do all of these things that people are suggesting, but what good will it do? I suggest you let this go. The village has organised such a big puja for the first time, and people from faraway villages are eagerly coming to witness it. At this stage if we start an immature brawl, the entire village's image will be spoilt. Just hold back for a while, and you will be the bigger person for it."

And so, tucking his anger and resentment into the darkest corner of his heart, Shankar decided to forget about it for now.

Forgive? He was not so sure.

This memory was embedded deep in Shankar's mind like a shard of glass, making him wince each time that he tried to move past it.

And as for Chitrasen? He might have dismissed Shankar's angry emotions and asked him to embrace peace, but his own heart refused to side with his intellect. He was of course deeply upset seeing his own caste brother humiliated in this manner, all in the name of some grand illusions of purity and pollution.

Those who had denied Shankar entry into the pandal were also troubled, for they knew they had not been in the right. They had held this festival in the hopes of embracing the modern culture that awaited them, and yet wronged someone in the midst of it, by dogmatically clinging to unsophisticated ancient beliefs and foolishly trying to preserve them. This was nothing but hypocrisy.

True, Shankar had not done anything to incriminate them, but their own guilty conscience held them in an iron grip, and shudders of foreboding slithered down their spines in fear of the possible consequences. Nevertheless, at least for the time being, they all buried their trepidation and consoled themselves under the pretence that everything was all right.

This aside, the puja was a tremendous success. So overjoyed were the villagers involved in the organisation that they never even asked the puja committee for an audit, claiming that they had full faith in the members.

Binay Panigrahi was of course smothered with praises, and a greasy smile sat on his lips as he raised his pudgy hands towards the heavens, saying this was all God's doing.

But the ones truly deserving of the praise were the villagers, no?

The way they had disowned their cultural, spiritual legacy in a flash in foolish hopes of becoming more advanced, more modern, more cultured, and, of course, more Aryan. The way they had blindly let the words of Binay Panigrahi twist their age-old, most deeply cherished beliefs askew and question their very basis, as the shrewd pundit thought of ways of exploiting their naiveté to the full, the cogs in his Brahmin brain busy spinning with entrepreneurial cunning. The way they had abandoned what had anchored them and sustained them culturally and spiritually as a people for longer than they could remember, only to indulge in a larger than life experience that reached its climactic end after a mere ten days of gay festivity.

One could still question: what was the difference? Nialimali and Durga were both beloved goddesses, and the choice lay with a devotee as to which deity they wished to turn to for displaying their piety. And, if one really considered, wasn't Dalkhai something that was a bit superfluous? After all, if a girl had a loving brother, he would protect her regardless of whether she tied a sacred jiuntia on his wrist or not. Wouldn't he?

Maybe. Maybe not.

Dalkhai wasn't just a festival; it was an emotion. One where sisters and brothers took time off their busy lives to meet and to express how grateful they were for the other's existence. One where girls could spend an entire day without worrying about the countless responsibilities that burdened their shoulders, laughing and singing their hearts out together, till they could no longer distinguish their heartbeats from the blood rushing past their ears in excitement.

Spinning a reverie of untold dreams and unbroken promises.

As the sun lapsed into its vermillion glory, they would return home with their hearts full, their minds light and their souls satisfied.

Satisfaction was what they got. Satisfaction was what the villagers got, from worshipping their dumas, taking a day to reconnect with their ancestry and the legacy of their bloodlines.

And they lived for it.

But not anymore.

With more and more people gradually making the shift from the mundane, intimate one-day celebration to ten days of endless social extravaganza, their traditional culture was dying out. Collapsing into itself and sinking to the ground as nobody took notice, blinded by the alluring aspect of soaring past new horizons, when all they were doing was tearing apart their own traditions that had kept them moored to Mother Earth.

In sharp contrast, Binay Panigrahi was flying high, his greasy smile turning greasier and his senses giddy at the exhilaration of gaining such recognition in such a short span of time. As he folded his palms together in response to the reverential greetings that he received from everyone these days, he couldn't help but feel victory surging through his bones.

What made this more significant were his humble beginnings at this very place. Fifteen years ago, his life here was nothing like what it was now. In fact, fifteen years ago, he didn't even live in Lathore.

Binay Panigrahi had been called from Sambalpur, as part of a band to sing the pala for someone's grandson.

That someone was Ratan Seth, the Marwari who headed the salt business. His son Kamalnath had become father to a beautiful baby boy, and blessed with his first grandchild, Ratan Seth had enthusiastically called for a pala band to celebrate the infant's *ekoishia*. That is how Binay Panigrahi had found himself in Lathore for the first time.

The pala was a huge success. People were mesmerised by Panigrahi's performance and his knowledge of the scriptures.

Along with fulsome praise, he was paid a hefty amount as fee and received many gifts as well. Thereafter, other people who had seen him perform also called him for auspicious occasions in their households. In fact, Panigrahi had never received as much appreciation and respect in his hometown. The ever observant Ratan Seth, having noticed all this, suggested, "Why don't you come and live here in Lathore, as a pundit? You can preside over all the religious rites and functions here, for there isn't any Brahmin in the surrounding villages who can handle events like this. And besides, the villagers here already worship you, so you would have a pretty good business."

Panigrahi's eyes lit up at Ratan Seth's suggestion. Given his irregular income, he was only too glad and took up the offer with alacrity. Slipping into the character of a knowledgeable priest, he started doing a whole lot more than he had initially thought he would. He started performing elaborate homas and yajnas, even took up stints in astrology and reading the future. The people adored him. He received so much dana-dakshina in kind that it was more than he could use, and he would sell it off to anyone willing to pay a reasonable price for it. Needless to say, Panigrahi flourished, and in fifteen years he found himself established as the indisputable purohit of Lathore.

Who would have imagined this would have been the fate of a humble nondescript pala singer?

Knowledge is power, after all.

And Panigrahi used this power well. It won't be wrong to claim that he had single-handedly helmed and authored the manifestation of an ambitious vision for Lathore: hosting the Durga puja.

Basking in the success of the first year, people enthusiastically set about planning the second year of the puja. Since the puja committee had done a good job of execution the first time, it was left unchanged, and assigned the charge of organisation once again. Again, like the year before, the committee members went to markets, offices, schools and institutions to collect funds, not to mention their own village households, of course.

On their way to collect funds from Ganapada, they came across a group of lads engaged in discussion. The boys said quite reasonably, "We have no problems contributing funds and we will gladly give you as much as you ask for. We only wish to add one member of our basti to the puja committee, in order to ensure representation of our caste."

The committee members, however, refused. They argued that the members had already been decided upon, and adding a new member at this point of time was near impossible. But the boys stood their stand as well, stating how the absence of a member of their caste in the puja committee was leading to discrimination against them, and their eventual isolation. They were reassured that the committee was not discriminating against them, and that it treated everyone as equal and would try its best to provide all facilities to everyone, regardless of what caste they belonged to. In fact, there were many other padas as well from which representatives had not been chosen.

The Gana lads were incredulous, and promptly cited how Shankar Suna had not even been allowed to offer the goddess the water lilies that he had gone out of his way to procure from the cold pond waters on a chilly morning. Then how could they be assured when the committee members said they were "not discriminating against them"? The alleged party tried to reason with them, saying that was a thing of the past and was best forgotten, and that this year, the celebrations would prove to mark a new beginning, so there was no need to stir up a storm needlessly.

The Gana boys scoffed. "It is the same committee and the same festivities. And you refuse to add a member of our community. Then how can we expect things to be different this time around?"

At this, one committee member lost it. "Aren't you Dalit punks getting too talkative these days? Just because we are holding back, don't think we cannot hold our own. As if we can't organise the festivities without you. Know your limits and stay within them. Fucking Gana bastards!"

For one moment, there was pin-drop silence.

Then the dam burst.

This was the limit for the Ganas. An acrimonious verbal battle followed.

"So you can manage without us, huh? All right, we will see how well you manage when we don't lend you our ganabaja and our players. Not a single musician from our community will play the ganabaja for you this year."

And so the fight went back and forth. Enraged at the ugly casteist slurs, which only got uglier, the Gana boys finally went to report the committee members to the police station. The thana in-charge summoned the committee members to the police station, and told them that a caste atrocity was a non-bailable offence, and could land them in jail for quite a significant amount of time. So it was best that they settle this matter peaceably amongst each other.

Upon hearing this, the committee members got worried, more than they cared to admit. Moreover, seething at all the casteist insults and abuses hurled at them, the Ganapada people refused to settle the matter with a compromise. At their wits' end, the upper-caste accused decided to call for Chitrasen Suna, for he was a wise and widely respected member of the Gana community, in the hope that he might be able to cool down the anger of the youngsters.

As expected, Chitrasen sat the boys down affectionately and explained to them patiently, "Anybody can hold grudges. But the greater souls choose to let them go. We all live in the same village. We wake up to see each other's faces every day. If we bear grudges, our hostile emotions will only intensify. And it's not like they will choose to remain quiet after they come out of jail either. If anything, they will possibly look for more ways to pay us back. And so it will go on endlessly. Why make each other's lives so difficult? Why not go in for a compromise instead? Are you really that desperate to waste days and nights of your vital energy fighting for something, only for it to result in nothing? Or worse, something catastrophic?"

Chitrasen Suna was an influential man. His words carried weight and were always backed by reason. So the boys gave in to his counsel, but on one condition: the committee members would have to apologise to them, publicly, standing on one leg, with hands holding their ears.

To the great dismay of the upper caste men, this was an even bigger price to pay. Who could bear the insult of having to publicly apologise, and to the Dalits, standing on one leg? To think that the very men who used to live so humbly, as was best for them, had now mustered the audacity to call *us* for an apology!

There was a time that they couldn't even stand in the same room as us. They would never dare to bathe at the same ghat, would stay metres away from us when passing us by on a road, and bow down a full ninety degrees in salutation. They would swallow their spit and suppress their sneezes and coughs so as not to pollute us if we were anywhere in the vicinity. In matters of law, they could never dream of approaching the courts without our prior permission. These same people are living outlandishly today, deciding penalties for us and dictating to us to apologise publicly to them while standing on one foot!

Given how things had been before, and how things are now, how can we possibly bring ourselves to just apologise to them like that? It is nauseating even to contemplate. How could we go back to living our normal lives in dignity and self-respect after this? We won't even be able to look our women in the eye after stooping to such a disgusting low.

Such volatile thoughts were raging in the minds of the accused.

To them, this was less of a brawl and more of a battle for the throne of dominance.

A war.

They were adamant on not backing down, and so they decided to find a way of evading the apology. All minds turned to Assistant Sub-inspector Kishore Sarangi, another upper-caste who was in a position of power, and who could possibly put an end to their troubles.

Mind you, in addition to being upper-caste, the puja committee members were powerful men of the village who also came from wealthy households. Men like Kamalnath Seth, Srikanth Meher, Himanshu Bagarti, Narottam Pradhan, Balabadhra Meher and Bhola Aggarwal.

Kamalnath Seth's petrol pump business had a turnover of crores. If properly invested in the development of Lathore, it could support the village for generations to come.

Srikanth Meher owned a cloth shop which did hefty business, and was chairman of the business association. His cloth stores were found in Raipur as well. He also dabbled very profitably in the diamond jewellery business.

Himanshu Bagarti owned a country liquor shop, which raked in more than he could count.

Narottam Pradhan was a railway contractor. From Kantabanji to Khariar Road, all the railway stations turned to him for their supply needs.

Bhola Aggarwal ran the business of *mahua*, *char* and other produce from all the forests of the area, and sold them in the *mandi*. In addition to this he also owned two rice mills.

These men weren't just millionaires. They wielded power and clout in their areas and beyond. The same police officers who were asking them for an apology today were the kind they could employ as their personal security officers any day, anytime.

And they were more than willing to make 'judicious' use of this power to bend the rules in their favour. The plan in their vile heads was simple: bring in ASI Kishore Sarangi into the picture; bribe him with some of their 'hard-earned' money to beat those Gana bastards into submission, and make the boys admit that their allegations were nothing but a figment of their delirious imagination.

So, in feverish haste to save their now flailing dignity, they had ASI Sarangi summoned in the dead of night, and told him, "Look here, ASI *saab*, you know perfectly well where we stand, and where those Gana punks stand. And they are asking us for a fucking apology, the sheer audacity of it. You know that we can't possibly give in to their command, right? You are a clever man, you would know." Slipping a bundle of hundred-rupee notes into his hands with a wink and a sickening smile, they supposed the message was crystal clear.

But Kishore Sarangi was plotting something else altogether.

Sometime ago, Himanshu Bagarti used to be a small-time underworld don of sorts, in league with other not-so-small-time gangsters, dabbling in the darker trades of business. However, as his age tilted towards the middle bracket, he settled for liquor enterprises, although he still stayed in touch with his powerful 'acquaintances': namely politicians, influential underworld goons, and the like. The fact that he was an unlicenced, unregistered liquor vendor and sold crude liquor straight from some illegal factory dungeons was something best kept secret.

Once, two men drunk to their gills started a stupid brawl right in front of Bagarti's shop, screaming their heads off. Much to Bagarti's dismay, this attracted a police squad, led by none other than Kishore Sarangi. Determined to put the drunken wretches behind bars, Sarangi was surprised when Bagarti bravely sided with his customers, stepping in despite the legal complications his shop could land him in.

So Sarangi chided the liquor shop owner, "Careful, Bagarti. Watch what you say and where; you could get these drunkards out of their well-deserved lockup, but might end up in jail yourself. I know the kind of shit you indulge in, and just how 'clean and honest' this business of yours is."

The officer did not expect the response he got. Forget cowering, Bagarti thrust his hands into his pockets, walked up slowly to Kishore and drawled, 'Ah yes, honest ASI Sarangi. I know you are practically drooling to land me in jail right now. And quite a good catch I would be. Perfect for promotion, right?" Then his saccharine smile dropped as he snarled, "But careful, officer *saab*. One wrong move, and I will make sure I have this uniform stripped off you. Right before my eyes."

Then, Bagarti extended a hand towards one of his men, who handed him a phone. Without breaking eye contact with Sarangi, he dialled Sarangi's senior, a police commissioner he had good relations with. When the call connected, his loud voice dripping honey said, "Ah, Commissioner sir! Greetings to you and your family. Hope you are doing well." As he heard the officer respond on the line, his lips curled in a malicious smirk as he said in a tone of complaint, "Oh you see, your junior here, what's his name... yes, Kishore Sarangi. He has been wagging his tail for funds, like I bestow upon you. He has been bugging me every week since quite some time, sir. Threatens to report my shop if I don't comply. How do I shake him off, sir?"

As Sarangi watched, his muscles taut with anger, the underworld don with a victorious smirk said, "Yes sir, I'll just hand over the phone to him," and held out the battered device to Sarangi. It took the officer some restraint to hold back a furious sneer from showing on his chiselled face. Calming his nerves, he plucked the phone out of Himanshu's grasp and put it next to his ear, "ASI Kishore Sarangi reporting, sir." And then he closed his eyes for the insults to rain down on him. And rain they did. His senior cussed him left and right, spewing bullshit over how naive Kishore was for messing around with the powerful. Then hoarse from all the shouting, the commissioner snapped, "Sarangi, do your nightly rounds like a good boy and stay perched in the police station as you are told to. No need to sprout wings and go about meddling in business that isn't yours. If I hear of you worrying Himanshu Bagarti one more time, I'll suspend you off the face of this earth."

And the line went dead.

Sarangi's jaw was hurting from how hard he had been clenching it, and if he had tightened his grip on the phone a bit more, it would have collapsed. Wordlessly, he turned back to Bagarti, who sat there with his head tilted smugly, an ugly smirk on his lips. Tossing the phone back to the gangster, Sarangi turned to the officer with him, "Get back into the jeep. Let this case rest. It was just a brawl after all." And then turning on his heel with as much dignity he could master, he went back to the driver's seat and drove off with his colleague. The two drunkards in question were sprawled on the ground, passed out. Bagarti let out an amused chuckle, asked his men to disperse the crowd that had gathered, and forgot all about the incident soon after.

But Kishore Sarangi wasn't so fortunate.

Even as he drove the jeep furiously through the *kachcha* roads, blowing dust, and his colleague frantically asking him to calm down, Kishore kept his foot down on the accelerator, his knuckles hot from how hard he was grabbing the steering wheel. The rational part of him was calmly asking him to unsee and unhear what had just happened, but his heart knew he would never forget it even if he tried.

Never.

The crowd.

The cuss words his senior had bathed him in.

The ugly cackle and the smirk on that monster's face.

The soul-crushing urge to just put a bullet through his skull.

The humiliation.

He would never forget that.

Sarangi drove on, fearing that if he stopped, his hands won't; unless they found themselves wrapped around Bagarti's throat, till his soul was forced to leave his body.

And so it was that the same Kishore Sarangi now stood towering over the puja committee members, his blood boiling at the sight of an oblivious Himanshu Bagarti, and his heart soaring at the chance that had planted itself in his grasp. A chance to get back at the devil. With Bagarti's guardian angel, the previous commissioner long gone, and replaced with another officer, Sarangi could easily use this opportunity to squelch out all the dignity Bagarti held dear, the way he himself had been forced to let go of his, all that time ago.

As a police officer, Sarangi wielded much more power now; he could dismiss the case of the Ganas with a flick of his little finger. He had many ways to bring this situation under control and save these anxious wealthy, powerful men from their precarious fall from grace.

But he wouldn't.

For the life of him, he couldn't.

Not after what he had suffered to get through that fateful day.

The bribe money would just add to the riches rotting away in his safe; and these men that he faintly recognised could go about licking the roadsides for all he cared. His reading and assessment of this situation was based on one factor, and one alone: Himanshu Bagarti. And Kishore Sarangi was willing to be dragged to hell, but not before he had given some of it back to the man who had toyed with him back then.

And so, mimicking the saccharine sweetness he had heard his nemesis use all those years ago, the ASI declared, "Dear sirs, there is no way I would want such respected and reputable men like you bow down to those lowly Ganas, that too in public. But what can we do? This is the era of RTI and mobile phones. If someone tips off information on this case to the SP, I would lose my job. And even if you somehow manage to evade this public apology with my help, you would still end up getting booked under a caste atrocity allegation, which is a hundred times worse. So, as much as it pains me to say this, I think it is better that you make the apology, and just get this over with as quickly as you can. Best to keep community matters to ourselves, isn't it?"

While he looked genuinely anxious and concerned, his facial muscles were fighting to keep a grin from creeping onto his face. Had he been alone, Sarangi might have given himself a pat on the back for his flawless performance. Not only had he convincingly portrayed himself as a true well-wisher of these men, but also snagged a chance of fulfilling his long-awaited desire for revenge in the process.

Suave, subtle and sublime.

Perfect.

Finally, the penultimate day arrived. The small Lathore police station compound and the area all around it was teeming with people, sagging under the weight of countless expectant feet. Although the crowd comprised hundreds of unnamed faces, one could still make out two distinct groups that stood separate from each other. On one side sat the Gana people, together with Chitrasen, waiting anxiously for the spectacle to unfold, while others were sceptical, half expecting the whole scene to evaporate just like a fever dream right before their eyes. On the other side sat a group of dejected men huddled together, with long, wary faces. They all looked familiar, yet not entirely, for the great anxiety and fear of having their dignity and pride publicly stripped had given their faces a ghostly pallor.

And right in the middle of the crowd stood ASI Kishore Sarangi, towering over the others as he took in the sheer numbers of people who had turned up to witness what would probably be a once-in-a-lifetime event for them. His eyes shone with the intense anticipation of someone who would finally see years of labour bear fruit in tangible form. His chest was out proudly, wearing the uniform he treasured, which had once been nearly snatched from him in the past. His smiling, shining eyes spoke far more than what he would have brought himself to.

All heads turned to ASI Sarangi as he solemnly addressed the crowd: "Since this is just a minor miscommunication that the village has embroiled itself in, it is best kept within its confines. Upon majority approval, we have therefore agreed that the puja committee members shall each stand on one leg, place both hands on their ears, and seek due apology for having offended the members of the Gana community."

The committee members then set about acting upon Sarangi's words. Standing on one leg and struggling to maintain their balance without toppling over as their hands reluctantly went to touch their ears, their faces a picture of misery, they took in deep breaths and spoke slowly and grudgingly, "Gana brothers, we acknowledge that we were wrong in speaking to you thus, using offensive words and casteist slurs against you, and behaving in a condescending manner. We beg your forgiveness and hope that you will put this behind you, and join us to celebrate the upcoming festivities together in the name of brotherhood."

They made the mistake of looking up at the crowd, and saw a few youths with their mobile phones out, joyfully clicking pictures of this epic and extraordinary event. Their blood surged in their veins as their hearts pounded with anger. Yet they stood still, letting their hands drop down their sides and their feet plant themselves on the ground, which they wished would swallow them and end their ordeal. Their faces contorted with the agony of humiliation as they let it sink into their bones: the excruciating feeling of having to lose their dignity, their pride. No longer able to bear the piercing gaze of the crowd, they hurried home quietly, willing themselves to become invisible, and fervently wishing that their actions and words could be undone and unspoken.

Then there was officer Sarangi.

He couldn't quite put his finger on this feeling of euphoria that had caught him unawares, making him feel as if he had suddenly grown wings. Was it happiness? Satisfaction? Peace? A sense of closure? He did not know. But what he did know was that he was willing to feel this a hundred times over and again, his senses were almost giddy he felt so high, so light.

And lastly, there were the Ganas.

Some stood there motionless, as if even the tiniest flurry of movement would break their incredible reverie, still telling themselves that this was not a dream but very much a reality that happened right before their eyes. Others stood with their mouths agape, too stunned to speak after having witnessed such powerful men vanquish their haughty selves and actually own up to their mistakes. Others were screaming their lungs off in sheer joy at the victory, for this was the best day of their lives. But one thing that united every soul in that crowd was a spark.

A spark they had felt when the men had declared themselves to be wrong, contrary to how they had brushed off their abusive language and behaviour as 'normal', just as they always had in the past. A spark they had felt when the men had asked them to join in the festivities, as brothers and equals.

A spark they had been longing to feel in their hearts since eternity.

And now, even when they got over their stupor and joined in the celebratory hooting and jubilant shouting and dancing, with beautiful smiles adorning their faces, they knew that something vital had shifted. Something had changed. They no longer cared if a member of their community was a part of the puja committee or not, because they had found something far more potent, more compelling to look forward to.

The spark.

Sixteen

Himanshu Bagarti could not get a wink of sleep.

After having returned home, he had been served dinner, but he had no appetite. He went straight to bed on an empty stomach, but there too, sleep evaded him. He was tossing and turning the entire night, sometimes visiting the bathroom in hopes of emptying his bladder, but could not.

His children were asleep in the next room. His wife noticed that he was disturbed, but she remained silent and did not comment. She knew Himanshu was battling an inner storm.

The nocturnal creatures were busy making their usual night sounds, but to Himanshu it sounded as if they were laughing at him. How could he stay quiet when they were mocking him so?

In a little while the sun would probably rise from behind the cottony clouds to mark the beginning of a new day. The annoying crickets would stop chirping, the cows would head to the meadows to graze, and the women would get busy with the day's chores. Everything would function normally just as usual. But how could he bring himself to blend into this normalcy when his heart was pounding abnormally and his soul felt like it was slowly ebbing out of him?

To think that he, a proud Bagarti, had to apologise to those Dalit nobodies publicly like that! Such humiliation!

Right after the Ganas and Gonds, the Bagartis had been among the first ones to settle in this village. They used to herd buffaloes. When Himanshu's ancestors had first come and settled in Lathore, it was the Ganas who used to help them with the breeding, feeding and animal husbandry. They used to clean up the buffalo sheds without complaint. They used to pay them obeisance from a respectful distance. And yet, those same subservient silent Ganas had today mustered the audacity to get him to apologise standing on one foot! Had they forgotten what business he was a part of? Had they forgotten how bad he could be if they provoked him enough?

Himanshu had built himself a large well-furnished home, with a latrine and a bathroom. Yet, he never used them himself. Growing up in a village, he was accustomed to defecating and bathing in the open. Every morning, he would pack his toothbrush, soap and towel, and ride lazily to the village pond on his motorbike. He would empty his bowels in the nearby fields first, before going into the pond for a leisurely bath, enjoying the cool green waters.

But today, Himanshu Bagarti was faced by a dilemma. Did we mention that the road to the village pond passed through Ganapada? So he was stuck at home, fervently praying for the sun not to rise, so he could evade stepping out of the house altogether. He kept muttering, "Oh God, please don't ever let me see those misbegotten Ganas ever again!"

Fury running through his veins, Himanshu decided he just couldn't take this anymore. He would pay them back, ten-fold if need be, teach them a lesson. He was not going to allow them to trample over him like this and get away with it. So, he took out his motorbike and set off. His wife asked him where he was headed, and he replied, "Kharli."

Kharli was a village adjacent to Lathore, and home to Himanshu's best friend, Srikanth Meher, whom he had decided to meet today. Besides, there were others he knew there. His wife let him go, hoping that a heart-to-heart talk with his old friend would help ease what was troubling him, burdening him.

Srikanth's ancestral home was in Kharli, but his businesses were based in Lathore. So he had homes in both villages. Srikanth had spent his childhood in Lathore, and had been a classmate and best friend of Himanshu. While he did go to inspect his ancestral property and the lands he owned in Kharli, he still spent most of his time in Lathore. As a member of the puja committee in Lathore, he too had to apologise to the Ganas along with the others. So, when Srikanth saw his friend's ashen face just a few hours after the public humiliation, that too in the wee hours of the morning, he obviously thought something similar had come up again. He greeted him briskly and asked him if everything was all right.

The two friends settled down, while Srikanth's daughter brought in tea. Once she left, the room was shrouded in a thick silence. The two looked at each other wordlessly, each cringing at what they had gone through the day before. Finally, Himanshu broke the silence and said, "You know, I have been losing sleep over this shit."

Srikanth looked up and instantly said, "Me too, friend, me too. In fact, I was actually thinking of calling you up. These bastards are going way out of their league. We have to keep them in check. Have to take revenge."

Srikanth might have said this in relation with the public apology, but he had other reasons as well. Reasons that he could neither live with quietly, nor share with anyone lest he lose face and his dignity. Reasons that involved his niece, Lipsa.

Lipsa was the daughter of Srikanth's elder brother. She studied in Lathore High School and went to Kantabanji to pursue a BA. Then she went to Sambalpur University to get a degree in MA Economics. There, she became friends with a Dalit boy from Lathore named Vikas, who was pursuing an MA in Sociology. He had been studying with her since high school, but they only started talking to each other in college, drawn together by the fact that they belonged to neighbouring villages, and both were living away from home. They started depending on one another increasingly, and soon feelings of friendship turned to love.

At first, Lipsa and Vikas managed to keep their relations secret. But soon, people began noticing them together. How could they not? They would be seen walking together between classes on the campus, studying together at the university library. On Sundays and holidays they would go to watch movies. Inevitably, their romance became a hot topic among their peers. Their names were seen engraved on walls and furniture, and they became a topic of discussion at tea stalls and canteens. So, news of their affair soon reached Lathore.

Srikanth's elder brother lived in Kharli, and ran a simple business. He would call weavers and artisans over to his house, where they would work on his looms and weaving machines, and he would sell the finished cloths to cloth merchants. It was a minimalist enterprise and he hardly came in contact with anyone except the merchants and weavers. Srikanth Meher, on the other hand, was quite well known. His cloth shops were the biggest in the area, and he came in contact with a wide spectrum of people. So, when Lipsa's affair with a lower caste boy became known, people would mention it more to Srikanth than to Lipsa's father, his brother. Suffice it to say that the rumours and gossip about his family made Srikanth angry.

But he could do nothing about it. What if he forbade Lipsa from meeting Vikas again, and she just eloped with him to rebel? Children these days were a different level of adamant. And, if he told Vikas to stay within his limits, he would probably answer him right back, saying he better keep an eye on his own family member first. Both involved consequences Srikanth preferred not to face, for they would mean an insult to his dignity. So he just kept shut.

Soon, the lovebirds were done with their MA courses, and returned home.

Lipsa was immediately grounded at her father's house in Kharli to keep her away from Vikas, who lived in Lathore. But she would always come up with excuses to visit Lathore with her sister. If Srikanth chided her, she would say that she was there to see his shop, and he couldn't say no to that. Vikas, knowing this, would try and pass by Srikanth's shop every day, to see if Lipsa was there. And if she was, they would exchange bashful eye contact and shy smiles of affection. Sometimes he would purposely loiter outside the shop with his friends, laughing and talking loudly or finding other ways of letting her know he was there.

Seeing all this would make Srikanth's blood boil. As far as he was concerned, Vikas's love for his niece was a personal affront to his dignity. He would try and busy himself in the shop to give the boy the impression that he wasn't aware of what was going on. He would randomly start talking to one of the salesmen, or on the phone, or just turn his back to them, gritting his teeth all the while.

He wanted to poison Lipsa.

"Would my brother and his family ever understand what this girl has done to my reputation?" Srikanth would curse in vexation. He was the one who bore the brunt of people's constant curiosity and their intrusive questions. He was the one who had to deal with people talking behind his brother's back. So, he decided to take matters into his own hands.

By that time, every gram panchayat had opened a college for universal education. Lipsa was a bright girl, so Srikanth decided to get her employed in one of those institutions. Perhaps working would take her mind off romance, he thought. But, of course, he would never get her employed in Lathore, for that would only mean her becoming even more wayward and things going out of hand. So he decided to send her off to Kantabanji instead. He spoke to the management, throwing some of his influence and weight to make the job easier. And, Lipsa's grades were well above average, so getting the favour wasn't that hard.

As planned, Lipsa went to Kantabanji. Srikanth heaved a sigh of relief. Finally, Lipsa would forget Vikas, and the family honour and pride would be saved.

Little did he know there was a storm brewing.

As soon as Lipsa arrived in Kantabanji, she was free from the constant prying and prodding of her family. She was free to do just as she pleased, for she was alone, with no one to chaperone and watch her all the time. She started meeting Vikas on a daily basis, ditching her lessons, and spending hours on end talking to him on the phone. If anything, she only got more wayward.

No matter what their dynamics were, it was clear that Lipsa's attachment was more evident than Vikas's. Soon, they decided to make their relationship physical and got intimate as well. Deep in her heart, she knew for sure that she wanted Vikas as her partner for life. But he was unemployed right now, and she didn't want to start a caste war in her village. So she told herself to be patient, and wait till her beloved got a job, so they could take the next big step in their lives as a financially independent couple. Meanwhile, news of her meetings with Vikas reached Srikanth's ear, which sent him over the edge and made him livid.

Vikas got admission into Jawaharlal Nehru University for his MPhil, and he had to leave for Delhi. So, Lipsa stopped commuting and, much to her uncle's relief, settled earnestly into her job.

But who was to say that they weren't in touch with each other on phone? Though these days, Srikanth was spared the daily humiliation of his niece being spotted with that disgusting pest by everyone, he still felt restless and wary. An ominous feeling was tugging at his guts. What if that bastard came back from Delhi? What if Lipsa, blinded by her foolish emotions, decided to elope with him?

Srikanth imagined the whole scenario, and shuddered. Imagine your niece living just three kilometres away, wedded into an untouchable household, while everyone else in your community looked down upon you and your family, because of her stupidity. It was a nightmare.

What did he do to deserve this?

Srikanth hated how helpless he had been rendered. He hated how all the dignity, the respect and the stature he had earned over many years of his life were now all in danger of being frivolously thrown out of the window, just because of this girl. And he hated the fact that he could do nothing about it.

Or, could he?

Turning to his friend, Srikanth gave vent to all the accumulated rage and bile that had poisoned his mind and body. "These untouchable bastards are getting out of our hands, Himanshu. We have been quiet for too long. So much so that they have started targeting the women of our households now. We have to get them back on the ground. Real hard. I am with you in whatever you are plotting for their demise. Just say the word, and I'll do anything you ask."

Himanshu and Srikanth were both been seething with fury against the Dalits, but they couldn't find a way of venting it and of avenging themselves. They wanted desperately to see to the destruction of the Dalits, yet couldn't find a way of doing so. Their anger was like the flickering flames of a bonfire. What they needed was to channel these unbridled emotions and let them take the form of a concrete, foolproof plan so they could bring the Dalits down from their high horse.

They thought and thought, but couldn't bring themselves to hatch such a plan, though morning turned to late afternoon. Restless, they decided to head to Lathore for a change of surroundings. They went to Srikanth's cloth store, and sat down to talk again while sipping coffee ordered from a nearby stall. Engaged in passionately roasting their arch rivals, they spotted Bhola Aggarwal, who had come to meet Srikanth at the shop, and ordered for another cup of coffee.

Making an attempt to continue the conversation, Bhola said, "Yesterday's nightmare has taken my breath away. I can't even walk on the streets anymore. Wherever I go, I hear people say that we have been taught the right lesson, and that the Dalits couldn't have done a better job. I feel like vomiting then and there. I slept all day today, and was feeling so lonely and so wronged. I feel a bit better now at the sight of you two."

At this, Himanshu lost it. "Feeling better? What the fuck do you mean you feel better? Those bastards literally stripped us of everything in broad daylight, and here you are, still high on life, 'feeling better'. Bullshit!"

The chirping of crickets filled the icy silence.

Taken aback by the outburst, Bhola was stunned. But trying not to take it to heart, he said, "Himanshu, I never said that I was 'high on life'. You know very well that I feel just as you do about this. This is something I'll probably never forget my whole life or even when I die. It's just that being cooped up at home all alone with my thoughts teetering on edge isn't a very pleasant or exciting experience. My mind was turning poisonous, and had I spent any more time in my room alone, I would have probably gone mad. So I stepped out for some fresh air, and spotted you guys. At this point of time, when lowlife scum who used to bow to me are whispering venomous things behind my back, I was just trying to find some empathy and solace in the two men who used to be my friends."

Srikanth gave him a subtle nod of understanding, and looked at Himanshu to make sure he didn't explode again. The latter, whose face had turned stone cold with rage, thawed somewhat and wore a displeased frown at having taken out his anger on his companion. Yet, he remained silent.

Having made sure that the atmosphere wasn't thick with tension anymore, Srikanth broke the silence, saying, "We were always your friends, Bhola, and will always remain so. And just as you said, this is something we'll never forget, not even in our graves. But this isn't the time to dwell on what happened; this is the time to think about what can be done. Himanshu and I were trying to come up with an action plan. Do you have any ideas?"

Himanshu cut in, "Utter destruction. Shake them to the core. Just wipe them out altogether. Looks like living among us has given them wings. Just leave them in shreds and watch them leave their 'thrones' with their tails between their legs. Fucking bastards think they can ruin us! I'll show them what messing with us really means!"

A ripple of hopeful enthusiasm washed over the three.

Srikanth piped up with a smirk, "You took the words out of my mouth. Yes. Just torch down their basti and watch them cry like the bloody cowards they are."

Nodding enthusiastically, Himanshu agreed, "Yes! That's good, Srikanth. In fact, I can't wait to watch their matchbox houses burn."

Bhola listened intently. His eyes went back and forth between Sriknath and Himanshu like he was watching a tennis match as they spoke heatedly. One would think that yesterday's event had taken a toll on him, and that he wanted relief.

But that wasn't the entire story.

Bhola's hatred for the Dalits may have peaked now due to the public apology, but it had originated much earlier. His story intertwined with that of two Dalit boys, even the mention of whose names made him burn with fury.

Manas and Vikas.

Sometime ago, in addition to transporting mahua, char, tol, paddy and latex that he used to buy from the people who gathered them from the forests, the avid businessman in Bhola decided to venture into transporting rice as well. He invested in a rice mill, or a rice processing unit, which used paddy as raw material, mechanically husked it, cleaned and filtered it, and then exported the finished rice to Balangir. Needless to say, it used up a lot of electricity. So much that the first time Bhola saw the electricity bill, his eyes turned as big as saucers and his jaw dropped to the floor.

Now, Bhola might have had to pay a little more for his energy expenses than he had anticipated, but his business was earning a lot of money, too. In fact, the profits were so high that his entrepreneurial instincts were telling him to invest in another rice mill. But, what was he to do with the electricity bills? So, he rigged the situation in his favour. Getting the line worker on his side, he got an illegal connection, so that he could use as much electricity as he liked, but there was no metre to record it, and consequently no bills to pay. Granted that this mill was mostly used by the villagers to husk their paddy grains, so it used less electricity compared to the large, fully mechanised mills, but paying no money was still better than having to pay some, right?

Besides, he would sell all the husk he got at high prices in the market as cattle feed.

In his defence, Bhola could argue that the village was already electricity-starved, so he was 'optimising' its use. The village only got electricity four days a week at most, and that too, it never lasted twenty-four hours. At least he was using the electricity to help the villagers get clean rice! In fact, being the 'good Samaritan' he was, he promised the line worker some of the husk, that Bhola got for free, so the line worker could feed his cattle, and keep quiet. Not to mention, Bhola would send fifteen hundred rupees as bribe to the junior engineer every month, even going so far as to treating him to exotic wine and lip-smacking meaty dishes every time he would arrive in the village.

But Bhola Aggarwal's tricks did not last for long.

One day, a Gana boy named Manas arrived at Bhola's mill to get a huge load of paddy husked. Manas was studying for his MA degree, came from a well-to-do family, that owned fifteen acres of arable land and as many as eighteen cattle to supplement the family income. In addition to being monetarily comfortable, Manas was a sharp lad, educationally equipped, and knew the workings of the government and the law. It was no surprise then that when his load of rice was given to him, but without the husk, he turned suspicious. He thanked the workers for their labour, and asked for the separated husk politely. But they just laughed it off, saying, "Boy, we don't give the husk back, okay? If you really need some, come in, and we'll sell you some. Instead, we did the husking for free." Manas had a feeling something was off, but continued in a light-hearted tone nonetheless. "Husking for free? Well, that is strange. Okay, maybe I'll forget that, but at least give my husk back. I have nearly twenty hungry cattle waiting at home to be fed, brother," he said half jokingly. He knew that they won't give it to him; still, he took a chance. Just as he had expected, one of the workers chuckled, and responded, "Boy, if our owner started giving away the husk for free, what would he earn, huh? We are not charging you for cleaning your rice. You aren't getting the husk back because this is what he sells, and uses the money to operate the mill. Otherwise, he won't be generously husking your paddy for free. We got your job done, now bugger off; we're busy."

But Manas was adamant. He wanted his husk back, whether the workers liked it or not. So, as much as he hated resorting to it, he created a ruckus and refused to back down. The workers stuck to their ground, and called up their owner instead. This actually surprised Manas. How serious did this have to be for them to call the owner himself? Bhola Aggarwal walked up to Manas, and demanded that he leave the premises immediately if he didn't want to get beaten to death. An aggressive shouting match followed. Bhola's workers pitched in to defend their master, naturally. Seeing that he was outnumbered, and being proven wrong in an audience that had quickly gathered, Manas finally withdrew with a sigh of defeat.

Bhola and his men walked off triumphantly, but Manas was left standing there. He quickly put the pieces together and inferred just how much of a shrewd businessman Bhola Aggarwal was. To think that he was offering to husk the villagers' rice for free, just so he could earn double from selling their husk back to them! And the naive villagers were paying such high prices for buying their own husk, just to feed their hardworking cattle. Then the pretence of benevolence and righteous, indignant innocence that the wily man had put on for the benefit of his audience, humiliating Manas before the villagers, to cover up his blatant malpractice was too much to bear. Manas was beyond enraged.

He was well aware of the laws of the country and also aware of Bhola's dirty little secret. Determined to expose him, Manas went and filed two cases: one in the District Electricity Office for his illegal connection, and the other in the Labour Department. Bhola was milking every paisa possible from those poor illiterate villagers; who was to say he wasn't piling profits by cutting on his workers' wages as well? So he filed a complaint, lest Bhola be defying any labour laws. If he wasn't, good for him. If not, he better be prepared for a storm coming.

The Labour Department officer was quick to act on the complaint, and promptly swooped down like a hungry vulture having spotted its meal. He started questioning Bhola and his workers about labour conditions at the mill. What were the wages? The working hours? Were the labourers made to work overtime? If so, were they paid for it? Were there any allowances for leaves? Were they made to work on holidays as well? What about the master's role? The workers' insurance? Bhola had been lousy at keeping records as it is. Need one really mention that he was neither the most honest nor the most just employer out there? The inquiry simply laid it all bare.

And then there was the Electricity Office. Bhola might have bribed the line worker and the junior engineer. But Manas had registered a complaint with the chief engineer, a no-nonsense officer who took his job seriously and wasn't one to be deterred with bribes or threats. He fired question upon question at Bhola, warning him that he would cross-check with his workers as well. Meticulous verification was done on the veracity of the consumer number, installation of the metre, the monthly loading of the transformer, the electricity charges, etc. Needless to say, all of this had been fudged or bypassed. Besides, the illegal connection itself served as the icing on the cake.

Bhola Aggarwal was neck-deep in trouble.

As a result, he had to pay a humongous fine for both cases, amounting to lakhs of rupees, and additionally had to promise due diligence and compliance in paying electricity bills, and improve labour conditions in his mills. Now Bhola earned a lot from his rice manufacturing unit; so the fines were probably not more than a week's earning for him, which he didn't have many qualms parting with. What really hurt and angered him the most was how he lost face and his dignity, not only before his own workers but the villagers as well, for now all the neighbouring villages also came to know how he operated his mills. Now, they wouldn't stop calling him a black-marketer and a cheat who not only duped the villagers but had no compunctions about denying his own workers their proper wages and making them work in subpar conditions.

All his humiliation manifested itself as pure vitriolic hatred for those who had landed him in trouble in the first place: Manas, and his best friend Vikas. Bhola hated them to his bones, to the point that he would fight the insane urge to kill them on sight. He hated how his face had been blackened and how his image ruined.

What enraged him much more was the fact that they were both Dalits.

Manas and Vikas were just young college students; they didn't have so much of an image to uphold and protect, as did Bhola.

But they did have a life.

If he couldn't land their image in jeopardy, he would ensure their lives did.

And so, like a dangerous alley cat sitting silently in a dark corner, he had been patiently waiting for the right opportunity to come his way, so he could pounce upon it with his merciless claws.

And that opportunity was finally here.

Bhola Aggarwal was a shrewd businessman who was used to getting his work done without getting his hands dirty (his mills broke his perfect record), so he practically jumped at this opportunity. Getting to exact a long-awaited revenge, without even having to engage in battle? He would have done anything to get this. Here, he could practically watch his enemies lose their all, with Himanshu and Srikanth working at the forefront, while he himself sat and enjoyed their doings from behind the scenes.

Torching the Dalit houses was the best idea, ever.

What pleased Bhola even more was the fact that now he would also be able to take down his arch rivals, the Mehers. The Marwari community, that Bhola Aggarwal was a part of, had been the only traders in Lathore for a while, thus enjoying sole monopoly. Until the Mehers arrived on the scene. Bhola couldn't wait for Srikanth Meher to get embroiled with the police after the arson, so that he could write the Mehers off the business scene for good, and the Marwaris could rule once again.

So, he provoked his friends further, saying, "Srikanth *bhai*, it isn't just an incident or two but a whole series of them. They are really getting out of their league now, trying to touch horizons that weren't even meant for them to see in the first place. We must definitely take action."

Srikanth was surprised by Bhola's sudden pitch-in, but satisfied nonetheless. He gave him an enthusiastic nod.

Bhola continued, "You go right ahead with your plan. Put their entire basti on fire. Let's see how much they wail and shout then. I am always with you, lending moral support. And if there is any financial requirement to be met, you can bank on me."

Himanshu and Srikanth exchanged meaningful glances. Despite his reputation in the area, there was no denying that Bhola Aggarwal was a man of means. To have him on their side meant that they could at least tackle all money-related matters with ease.

Having thus arrived at a definite plan of action with mutual support, they settled back into their seats, visibly more at ease now. Then, with a deep sigh of satisfaction, Bhola got up and said, "Brothers, I'll get going now. I hope we will continue to keep each other's spirits alive, until this mission succeeds." And, winking at Himanshu, added, "And when it does, we can all get 'high on life' together."

Himanshu gave a wry chuckle and waved him off, saying, "All right, enough with the jokes, get going now."

As the two friends watched, thin smiles floating on their lips, their heads much clearer than before, Bhola leisurely got onto his motorbike and kick-started it with extra vigour. Then playfully shooting a finger gun at Srikanth, he sped away in a cloud of dust, his fat face momentarily souring as some passers-by gave him dirty looks.

"Bhola and his antics," Srikanth muttered with a shake of his head as the two men looked at each other and shared a chuckle. Then they turned to look into the distance where the setting sun was painting the sky in hues of vermillion.

The war had begun.

Seventeen

Humans are forever rushing about their lives waiting for a miracle to guide them out of their misery. The right college, the right career, the right post, the right life companion.

They are always waiting.

But seasons? They wait for none.

Whether it is the blazing summers with their ruthless heat waves, the thundering monsoons with their unending downpours, the cold winters with their cosy quilts and warm bonfires or the jubilance of springs that bring a burst of colours and a reviving breath of pleasant winds, they all roll into one another, forever intertwined in their periodic cycle.

And so, Lathore found itself in the midst of January, braving chilly winds, as the winter crops ripened into a promising harvest.

Lathore and Kharli were a mere three kilometres apart, separated by rolling fields of bamboo. Directly across those villages were the magnificent peaks of Gandhamardhan flanked on either side by Harishankar and Nrusinghanath. The expansive mountain ranges were home to icy-cold winds that blew down the slopes. Those, coupled with the bamboo thickets, always ensured that Lathore and Kharli were enveloped in bitter cold in the early months of the year.

Thankfully, the people of Lathore didn't have to brave this chilly weather for long hours out in the fields. Nearly all the paddy, which was the major crop of this season, got harvested by then and people stashed the crops away, using the time to unwind and relax while warming themselves and chatting around bonfires. However, the lands of the villages were really fertile, so some people went the extra mile and sowed green and black gram as well. Those would take a little more time to ripen; so farmers had to sometimes guard their crops while sitting out in the field, lest any grazing cattle or birds ate away months of their hard work.

Overall, winters in Lathore were a contrast of cold and comforting as people brought out their warm blankets and wrapped themselves in layers of clothing, craving cuddles and crackers and hot teas.

The days would start off misty and slow, with the pearl-like dewdrops glistening in the early morning sunshine, adorning the barks of trees, giving a bejewelled charm to the muted hues of hickory, sepia and cinnamon. They wouldn't melt till the day had rolled into early noon and would take their time trickling down the rugged barks. People would gather dry twigs and light them to make little bonfires, huddling around them in batches as they reminisced about the day before and revelled in their temporary warmth.

They would trudge leisurely to the village pond, for the water looked anything but inviting. They would let the smiling sun warm the cold waters a little before wading in, as they congregated in small groups to catch up on the day's gossip. By the time they finished with their bath, it would be nearly ten. But who cared? They had all the time in the world, with months of their hard work now harvested and stored away safely, giving them time they had rightfully earned to relax. As the day would rise onto her youthful glory, the horizon would glimmer with a crimson sheen, the sun splattering colours onto benevolent blue skies.

On one such winter morning, an adolescent was gazing at the endless sky, taking in the beauty of the enormous white clouds and the mist-enshrouded foliage. He had woken up in the wee hours, and tried to keep off the nail-biting cold by lighting up some twigs for warmth. Now, as he watched the smouldering embers and soot lying in a soft heap of orange, black and grey, he decided it was time to go for his bath.

This teenager went by the name of Ganesh Suna, of Ganapada. A pleasant, polite and witty boy, Ganesh studied at the Ashram school for free, and was in class nine. He stayed in the school hostel, but had briefly come home to spend the winter holidays with his family and friends.

Ganesh was on his way to the village pond. As he made his way, weaving through the little creepers and the wet, dewy grass, he walked with leisurely steps, breathing in the clean cold air, alive with bird calls, enjoying the scenery that he had come to love since his childhood. He knew he would miss this when he returned to his hostel. Today was 21 January, the day of his departure.

Ganesh was recalling the conversation he'd had with his father that morning. He had packed most of his belongings, but had expressed the need for a new vest, for the old ones had been torn with repeated use. His father had assured him that he could go and buy some later in the day, after he was done with his bath and lunch.

Hence, here he was, all freshened up after his bath, donning formal clothes, with his belly full, and now on his way to the market to buy a vest. It was eleven already, and Ganesh knew that he had a bus to catch, so he hurried towards Kishore Meher's cloth shop, which was in the middle of the marketplace. If he missed his bus, he would only get the next one in the evening, which meant arriving at the hostel at night, and no dinner at the mess. Not to mention that his father would definitely not be pleased about it.

Thus guided by the urgency of the situation, young Ganesh entered the shop with a single-minded focus, uttered some brisk greetings and politely asked for some vests. The sales boy deftly laid out some for him. Ganesh quickly slipped on one that he thought was his size, but it was a bit too tight. So he picked the next one, which was bigger. This seemed tailor-made for him and it fit him perfectly. With a smile of satisfaction, he told the sales boy he would have the one he was wearing and requested him to bill it. Then, hurriedly slipping on his shirt over the vest, he paid the amount asked and, with a quick thank you, proceeded to walk out of the shop.

Now, on the counter sat two of Kishore Meher's sons, managing the shop in place of him. The younger one of the two, around twenty-two or twenty-three, had his eyes trained on an oblivious Ganesh. He was sure that Ganesh had tried on two vests at one point of time, but wasn't sure if he had seen him take both of them off. What if he was wearing two vests, but had only paid for one? The fact that he was rushing out of the shop in such a hurry also made him suspicious. So he warily called out to the young boy, "Hey Ganesh! Come here for a bit, will you?"

On hearing his name called, Ganesh briskly turned back and said, "Sorry sir, but I have a bus to catch! Please just tell me what it is quickly." At this the man's suspicions solidified into certainty. Did the brat just refuse to listen to him? The thieving bastard must be scared of being caught. Getting angrier now, the man shouted, "COME HERE, I said! You cannot walk out of here wearing two vests when you have paid for just one!" At this, Ganesh paused, very surprised, and with a shrug, said, "Why would I wear two vests at the same time? I am wearing just one vest, and I *have* paid for it, sir. Well, I am off now."

At this, Meher lost it.

Not only had this untouchable son of a bitch turned up at his shop and polluted it, he had also ruined his luck for the day by stepping in as the first customer. And then he had the audacity to steal from right under his nose, and talk back! He shouted so loud his throat hurt, "You come back here, you motherfucker! *Sala*, stealing a vest right before my eyes! You get your thieving ass back in here or I'll punch your shit-eating face into the next century!"

Thieving?

This got to Ganesh. He was not thieving! He was just trying to hurry so he won't be late in catching his bus! Why on earth was the owner picking on him like this?

But he wasn't about to be bullied. He had duly paid for his vest, so why should he let anyone brand him a thief. He would stand up for himself. He had nothing to be afraid of. Let him be late if need be.

So, Ganesh marched back into the shop, saying, "Sir, you've got it all wrong. I have not stolen—"

Smack.

Ganesh brought up a hand to his stinging cheek in stunned silence, his ears ringing from the hard slap.

He had been slapped. For no fault of his own.

"Think I will let you get away with this, you thieving bastard! Here, let the world see your filthy low-caste antics," the man was shouting. He grabbed hold of a dazed Ganesh's collar and ripped his shirt open, leaving his half-naked torso for everyone to see. "Take off your shirt and then tell me you have not stolen two vests from my shop!"

Ganesh stared and stared. With his half-torn shirt hanging loosely from his frame, he looked straight into Meher's eyes. Then, as a hot tear fell from his eye, he clenched his jaw hard so that he wouldn't cry. His voice dropped as he uttered a single word.

"Fine."

Then, with eyes still trained on his assaulter, he slowly took off his shirt with unsteady hands. Then he peeled off his vest as well, and stood with his torso bared in front of the stunned shop workers, his cheeks burning, as the chilly morning air left goose bumps on his skin.

Meher's son stood there, his eyes bulging stupidly out of their sockets, open-mouthed in dismay at being proven wrong. As

Ganesh glared at him with all the ferocity he could muster, Meher guiltily looked away, unable to bear the boy's gaze. When Ganesh felt a sob threatening to break out of his trembling lips, he cast a hurt, accusing look at everyone around him and stormed out of the shop, wiping his tears with his palms.

He didn't want to go to school anymore.

As fresh tears ran down his cheeks and a gust of cold air enveloped his half-naked torso, he half ran, half walked home, his angry feet stumbling with the terrible hurt of the humiliation.

On the outskirts of Ganapada, Manas, Vikas and Suresh were sitting leisurely and chatting, when they spotted Ganesh, stumbling along, half-running, his torn shirt hanging from his torso, eyes red with tears, distress writ large on his face. Concerned, they called out to him and asked him what had happened and was he all right. Ganesh, whose cheerful world had just been turned upside down for no fault of his, broke down on receiving such genuine concern from these kind souls. He started sobbing uncontrollably.

Making his way to where they sat, he recounted between sobs the morning's cruel episode, as they listened attentively, the frowns slowly deepening on their faces. Absorbed in describing how that "demon" of a shopkeeper had abused him, called him a thief, mercilessly torn his shirt and made him strip, Ganesh did not realise the powerful impact that his words were making on the emotions of his listeners. They were overcome with concern, empathy, incredulity and finally, blinding rage.

Who did that Meher's son think he was, treating an innocent child like that?

The three youths were livid. With fury coursing through their veins to teach the arrogant Meher a lesson, they got up. Hands balled into angry fists, they marched to the market place, with Ganesh in tow, causing a ripple in the general humdrum of vendors and shopkeepers, who sensed something was wrong.

Barging into Meher's shop, Vikas shouted, "Where's that bloody thief's son who dared to slap this innocent boy? Come out, and I'll show you just who is a thief!" Meher's younger son, who was sitting at the shop counter with his elder brother, was shell-shocked. They both froze momentarily, their hands pausing whatever they had been doing till then. Vikas glared at the younger Meher, demanding to know how he could have possibly been so barbaric as to inflict such trauma upon an innocent and honest child.

Incredulous at the disrespect and ignominy, which cut them all the more for they knew full well where the guilt lay, the brothers came out of their stupor and retorted with vulgar caste abuses at the group of four. This infuriated Manas even more. He had thought that they might own up that it was a mistake; and here they were, not only blaming poor Ganesh but concocting details that the boy had neither spoken of nor, he was certain, had occurred in the first place. Utter lies and rubbish! Manas was so angry that before anyone knew it, he had moved from holding a trembling Ganesh's shoulders, and grabbed the younger Meher by his collar and landed one stinging slap across his right cheek.

As the stunned man clutched his cheek, glaring at Manas with pure hatred and fear, Manas quietly said, "*Sala*, son of a thief, now do you know what it feels like?" Enraged, the older brother lunged viciously at Manas, who dodged and punched him one in the face; then the younger Meher hit back. At this Vikas and Suresh threw themselves into it, and fists and abuses flew fast and furious in a free for all.

Poor Ganesh watched in horror, unable to move, his feet numb with terror. He desperately wished to stop this ugly brawl, yet couldn't. His conscience was eating into him, telling him this was all his fault. Yet all he could do was watch in stunned silence as the fight between the five men raged on.

With a sixth man orbiting them in futile panic.

It was Chitrasen, who had seen the trio leave with a very perturbed Ganesh in tow a while ago. Worried by the grim looks on the young men's faces, he had decided to follow them, almost certain that they were going to do something rash. It had just been a hunch based on instinct, but he was certain that these boys were not on their way to play football.

Oh lord, and how he hated being right.

So here was Chitrasen, hating his decision to tail them in the first place, yet trying his level best to intervene and separate the men from the furious tangle of flying limbs they had ended up in, reminding himself now and again to wash his ears later in hopes of unhearing the string of blood-curdling, murderous abuses that were being thrown around. Visibly flinching with every kick or punch that landed on god knows who, Chitrasen was trying his best to drown their screaming, snarling, shouting voices with his own, trying to calm them down while anxiously circling them in hopes of finding a way of separating them.

Part of Chitrasen wanted to just let them fight, and instead solace and comfort the terrified child who stood rooted to the spot, his eyes widened in fear, but he could not. He was a responsible and revered elder of the village, and he felt responsible. Having come here, if he just left midway, he would become the laughing stock of the village and people would accuse him of tailing the youths only to enjoy some entertainment. Chitrasen didn't want to be labelled a safe player or a hypocrite; so once again he turned to the group, infusing extra vigour into his limbs, trying to separate them physically, and raising his voice a few decibels higher in trying to calm them down.

By now, a large market crowd had gathered outside the Mehers' shop to enjoy the mid-morning brawl. Among the curious onlookers were other shopkeepers as well, one of them being Srikanth Meher, whose enterprise was a few shops away. The audience was high on adrenaline, hooting and cheering lustily for the bloodthirsty opponents to tear each other's throats (some were even booing at a frustrated Chitrasen). Much to their delight, Vikas landed such a strong punch that the young Meher keeled over and hit the edge of the counter with a thud. When he got up, with some effort, there was a gash on his temple oozing blood.

Vikas staggered back in dismay and surprise, almost colliding with Suresh, who quit fighting and held onto him for support. The other Meher, who had been fighting with Manas, saw his brother fall and, seeing the blood on his head, instantly ran to his side to nurse him. Manas took in the situation, catching Vikas's eyes and looking at him in disbelief. Seeing the result of their actions, the three young men now realised that perhaps they had let their emotions govern their rationality. As the crowd's noises died down, the three proceeded to exit the shop, their eyes evading everyone's; Vikas muttered a curse under his breath, partly to cushion the blow of his own guilt.

Ganesh followed the three, his body convulsed by silent sobs as the consequences of his own little encounter hit him in the face like a truck. He was followed by an apologetic Chitrasen, still trying his best to douse the situation by politely asking everyone to return home, while secretly heaving a sigh of relief that the brawl was finally over.

Quick on his feet, Srikanth promptly called for an ambulance to take an injured Meher. Then he placed a second call, to Himanshu, and called him to the cloth store. There, he filled him in the details about what led to the injury. Meanwhile, the crowd had swelled as more and more people had collected, drawn by news of the fight. They had grown increasingly sympathetic towards the shop owners, and the upper castes in general, upon seeing the young Meher injured and bleeding. Exploiting the anger and charged emotions of the crowd, Srikanth used it to their advantage and provoked them further, "Did you all see that? Did you see how brazen those Ganas have become? When open fights didn't satisfy them, they started entering shops to beat us up. One day, they'll even start entering our homes, not sparing anyone. If we don't fight back now, we'll have to bear their reign of terror forever. Those atrocious bastards must be taught a lesson."

At this, the crowd hollered back in agreement. They, too, felt that the Ganas were becoming too high-handed. They started shouting vulgar caste invectives and slogans voicing their enthusiasm. Himanshu rejoined, adding his bit and said, "If this continues, we won't be able to live in the village anymore. They will definitely start bossing over us next. But we aren't flower girls either. We will show them what it means to challenge us!" Another round of shouts followed. The crowd had turned into an angry mob that was growing more agitated by the second, ready to attack and take down the Dalits there and then.

Srikanth and Himanshu turned to each other, trying to stop themselves from grinning in glee. Every ounce of hatred they had borne the past four months, every shred of anger they had forced themselves to bury in their hearts, every howl of fury they had shoved down their throats, had been worth it. Now was the time to let all the pent-up energy manifest into a destruction plan for the untouchables. After everything they had been through, it was finally time to get back at their enemies. It was payback time.

In order to escalate matters further, they sent the injured man to the Veer Surendra Sai Institute of Medical Sciences and Research (VIMSAR) in Burla. Although his injury was just a hairline gash on the temple, they spread word that the injury was so bad he had to be sent to Burla for treatment. Then, they spread the rumour that young Meher had suffered a head concussion and died on his way to the hospital. At this, the mob turned murderous. They started gathering sticks and stones as ammunition, and scattered in all directions to hunt for Manas, Vikas, Suresh and Ganesh.

Armed with lathis, iron rods, hockey sticks, sickles and whatever they could lay their hands on, the furious mob marched to Ganapada, determined to raise hell and create havoc. On learning that an armed mob was on its way, and seeing the dogs, livestock and domestic animals running helter-skelter, the Ganas anticipated disaster and ran for their lives.

The angry mob reached Ganapada soon after, only to find the place empty of people. Undeterred, they decided to ransack the houses for whatever valuables they could lay their hands on. They broke open cupboards, boxes, shelves, emptied everything and destroyed the rest mercilessly.

Then, Himanshu and Srikanth decided to have their vile plans executed. "*Arrey*, looting them won't do any permanent harm. Just burn down their fucking houses so they have nowhere to live." The mob thought this was a brilliant idea. So, they went about setting fire to the houses of Manas, Vikas, Suresh and Ganesh.

But still not satisfied, Himanshu goaded them on, "What good will it do to burn just four houses out of so many? Torch the entire goddamn basti, for heaven's sake!"

At this, the crowd held back, some confused, others hesitant.

Srikanth added, "What are you waiting for? Whether you burn four houses or four hundred, you will all be accused nonetheless. If we are going to be convicted anyway, might as well do something worth being convicted for, right?" he said half jokingly, but then went on to add grimly, "Burn down every single house in this fucking pada. I don't want a single one standing after we are done. And make sure you burn that Chitrasen Suna's house real good. That old man's been flexing his riches a bit too much these days. Burn it all down! Turn Ganapada to soot!"

The mob blindly obeyed. They tried setting the colony on fire, but it was difficult as not everything was inflammable. So Kamalnath Seth opened his petrol pump, letting them take the fuel for free. Himanshu Bagarti distributed free liquor, so they could get themselves drunk and carry out this heinous task without any qualms. After they set the houses burning, they went to the main road of the village and dumped wooden logs on it. Then, they lit those as well, effectively blocking the road, thus stopping anyone who might arrive with help from outside, like the police, or the Dalits.

The horrified Dalits, who had to run to save their lives from the murderous mob, stood and helplessly watched their belongings, their houses, their lives, everything being burnt down before their eyes. They could do nothing. They were powerless.

The people of Ganapada couldn't understand what they had done to deserve this. For generations, they had coexisted with the upper castes, even if unequally, depending on each other in relations of mutuality. Despite the daily insults and humiliation and worse that they had to suffer, for generations, they had persevered, dedicating their lives to serving the upper castes, hoping that one day they would change for the better. But alas, not one of them had hesitated or stopped for a moment to consider; they had torched down every single house. The Dalits had always addressed them as older brothers and sisters, uncles and aunts. But the upper castes did not even consider them human, forget equals. All that was left between the communities was an abyss of fear and loathing, swallowing all trust, humanity and rationality.

The Dalits were left alone to fend for themselves.

They immediately called the fire brigade, hoping they could help save at least whatever little could be saved. The firemen arrived promptly. But they found the road to Ganapada blocked by burning logs. So, they started by putting out the flames on the road in front of them first. At this, a fragment of the mob marched up to them, shouting aggressive slogans and threatening the firemen that they would not let them go further.

"You already see what we are capable of. If you move another step, you will be dead!" one hooligan shouted. "Yes...Yes! You better turn back. Or we'll finish you!" said another. The firemen cautiously assessed the mob's mood. One drunken goon walked up swaggering to the brigade in what he thought was intimidating fashion, stumbling thrice on the way. Then snatching the water hose from the hands of a fireman, he turned to the crowd like a saint addressing his devotees, and said, "Why trust these idiots? Let's just break their pipe and shut them down..." The firemen looked aghast at this, and one of them stepped forward to reason with the mobster.

At this, some drunkards lunged at the pipe, hitting it with rods and sharp objects, while others viciously attacked the firemen. The air was filled with soot, carbon dioxide and abuses. The water pipe was damaged, and some twenty firemen badly beaten. Not equipped to fight the belligerent armed mob, the firemen had little choice but to turn back and leave the site.

Last came those who were supposed to arrive first: the police.

The police contingent arrived at 6 pm, hours after the torching. The dedicated men in uniform had hoped that the mob would have cooled down by then, and so, they could have been last-minute heroes, trying their valiant best to salvage the situation, knowing that the damage was already done.

Unfortunately for them, however, the mob was still on the rampage, with the drunken louts going around admiring the fireworks, and laughing, cackling and celebrating like maniacs as the tall flames enveloped the basti, destroying anything that the fire did not. They had also called in friends and acquaintances from nearby villages to swell their numbers, so that the size of the crowd would intimidate any rival forces that arrived to help.

Seeing that mob, being the brave lot that they were, the police silently retreated from the site and drove away in their jeeps, annoyed that they would get no credit for coming this far. But at least they were alive and unhurt.

The bribe-stuffed bastards.

It may have been a different situation had Kishore Sarangi been there; but apparently he had been transferred. So the Dalits were left at the mercy of these dedicated law-abiding officers.

Some people went to lodge a complaint with the District Collector. But unsurprisingly, he too heard their story dismissively with scant attention, and took no action regarding the incident.

The other strange thing was that practically no media personnel turned up to report or even to take a look at the scene of crime. To think that local reporters, who had once chided the authorities for potholes on the road to Lathore, didn't think that an entire locality of Lathore being burned down was newsworthy enough for them was certainly very odd.

Were the news agencies genuinely not interested or curious about such a gruesome incident? Or had they been bribed and threatened to keep their mouths shut by a political party?

The police arrived again at the burning basti, this time at two in the dead of night, hugely relieved at the absence of the drunken mob of hooligans. The lot had dispersed after a round of celebrations; and the mob leaders, Himanshu, Srikanth and Bhola, had fled to Raipur, where they had stable businesses, and could evade any police interrogation for the meantime.

The perpetrators might have fled, but the aftermath of their destructive hate was there for the world to see. The Dalit locality was still in flames. So, the police briskly piled out of their jeeps, coordinated their positions after intense discussions, took up positions armed with their deadly rifles, and...just stood there.

That's about it.

They just stood there poised like the guardians of the galaxy, as if ready to face any disaster that might befall the burning basti. But, who were they trying to fool?

It was January. The Ganas were stranded in the middle of the fields, shivering in the cold, with hungry children and helpless elders by their side, no shelter, no food, only the clothes they wore, and devastated hearts and minds. There were forests nearby and bears and jackals sometimes wandered into the fields at night. So the homeless victims were also at risk of attacks by wild animals. Yet, this was not a fear anywhere as crippling as the fear that now sat in their hearts.

The fear of men.

With bellies growling in hunger as they struggled against the bitter cold, and their hearts wailed in anger and anguish, the moon rose and night stealthily crept past, to beckon the sun to start a new day.

As the Dalits slowly came out of hiding one by one, the firemen arrived on the scene again as well, as did the police, with reinforcements. The fire workers first doused the flames on the pile of logs blocking the road. Then they moved into the basti and set to work in earnest, aiming their long pipes to hose down the still burning houses, the powerful jets of water covering great distances with impressive force. But, of what use was it now? Nearly all the houses had been burnt down, with the remains smouldering. Spraying water only made it look even worse now, if that was possible: all of Ganapada was charred black, with the debris, ashes, the skeletal, burnt remains of houses, all mixing with the water and floating about in an unholy mess. A terrible smell pervaded the air. It was a nightmarish, ghastly sight.

That was the first sight the Dalits were met with when they went back to see what was left of their homes.

As they rushed forward in disbelief and horror, the police held them back. Some started wailing, others screamed and howled, others just collapsed on their knees. They looked like their souls had been sucked out of their bodies, and they had been left to fend for themselves as lifeless corpses.

Even so, they tried to comply with the surly police forces, and courageously began lodging FIRs for those they had seen involved in the crime. The list of suspects went on and on; there were a staggering two hundred eighty names. Some of the policemen dispersed to work on the complaints lodged. But only about forty individuals could be caught eventually. The rest had, quite conveniently, fled.

Meanwhile, two Dalit correspondents from Khariar arrived and went around taking pictures of the devastation and talking to the victims of the mayhem. They went on to publish an article on the atrocities against Dalits in the local newspapers. This attracted some attention of the outside media, that followed suit, publishing half-baked articles in their respective editorials, using the self-same photographs over and over again.

This was nothing new.

It had always been like this.

And, in absence of radical change, it was likely to remain so.

The main accused, or 'masterminds' as they were glorified, invariably fled the scene and managed to elude justice. If caught, they simply used their influence or their money as a shield they would thrust with impunity into the face of the law. If any of the guilty were ever caught, they would get out on bail. With the police, politicians and authorities in collusion, no evidence ever reached the courts of law untampered, if it reached them at all. Eventually, as the case dragged on interminably, people forgot about it, along with the fate of the victims.

The victims, the former residents of Ganapada, were herded into the hastily put up makeshift relief camp at the school in Lathore, and given stale flattened rice and jaggery for breakfast. The officials had thought that some food would liven them up, especially after the day-long fast they were forced to undergo the day before. To their dismay, however, they simply clutched their food packets, beating their chests and sobbing disconsolately. Now that everything was lost, even a bowl of homemade *pakhal* seemed like a luxury.

As the grief of their unfathomable loss settled on their limbs like leaden dust, they could not find themselves able to move. They could not even find themselves able to speak. Not even amongst themselves. Only their bewildered and bereft souls whispered silently to God, repeatedly asking what wrong had they done, to whom.

They never got any answers.

They had lost everything: their homes, their possessions, their livelihood, their freedom, their dreams, their hopes and their dignity.

Their souls.

Their future glared at them mercilessly through the haze of uncertainty. They did not know what lay ahead, or if anything did. No one has ever known what the future holds, and this is what frightens human beings the most: the fear of the unknown. But in their present nightmarish predicament, that fear assumed far greater, far more monstrous proportions than ever before. The fear of tomorrow. That fear crept up their limbs, slithered down their spines and curled itself around their hearts numbed with terror.

Their future was uncertain and unforeseeable.

Did they have a future at all?

Eighteen

The long night was coming to an end, the glimmering stars were receding one by one as they left the stage for the next day. The crickets had stopped chirping and the first roosters could be heard crowing. A goods train passed Lathore station, its wheels rattling on the tracks.

Makaru abruptly woke up. He urgently wanted to pee. Through sleep-heavy eyes, he saw Chitrasen awake in his makeshift bed, sitting with his forehead resting on his folded knees. A few feet away, another man was also sitting up, clearly unable to sleep. But for someone who had lost everything, would losing sleep matter?

A part of Makaru wanted to ask his dada if he was all right, but he couldn't bring himself to. So he got up as soundlessly as possible and, focusing on the urgent task at hand, quietly walked outside.

He saw the police van empty, the men on duty fast asleep. What a stark contrast. The cops peacefully snoring their troubles away, while the troubles of the victims kept their sleep and peace at bay. He walked outside the camp to look for an isolated clearing to empty his bursting bladder.

As he looked up, he saw a tranquil moon, radiating its cool milky whiteness. It must have been the eleventh or twelfth night of the lunar month. Having stood in its solitary corner of the sky all night, the moon would soon set, lowering itself behind the majestic Gandhamardhan hills. Anticipating sunrise, Makaru hurried on.

He saw a street dog curled up alone in a corner. As soon as it heard Makaru's footsteps, it got up, stretched its thin body to shake off the lethargy and came up to Makaru, wagging its tail. The dog and Makaru looked meaningfully at each other for a few moments, sole companions of the night. Makaru thought: Just see the paradox. Here's this dumb animal, who is seeing me for the first time in its life and yet came forward without hesitation to greet me. And then there are those inhuman upper castes, who have lived with us for generations and yet did not hesitate a moment to burn our homes down to the ground.

Oblivious to Makaru's thoughts, the dog trotted away after a while, seemingly bored.

Having emptied his bladder, Makaru walked back to the school compound. He saw Chitra-da, who had been previously sitting awake, now lying huddled under his thin bed sheet. Makaru tiptoed to his own spot and sat down. Now that he was wide awake, he didn't feel like putting himself back to sleep.

A cold wind was blowing in the wintry silence before dawn. He heard the wailing of a baby somewhere. It might have wet its bed, he thought. True to his suspicions, as he located the source of the sound coming from a far corner, the mother woke up, changed the cloth to a fresh dry one, and patted her baby to sleep once again.

Just then, Makaru heard someone's sniffles. It was Chitra-da. Makaru wanted fervently to be able to comfort him, to console him somehow. But he could not. He could not even muster the courage to go up to him; for each time he tried, his soul would shrink, weighed down by the enormity of Chitra-da's loss and his grief, which Makaru could not share.

Unconcerned by the mundane cares and worries of mortals, the bright golden sun rose on another day, dispelling the darkness of the night. Men and women set about scurrying to get done with their morning ablutions. While the women went to the latrines in groups, the men trudged off to the village pond. Among them were Chitrasen and Makaru.

On their way, Chitrasen came across a neem tree. So he wordlessly broke off two twigs, keeping one for himself and giving the other to Makaru. The receiver accepted the neem twig with extended hands and palms folded in gratitude, as was the tradition.

Soon they reached the ridge of the pond. Having finished their ablutions, Chitrasen and Makaru sat there in silence. Going about his daily rituals this late in the day was unusual for the older man. He had always been a workaholic, rising before dawn and getting ready for the day's work when half the world was still asleep. He quietly rued the change as he reflected on the recent developments in his life.

Before this, Chitrasen Suna had never had a moment's pause; he was always immersed in work, surveying this, inspecting that, managing, advising, overseeing. He had always taken pride and joy in completing all his tasks well and efficiently. Yet here he was, with nothing to do now but indulge endlessly in his despair and dwell repeatedly on all that he had lost. Back then, time would simply fly through the day, and before he knew it, a brand new day would be beckoning him back to work. He had absolutely no time to brood. But now, spending even a minute without tearing at his hair and screaming his lungs out in frustration and despair seemed daunting.

Reluctant to break the silence and Chitra-da's thoughts, Makaru hesitantly asked, "Dada, have you received any kind of help from the government?"

Chitrasen scoffed and replied, "Hardly. All they have done so far is to herd us and dump us together in little matchbox rooms. There is some free food to keep us alive, that is all. And there is this...Relief Fund that someone mentioned, but it involves too many complications. One has to go through a hellishly cumbersome bureaucratic process, and at the end of all that running around, it amounts to just one lakh per family. Who would be content with that, when the losses they have incurred are many times that?"

Makaru wasn't surprised to hear this, but it broke his heart all the same. Nevertheless, he couldn't stop himself from asking, "And what about the case itself? Has the government enlisted any actions it will take...to apprehend the accused?"

Chitrasen chuckled bitterly. "Do you really think they intend to do anything about it, when it is literally a win-win situation for them? Just think for yourself: are the upper castes who vandalised our basti and those who run the government any different? It is us Dalits who are dying here, Makaru. They don't give a damn about us."

Deep down, Makaru was aware of this. But what surprised him was the brutal honesty with which Chitra-da spoke of their mistreatment. But then again, Chitrasen Suna had never been one to mince his words.

He continued, "Just the other day, we were visited by this influential Congress politician. And he got full marks for showing fake sympathy. He did everything: walked through our destroyed basti, shed a few tears, went around consoling people at the relief camp, even gave a speech on how inhuman and barbaric it was, how we didn't deserve to be put through this, and whatnot. But did he ever say any of this publicly to the media? In any press conference? No. Not a word or mention of it anywhere. He was one hell of a good actor, that man."

Makaru was speechless. He could see Chitra-da had more to say, so he kept mum. Sure enough, he went on angrily, "And you know what, he knew me personally as well. I was the Sarpanch, wasn't I? But did he utter a word of acknowledgement? No. He just gave me a condescending pat on the back. As if I was a pathetic homeless puppy waiting to be petted."

Chitra-da paused here, and bitterly added, "Or perhaps…I am one now."

Makaru wished he could have assuaged the old man's anguish somewhat, and told him he was so wrong, but he knew it would be no use. Chitrasen Suna was a creature of thought. Once he had dived into the ocean of his thoughts, he only emerged when he wished to. So, to distract him from this train of thought, Makaru asked, "So, you didn't talk to him at all then? Maybe he couldn't recognise you at first and perhaps he would have done so eventually? You could have told him about what you all suffered. Hearing about a tragedy from the victims' point of view usually does evoke genuine sympathy."

For some time, Chitrasen remained silent, immersed in his world, his eyes on the far horizon where the land met the sky. Then he abruptly said, "Sympathy, huh? You think *sympathy* is what would have driven that shrewd man to help us? Open your eyes to the world, my boy, you are far too naive. If there is anything that politicians would ever help us for, talk to us for, breathe for, it is their own personal benefit, and that alone. You know, we would still have got a word or two of empathy from outside. The reason that that cunning man is still quiet is because of the coming elections, in February, which is just round the corner. If that gangster wants to win these elections, he needs to have all the Mehers, the Marwaris and the Gaudas on his side. Himanshu Bagarti is giving him free liquor for campaigning. The Mehers have promised him a huge vote bank. How would he secure these if he speaks to the media in our support?"

Makaru was stunned; he could never have thought of that.

As he listened in silence, Chitra went on, "And, talk to him about our sufferings? What good would that do? He has already seen the destruction with his own eyes. What more is there for me or anyone else to elaborate?" he said, his voice slightly quivering at the last part.

Chitrasen was broken. Yet he was trying to keep a firm hold on himself, and move on. For that alone, Makaru had the greatest respect for him.

"And besides, you see, it isn't just the politicians themselves, but the entire system they are a part of. As much as it pains me to say so, this is one of the biggest caste atrocities that Odisha has seen. Had things really been as 'transparent' as they claimed, pictures of our pada would have been flashing on every broadcasting channel as breaking news at least by now."

Makaru considered this seriously. A world where they had a voice, a vision? It lurked in his dreams like a phantom, sometimes tantalisingly within reach, yet light years away. A dream too agonisingly idyllic, yet as real as the passion in their hearts to strive for a better future, a future of equality.

But yes, what Chitra-da said was very true. Regardless of the party a political leader belonged to, every politician was much the same: forever recruiting allies, building a foolproof support system, going out of his way to tip the scales in his favour, to his advantage and his benefit. And so Makaru went on to ask, "Did political figures from any other party pay a visit as well? Or...", he trailed off.

"Well, there was one who came from the Bharatiya Janata Party. And guess who it was? Our own dear MLA. He too went over the same nonsense. Visiting the site of destruction, shedding a crocodile tear or two, and then 'reassuring' us that he would do whatever he can in his capacity. Hmph! As if we have no clue whose side he is on. Those bastards who torched down our settlements are all his party workers. Forget about getting justice, he probably knew about this sick plan well before it was even put into action."

Makaru heaved a hopeless sigh. He was overwhelmed.

He had been in denial so far, hoping, wishing against hope that maybe, just maybe the isolation was only a coincidence. Maybe, the hatred wasn't as insidious, as deep, as widespread as it seemed.

But it was.

The fact that every little detail of this diabolic plan had been cold-bloodedly, meticulously discussed, envisaged and implemented was like an arrow to his heart. Makaru couldn't decide which was worse: that Chitra knew that this was an entirely premeditated attack; or that he had come to terms with it. How much could this old man possibly endure?

Chitra-da said in a voice weighed down by the burden of what he knew, "Take this as a lesson, my boy. No one will ever be here for us, except we ourselves. People will come and people will go, and if we keep relying on passing souls to heave us out of our misery, we will forever be deserving of doom. We Dalits must stick together, for we are the only ones who can get ourselves out of this hell. This is what my life has also taught me."

Makaru said, "That is a powerful lesson, da. But aren't we learning it a little too late? Even if we look at the petty vest incident in Meher's shop, it could have been settled by taking the legal route. Meher would have been accused of assaulting Ganesh; or Manas, Suresh, Vikas would have been accused of assaulting Meher. But what happened instead? An entire basti was razed to ashes! Had this lesson come even a little earlier, perhaps things would not have been as bad as they are now, would they?"

Despite the tragic circumstances, Chitrasen had not lost his calm or his clarity. He proceeded to explain and said, "We all realised it late, my boy. We all are somewhat guilty and have some fault or the other that led to this catastrophe. I myself was not aware of how much I was at fault. I only realised it much later."

Makaru, who had till now been going with the flow of the conversation, suddenly stopped perplexed and confused. Had he heard it right? Did Chitra Suna, a victim of one of the worst caste atrocities, just claim that he, too, was responsible for what he had to suffer?

That made no sense to him at all.

He had finished brushing his teeth and cleaning his tongue; rinsing his mouth, he patted his mouth dry, then put his things on his towel. Then he sat down and, resting his elbows on his folded knees, looked up at Chitra and asked, "But how are *you* at fault, Chitra-da?"

Taking a deep breath, Chitrasen proceeded patiently to explain. "As I said, for the longest time, even I myself was not aware of it. But you see, someone opened my eyes. It was none other than the Chairman of the Scheduled Caste/Scheduled Tribe Commission of Delhi. He had come over here recently, with several members of the Commission accompanying him. After making a quick survey of our Ganapada, he told us that this had happened as a result of us trying too hard to be people we are not. We were going out of our way to become like the upper castes; so the heavens had struck down on us to make us suffer for our misdeeds."

Makaru threw an even more perplexed look his way, so Chitrasen further elaborated.

"We left all our ancestral traditions behind, vanquishing our caste identities, in the hope of becoming like the touchables. We stopped worshipping Gadia Gajapati, Chhuti Gudi, Nialimali and Mahalakshmi. And we started worshipping Shiva, Vishnu, Durga and Hanuman instead. In our foolish short-sightedness, we thought that doing so would make us 'Sanskritised'. Which is also why we were aspiring for a place in the Durga puja committee. Then we demanded to be allowed to offer flowers to the deities' idols. And so on and so forth. Consequently, one thing led to another, and we became enemies of the upper castes. So much so that they burned down our homes. Had we stuck to our own traditions, our own deities, and not tried to covet theirs, had we not been greedy to become 'Sanskitised', and ready to abandon our own customs and culture, could we not have avoided the situation we got ourselves into? To be honest, I think that we are evolving, only not for the better, but for the worse.

"I myself had been so delusional, hanging portrait upon portrait of every deity I knew. But the Chairman of the Commission came to me personally and told me how wrong I had been. Think for yourself, Makaru, when those hooligans burnt down my house, the deities got burnt too. Could they not have stopped it if they had wished to? When the mobsters torched down my house, couldn't the gods have orchestrated a divine intervention, or influenced their minds for the better? But they did not. Simply the sight of so many gods should have deterred them from carrying forward that heinous task. But it did not. Do you understand now?"

Makaru nodded. He did begin to understand what Chitra-da was saying. His thoughts drifted to the Hanuman temple of his basti back in Raipur. There, too, the lower-caste residents could only worship the god from outside, because the head priest did not allow them to enter the temple, claiming they would 'pollute' it. This convinced him that the caste system of the village and that of the city were ultimately not that different.

But there was something still troubling him. "Da, so then, should we just stop worshipping gods and goddesses altogether?"

"*Arey* Makaru," Chitra-da chided him lightly, "You are missing my point altogether! See, we used to worship our own gods before. They gave us courage, spirit, determination, and we turned to them to share our grievances, our joys and troubles, and to pay our obeisance. Well and good. But now these shrewd upper castes convinced us to worship their gods. And so began the catastrophe. Their gods don't understand us, our language or our traditions. And we are not accustomed to worshipping them, so we struggle in the process as well. There is always a gap somewhere that just cannot be filled. I guess it serves us right for blindly abandoning our own customs, without even trying to understand why and what we are losing."

"Hmm," Makaru agreed, then added with a chuckle, "Perhaps we should rather worship the politicians. In the present day and age, it is they who hold absolute power. At least, the returns of our 'piety' would be tangible!"

The two men shared a laugh.

Then Chitrasen said, "That may be true, my boy, but just worshipping them won't tip the scales in our favour. See, here we are, rendered utterly homeless. Did they care to even pay us a wholehearted visit? Our votes have contributed significantly to help them secure their seats. The least they could do is provide us help in times of crisis."

Makaru said, "Why not just prepare a list of casualties yourself and submit it to the government? Perhaps help would arrive faster that way?"

"No use, Makaru," Chitra sighed. "The government only accepts lists made by the government officials themselves. We have to first get them to come over here, then give them bribes to get the work done correctly, then answer their endless stream of questions, and finally get them to submit the proper list by giving more bribes. The system is hollowed inside out."

Chitra and Makaru had been so engrossed in their discussions that they never realised when the noon sun had climbed to its full glory. Hurrying to take a bath, they dived into the tranquil green waters of the pond. Having scrubbed themselves clean, they emerged, dried and clothed themselves, draping their wet towels around their heads. It was a common village habit; this way one's head was shielded from the hot sun, and the towel would dry quickly too.

On reaching the relief camp, they hung their wet clothes on the compound wall. Then they went to see what was there for breakfast: *poha*. The Anganwadi workers were doing their best to ensure that the victims got timely and nutritious meals. But curse this tragedy, the Ganas had lost their appetite.

Fortunately, the children weren't as badly affected, and they would hungrily eat up the meal given to them, spending their days in the camp largely content, their parents always by their side. The only thing that suffered was their schooling. Nobody was attending classes, since the classrooms of Lathore High School had become a relief camp. Nobody included not just the Dalits who lost their homes in the fire, but the other children who attended Lathore High School as well.

Makaru had started feeling that now he should head back home soon. He had already spent quite some time here in Lathore, in his efforts to offer some measure of solace to Chitra-da. But how much solace was he bringing him anyway? True, this visit had been like a break for him. But he couldn't stay here for ever, could he?

"Da, I think I should be returning soon," Makaru said hesitantly, looking at Chitra-da carefully to gauge his reaction.

Chitra-da was silent for one long moment. When his eyes met Makaru's, they were distant and glistened with unshed tears.

"Yes, you should. How long can I keep you here to myself? You've got a little grandson and your own family back in the city. You must return to them soon. At least I have my family, my relatives and my neighbours here. But you are all alone. Your family back there, too, is alone. Yes, you should return to them soon. That would be best. In fact, it is better that you leave this afternoon itself."

A proud man, Chitra-da struggled to keep his voice steady, trembling as he spoke, each word weighed down by the melancholy he was fiercely trying to hide.

This brought tears to Makaru's eyes, but he too fought to not let them fall.

Both men were silent, each lost in a storm of his thoughts.

Nineteen

Tragedies are ruthless. They bring untold misery and tears. But they also reveal something that no one wishes to confront: the ugly truth.

The truth about people and their relentless striving to survive the tragedy at any cost. At the cost of other humans, at the cost of humanity, even at the cost of their own people.

Chitrasen Suna found himself in the midst of a crisis of epic proportions, and all he could do was to look around aghast, bewildered at the workings of the human mind, and the instinctive selfishness and cunning and mechanical ruthlessness with which it eliminated obstructions in its path in order to survive.

The torching of the houses in Ganapada had brought numbing grief in its wake, but it also brought a rude awakening for Chitrasen. He now knew how dangerously close to insanity the human mind could go, and he didn't wish to test the boundaries of his own sanity any further. So, although he had tried initially, he had now stopped advising and counselling people, giving them suggestions. He could no longer bring himself to do so, for he knew that it was futile; his words could do nothing to help anyone. He also knew that nothing could shield him from the nightmare that surrounded him.

He watched as a constant stream of visitors came and went, not a soul trying to understand the plight of the victims. Reporters came for their interviews, photographers came for their pictures, relatives came to offer sympathies, and they all left soon after.

By this time, Chitrasen was practically numb to everyone's existence, including his own, just quietly going along wherever life chose to take him next.

One day, there was a new visitor at the relief camp: the Tehsildar.

Since he was a Gana himself, the victims had hoped that he would at least help them in the tedious process of procuring government aid, to give them what was their due. But the Tehsildar had no interest whatsoever in helping them. Instead, he shot question upon question, interrogating them relentlessly. This, coupled with their already fragile and desperate state, only exasperated them further, even driving some of them to lash out at him. In fact, the Tehsildar and the victims got into ugly verbal brawls several times in just the few days that he was there.

But even this wasn't as bad as the complete violation of faith and betrayal that the *basti* people had to face from their own acquaintances.

How was that, you ask.

Well, here is how.

The Gana basti of Lathore was yet to achieve significant literacy. When counting those who had achieved higher education, only six individuals made it to the list: a private college teacher; Vikas, an MPhil. Student; Manas, an M.A. student; and three primary school teachers. The rest of the adults were, so to say, uneducated and illiterate. Whenever any government officials would condescend to pay the relief camp a visit, or when reporters would come with their tech-savvy cameramen in tow, they would prefer to converse with these 'educated' men. So it wasn't surprising that these individuals offered themselves as 'volunteers', assuring the villagers that they would be the bridge between them and outsiders. The villagers gladly agreed, trusting them as members of their own community.

When the Chief Minister's Relief Fund sent compensation amounting to one lakh rupees for every family, the same volunteers breached the people's trust, like vile bloodthirsty leeches.

They explained to the villagers how the Tehsildar and Sub-Collector wanted bribes in order to truthfully and fully report the damages caused to the higher authorities. Falling into their honeyed trap, the innocent villagers shelled out ten thousand rupees for the supposed 'bribes'.

Little did they know that the money never made its way to the intended recipients.

No, it went into the pockets of those shrewd, educated individuals instead, who collected the lump sum and divided it amongst themselves without any qualms. Leaving aside a meagre amount for the supposed bribes they actually had to pay, they went to the Tehsildar, and then the Sub-Collector, respectively, and put on an act in a half-baked attempt to extract sympathy from the corrupt officers.

They went to them and pleaded, "Sir, you know very well where we come from and what our dismal resources amount to, especially now in the aftermath of this huge tragedy. How could we possibly put together all the money? This is what we have been able to collect, with great difficulty. Sir, please do what you can."

Of course, this did not remotely satisfy either officer. So the damage reports were not written satisfactorily either.

All through this, the villagers had no idea what was going on behind their backs.

Nature worked on a principle of balance.

But the evil human mind did not. It worked on weakness, feeding on it relentlessly like termites, hollowing out its victims, till they had nothing left to live for. Pushing already desperate people down into an abyss of despair and helplessness, denying even the possibility of hope and redemption to already hopeless souls.

If Manas, Vikas and the others had only sat down and spent just a little thought, genuinely, sincerely, about the catastrophe that had struck their own people, about what they could have done to emerge out of the storm together stronger, they wouldn't have stooped to such disgusting lows. Had they appealed to their truly educated, humane selves and envisioned a better future for their people, they wouldn't have had the heart to author such an abominable betrayal and exploit such innocent trusting souls.

Were they really any different from those ruthlessly exploitative, oppressive upper castes?

They were Ganas, but how were they any different from the Himanshu Bagartis, Srikanth Mehers and Bhola Aggarwals?

Could they really call themselves educated?

Educated enough to embrace the empathy that resided within their souls? Educated enough to put aside their selfishness and extend a helping hand to people in distress? Educated enough to acknowledge the sharp pangs of guilt that their conscience made them alive to when they proceeded to betray the very trust reposed in them by so many helpless people?

Educated enough simply to be human and humane?

Of the two officials, the Sub-Collector was an upper-caste man who had no qualms about demanding his dues in bribes just to do his job. But the Tehsildar was a Gana; had he wanted to, he could have at least shown the victims a little sympathy. But he did not. On the contrary, he added fuel to the fire by further downgrading the Ganas before the Sub-Collector. The latter was already aware of how the literate representatives of the victims were greedily siphoning away the compensation money. To make matters worse, the Tehsildar openly ridiculed certain complex social customs of the villagers.

For instance, every traditional Gana family followed a rather intricate system of household planning. When the sons would marry and the family would enlarge, it would also bifurcate. Perhaps not so much explicitly as implicitly. The families of different generations that co-habited under a single roof would limit themselves to certain parts of the house, cook their own meals, and lead largely autonomous lives. They would all live in the same house, like one joint family, but would have different households.

One house, many homes.

One family, many households.

This was a tradition so entrenched and pronounced that whenever any volunteer made their rounds to collect funds for some important occasion in Ganapada, they would ask for sums based on the number of households in one house, not families. So, say a family has two wedded sons, they would have to pay thrice as much as the usual one household setting: one part from the older brother, a second part from the younger brother, and a third part from the parents.

Perhaps nuclear families are a better option after all! Anyhow. Bifurcated and trifurcated families, demarcated costs, ailing victims, and a corrupt officer. It doesn't take much to put two and two together and figure out just how desperate the situation was.

The Tehsildar, hell-bent on ensuring that the Ganas got nothing more than the bare minimum in relief, devised a convoluted plan so that he could pocket the bulk of the money himself. Counting multiple households under one family, he strictly allotted one lakh each to every house that had been burnt. The apathetic monster that he was, or had become, he deliberately ignored the distressed pleas of the many families that had been lumped together as one unit for receiving compensation. He did not care if or how they came to terms with surviving on just a fraction of what they were entitled to for sustenance. He turned deaf to the calls of humanity.

The District Collector paid Lathore a visit a few days after this, and he proposed setting up a 'peace committee' which would forge a compromise between the two sides: the aggressors and the victims.

What was this peace that he talked about?

And what fault was it of the Dalits for them to take the first step in initiating such peace?

The District Collector was proposing that both parties come forward and try to forge peace. As if one party had not isolated, humiliated, subjugated and oppressed the other for generations. As if they had not demolished and burnt down an entire locality like toy houses. Given that, one had to be really optimistic or stupid to hope that a 'peace' like this one wouldn't fall through.

Clearly, all the Collector really wanted was to add this to his list of achievements. As soon as the Dalits and the upper castes signed the dotted line, he could go to press, citing how hard he had worked to bring the two warring communities together and how he had mediated to aid them in reaching a settlement. Again, another measly human who cared about nothing but himself.

The Ganas had registered an FIR, and the police had acted on it too, but it had all been for show. Out of the two hundred eighty named, the police arrested forty people, all of whom sat in the jeep and went to the police station chatting nonchalantly. They knew they had the money, the power and the lawyers at their disposal. They were also friendly with some of the police officers concerned. And so, the next day they were out of lockup, just like that.

The mobsters and minor culprits all got out on bail. The main culprits, the mob leaders Himanshu Bagarti, Srikanth Meher and Bhola Aggarwal, didn't even go to jail. The police could never lay their hands on them. The main accused knew they had powerful connections, and so did the police officers.

The perpetrators were fearlessly strutting about the village with their chests out, spitting on the streets of Lathore, while their homeless neighbours lived from day to day, crammed into schoolrooms, with little or no hope of justice. Did the aggressors feel any remorse? No. If anything, they were more arrogant and smug now, knowing that they could commit such a heinous crime, and get away with it.

While the guilty men evaded every conceivable punishment and repercussion that they would have suffered in the normal course of justice, and continued with their lives as if nothing had happened, for the victims, it was raining blows from everywhere.

No help, no support was forthcoming from any quarter. Ever since the arson and looting, the police had been guarding them at the relief camp, as if they were naughty children who would escape if left unguarded and do something mischievous. Police were also standing guard near the burnt skeletons of their homes. But, what was left there to guard now? All through this, had a single concerned conscientious citizen offered to help? No. Even their own Gana officials had grown sluggish, citing one lame reason or another to postpone urgent work.

Little did they know.

The upper castes had, with extraordinary foresight and industriousness, already devised intelligent plans to ensure the ultimate damnation of the Dalits. They had pitched in money, influence and resources to fragment their community. They had bribed the so-called Dalit 'volunteers' with hefty sums of money and brainwashed them to go against their own people. Which perhaps explained why Manas, Vikas, Suresh and the rest weren't so enthusiastic about standing up for their rights anymore. Vikas had more than one reason. His beloved, Lipsa, was a part of Srikanth Meher's family; so he was unwilling to seriously displease them in any way.

Civil activists, litterateurs and NGOs arranged awareness programmes, inviting the Ganas to speak out and share their sufferings. If the educated, articulate ones among them had spoken on behalf of the community and shared their trauma and grievances, they could have made the larger society more aware, rallied more people in their support, and demanded better relief and compensation measures, so that the victims could be rehabilitated and could return to normalcy sooner.

However, those volunteers not only declined to participate in these programmes themselves, they also prevented the villagers from attending them. "What good would it do us to attend these ridiculous circuses now? Will it bring back our homes? Will it undo what life inflicted upon us? No, right? Then why thrust ourselves into such useless things?" they argued.

But, to outsiders, this painted an entirely different picture altogether. The administration, already apathetic, now alleged that the Gana victims of the caste atrocity had refused to cooperate with them, and were not reporting their losses, and hence could not be compensated properly. The upper castes rejoiced at the success of their scheme to divide and pull apart the Dalit community from its roots. Manas, Vikas, Suresh and others were satisfied with the money they got in return for betraying and duping their own people. The rest of the victims tossed and turned on the nail bed of misery, hoping for change and for better times.

And then there was Chitrasen Suna.

A self-made, prosperous man of means, a man of integrity trusted by his people, a man who had held a position of authority, influence, respect and affection in his community before the disaster, one would have thought that Chitrasen would rise to the occasion and rally every Gana around to raise their collective voice to demand justice.

But he did not.

Chitrasen had sunk into his own little dark corner, never to rise from it again.

And it was because of those scheming, lowly upper castes.

They had spread word and registered a false FIR, claiming that Chitrasen was not only present on the day that Kishore Meher's son got beaten in his shop, but that he had also lent a hand in the assault on the innocent young boy, Ganesh Suna. This meant that nobody in the Gana community trusted Chitrasen anymore, and he sank further below his moral ground and even lower in his own eyes, and theirs.

But he hadn't always been like this.

The old Chitrasen would have fought back hard and fierce. He would have ripped those Gana traitors to shreds. He would have used the power and position he commanded to the best of his ability, bringing everyone together and uniting them for the common cause of a revolution, like a true leader. He would have made sure that their voice was not suppressed anymore, and he would have let their grief, loss and indignation do the talking, such that it created shockwaves so huge they would have sent ripples throughout Odisha and beyond.

He would have ensured their screams of agony were laid bare on every newspaper, every magazine, every news telecast.

Screams so loud they would have made their way up to the Parliament.

But he did not.

Because he could not.

How could he, when he was entangled in a brawl that he had merely tried to stop, and was no longer trusted by his own people? He wallowed in his despair and let it consume him. He had been driven past the point of insanity, and now he was just waiting and watching to see how much he could endure, till his soul and spirit gave in completely and left his hollow mortal shell forever.

As his angry, hot tears fell on the dry ground, Chitra took in short ragged breaths, waiting for when he would breathe his last.

One could say he was waiting for death. But he wasn't.

He was dead already.

Twenty

A cool wind cascaded down the hills of Nrusinghanath, making people at the relief camp shiver in their skins. It was two o' clock in the afternoon. Had this been any other day, people would have already left home for the fields after their afternoon meal, for the second time in the day. Instead, they were huddled within the dilapidated walls of the schoolrooms, contemplating life.

The afternoon sun cast a pallid shadow of gloom on the flat insipid skies and the still earth. Passing clouds briefly shielded the eyes from the sun, leaving dappled patches of light and shadow over the undulating land. The wind raked shudders through the spines of people in the relief camp.

Leaves in all shades of yellow and brown were falling softly to the ground as if with a sigh, chasing their youth as their senescence rushed to embrace them. A nondescript emotion hung in the air as nature slowly metamorphosed into yet another entrancing guise of hers, and the seasons changed.

Yet again.

Makaru went up to the school compound wall where he had hung his clothes to soak up the sun and dry. As he collected them, he was careful to dust the yellowing leaves from the garments, which looked like fallen angels in the sunshine. His ears caught the solitary crow of a cock in the distance. On other days, Makaru would have found it odd to hear a cock crowing in the middle of the day. But today was different. He felt a warmth envelop his shivering body, and felt as if the bird was crowing to get his attention. As if reminding him that he had a train to catch.

The train back to Raipur.

Yes, Makaru was returning to the city, back to the chaotic humdrum of car engines and grey concrete roads. He was going back home, to his wife, his son, his family.

But a part of him didn't want to leave.

For he had a family here, too. Chitra-da.

He had so many memories attached to the village, to his pada, now reduced to soot and ashes and crushed beneath the weight of the all-consuming fire of hatred. Would he be able to hear the cock crow in Raipur in the middle of the afternoon, or even in the morning? No. All he would hear was the mundane chatter of the slum residents, the impatient honks of the office-goers as they sat frowning in their air-conditioned cars, the blaring horns of the train as its wheels wrestled with the tracks laid out for them, and the sound of his soul as it wailed in agony.

Shaking himself out of his thoughts, Makaru neatly folded his clothes and thrust them into his bag one by one. Beside him sat Chitrasen hugging his gaunt frame, silently following his every move with his eyes.

The station was very close to the relief camp. So close that the warning bells before any train departed could be distinctly heard from the camp itself.

What pained him was the fact that he was leaving.

As Makaru hoisted his bag onto his shoulder, Chitra stood up too, perhaps wishing to accompany him to the station. Makaru looked behind him, hoping for anything, literally anything, to intercept or delay his departure.

As they walked to the station, Makaru deliberately slowed his steps so that Chitra would be the one leading.

Sensing his brooding companion's steps become progressively slower and slower, Chitrasen turned around and said with a dry chuckle, "Come on Makaru, you have a train to catch. You don't want to miss it, do you?"

Makaru was perplexed.

Part of him actually *wanted* to miss it.

He didn't want to board the train, his feet growing heavier, more reluctant, by the minute as his mind struggled to reason and remind him that he really ought to hurry on.

Wrestling fiercely with himself, Makaru speeded up a bit, but only enough to catch up with Chitra-da, not to overtake him. As much as he wished to turn back, and turn back time itself, he knew he could not do either. There was something irresistible about facing one's deepest fears, which in this case was Makaru's fear of leaving his village behind, once again.

But then, wasn't this what people always did? Leaving their native village behind, leaving the land that had birthed them and anchored them all their lives. Leaving behind a Pandora's box of memories and nostalgia to haunt them lifelong. Leaving behind homes, every inch of whose walls and roofs and floors they had built from scratch with their bare hands.

But, did they always leave of their own accord? No.

Sometimes, they were forced to leave.

Just like he had been forced to, all those years ago, due to the mishap that his father had got embroiled himself in (or, one that Makaru had embroiled him in, but we won't go there).

And now, as heartbreaking images flit past his floundering mind, he found himself confronting a cold revelation.

This was what would happen to his Gana brothers and sisters, too.

They would leave Lathore, having been forced out of their pada thanks to mindless bloodlust and caste hatred.

And much as he loathed himself for it, he could do nothing about it. Absolutely nothing.

How he hated that.

Makaru's feet moved forward mechanically, following each other in an urgent yet seemingly unhurried pace, both determined yet hesitant. With every step he took, one thought in his head replaced another. And with every new thought, he struggled to maintain his composure and sanity, but felt them slowly but incessantly slipping out of his control.

As Chitrasen and Makaru walked on in silence, Makaru's eyes fell on the gudis of goddess Pardeshen and goddess Nialimali by the roadside. He stepped off the road to pay his obeisance to the two deities, now two sadly neglected stone sculptures. Dust had settled on them, and from the carelessness with which religious paraphernalia had been scattered around them, it seemed as if nobody really cared for them anymore. Many of the Gana people had in fact stopped worshipping these goddesses ever since the advent of Durga puja, as Makaru recalled.

Especially people like Chitrasen.

As he quickly glanced over his shoulders, Makaru caught sight of the determined form of the older man marching ahead without breaking his stride, his eyes staring into the distance. Makaru could not blame him. Chitra's aggrieved heart and exhausted mind no longer had the capacity or the energy to pray, perhaps. Shocked at the betrayal, all his beliefs and his faith had been shattered to the core.

As Makaru slowly traced his memories back to the many events past, his thoughts converged on one point in time, when, he thought, all the madness had actually begun.

The Durga puja celebrations.

The fateful day that the Ganas had decided to denounce their ancestral goddess for another, looking for momentary comfort in the misleading allure of grandeur, cultural advancement, sophistication.

These were nothing but delusional kites, blinded by the freedom that came momentarily when their string was cut, before they fell crashing to the ground, never to be able to pick themselves up again.

The quietest of sighs escaped Makaru's lips, hung upon the air a moment and dissolved.

As he buried himself deeper into his thoughts and memories, he had a sudden epiphany.

As children, we all struggled to sit upright, to walk with steady steps, to run. If we can do so effortlessly today, it is because of our parents. Our parents who brought us up, showering us constantly with unconditional love, care and affection, making countless sacrifices everyday, pouring themselves, their ideals into our upbringing, hoping we would adhere to some of those ideals as we blossomed into adults.

As time walked, ran, and flew, fate played its wizardry again, switching our roles with that of our selfless caregivers and benefactors. We found that things had changed.

Our parents had become the children, and we children the parents.

Now the ageing parents would be the ones hoping for their adult children to take out some time from their busy lives; yet, if they didn't, they would quickly dismiss it, feigning consolation and claiming that their sunshine was probably working very hard to earn for their family. They would spend long days and even longer nights hoping for just one small acknowledgement of their existence from the no longer recognisable adult who went about their daily activities in front of them every day, holding their hearts for just one glimpse of the tiny person they had once brought up selflessly with their blood and sweat and kisses and tears.

They didn't want us, no.

They needed us.

But did any one of us acknowledge their needs? No. We would heartlessly turn our backs to their slowly receding, diminishing existence, pretending that they had as much time left with us as we did on this earth. We would test their patience and our conscience a little more everyday, putting off a heart-to-heart talk, a quiet companionable walk, firmly ignoring all the pangs of guilt that fed on our soul. Sometimes, we would even let our stupid intellect get in the way of our feelings, cruelly lashing out at them without reason for having seemingly interfered with things more 'important'.

This would break them.

Break their heart into innumerable pieces.

Yet, they would slowly pick up those pieces one by one with a heartbreaking smile, forgiving us with a generosity only they could possess, still hoping there would come a day when the apple of their eyes would come bounding into their room with a smile on their face, and hug them so tight they would never let go.

Alas, so many parents around the world take this wish to their graves.

We never deserved our parents and we never will. Neglect on our part has always led to their pain, their loneliness, their desolation and their sadness.

And neglect on part of the Ganas had led to the decline of their deities.

For what else were devotees but the children of their deities?

As Makaru gave the dusty stones a last look and let his tired eyes wash over the desolate ruins the goddesses stood in, he couldn't help but feel that he and his people had failed them.

Failed as devotees, failed as humans, failed as children.

Makaru probed further, thinking of the conditions back in the city. There too, abandoning their own Gana deity, they had poured in everything into building a shrine for Hanuman, only to be prohibited from worshipping the god by the Brahmin priest, who barred their entry into the shrine on casteist grounds.

Makaru felt like hiding himself away somewhere, vanishing out of existence. The onism that life had confronted him with in his mature years left him acutely aware that he would experience only a little of this world in his lifetime, yet he couldn't help but acknowledge how little the world itself was. Broken promises and dreams lay scattered over the uncertain terrain of life like shards of glass at every turn. Everywhere, he saw the same hatred, the same irrational fear, the same cruelty, the same insanity.

As he stood up on his feet, Makaru couldn't help feeling as if he too was slowly but imperceptibly giving in to the insanity.

Propelling himself forward, he willed his legs to fall into a regular rhythm, and soon he could see Lathore station appear in the distance before him. How ridiculously small it looked! So small that a series of just three bell chimes sufficed to announce the arrival or departure of the train. Makaru compared it to the sprawling Raipur station, which was enormous and forever bustling so full of people, noise and frenetic activity that it would put a fish market to shame.

Yet, what mattered was not the differences, but the similarities.

And the similarity lay in the anxiety that would grip him whenever he travelled to any station, his heart threatening to jump out of his chest in fear. The similarity lay in how endless reels of undesirable memories would come crashing down on him, memories of his childhood that he had always wanted and tried to forget, that would choke him in a stranglehold, but never really bless him with death. The similarity lay in how his mind would always take him back to that ominous day more than five decades ago, when he was compelled to flee his homeland and was uprooted from his native village forever.

As much as he wanted to shrug it off, calling it bad luck, a rotten fate, he could not. Because he knew exactly what was to blame for the predicament that he, his parents, and his subsequent family had landed in: the caste system.

A villainous conjuring of the vile human mind, the system had been blindingly fast in spreading its roots into every docile soul's mindset. Stirring its poison into the innocent thoughts that pervaded one's mind, it burrowed and burrowed, till it had installed itself as an emotion, an object irreplaceable, indomitable, to the point that it led to the enslavement of one community for no fault of their own.

But Makaru wasn't as troubled by its origins as he was by its existence.

To think that such a barbaric mechanism still pervaded in its monstrous glory in today's world, in today's society, shielding vile humans from the wrath of intellect and reason, as they sank deeper into the void of pointless hatred. To think that it had claws so far-reaching that it had led to the abhorrence his community had suffered today.

He knew of the origins, but what of the end?

When would the day arrive when caste would cease to exist altogether?

Would such a day ever come?

He had even been told that education was the key to fighting caste. Because educated people were supposed to be sensible, rational, empathetic, humane. Several volunteers had come to the slums too, encouraging them to educate as many members of the family as they could, for even if it took a toll on their expenses, it was a worthy investment. Makaru had always believed them wholeheartedly, believed that a good education was the key to humanity and progress.

Now, he was not so sure anymore.

He thought back to his father and his employers, the gauntia and his son Nandakumar. How they had treated his father despite being well educated. He thought back to Himanshu Bagarti, Srikant Meher, and the others. How they had treated the Ganas despite being well educated.

Education alone didn't always grant emancipation, no.

One could still be caged by the shackles of mindless hatred and bigotry despite being educated.

Could we really call those caged beasts human?

Could we really call those apathetic monsters vessels of empathy?

Did education really bring sensibility and reason as many claimed?

No. Education had nothing to do with empathy; it did not guarantee humanity. He would rather meet someone uneducated but humane than someone educated but inhuman.

Shaking himself out of his thoughts, Makaru saw Chitrasen walk up to a bench and sit on one end of it. He did the same, sitting down at the other end wordlessly. He was surprised to see the same dog that he had seen some days ago, now nestled comfortably near Chitrasen's feet.

As Makaru's eyes came to rest on the animal, he was startled when the dog looked back at him, with what seemed like pity in its eyes, as if reassuring him, "Don't worry, I never heard your thoughts."

Turning away from the dog, Makaru looked around him and saw the station master's makeshift office. Beams of glorious golden sunlight were filtering through the windows of the tiny office, one of which was falling on the bench they sat on. The warm, fuzzy beam of sunlight was in contrast to the biting cold which enveloped them in the small train station.

Just then, the three were jolted out of their tranquillity upon hearing the second honk, signalling the train's due arrival.

Makaru sucked in his lips, exhaling a long breath as he prepared himself to board the train, something he didn't really want to do. True, he had his family waiting for him in Raipur, and yes, he too had started to miss them. But that emotion was dwarfed by the other emotions he was at the moment holding in.

Guilt. Torment. Agony.

He wanted to talk to Chitra, he really did, but couldn't because of the emotional wreck he was. In fact, if he could, he would have also made the effort of going up to the other victims at the relief camp and talking to them. They were his brothers and sisters after all. But he couldn't, for they were all enveloped in their own cocoons of misery.

Makaru, too, had been enveloped in his own cocoon when he had escaped from Banjipali all those years ago. Why? Because he had a guardian angel by his side.

His father.

His father, despite facing the acute anxiety of having the life of his son threatened, had brought a sense of peace, a sense of security to Makaru. His father had told him to board a train, and he had. His father had guided him to leave his homeland behind, and he had. His father had asked him to make a completely foreign city his home, and he had.

But now, he was all alone.

And he had no father to stand by his side.

His eternal shield now gone, Makaru could feel his emotions raining down on him. He felt everything he hadn't felt when he had been in the same predicament, in the same place, more than fifty years ago.

Unbeknownst to him, a single tear rolled down his eye.

On the other end of the bench sat Chitrasen, completely still, his eyes resolutely, calmly fixed on the empty rail tracks before him, unblinking.

In his large liquid eyes, one could see time unravel the events that had led to the downfall of the basti. Chitra's eyes told a story.

The story of his basti.

The sickly sweet smile of pundit Binay Panigrahi as he blessed them with his pudgy hands when they agreed to worship Ma Durga.

The acrid stench of the petrol as it was thrown onto their homes, and lit, engulfing them in hungry flames that collapsed their world onto itself.

The maniacal laughter of Himanshu Bagarti, Srikanth Meher and Bhola Aggarwal as they watched the Dalit basti fall.

The soot, ashes, skeletal remains of their homes and debris scattered amidst the glowing embers, reminders of the angry crimson flames of hate.

His eyes held all this, and more.

He had turned into an ancient medieval stone statue, lined with deep cracks, broken in places, such that one touch could leave him crumbling.

His mind chaotic with memories, an unbearable cacophony of thoughts, emotions, regrets, Chitra-da sat completely still. A hair's breadth away from destruction.

As if he was about to...die.

Shut up! Makaru told himself harshly, fiercely reigning in his thoughts. How could he even think of his Chitra-da dying! He would rather be crushed under the wheels of the coming train than envisage the death of his dear Chitra-da.

And then, the bell rang.

The train would arrive any moment now. Makaru felt his heart pounding in its ribcage as he heaved a final sigh full of indescribable emotions. Torn between reluctance, melancholy, latent fury and burning guilt, he just wanted to scream aloud, till his throat turned raw. He wanted to break the heavy chains that burdened his leaden heart and set himself free.

But he just stood there, doing nothing.

Suddenly, the ear-splitting horn of the train pierced the deafening silence. As its worn out wheels squealed onto the gleaming steel tracks, the crowd on the platform burst into frenetic activity and commotion, as noisy commands were given to load luggage, grab seats, and tearful goodbyes were made, relatives hugged, feet of elders touched in farewell. Knowing that the train didn't make a long stop at this station, Makaru hurried to hoist his solitary cloth bag over his shoulder, and bent down to touch his da's feet.

Chitrasen, however, stood stone still.

With the moment of departure now breathing down their necks, and with Makaru finally about to depart for real, it seemed as if old Chitrasen was on the verge of breaking down. All the constant effort and struggle he had made all this while to firmly reign in his emotions was now threatening to give way and crumble.

The expressions on his face seemed to reflect the emotions of experiencing the five stages of grief all at once: denial, anger, negotiation, despair and acceptance. The last one he was still struggling with.

He looked as if he yearned to get up and embrace Makaru tightly in a bear hug and not let go, and yet, he remained there on the bench, motionless, his limbs as if frozen.

Until the train blew its final whistle of departure.

Makaru, too, dearly wanted to hold Chitrasen and console him, reassure him that time will heal all. But, hesitant and unsure as always, he only exchanged one long last look with Chitra-da, and climbed onto the bogey, made his way past the other passengers and sank wordlessly into his seat.

Time.

The most powerful precursor.

Forever transient, sometimes walking by, sometimes rushing past, but never stagnant.

It came and it went, but it never stayed.

Worlds could come to a standstill, universes collide, but time never stopped.

It never stopped when Chitra's world did, and his universe was tipped askew.

It never stopped when the upper castes' compassion did, and they rendered the Dalits' dignity naked.

It never stopped when Makaru's train started inching away from the platform with slow chugs, releasing puffs of steam.

Time never stopped.

And time never will.

Glossary

antador: threads traditionally tied around the waist by men, women and children to ward off evil

antra: in rural Odisha a small fire lit to keep warm in the biting cold of winter; villagers make an antra outside their houses, or in their fields when guarding crops from animals

badipala: musical contest between two groups of **pala** folk artistes and performers

bedi: temporary rectangular platform on which wedding rites are conducted

beheran: village meeting to resolve conflicts and discuss important issues, like a panchayat

bheluan: *Semecarpus anacardium*, a medicinal plant, the oil extracted from its fruit is traditionally used to heal deep cracks in human feet as well as animal hoofs

birtia: the chronicler of the Gana community who visits them annually without fail and narrates the saga of their ancestors, their cultural heritage, and sings to the accompaniment of a **damru**

chirangul/chiruguni: spirit of a woman who dies with a child in her womb

chopkania: indigenous glue prepared from tree latex and castor oil

damru: small two-headed drum common across the Indian subcontinent; it is associated with Lord Siva who plays it when he dances the *tandava* and is believed to generate spiritual, cosmic energy

daskathia: Important traditional Odia folk art form performed by two male balladeers, identifying as **dasas** or devotees and servants of Lord Shiva, who sing and narrate stories from mythology and history to the accompaniment of a **kathia**, a wooden musical instrument to keep the rhythm

dhol: large double-sided barrel drum played with either one or two sticks, an essential feature of traditional and folk music and dance, and popular across northern India, Bangladesh and Pakistan; it is still used to make public announcements in some rural areas

duma: ancestral spirit worshipped as a deity

ekoisa/ekoishia: ritual performed on the twenty-first day of the child birth

feni: a reed or comb-like component in a loom that separates and spaces the warp threads, allowing the weft threads to move across the loom

fusha: child-lifter

gadi puja: ritual festival to remember and worship one's ancestors

ganabaja: special traditional musical instruments played by members of the Gana community in Odisha in almost all social, religious and cultural events in the village

gani: leftover food given in lieu of labour provided or services rendered, such as grazing and tending livestock

gardi: shaman, healer or village doctor

gauntia: village head or chief

gudi: mud hut built for a deity

gunia: seer, healer or village shaman who cures ailments by exorcising evil spirits

halia: bonded labourer, usually landless and of a lower caste than the landed employer or zamindar

jhankar: village priest, usually belonging to the Adivasi communities

jiuntia: auspicious thread tied by a sister on her brother's wrist as a symbol of protection on the festival of **bhai jiuntia** when sisters fast and pray for the wellbeing of their brothers; **pua jiuntia** is an Odia festival when mothers fast and pray for the safety of their sons.

kankada: *Momordica dioica* or spine gourd, consumed as a vegetable across India and South Asia

kantha: traditional hand-stitched, embroidered patchwork quilt

kakan: considered auspicious, folded mango leaves tied to threads given by a newly-wed bride and groom to close relatives, who bless them in return

khagla: ornament with a specific design worn around the neck

khala: threshing yard where harvested crops are collected and processed

khamar: traditional granary; the owner is called a **khamari**

khani: unit of measuring grain roughly equivalent to 80 kilos

khenjed: group of vagabonds, gypsies, nomads

mahuria: traditionally, a trumpet blower from the Odia Gana community

mahuri and **tasha**: traditional musical instruments played by the Gana community

makaddam: officer in charge of measuring land and fixing revenues

meeta: friend, companion

mundan: as per Hindu custom, the first ritual tonsuring of a male child

nissan: traditional folk percussion instrument made of iron and leather, played with two sticks called **chimta**

Nuakhai: major agricultural festival observed predominantly in western Odisha and southern Chhattisgarh on **panchami tithi** (fifth day of the lunar calendar) to ceremonially welcome the new rice of the season with a rice-eating ritual

pakhal: traditional Odia dish made of watered rice seasoned with spices, a popular summer staple

pala: traditional Odia folk performance of song and dance where popular religious folk narratives are sung and narrated

pidar: house altar where household deities and ancestors are worshipped

pika: intoxicant made of strong tobacco

pitha: a group of traditional, festive delicacies in Odisha usually prepared on ritual days, typically made of rice flour, can be both sweet or savoury depending on the fillings used; popular across eastern and north-eastern India, and Bangladesh, with distinctive regional variations

Puspuni: major harvest festival of western Odisha held on Poush Purnima when farming families celebrate their annual harvest of paddy

telghar and **dashaghar**: rituals followed on the third and tenth day, respectively, after death

tendu: *Diospyros menanoxylol* or East Indian ebony, also known as **kendu** in Odisha, Jharkhand and Assam, is a versatile tree nicknamed 'green gold' for its economic value, especially for forest-dependent Adivasis, for whom it also holds cultural and mythological significance; dried tendu leaves are used to wrap tobacco to make bidis; the green fruit is edible, rich in minerals and has cooling properties (for details, see: https://www.downtoearth.org.in/food/out-of-wilderness)

unjli: wedding ritual in which the bride or groom is taken around the marriage altar holding rice cupped in their palms